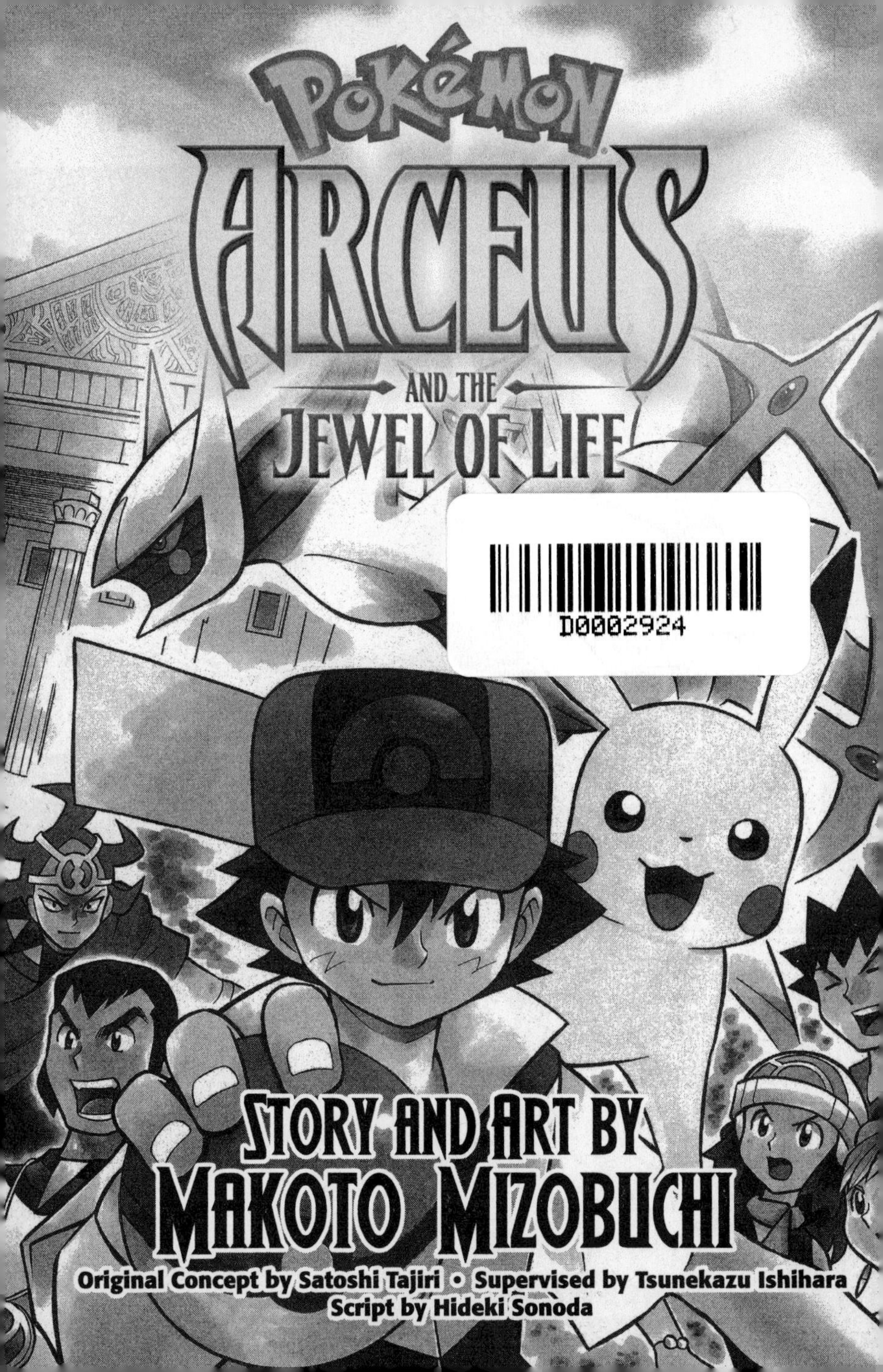

Pokémon
Arceus and the Jewel of Life

Story and Art by Makoto Mizobuchi

Original Concept by Satoshi Tajiri • Supervised by Tsunekazu Ishihara
Script by Hideki Sonoda

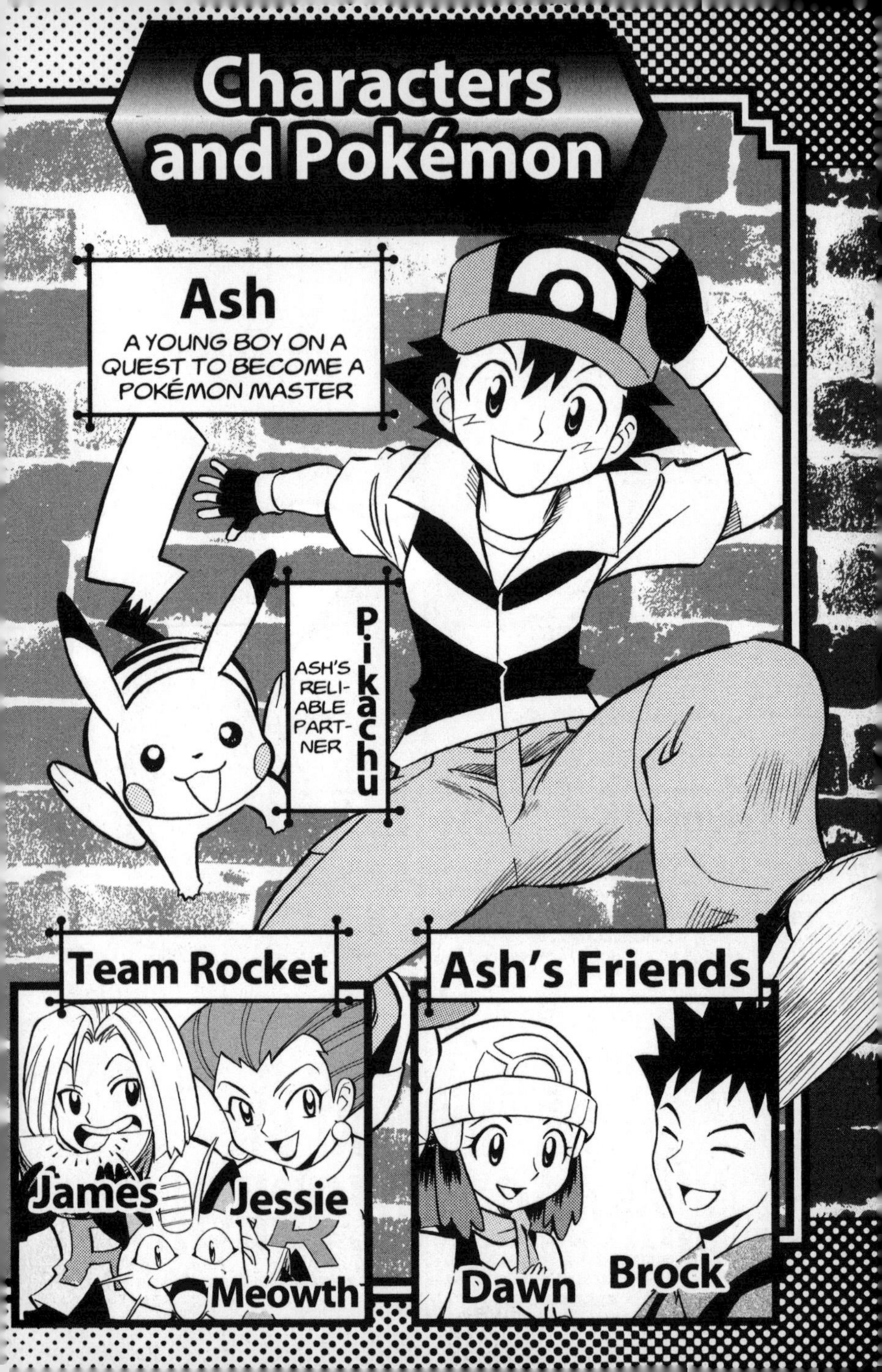
Characters and Pokémon
Ash
A YOUNG BOY ON A QUEST TO BECOME A POKÉMON MASTER
Pikachu
ASH'S RELI-ABLE PART-NER
Team Rocket
James
Jessie
Meowth
Ash's Friends
Dawn
Brock

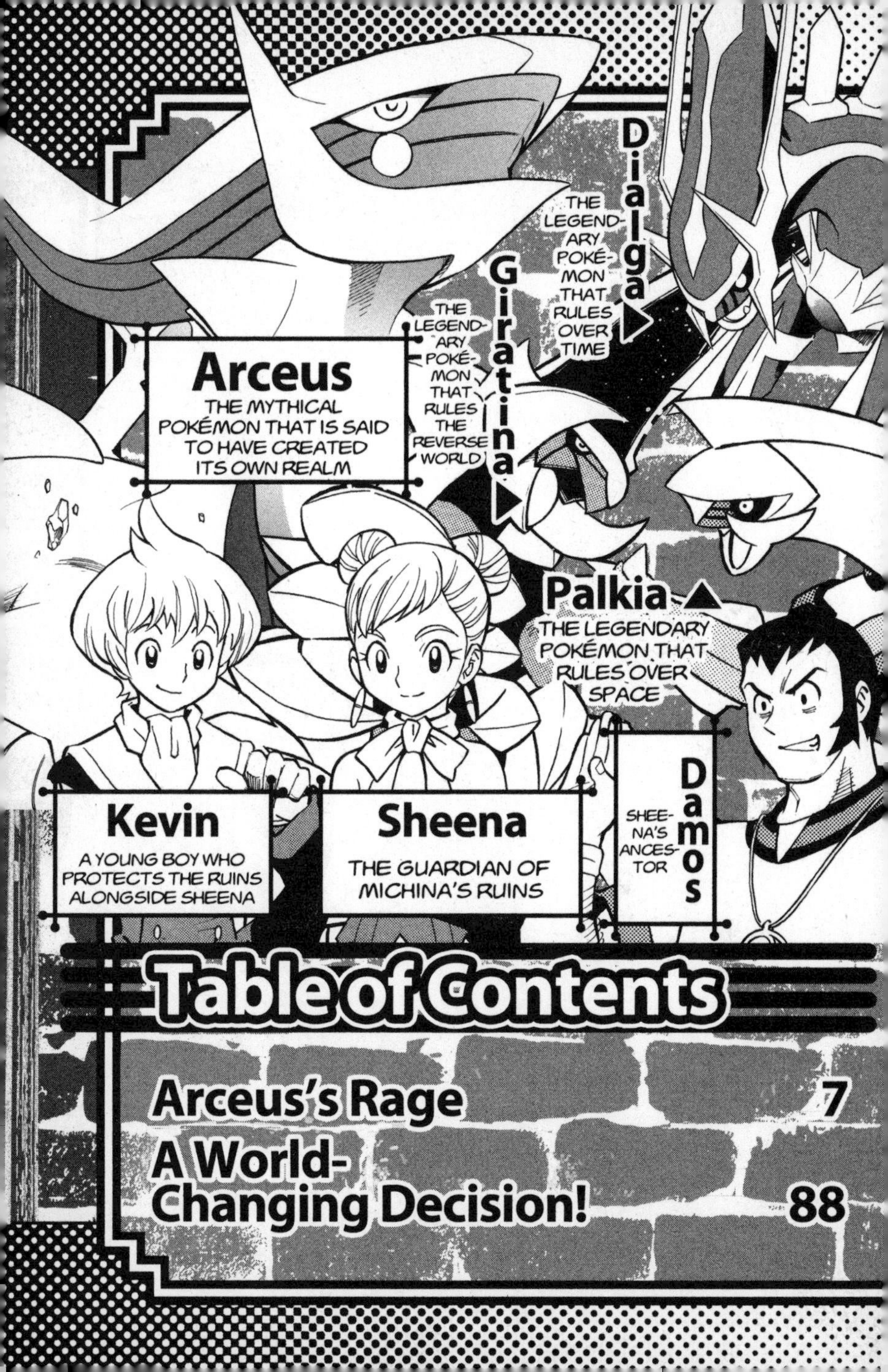
Dialga ▶
THE LEGENDARY POKÉMON THAT RULES OVER TIME
Giratina ▶
THE LEGENDARY POKÉMON THAT RULES THE REVERSE WORLD
Arceus
THE MYTHICAL POKÉMON THAT IS SAID TO HAVE CREATED ITS OWN REALM
Palkia ▲
THE LEGENDARY POKÉMON THAT RULES OVER SPACE
Damos
SHEENA'S ANCESTOR
Sheena
THE GUARDIAN OF MICHINA'S RUINS
Kevin
A YOUNG BOY WHO PROTECTS THE RUINS ALONGSIDE SHEENA

Table of Contents

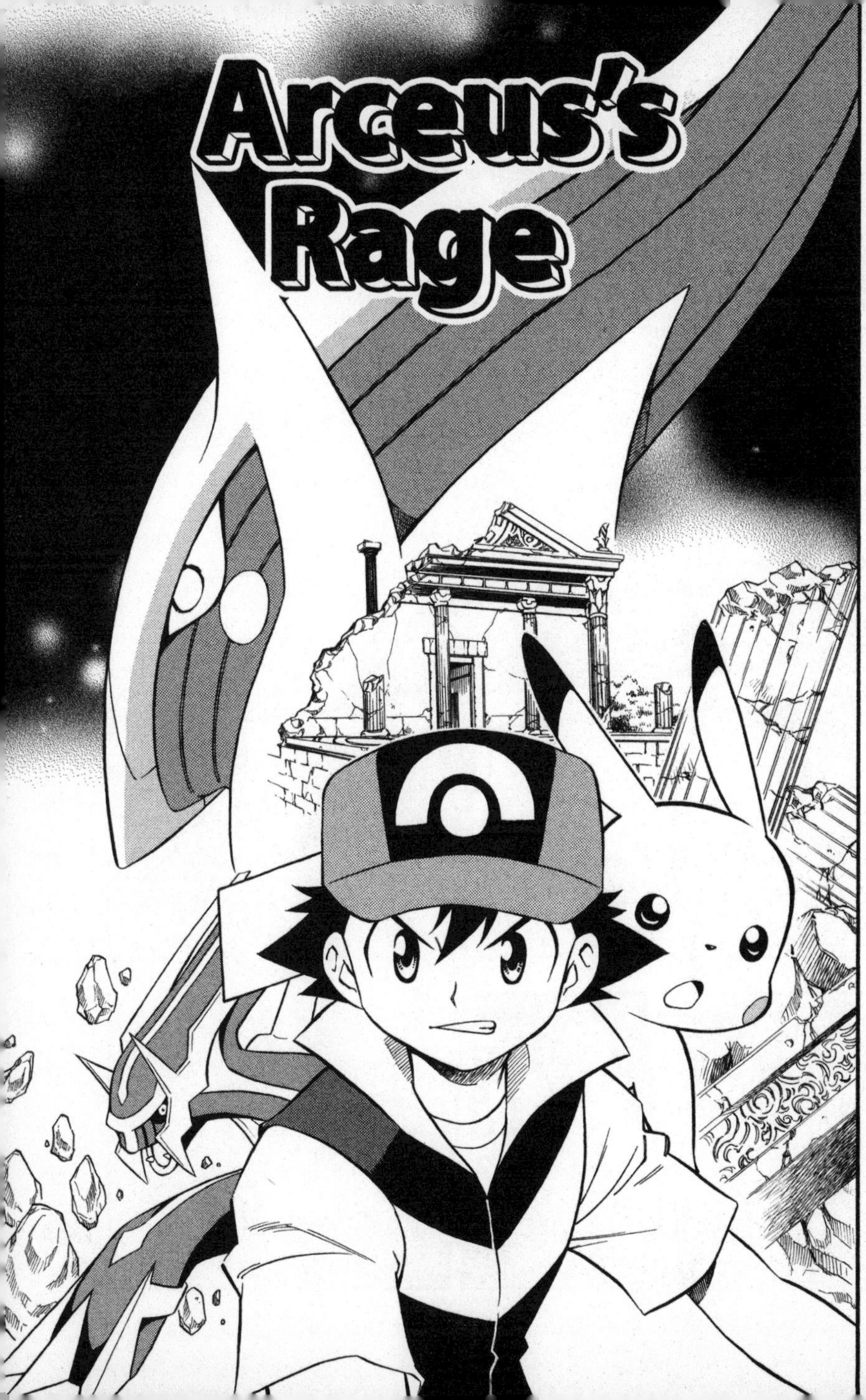
Arceus's Rage

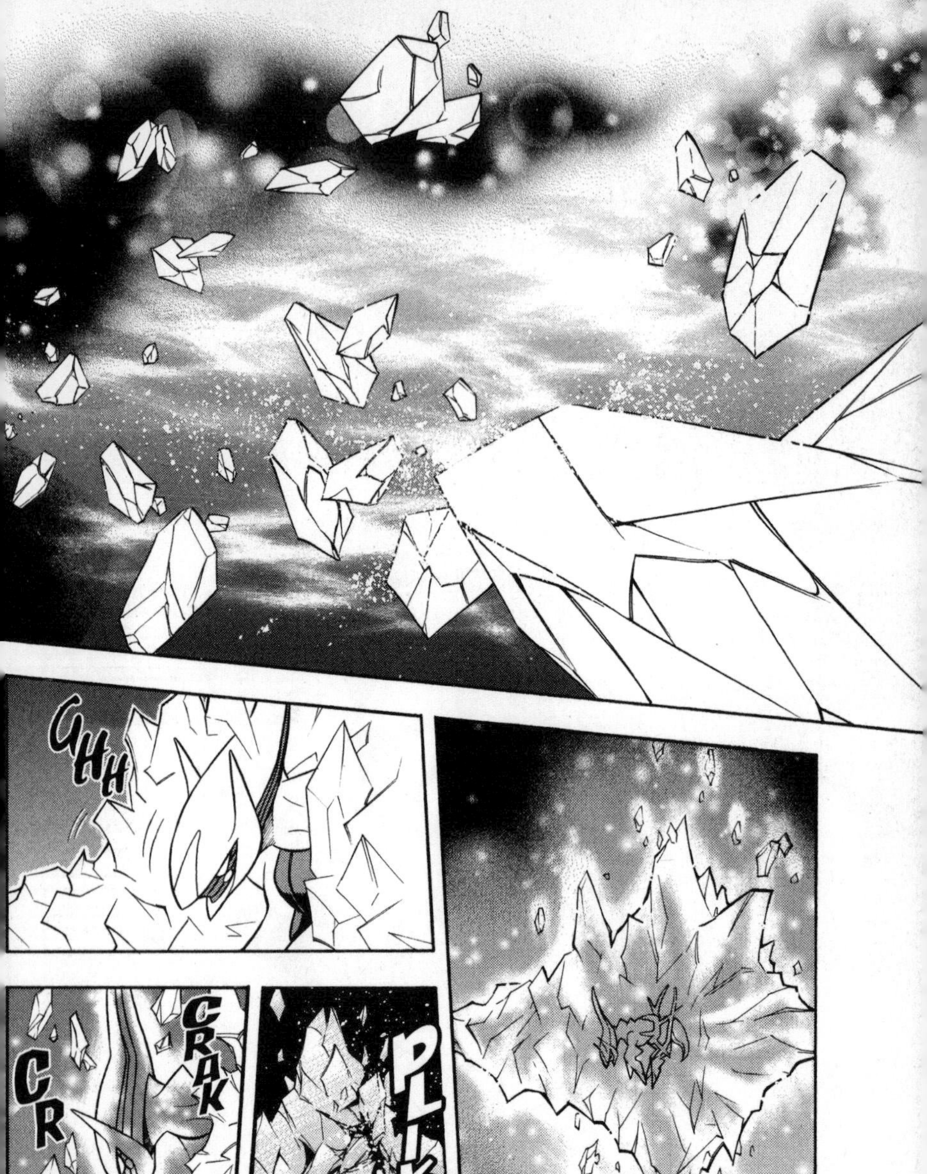
UHH
PLIK
CRAK
CRIK

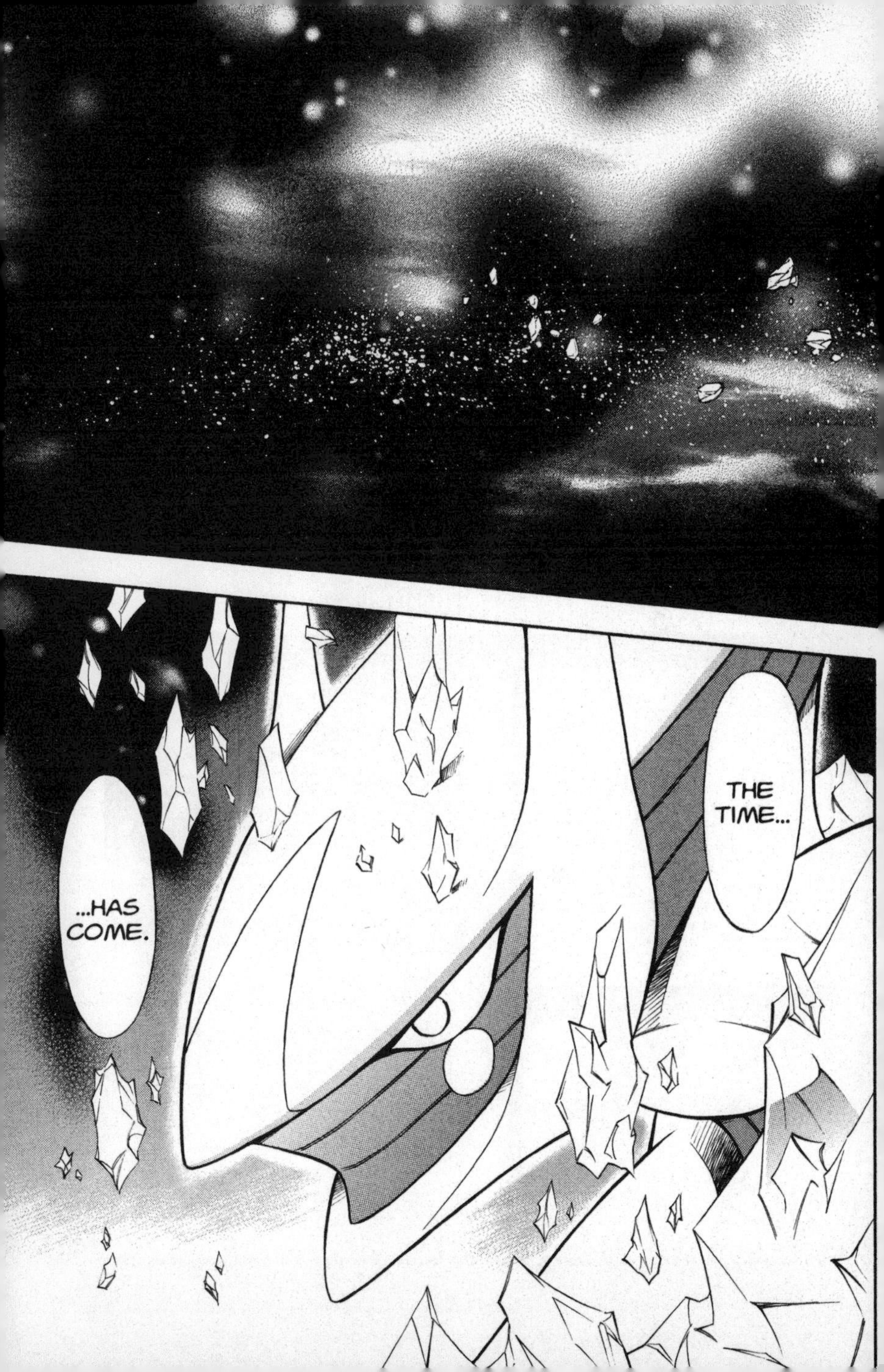
THE TIME...
...HAS COME.

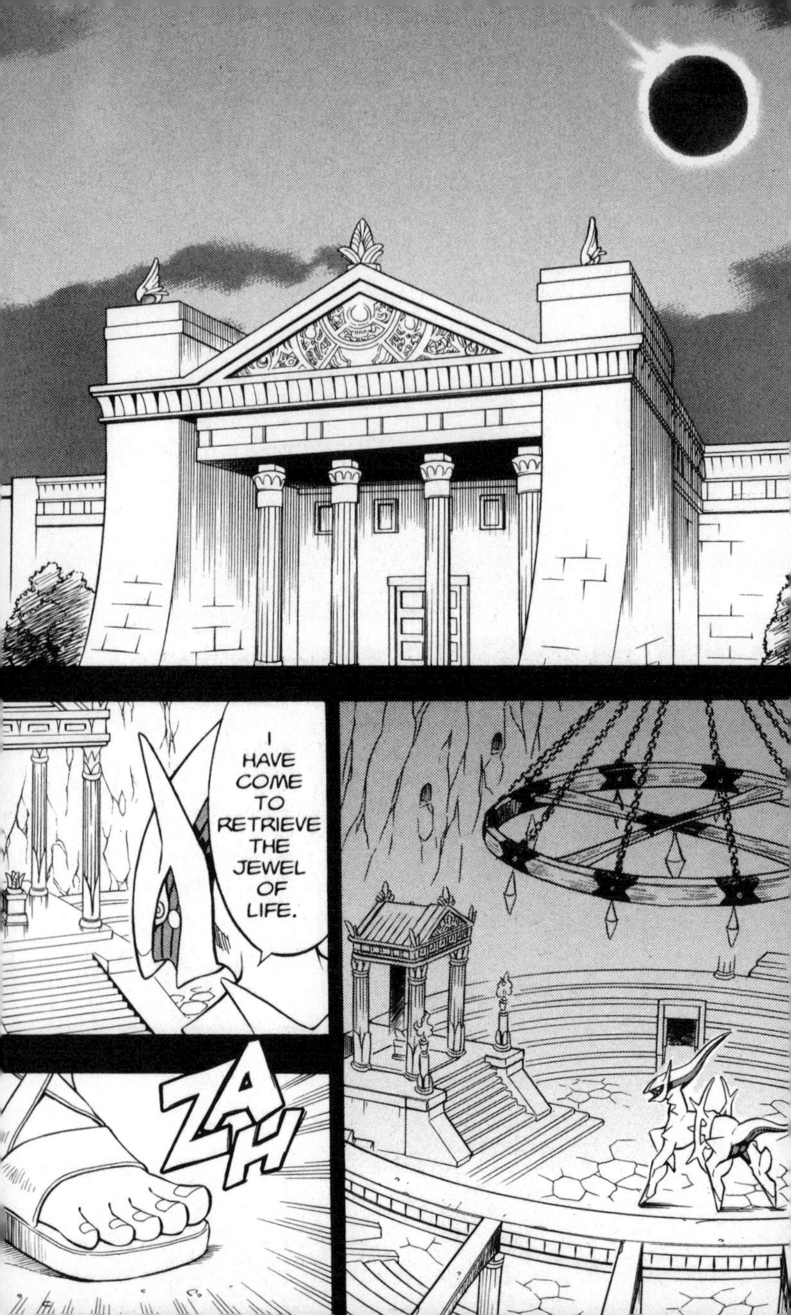
I HAVE COME TO RETRIEVE THE JEWEL OF LIFE.
ZAH

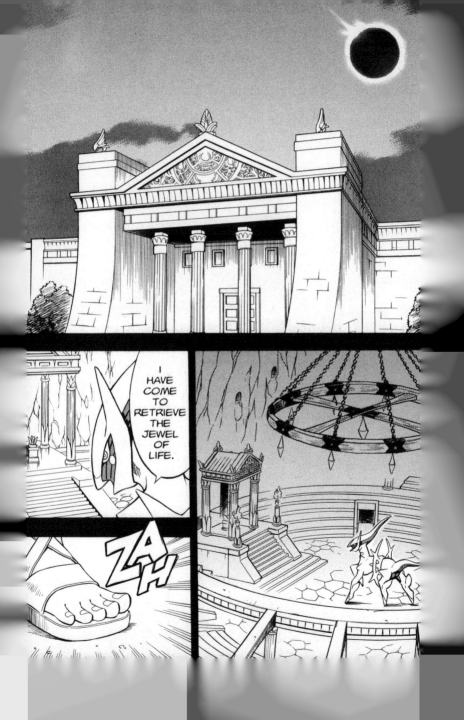

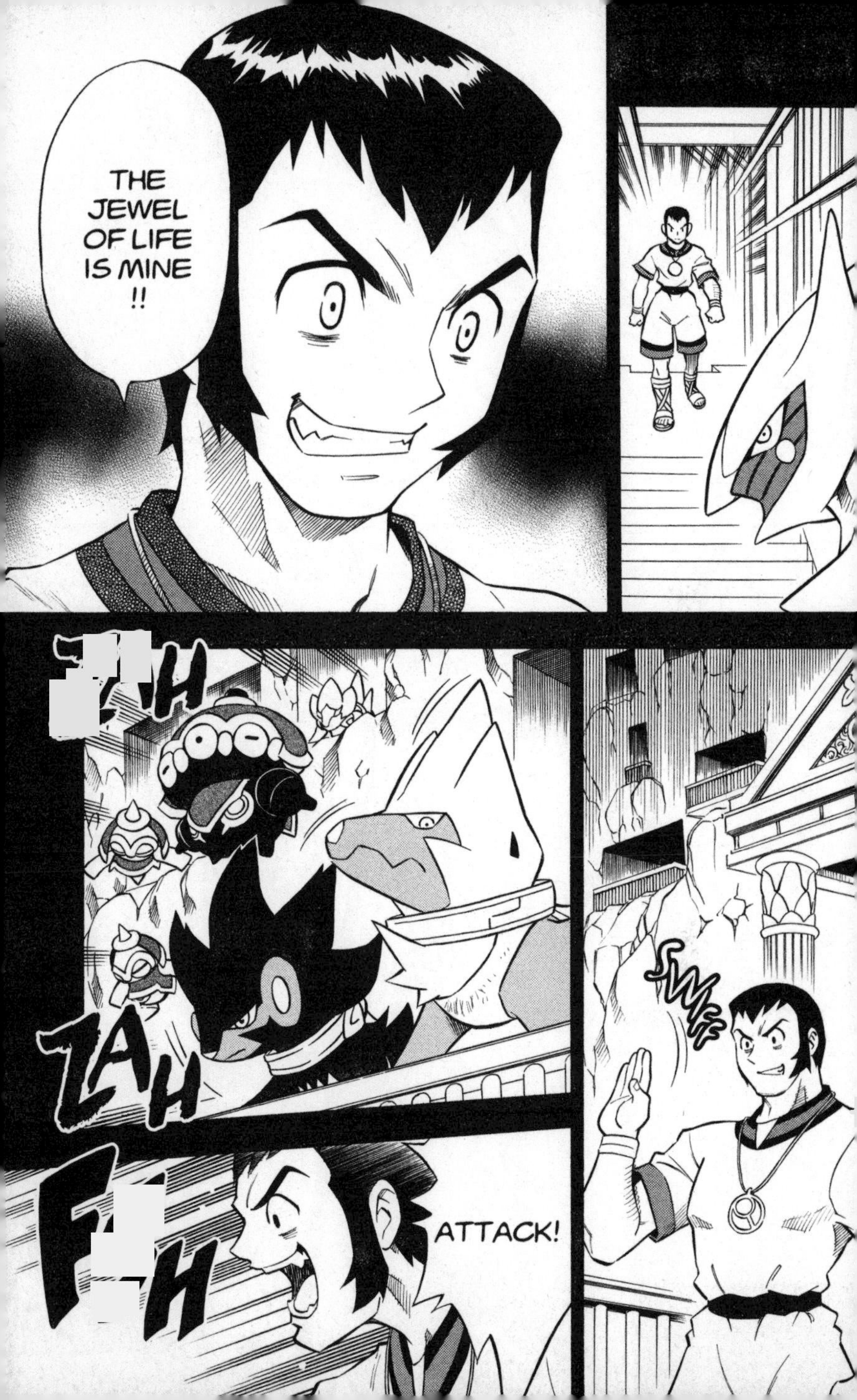
THE JEWEL OF LIFE IS MINE !!
ZAH
ATTACK!

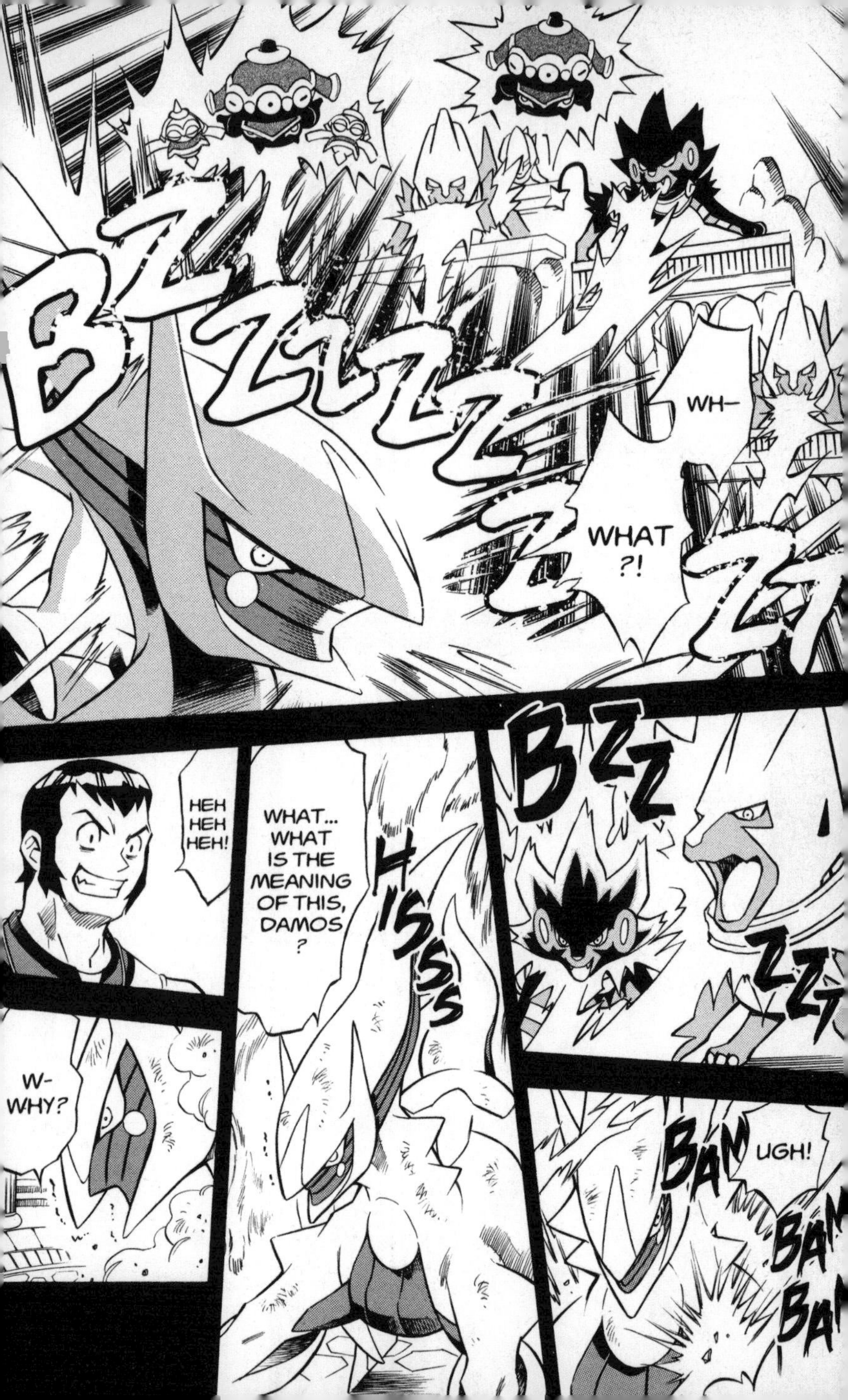
WH-
WHAT ?!
ZZT
BZZZZZZZZZZ
BZZ
ZZT
UGH!
BAM
BAM
BAM
WHAT... WHAT IS THE MEANING OF THIS, DAMOS ?
HISSS
HEH HEH HEH!
W- WHY?

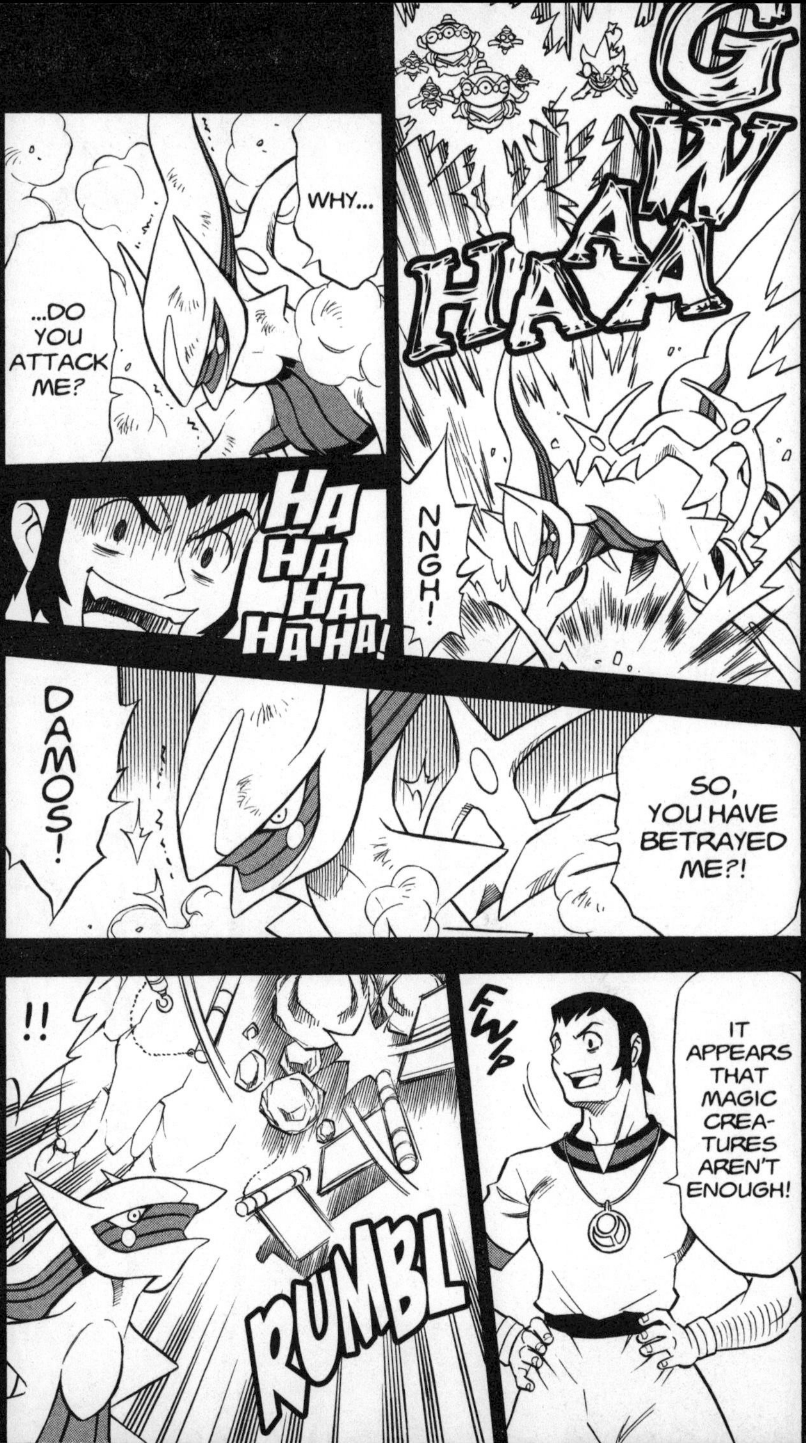
GWAA HAA
NNGH!
WHY...
...DO YOU ATTACK ME?
HA HA HA HA HA HA!
SO, YOU HAVE BETRAYED ME?!
DAMOS!
IT APPEARS THAT MAGIC CREA-TURES AREN'T ENOUGH!
FWP
!!
RUMBL

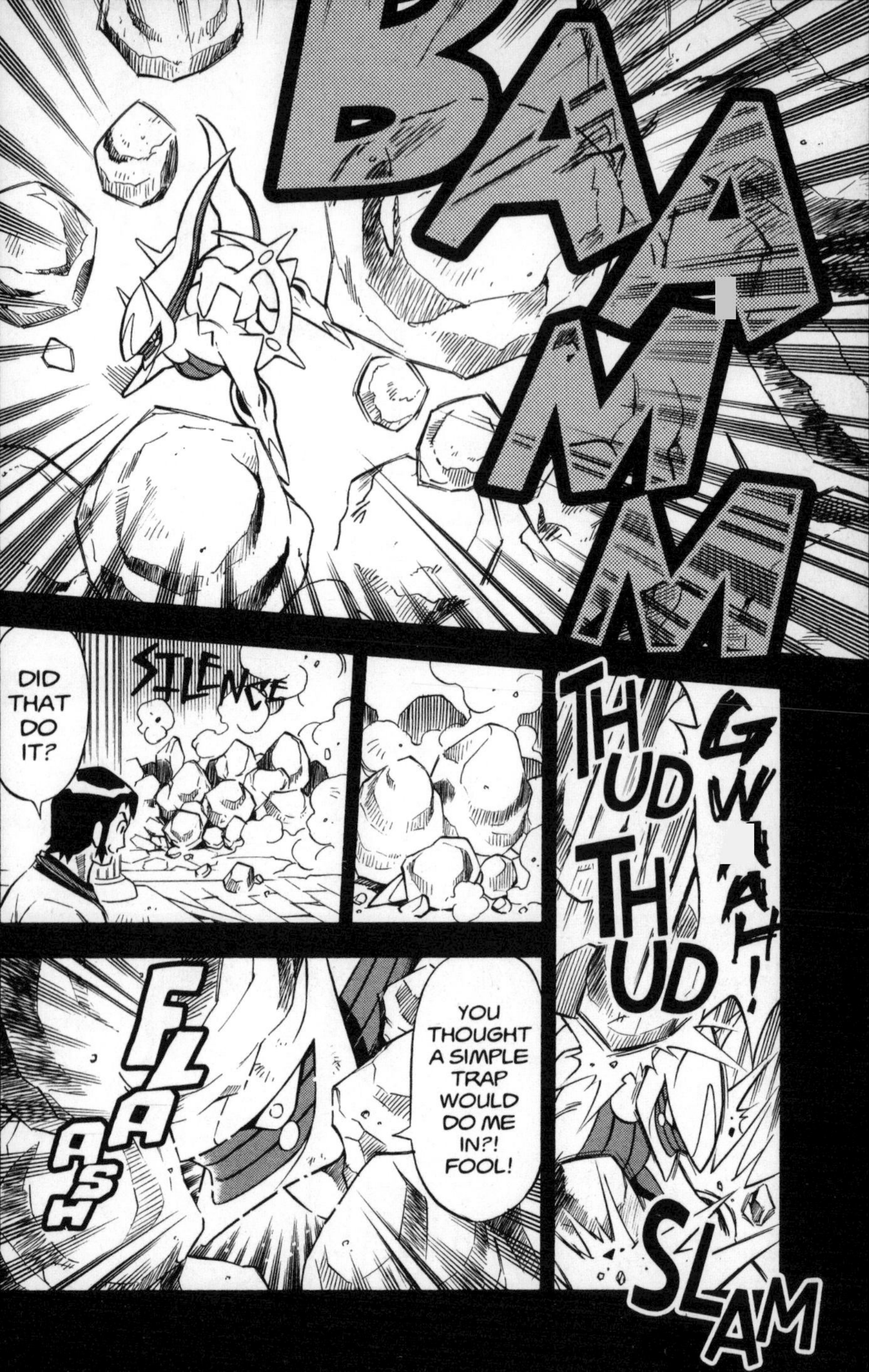
THUD THUD
GWAH!
SILENCE
DID THAT DO IT?
SLAM
YOU THOUGHT A SIMPLE TRAP WOULD DO ME IN?! FOOL!
FLAASH

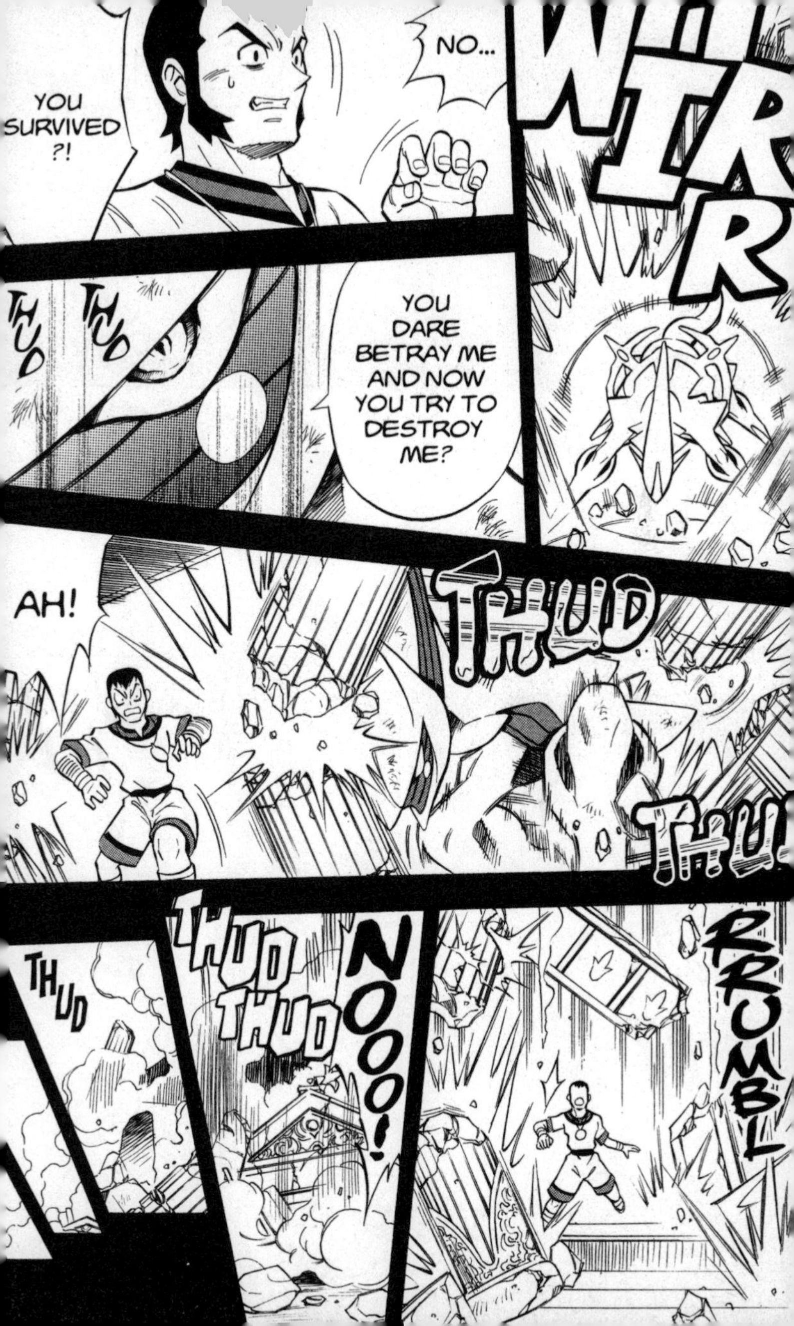
NO...
YOU SURVIVED ?!
YOU DARE BETRAY ME AND NOW YOU TRY TO DESTROY ME?
THUD
THUD
THUD
THU
AH!
RRUMBL
NOOOO!
THUD
THUD
THUD

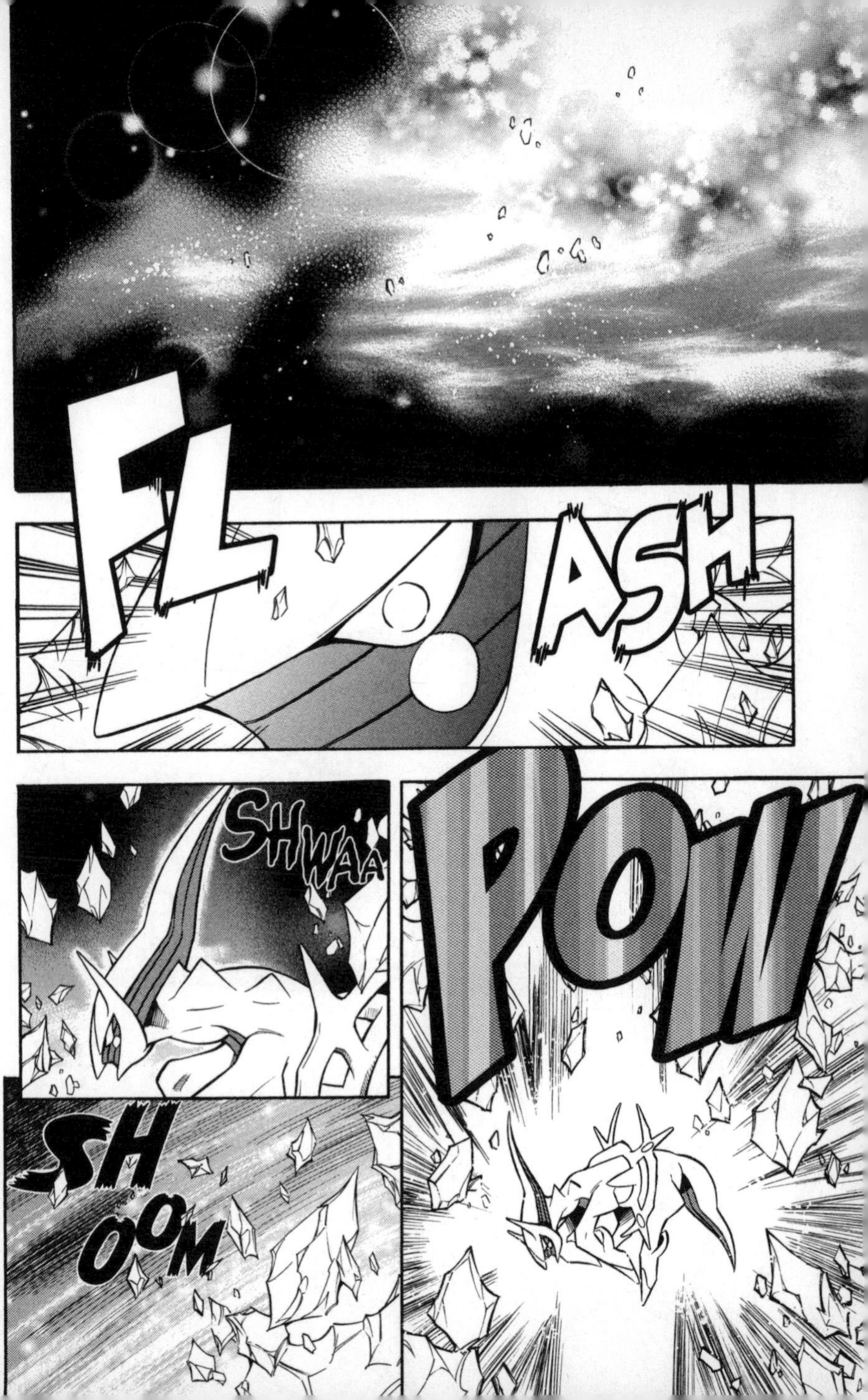
FLASH
POW
SHWAA
SHOOM

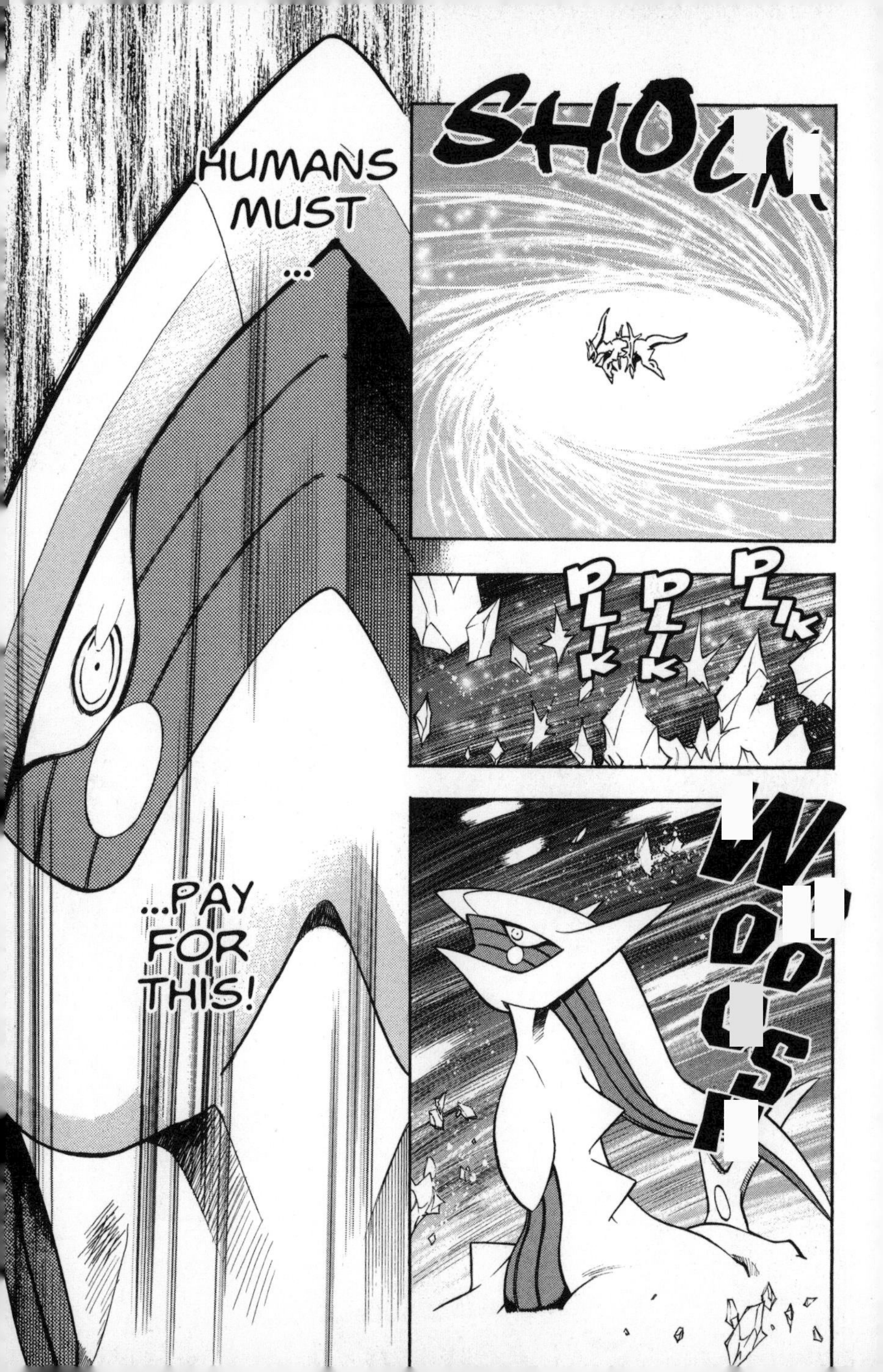
PLIK PLIK PLIK
HUMANS MUST ...
...PAY FOR THIS!

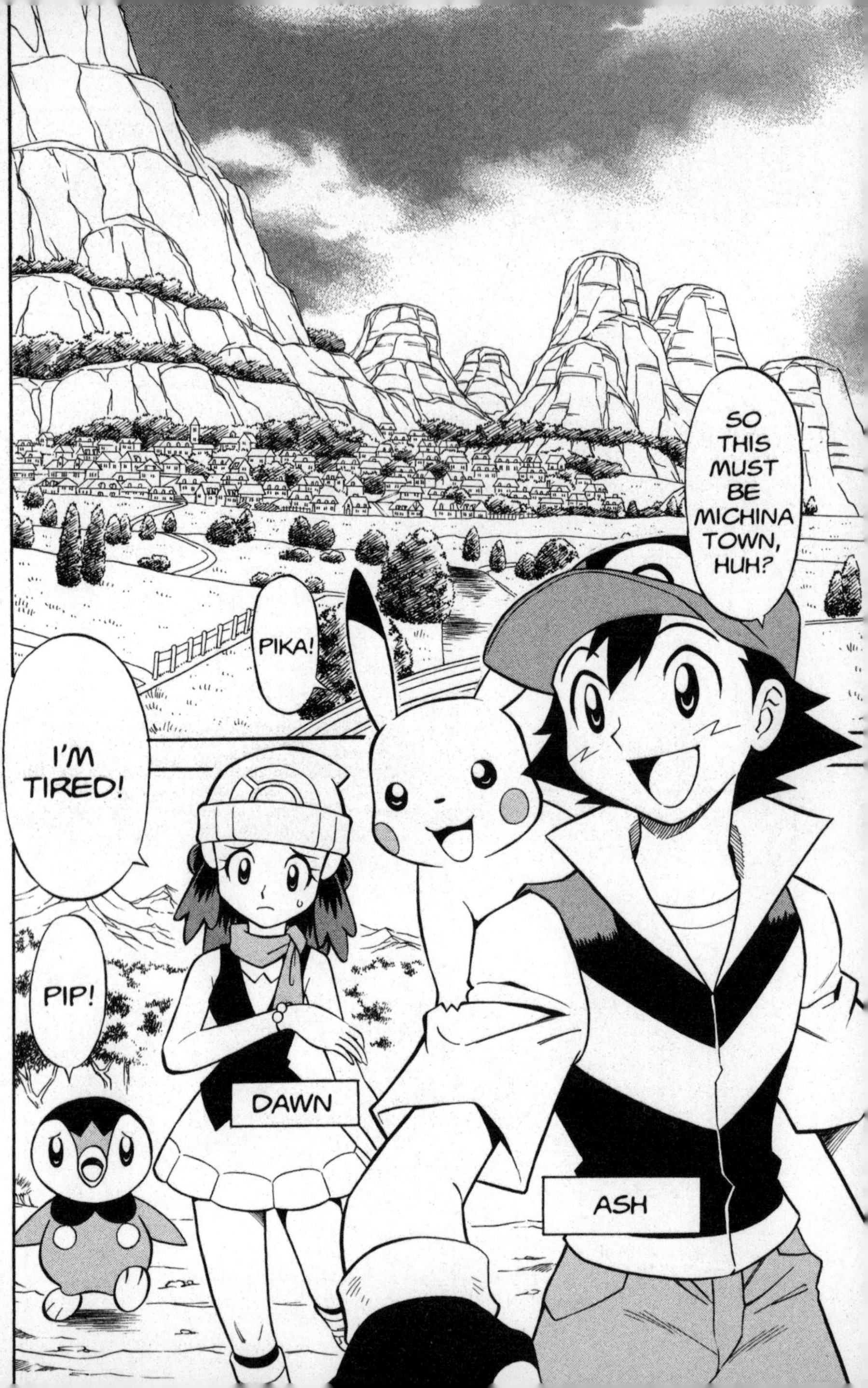
SO THIS MUST BE MICHINA TOWN, HUH?
PIKA!
I'M TIRED!
PIP!
DAWN
ASH

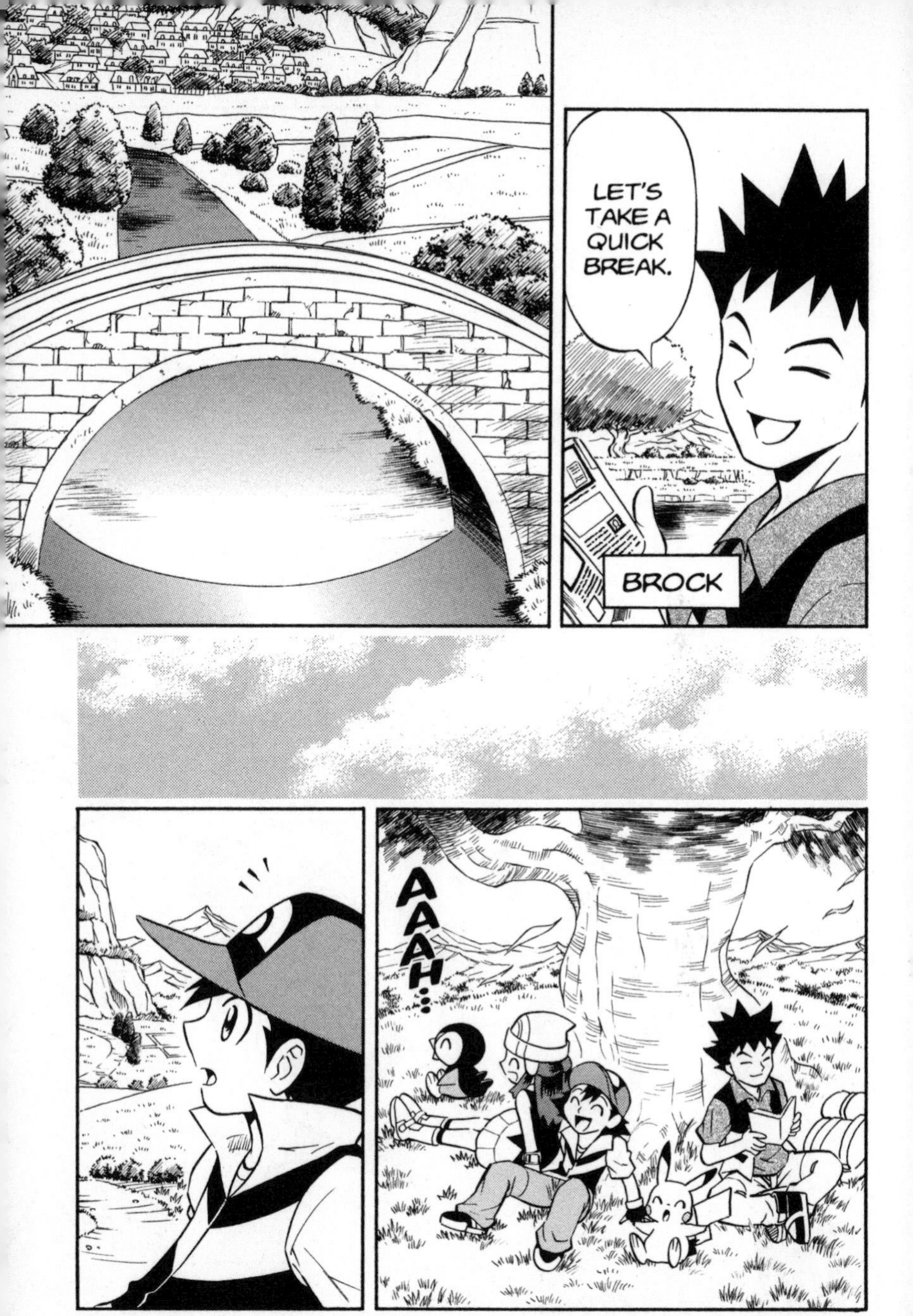
LET'S TAKE A QUICK BREAK.
BROCK
AAAH…

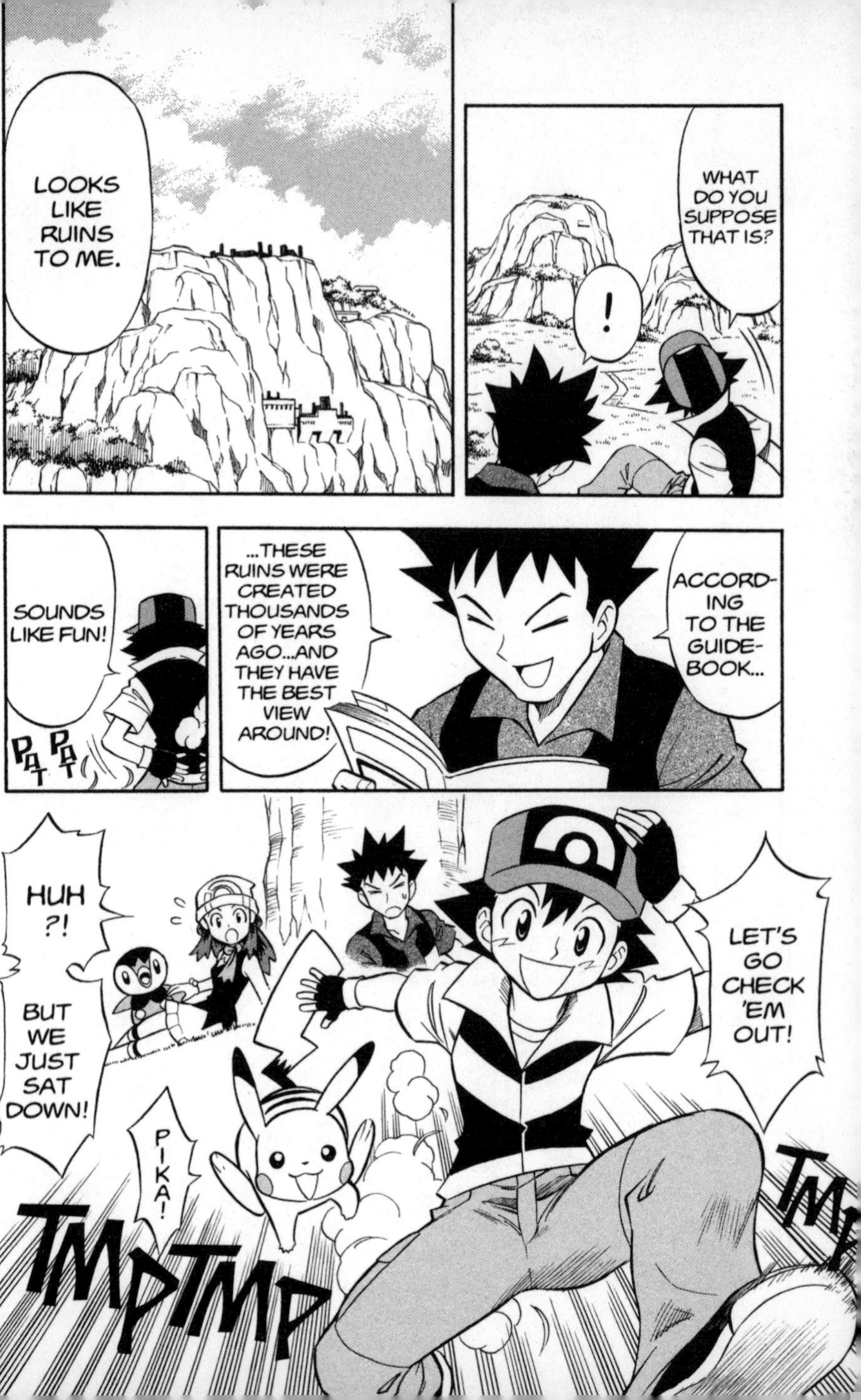
WHAT DO YOU SUPPOSE THAT IS?
!
LOOKS LIKE RUINS TO ME.
ACCORD-ING TO THE GUIDE-BOOK...
...THESE RUINS WERE CREATED THOUSANDS OF YEARS AGO...AND THEY HAVE THE BEST VIEW AROUND!
SOUNDS LIKE FUN!
PAT PAT
LET'S GO CHECK 'EM OUT!
HUH?!
BUT WE JUST SAT DOWN!
PIKA!
TMPTMP
TMP

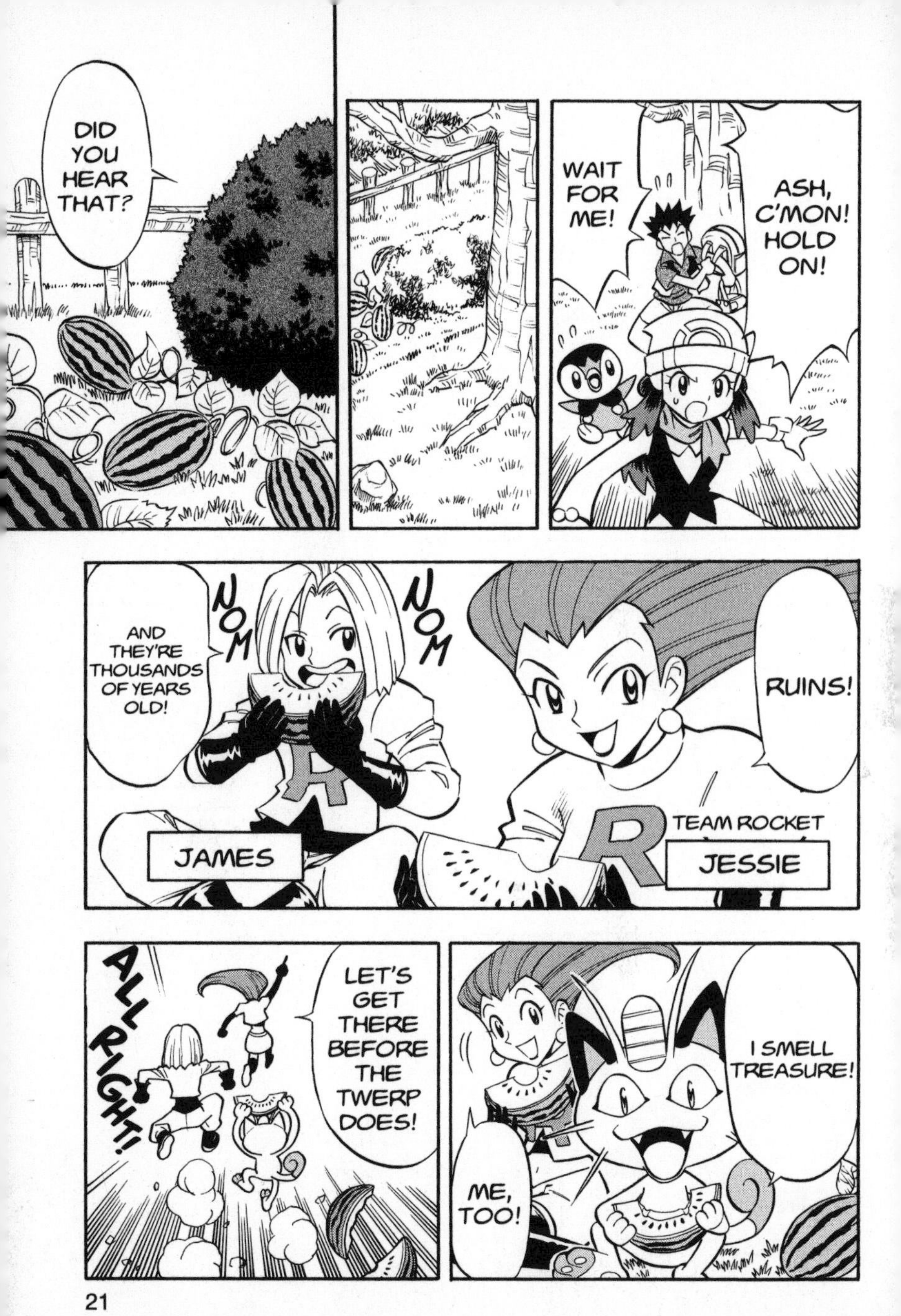
ASH, C'MON! HOLD ON!
WAIT FOR ME!
DID YOU HEAR THAT?
RUINS!
TEAM ROCKET
JESSIE
NOM
AND THEY'RE THOUSANDS OF YEARS OLD!
NOM
JAMES
I SMELL TREASURE!
ME, TOO!
LET'S GET THERE BEFORE THE TWERP DOES!
ALL RIGHT!!

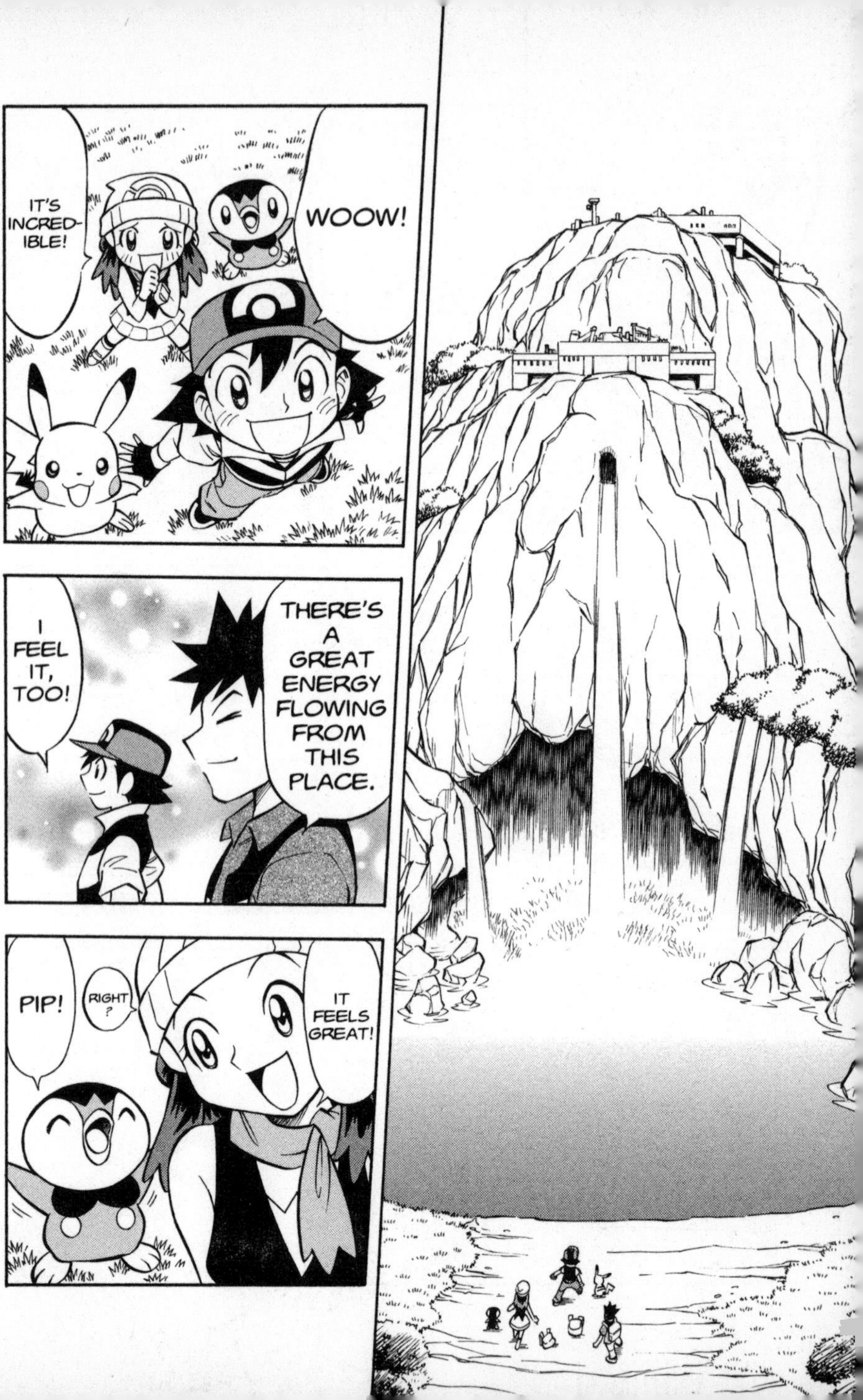
WOOW!
IT'S INCREDIBLE!
THERE'S A GREAT ENERGY FLOWING FROM THIS PLACE.
I FEEL IT, TOO!
IT FEELS GREAT!
RIGHT?
PIP!

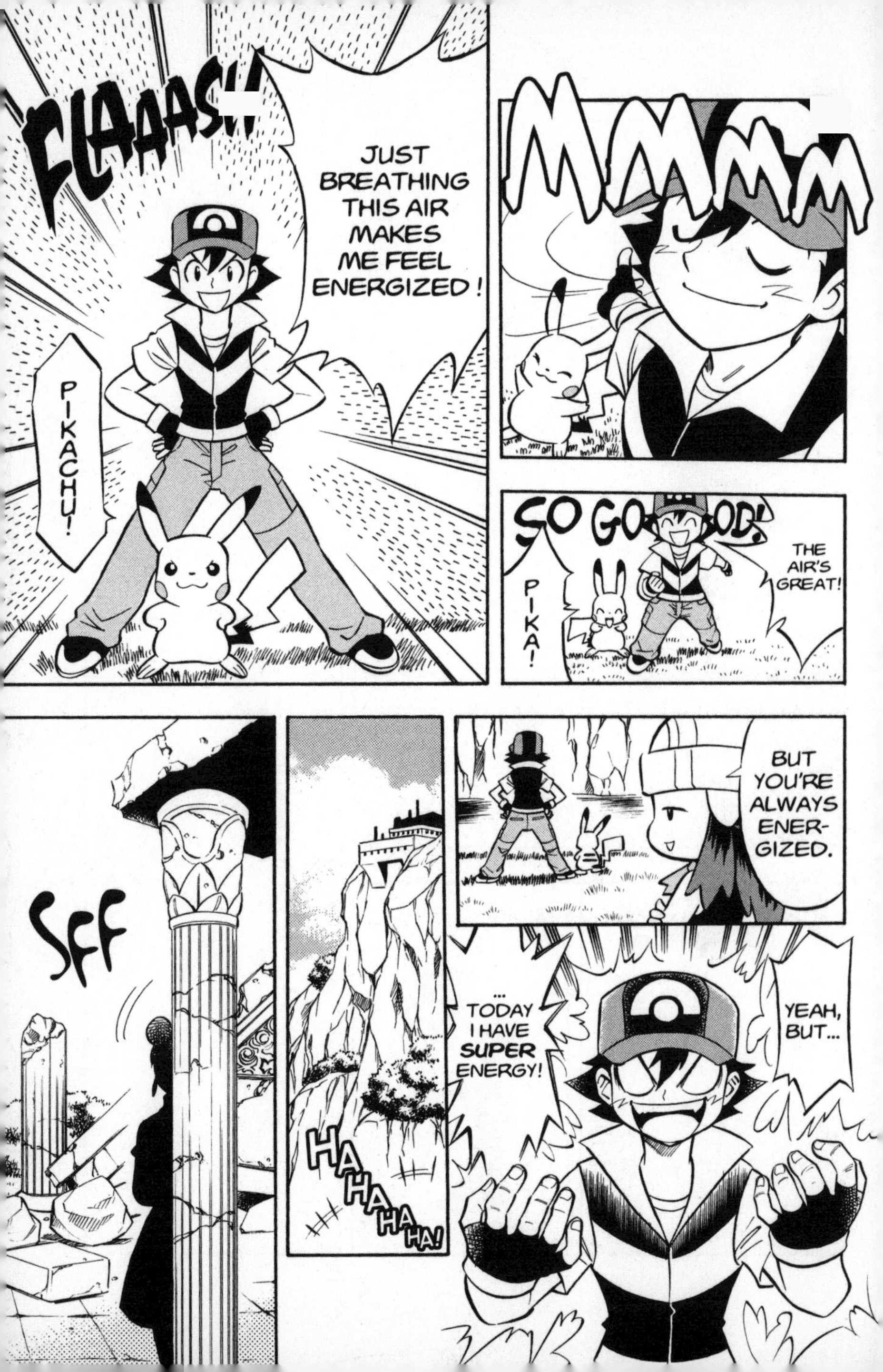
MMMMM
SO GOOD!
THE AIR'S GREAT!
PIKA!
FLAAASH
JUST BREATHING THIS AIR MAKES ME FEEL ENERGIZED!
PIKACHU!
BUT YOU'RE ALWAYS ENER-GIZED.
YEAH, BUT...
...TODAY I HAVE SUPER ENERGY!
HAHAHAHAHA!
SFF

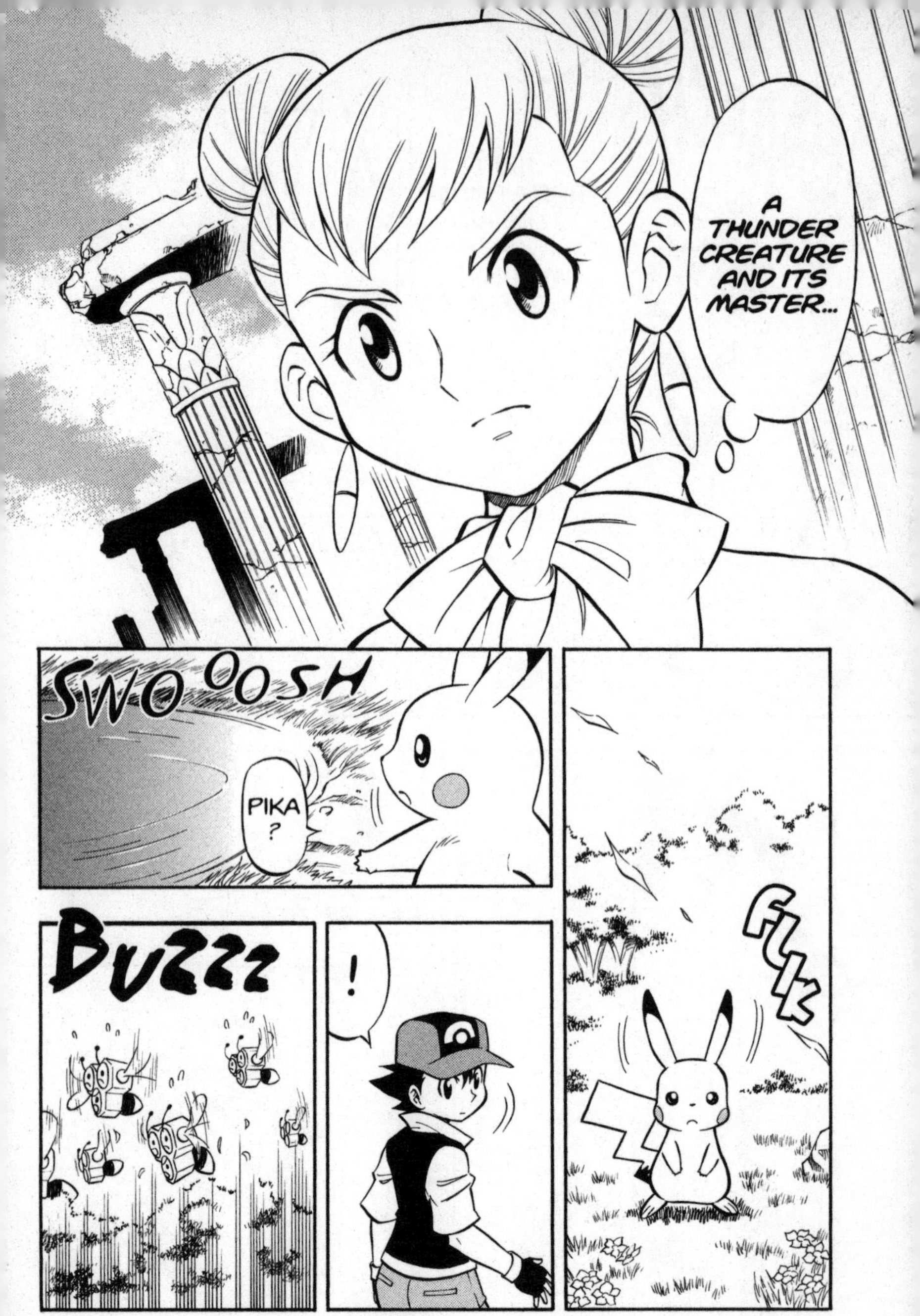
A THUNDER CREATURE AND ITS MASTER...
FLIK
SWOOOSH
PIKA ?
!
BUZZZ

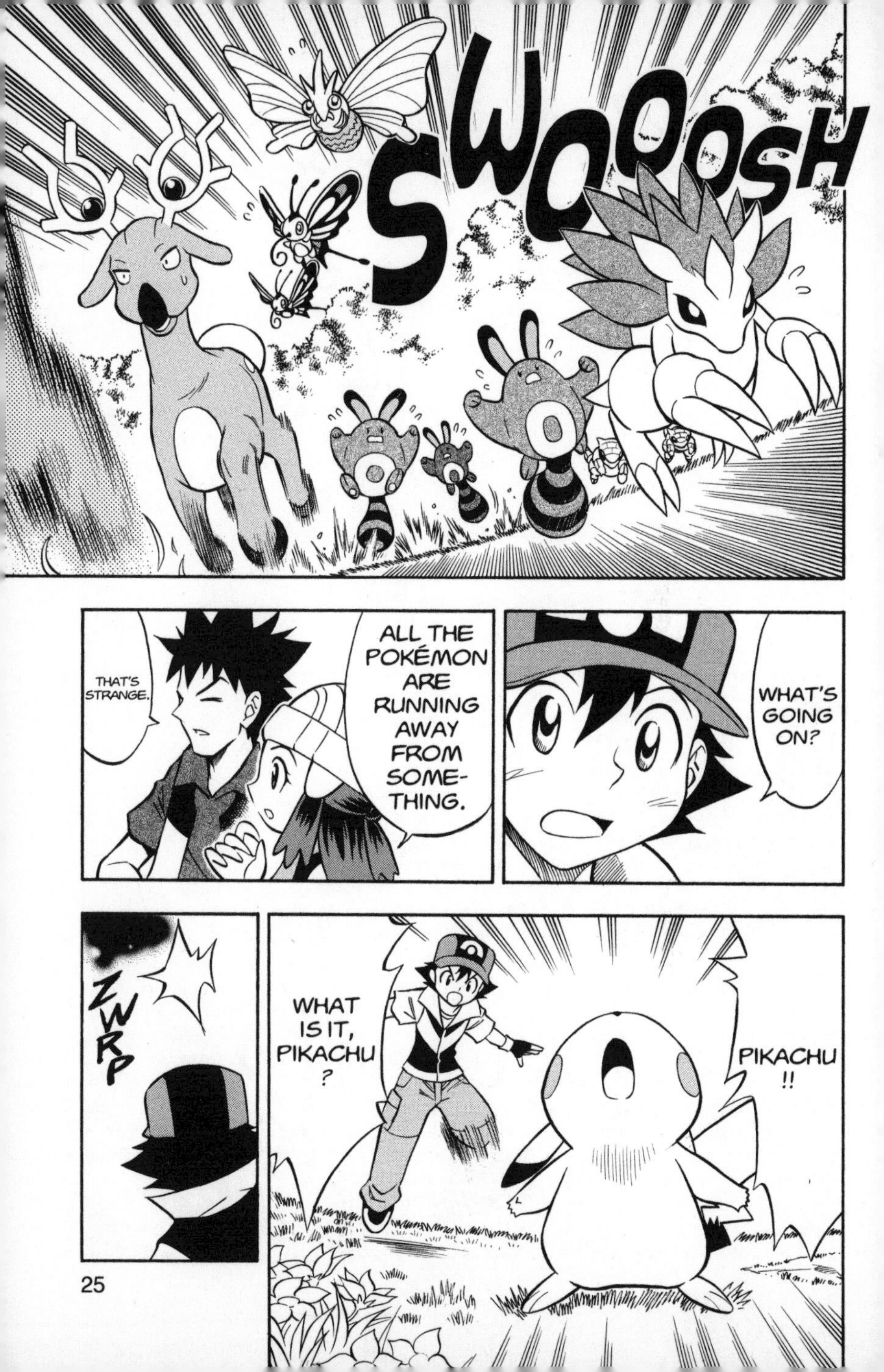
SWOOOSH
WHAT'S GOING ON?
ALL THE POKÉMON ARE RUNNING AWAY FROM SOMETHING.
THAT'S STRANGE.
PIKACHU!!
WHAT IS IT, PIKACHU?
ZWRP

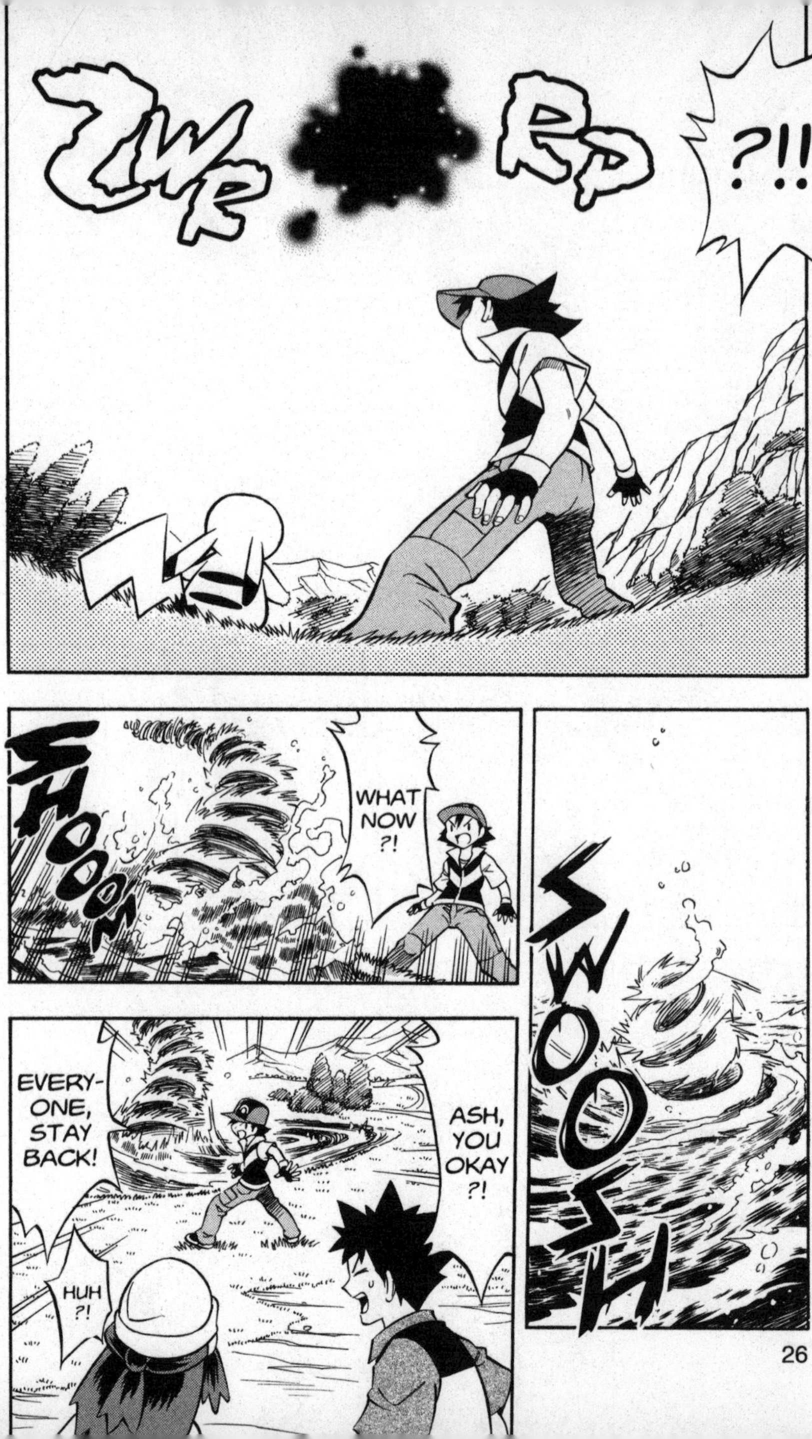
?!!
SWOOOSH
FHOOOM
WHAT NOW ?!
ASH, YOU OKAY ?!
EVERY-ONE, STAY BACK!
HUH ?!

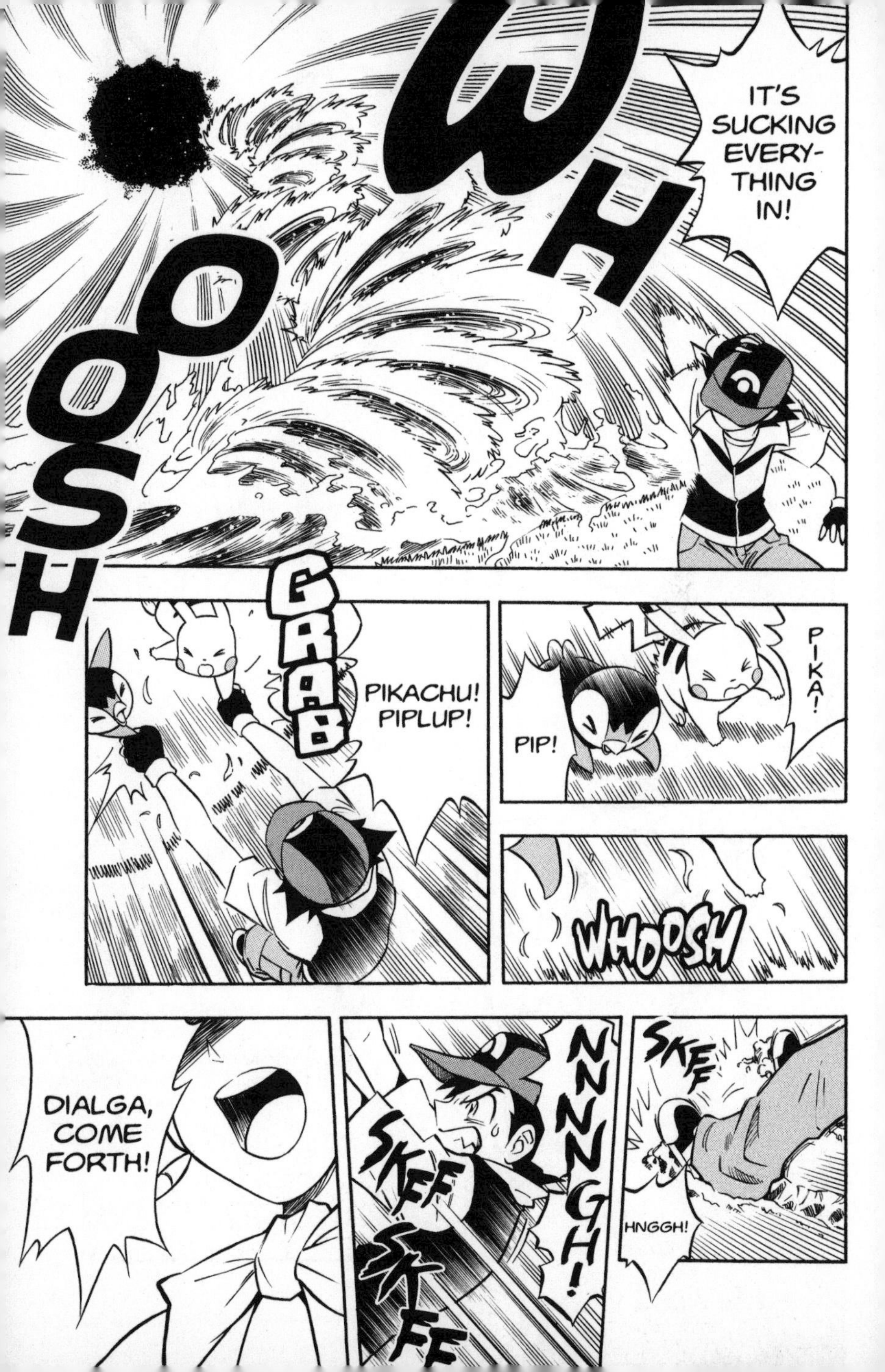
IT'S SUCKING EVERY-THING IN!
WHOOSH
PIKA!
PIP!
WHOOSH
GRAB
PIKACHU! PIPLUP!
SKEF
HNGGH!
NNNNGH!
SKEFF
SKEF
SKEFF
DIALGA, COME FORTH!

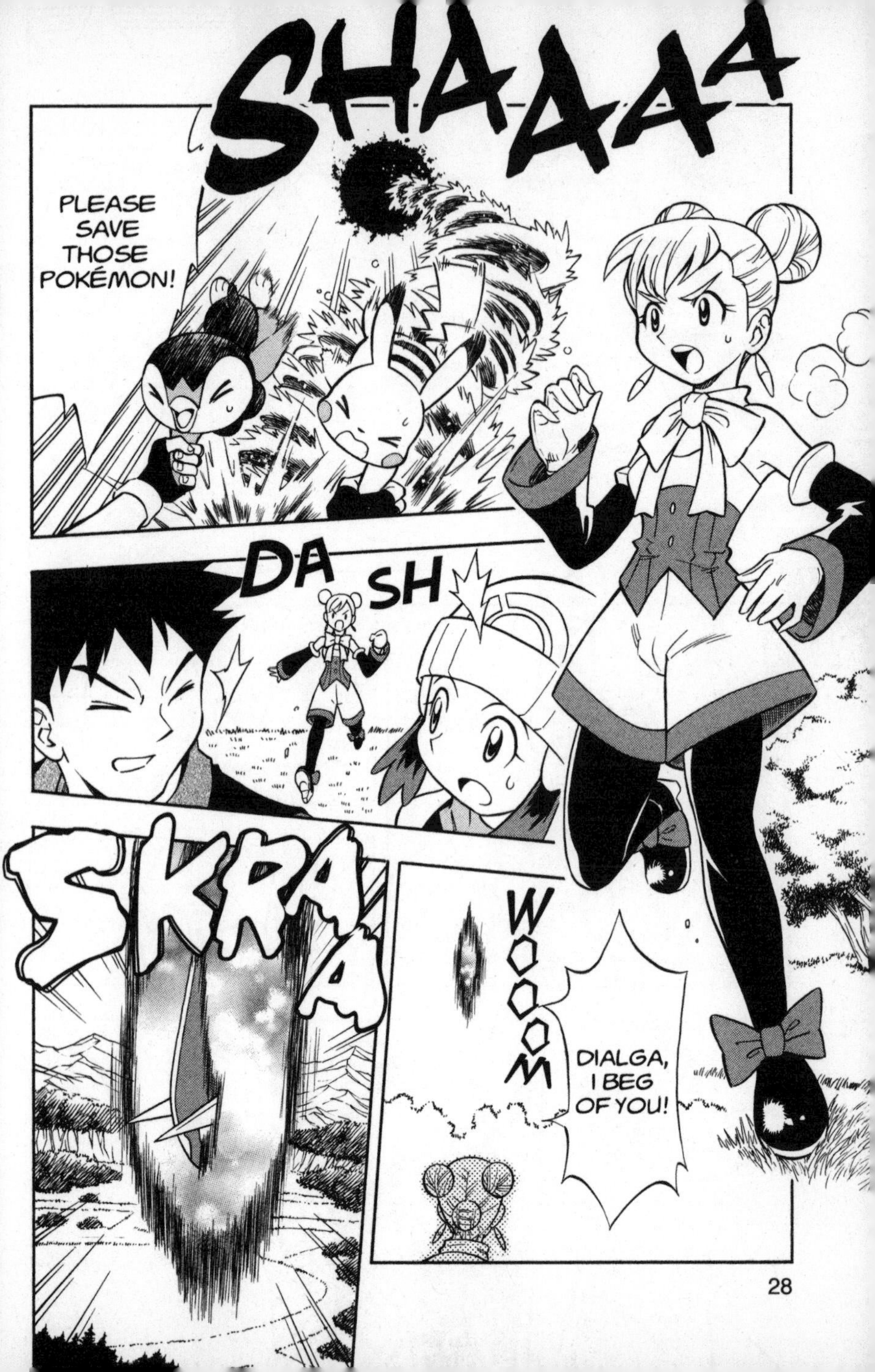
SHAAAA
PLEASE SAVE THOSE POKÉMON!
DASH
WOOOM
DIALGA, I BEG OF YOU!
SKRAA

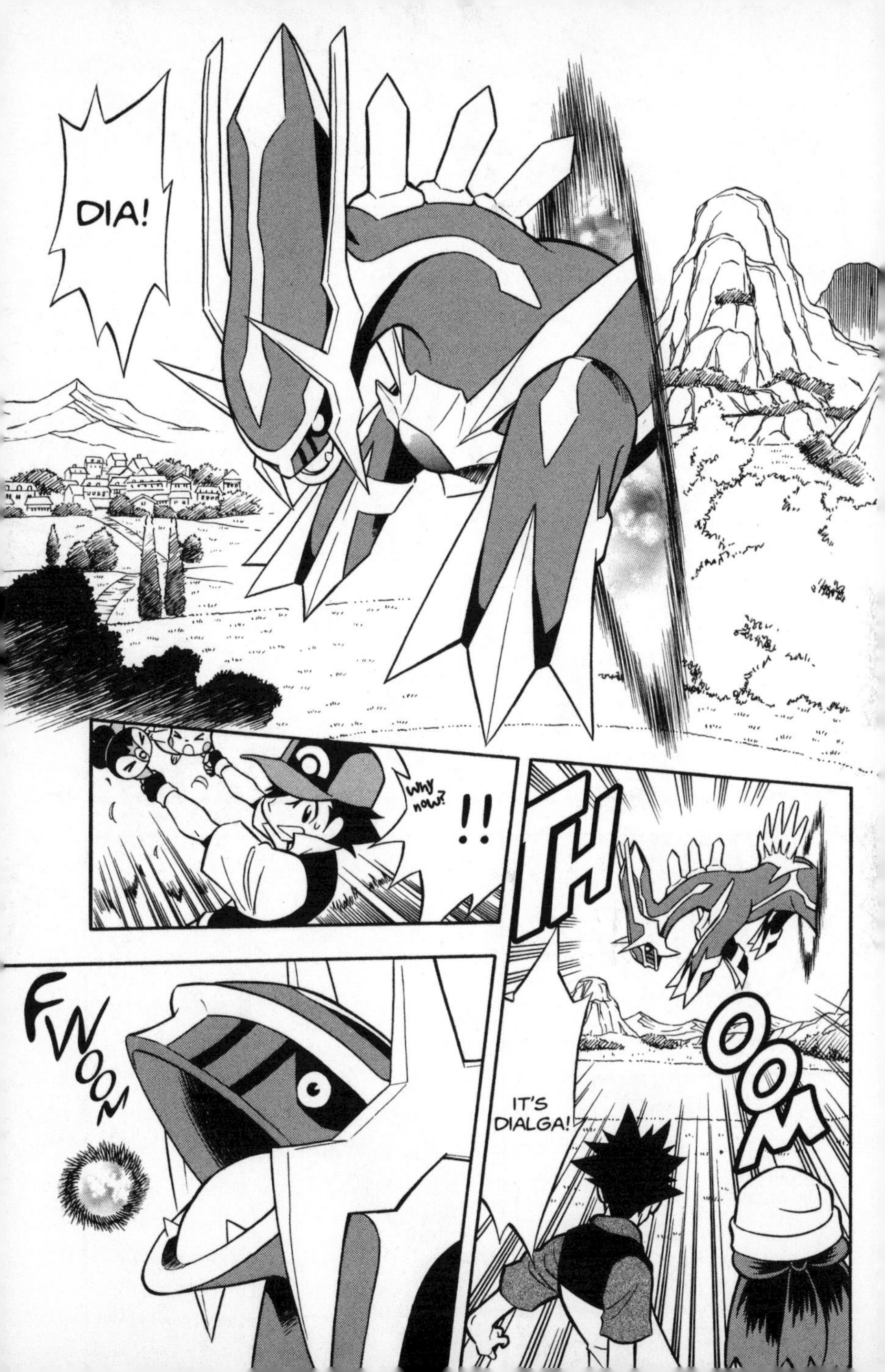
DIA!
THOOOM
IT'S DIALGA!
Why now?
!!
FWOOM

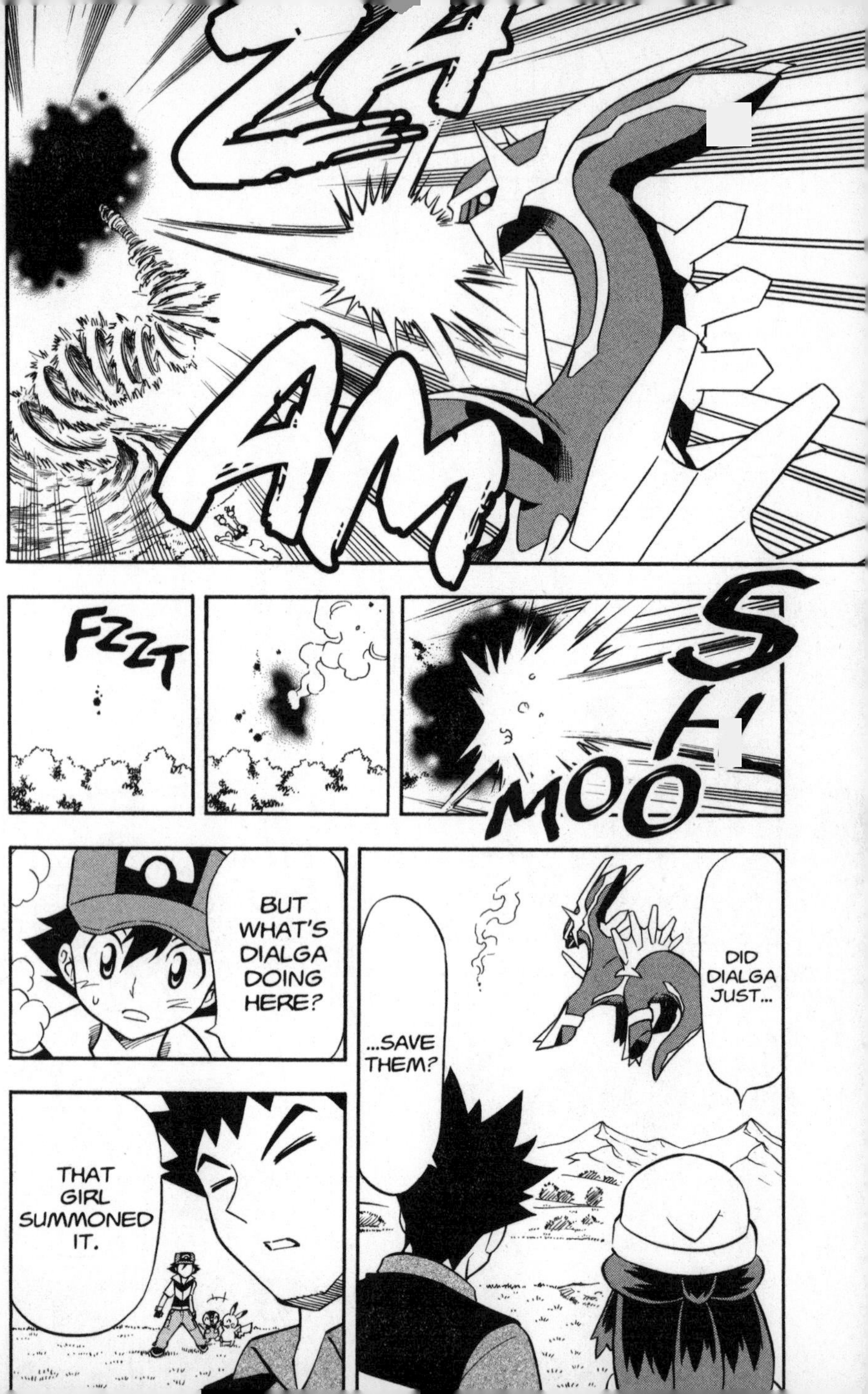
ZA
AM
SHMOO
FZZZT
DID DIALGA JUST...
...SAVE THEM?
BUT WHAT'S DIALGA DOING HERE?
THAT GIRL SUMMONED IT.

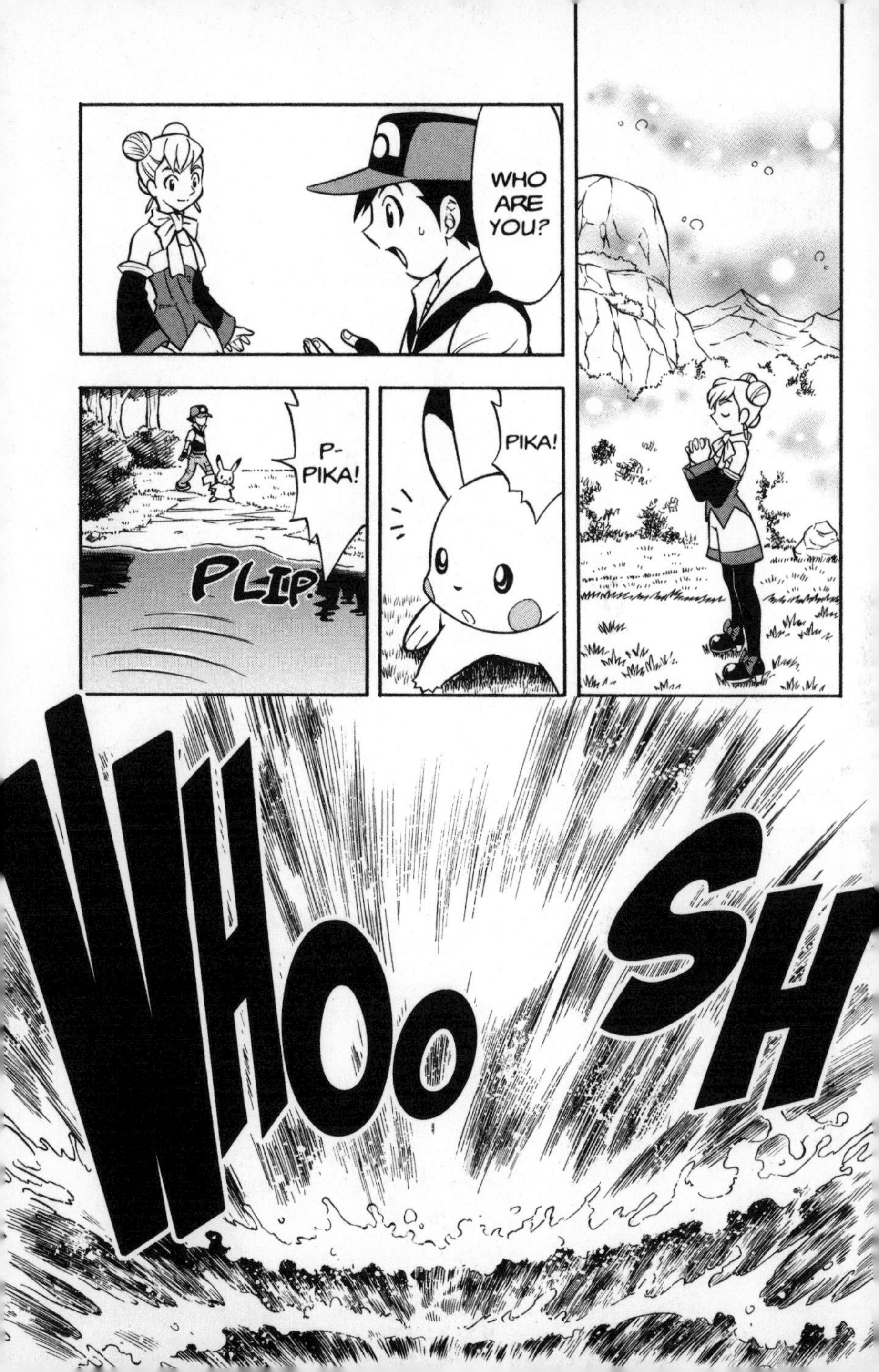
WHO ARE YOU?
PIKA!
P- PIKA!
PLIP.
WHOOSH

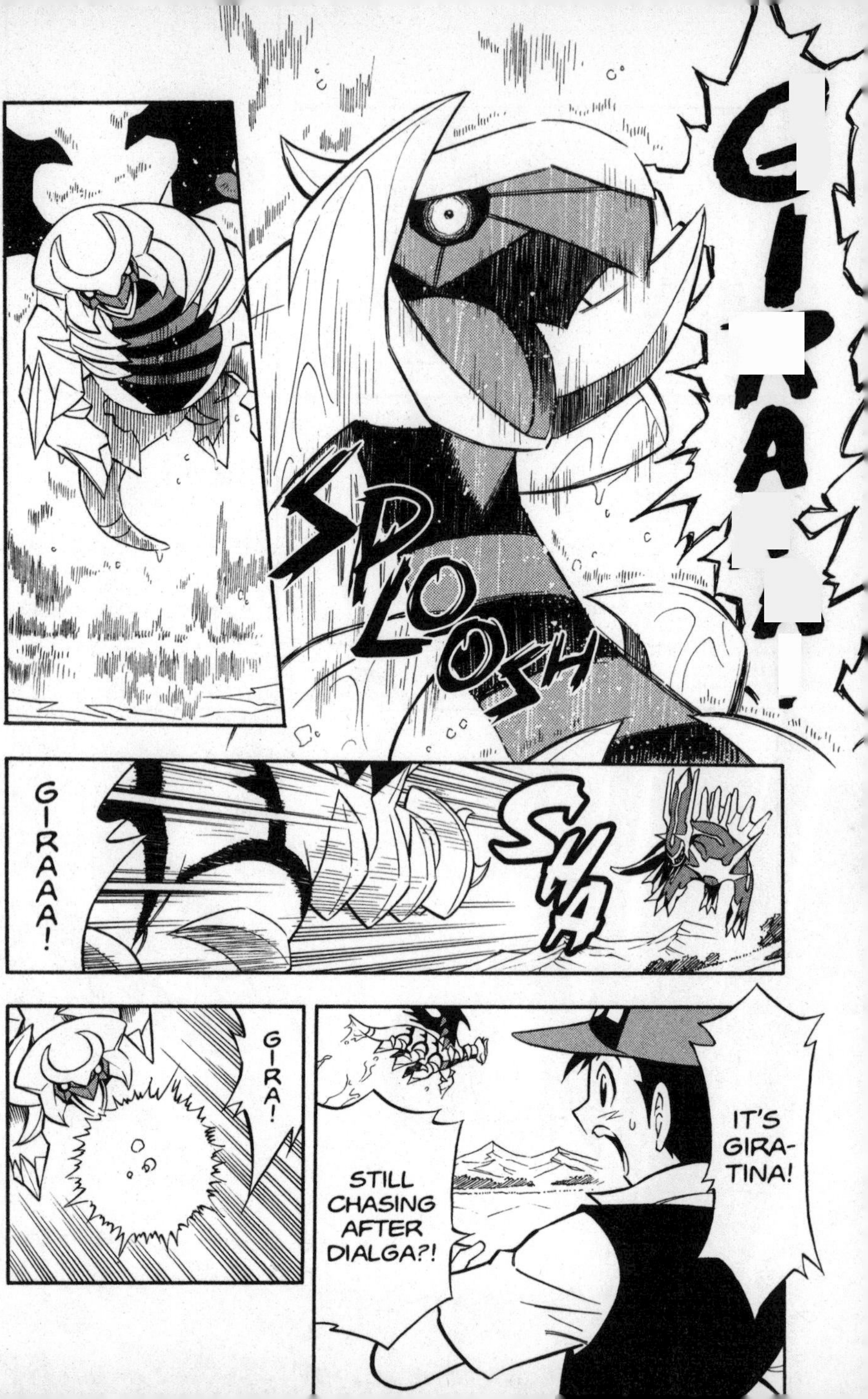
GIRAAAA!
SPLOOSH
SHA
GIRAAAA!
IT'S GIRA-TINA!
STILL CHASING AFTER DIALGA?!
GIRA!

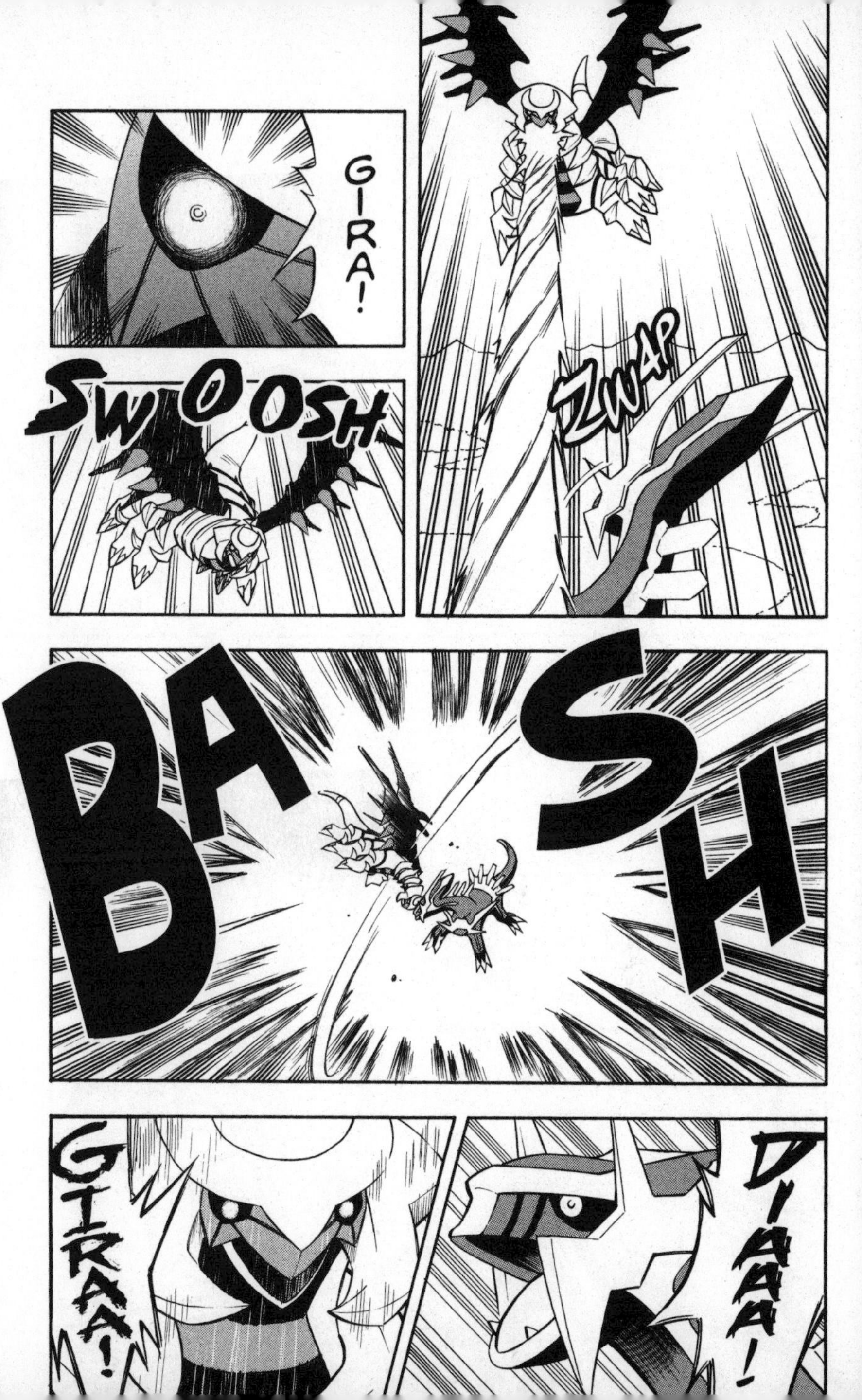
ZWAP
GIRA!
SWOOSH
BASH
DIAAAA!
GIRAA!

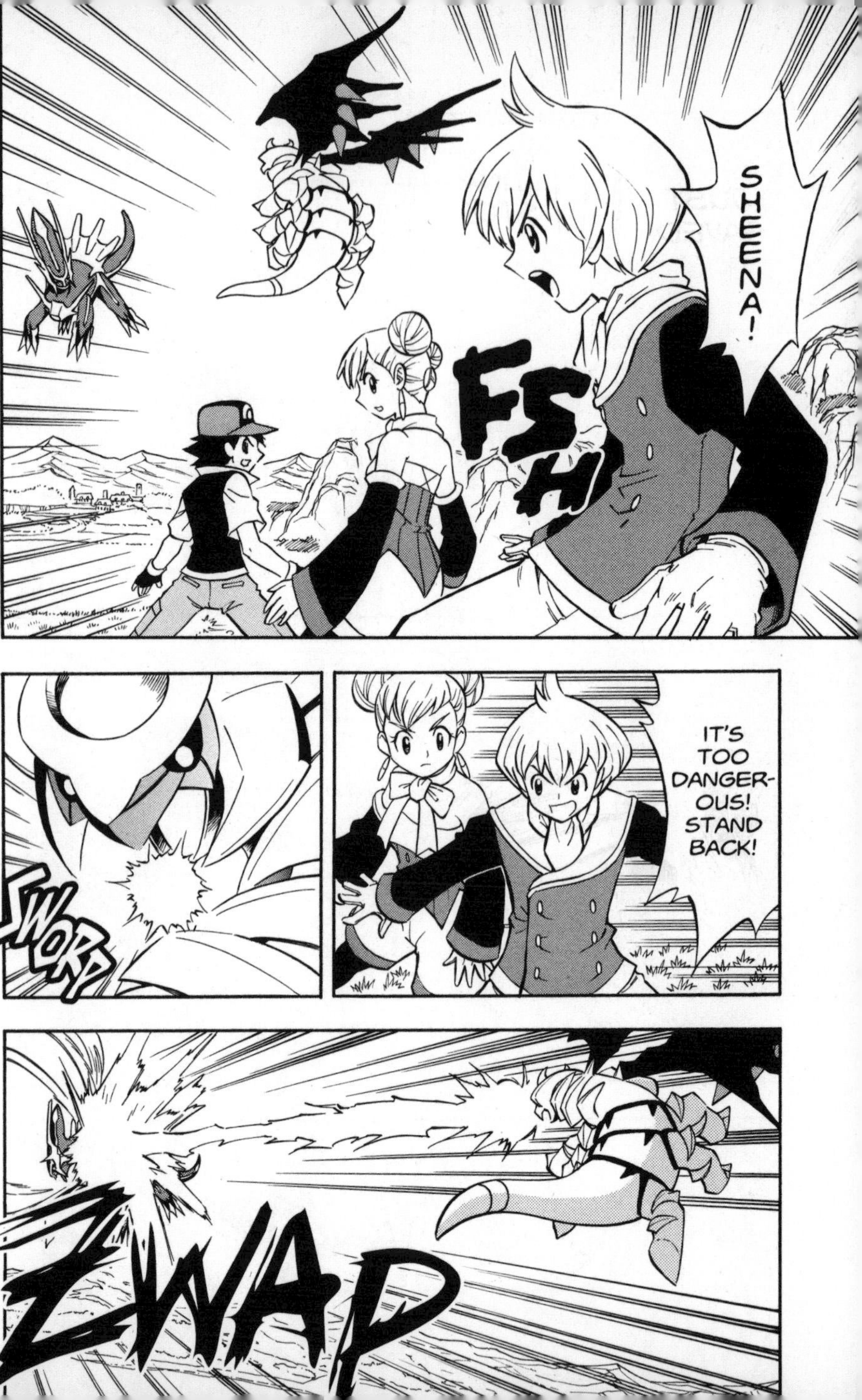
SHEENA!
FSH
IT'S TOO DANGER-OUS! STAND BACK!
SWORP
ZWAP

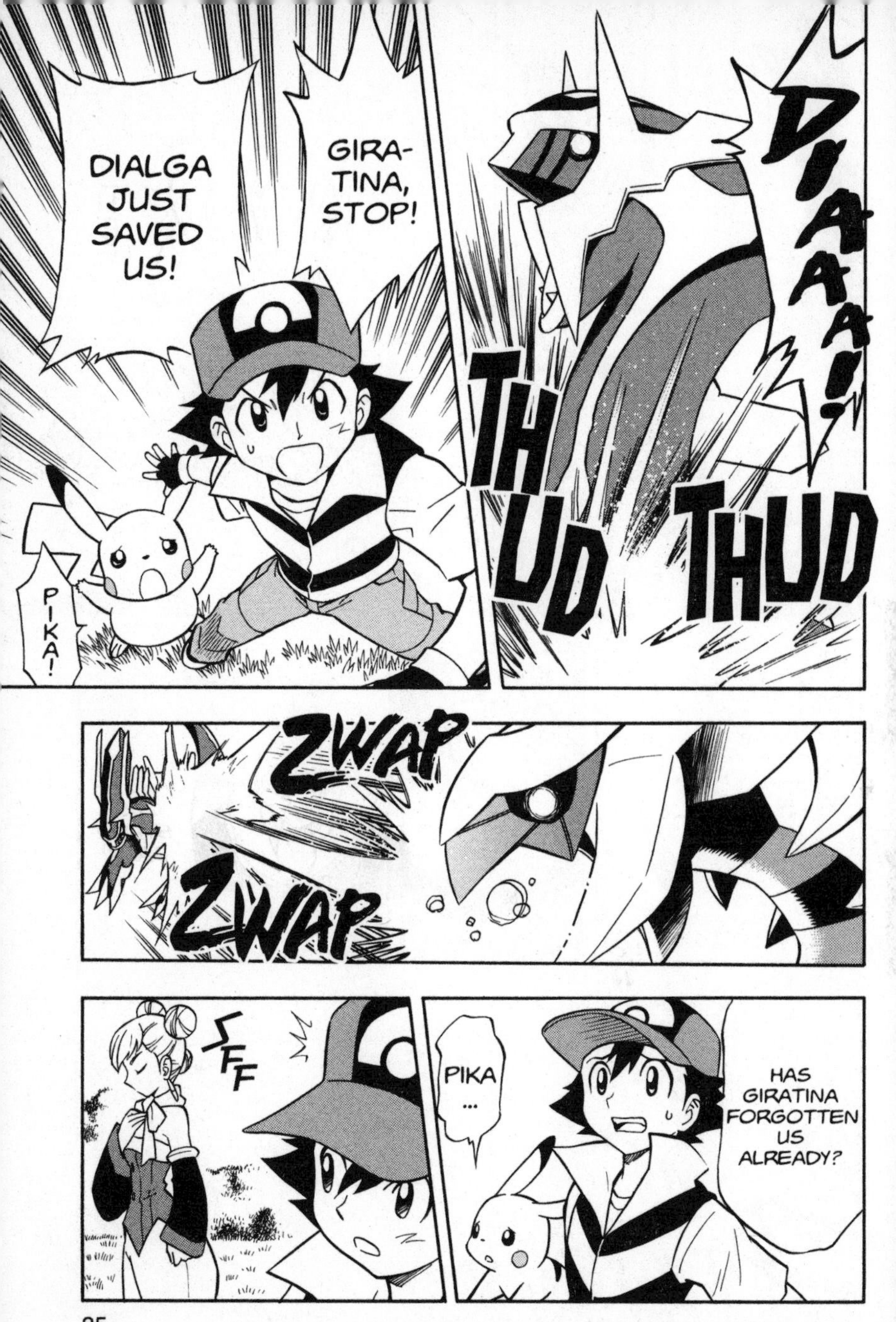
DIAAAA!!
THUD
THUD
GIRA-TINA, STOP!
DIALGA JUST SAVED US!
PIKA!
ZWAP
ZWAP
HAS GIRATINA FORGOTTEN US ALREADY?
PIKA...
SFF

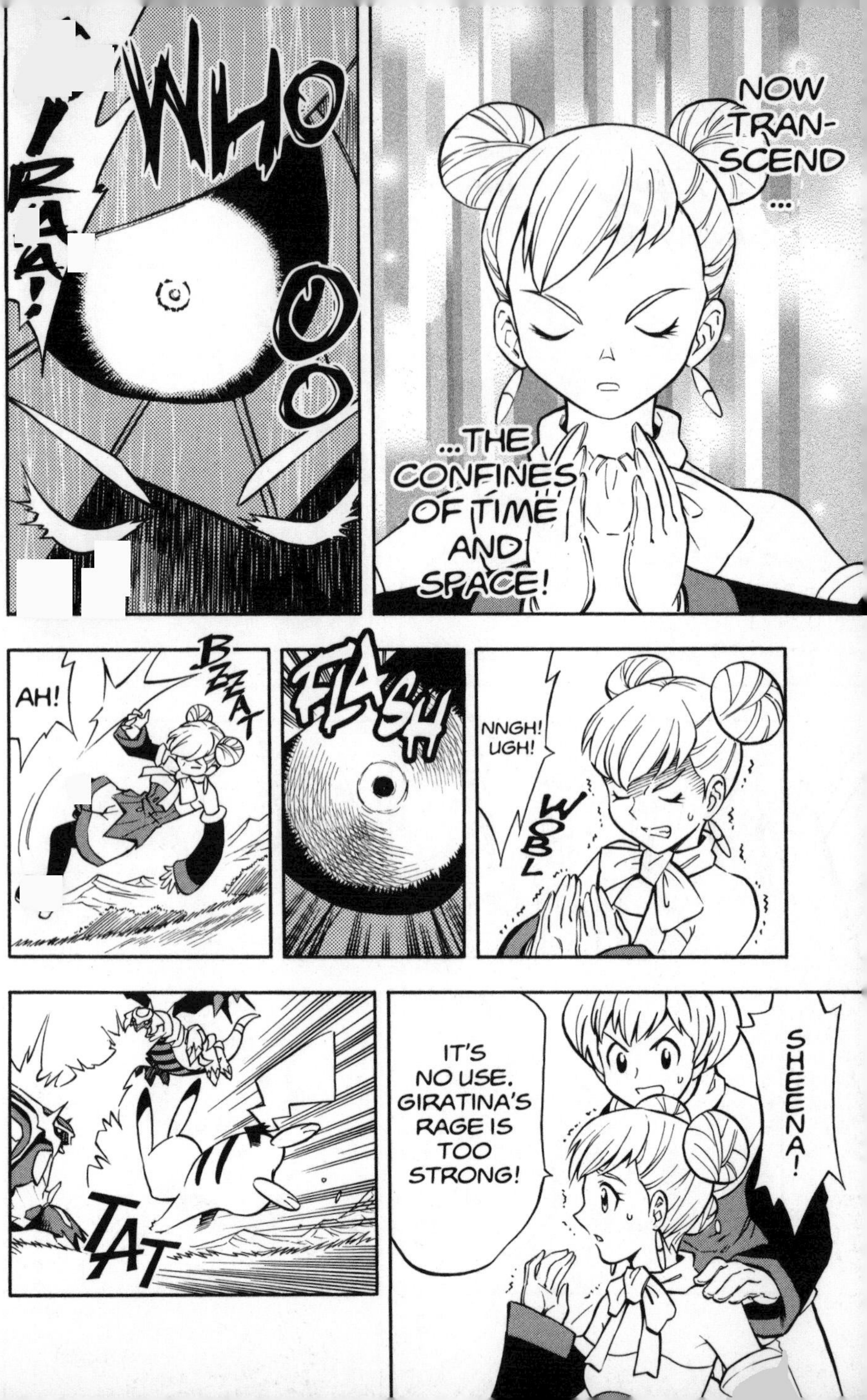
NOW TRAN-SCEND ...
...THE CONFINES OF TIME AND SPACE!
WHOOOO
NNGH! UGH!
WOBL
FLASH
BZZAT
AH!
SHEENA!
IT'S NO USE. GIRATINA'S RAGE IS TOO STRONG!
TAT

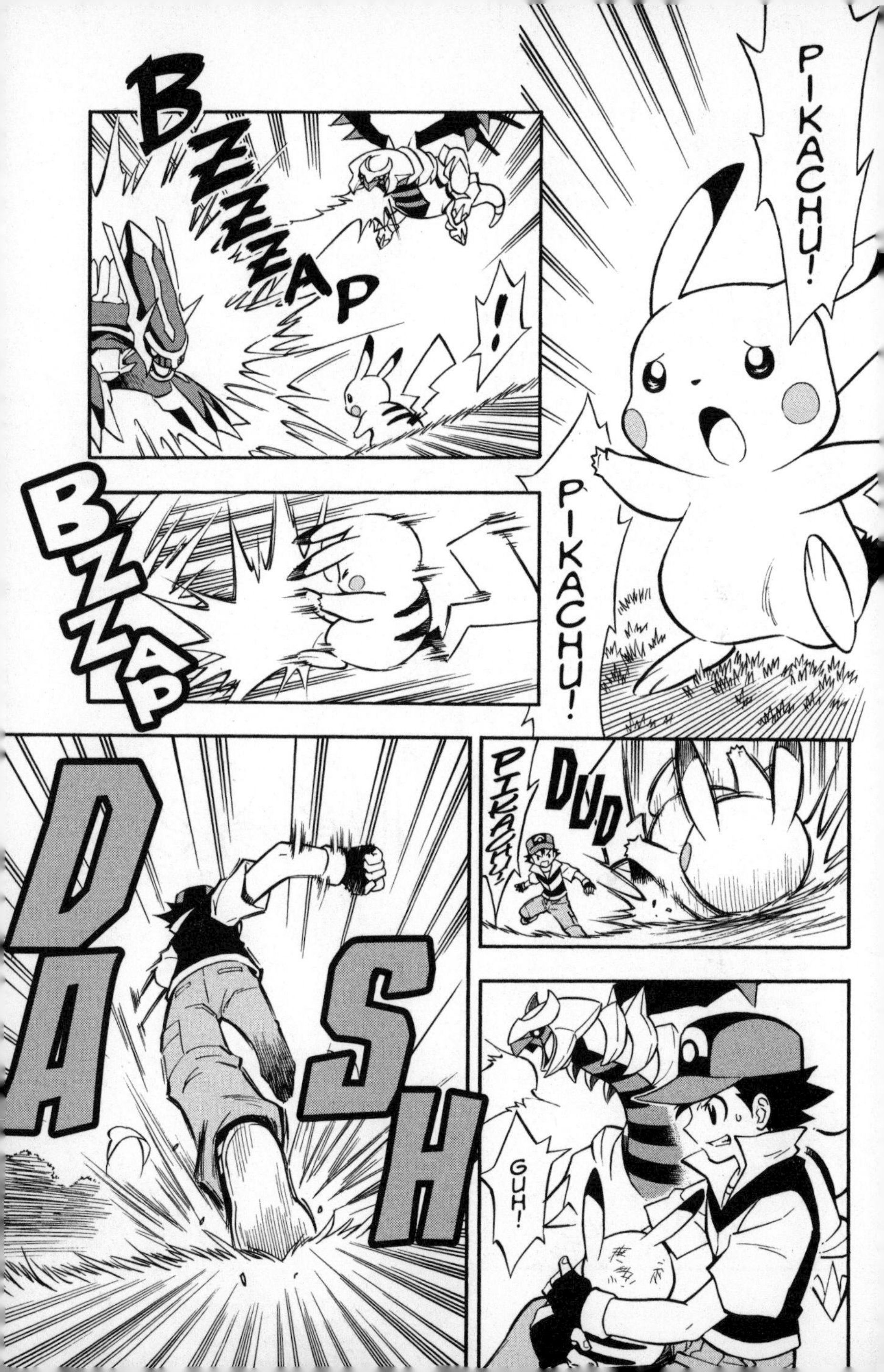
PIKACHU!
PIKACHU!
BZZZZAP
!
BZZZAP
PIKACHU!
DUDD
DASH
GUH!

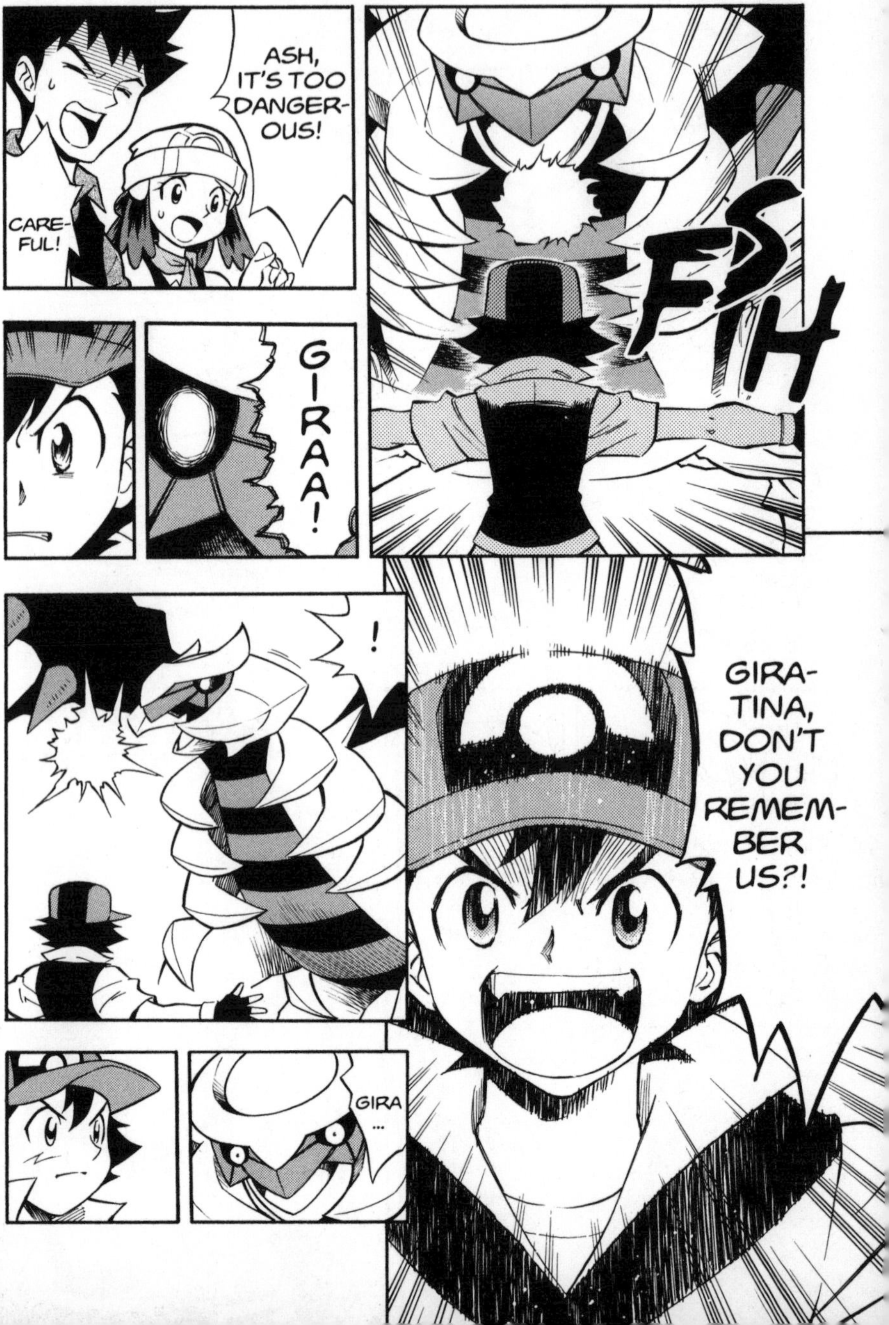
FSH
ASH, IT'S TOO DANGER-OUS!
CARE-FUL!
GIRAAA!
GIRA-TINA, DON'T YOU REMEM-BER US?!
!
GIRA ...

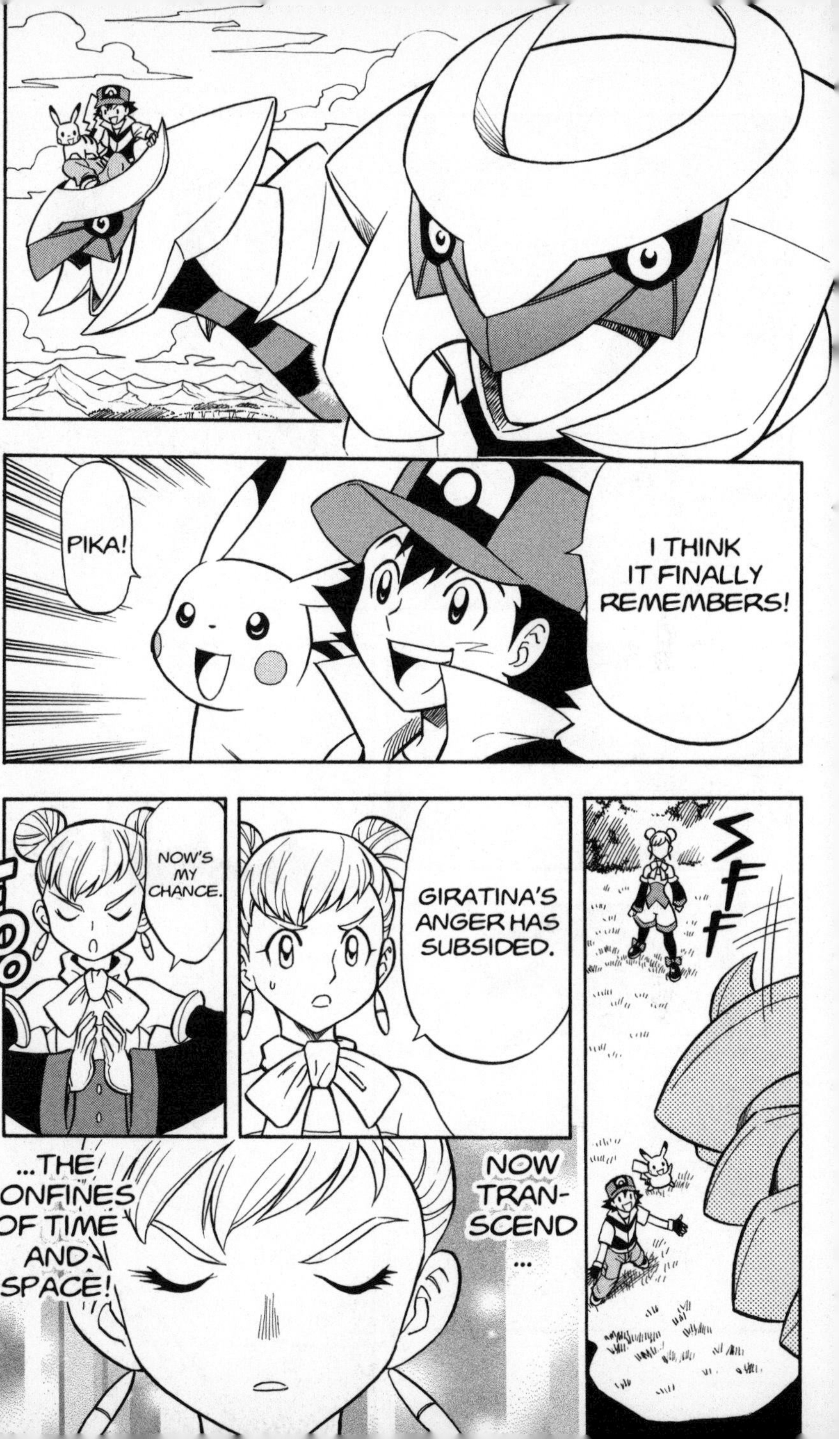
I THINK IT FINALLY REMEMBERS!
PIKA!
SFF
GIRATINA'S ANGER HAS SUBSIDED.
NOW'S MY CHANCE.
FOO
NOW TRAN-SCEND...
...THE CONFINES OF TIME AND SPACE!

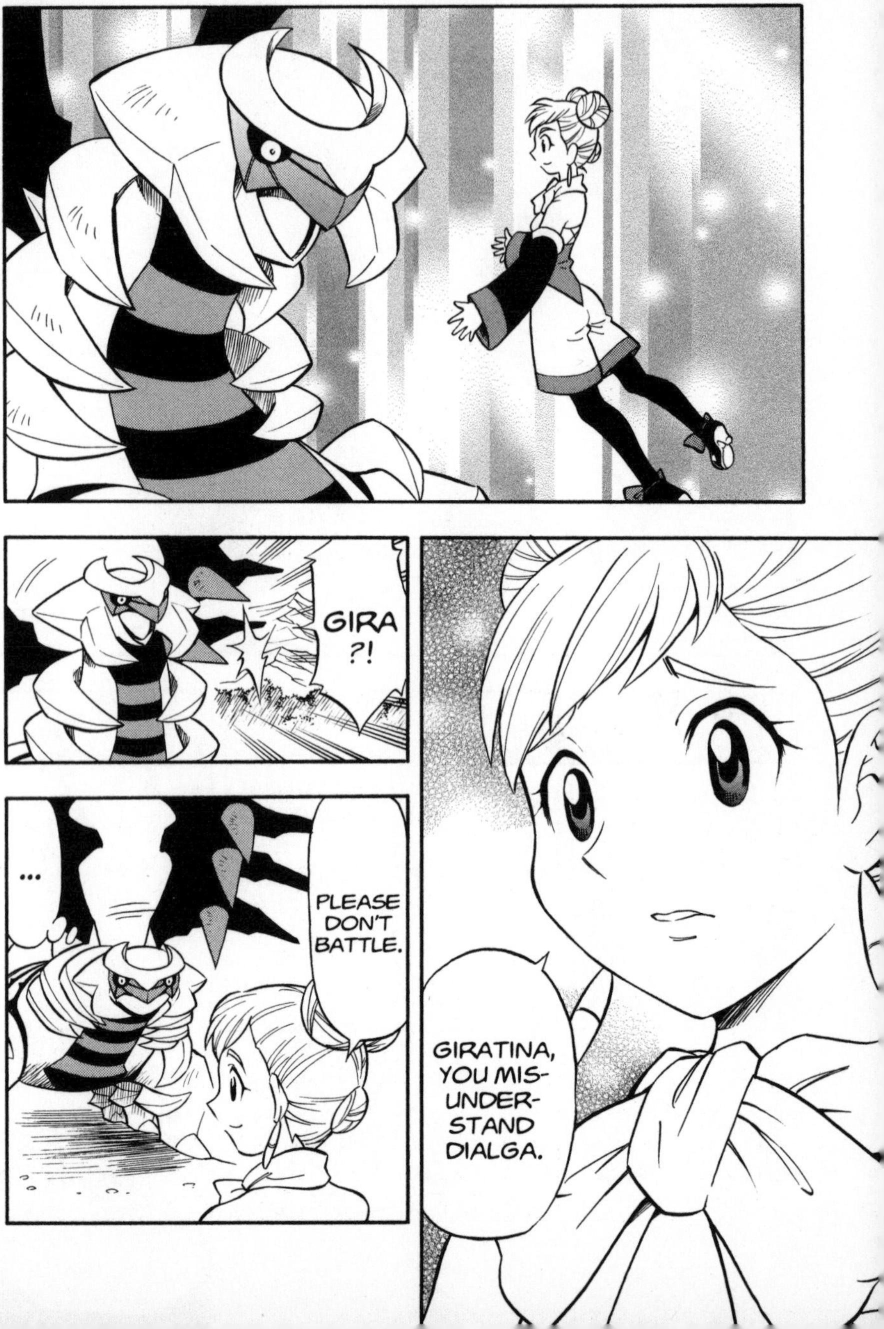
GIRATINA, YOU MIS-UNDER-STAND DIALGA.
GIRA ?!
PLEASE DON'T BATTLE.
...

WORRRP
DID GIRA-TINA'S ANGER ...
...JUST DISAP-PEAR?
PIKA!
YEAH. I'M GLAD TOO, PIKACHU.
BUT ...

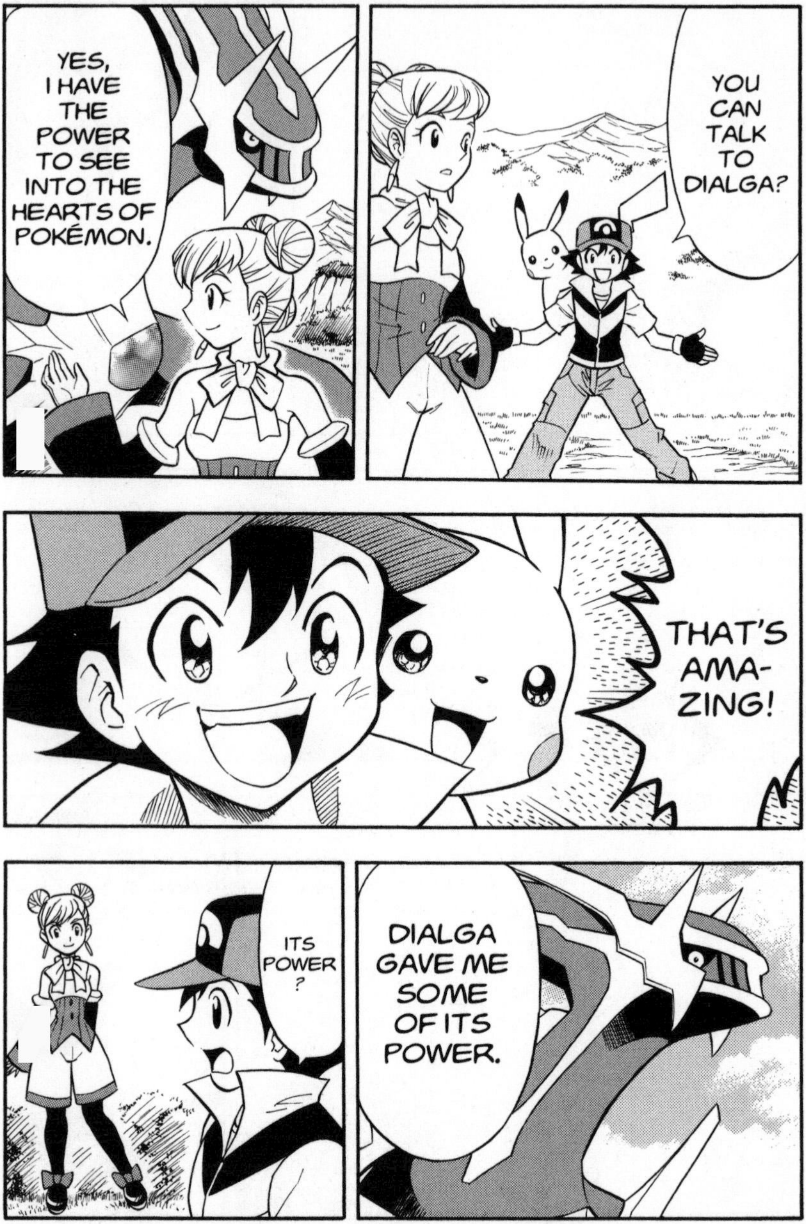
YOU CAN TALK TO DIALGA?
YES, I HAVE THE POWER TO SEE INTO THE HEARTS OF POKÉMON.
THAT'S AMA-ZING!
DIALGA GAVE ME SOME OF ITS POWER.
ITS POWER?

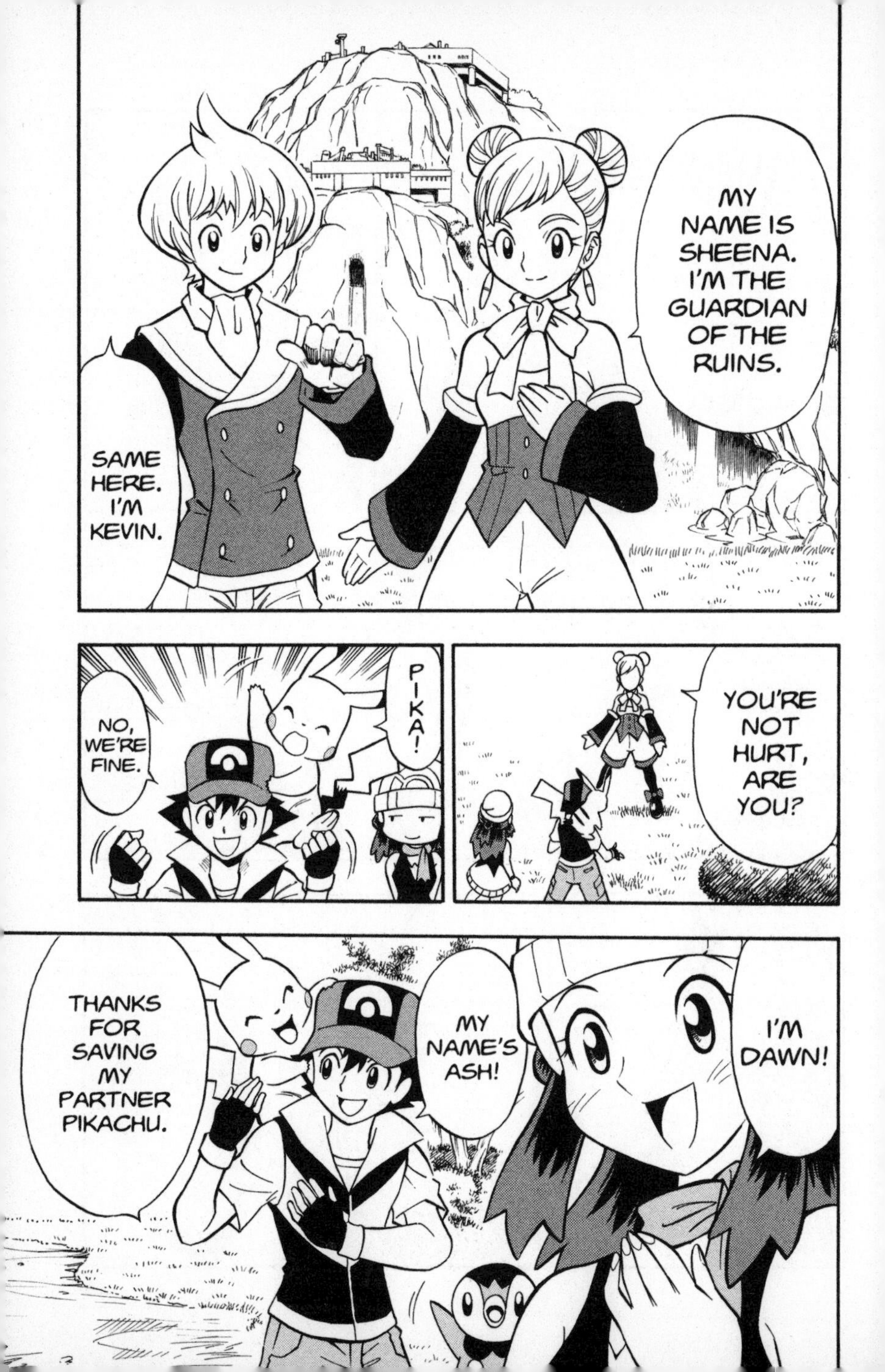

MY NAME IS SHEENA. I'M THE GUARDIAN OF THE RUINS.
SAME HERE. I'M KEVIN.
YOU'RE NOT HURT, ARE YOU?
PIKA!
NO, WE'RE FINE.
I'M DAWN!
MY NAME'S ASH!
THANKS FOR SAVING MY PARTNER PIKACHU.

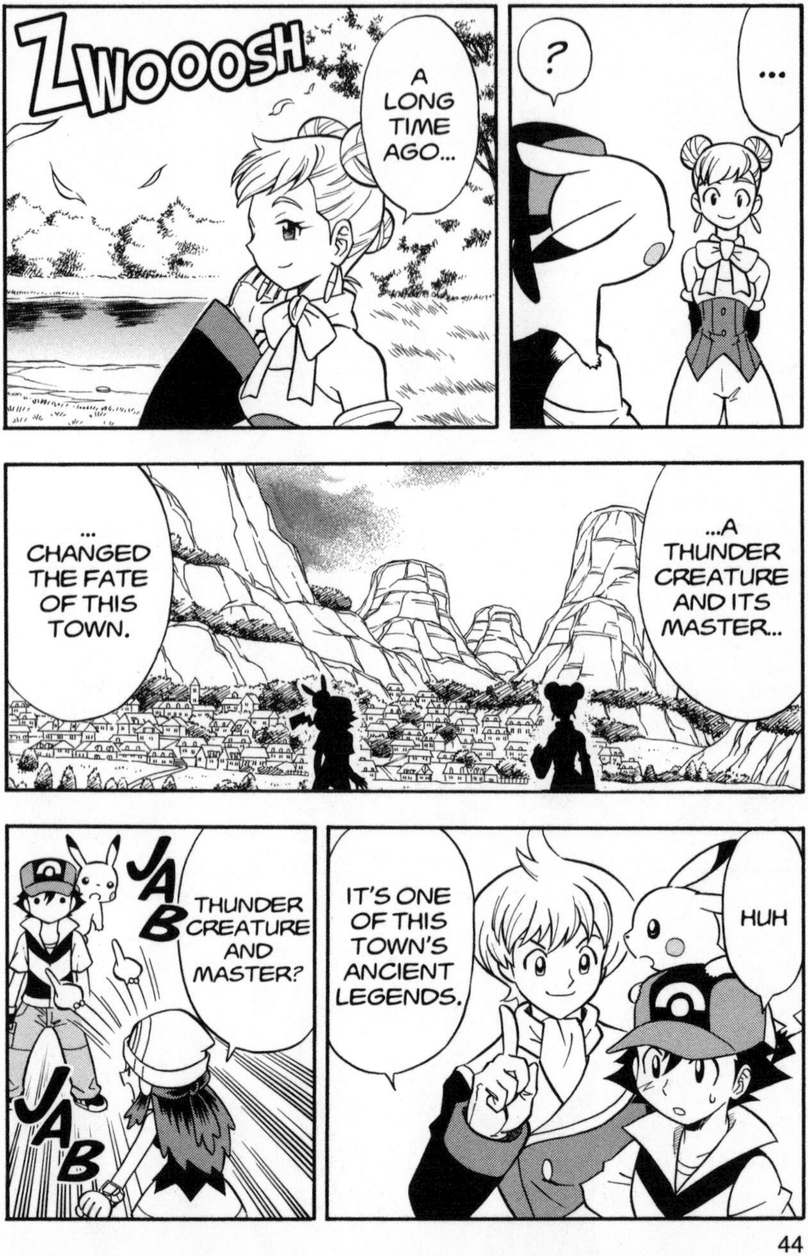
...
?
A LONG TIME AGO...
ZWOOOSH
...A THUNDER CREATURE AND ITS MASTER...
...CHANGED THE FATE OF THIS TOWN.
HUH
IT'S ONE OF THIS TOWN'S ANCIENT LEGENDS.
THUNDER CREATURE AND MASTER?
JAB
JAB

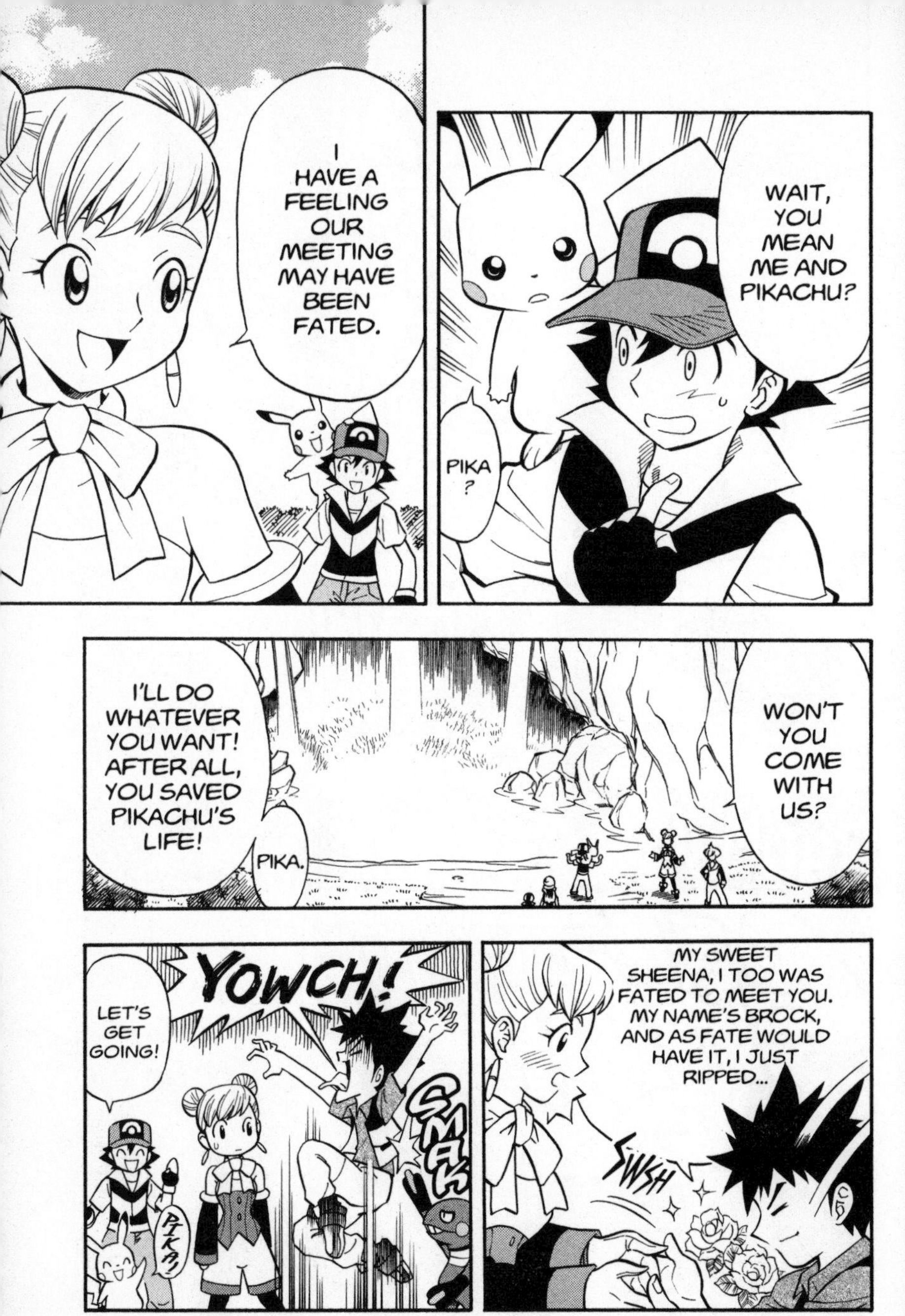
WAIT, YOU MEAN ME AND PIKACHU?
PIKA ?
I HAVE A FEELING OUR MEETING MAY HAVE BEEN FATED.
WON'T YOU COME WITH US?
I'LL DO WHATEVER YOU WANT! AFTER ALL, YOU SAVED PIKACHU'S LIFE!
PIKA.
MY SWEET SHEENA, I TOO WAS FATED TO MEET YOU. MY NAME'S BROCK, AND AS FATE WOULD HAVE IT, I JUST RIPPED...
SWSH
YOWCH!
SMAK
LET'S GET GOING!
PIKA!

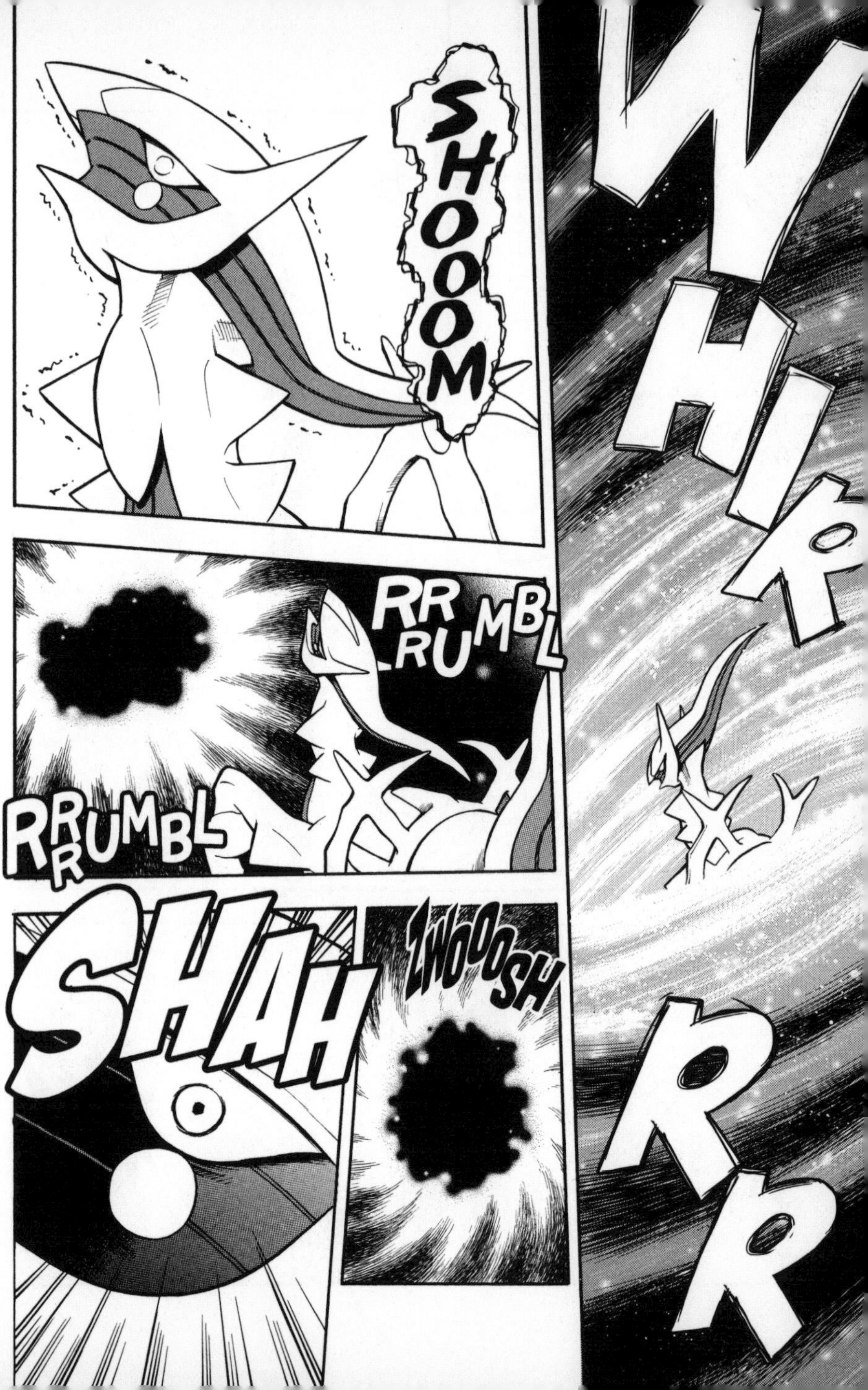
WHIRRRR
SHOOOM
RRRUMBL
RRRUMBL
SHAH
ZWOOOSH

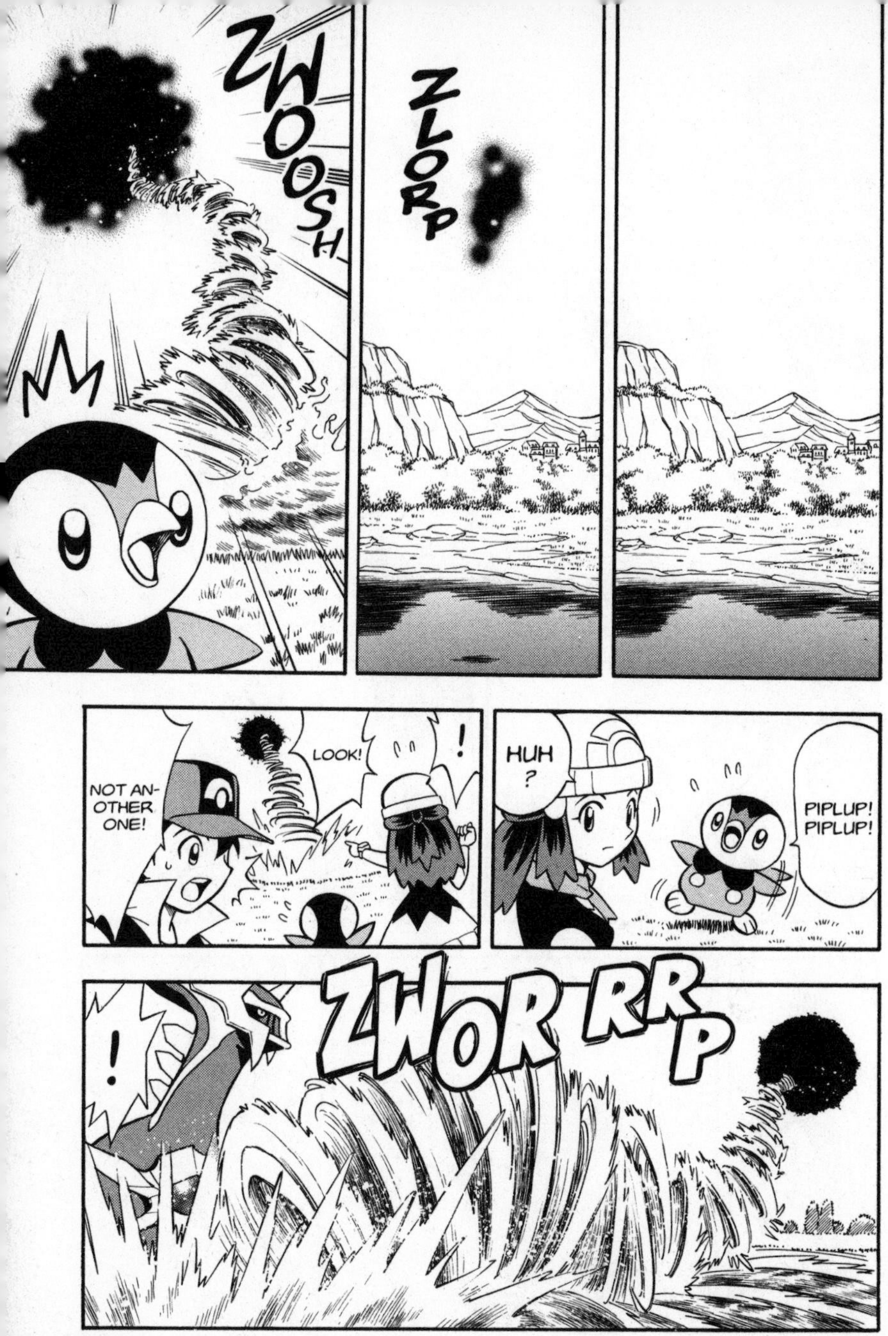
ZLORP
ZWOOSH
PIPLUP! PIPLUP!
HUH?
!
LOOK!
NOT AN-OTHER ONE!
ZWORRRP
!

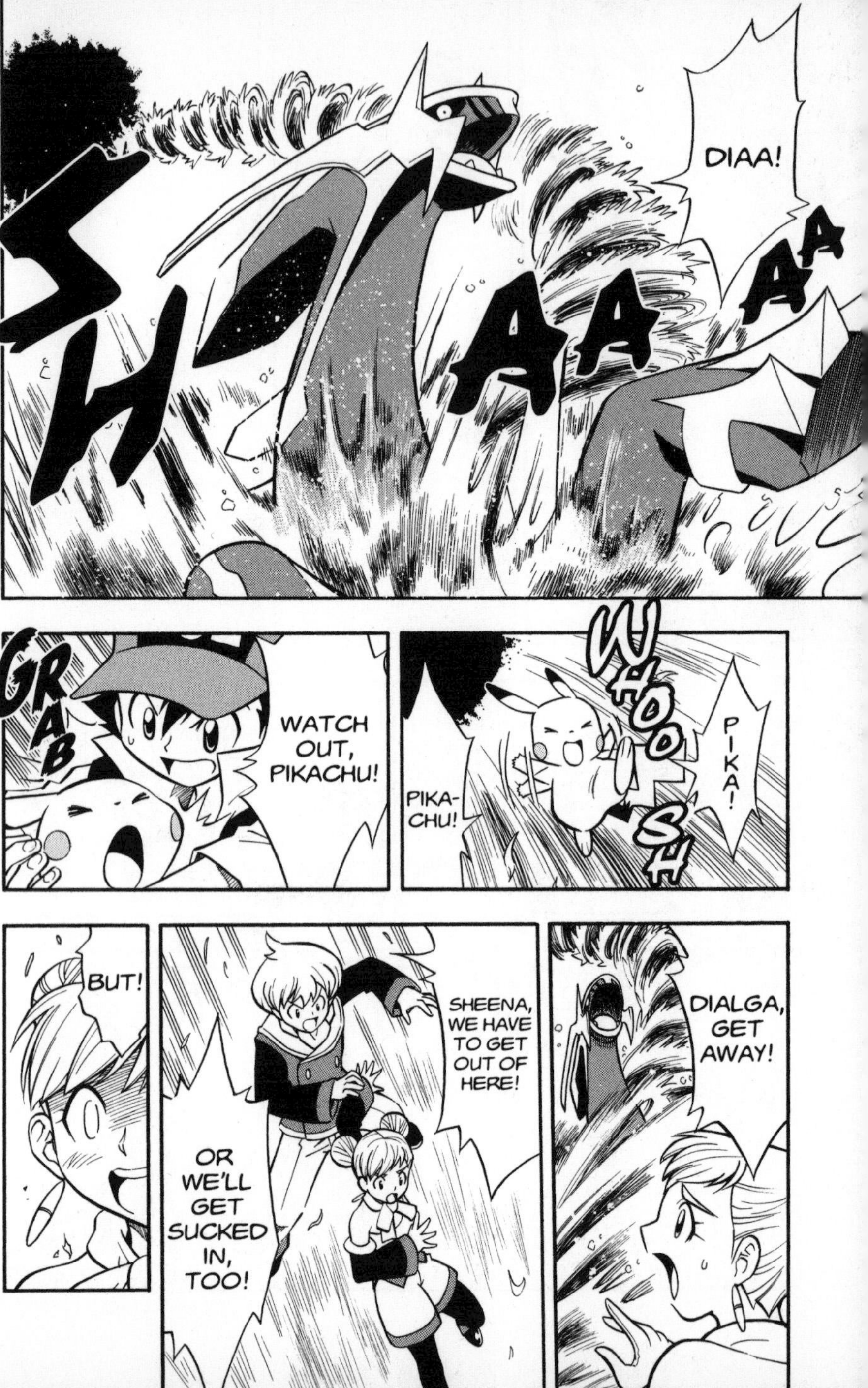
DIAA!
SHAAAAA
PIKA!
WHOOOSH
PIKA-CHU!
WATCH OUT, PIKACHU!
GRAB
DIALGA, GET AWAY!
SHEENA, WE HAVE TO GET OUT OF HERE!
OR WE'LL GET SUCKED IN, TOO!
BUT!

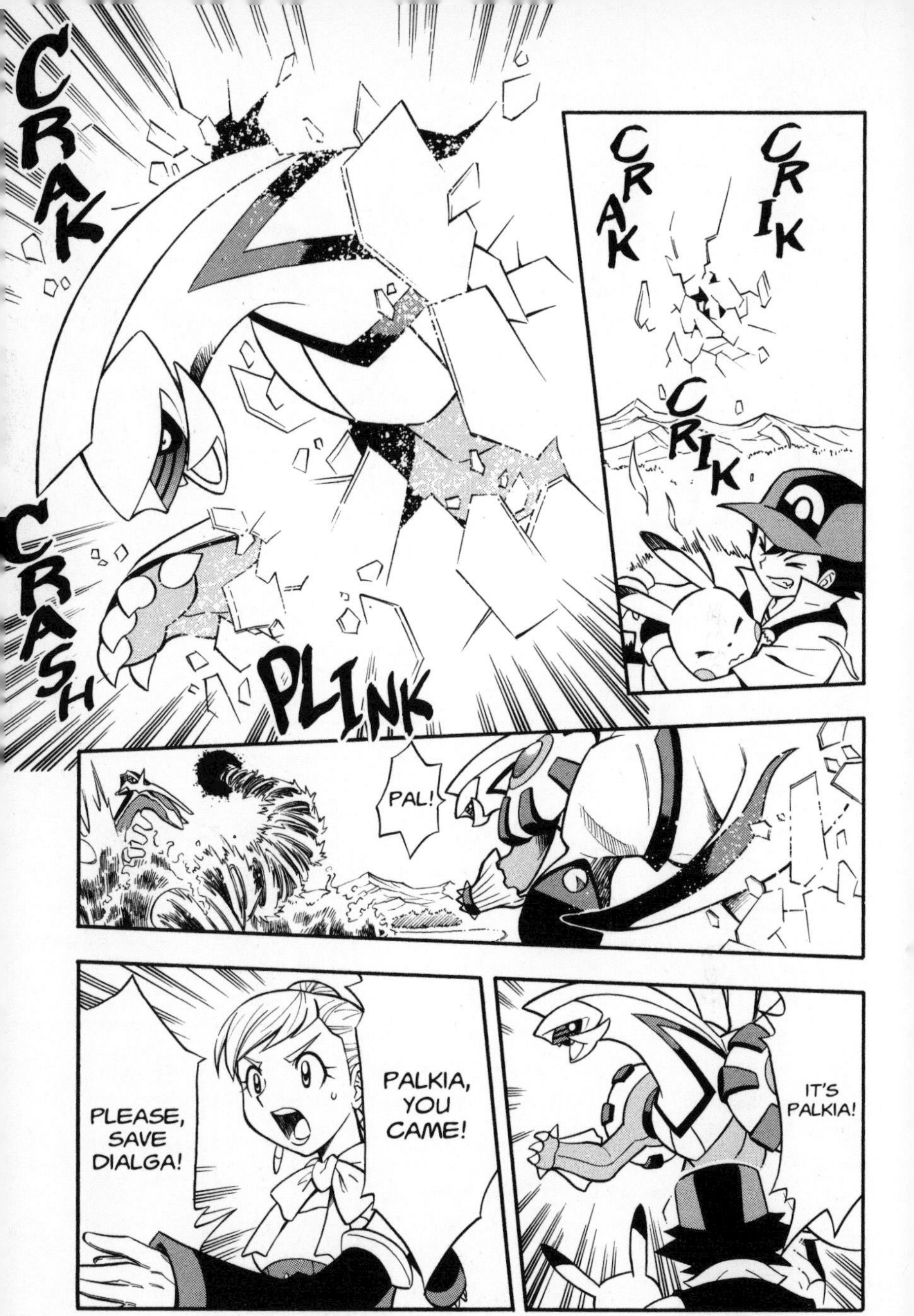
CRAK
CRIK
CRIK
CRAK
CRASH
PLINK
PAL!
IT'S PALKIA!
PALKIA, YOU CAME!
PLEASE, SAVE DIALGA!

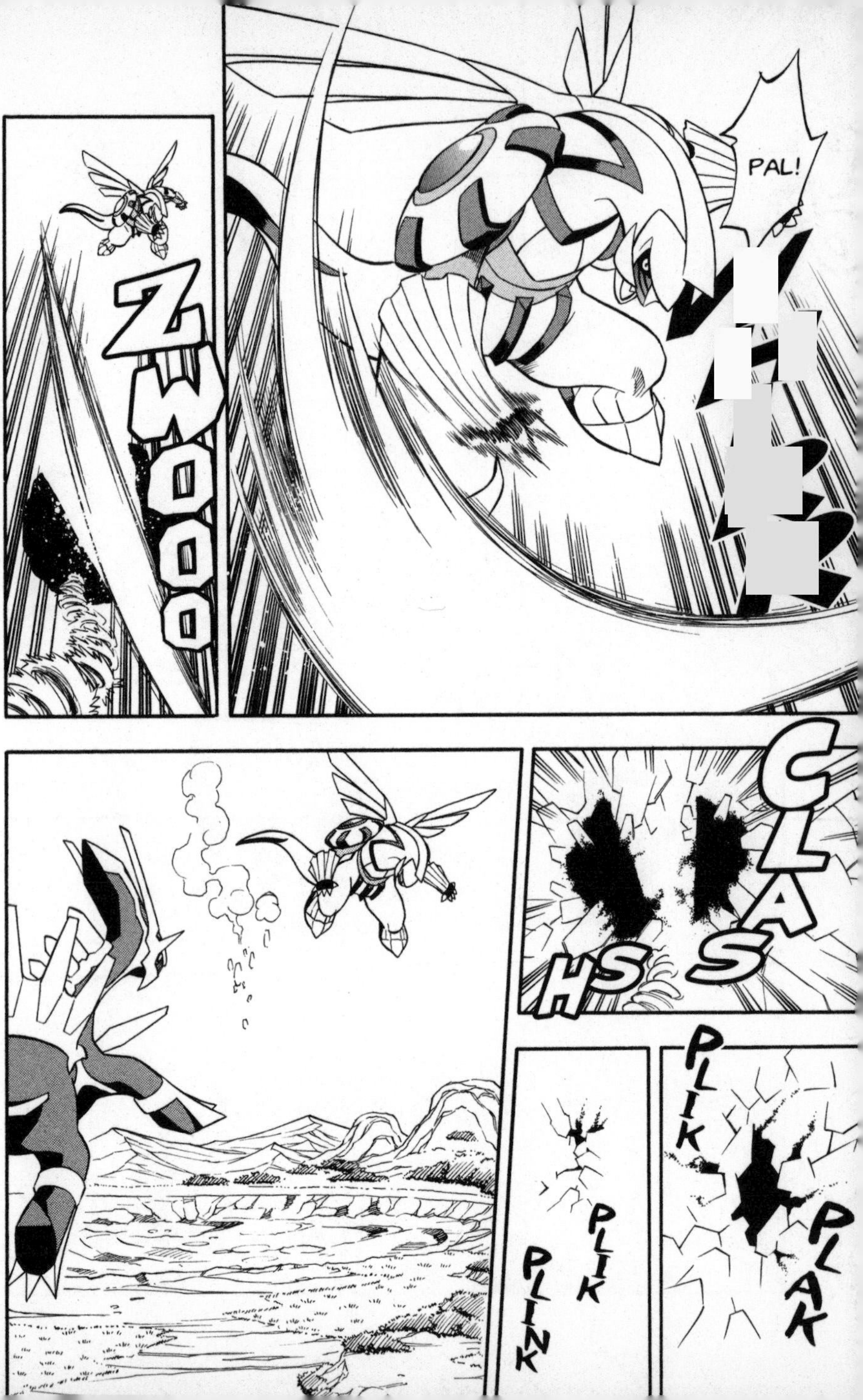
PAL!
ZWOOO
CLASSH
PLIK
PLAK
PLIK
PLINK

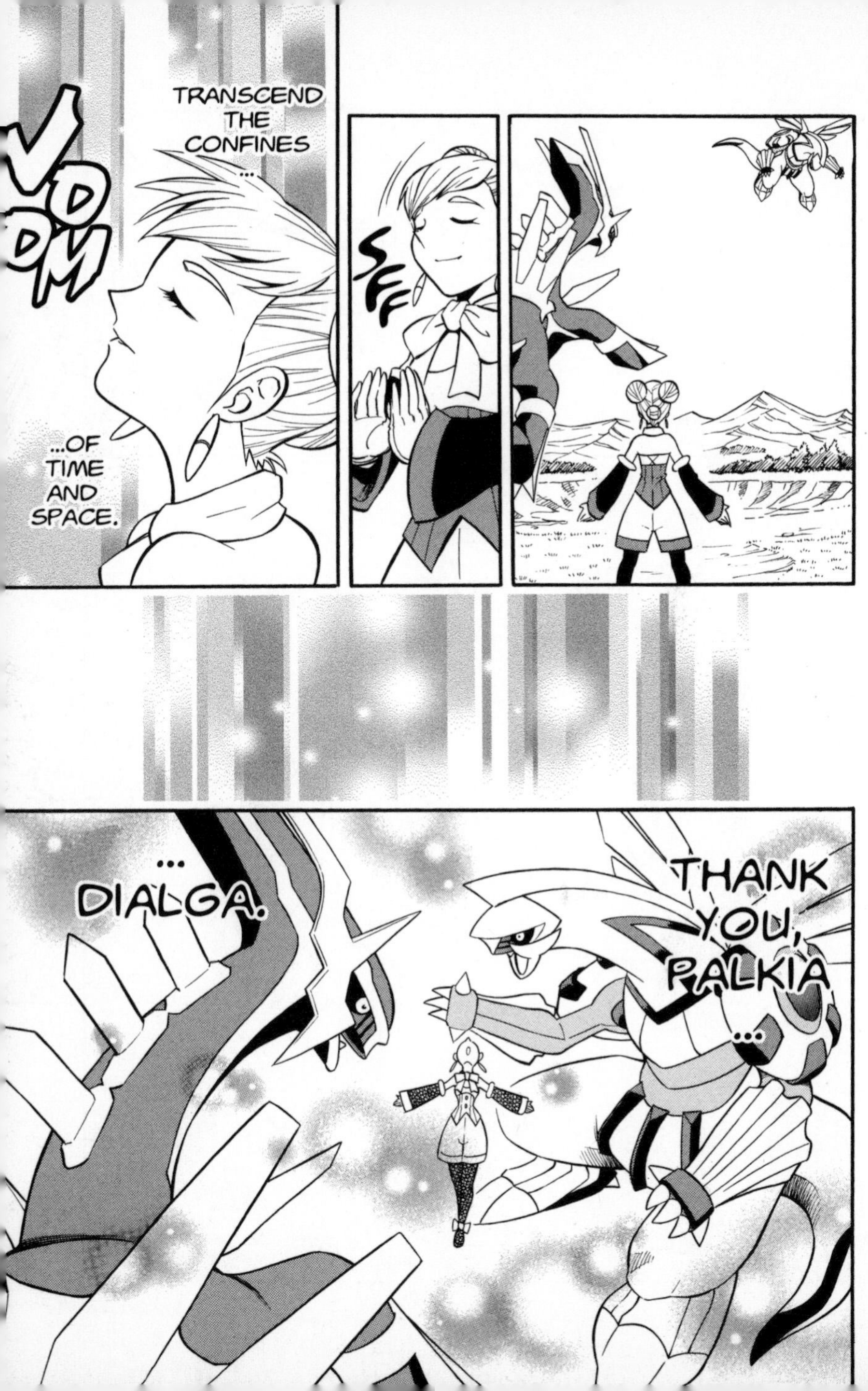
SFF
VOOM
TRANSCEND THE CONFINES...
...OF TIME AND SPACE.
THANK YOU, PALKIA...
...DIALGA.

RIGHT NOW, SHEENA'S CONNECTING WITH THE HEARTS OF TWO POKÉMON.
SHE'S SYNCHING WITH THEM!
WHAT'S "TRAN-SCEND" MEAN?
TO RISE ABOVE.
PIKA.
WHOA.
CRAK
PLK
VOOM

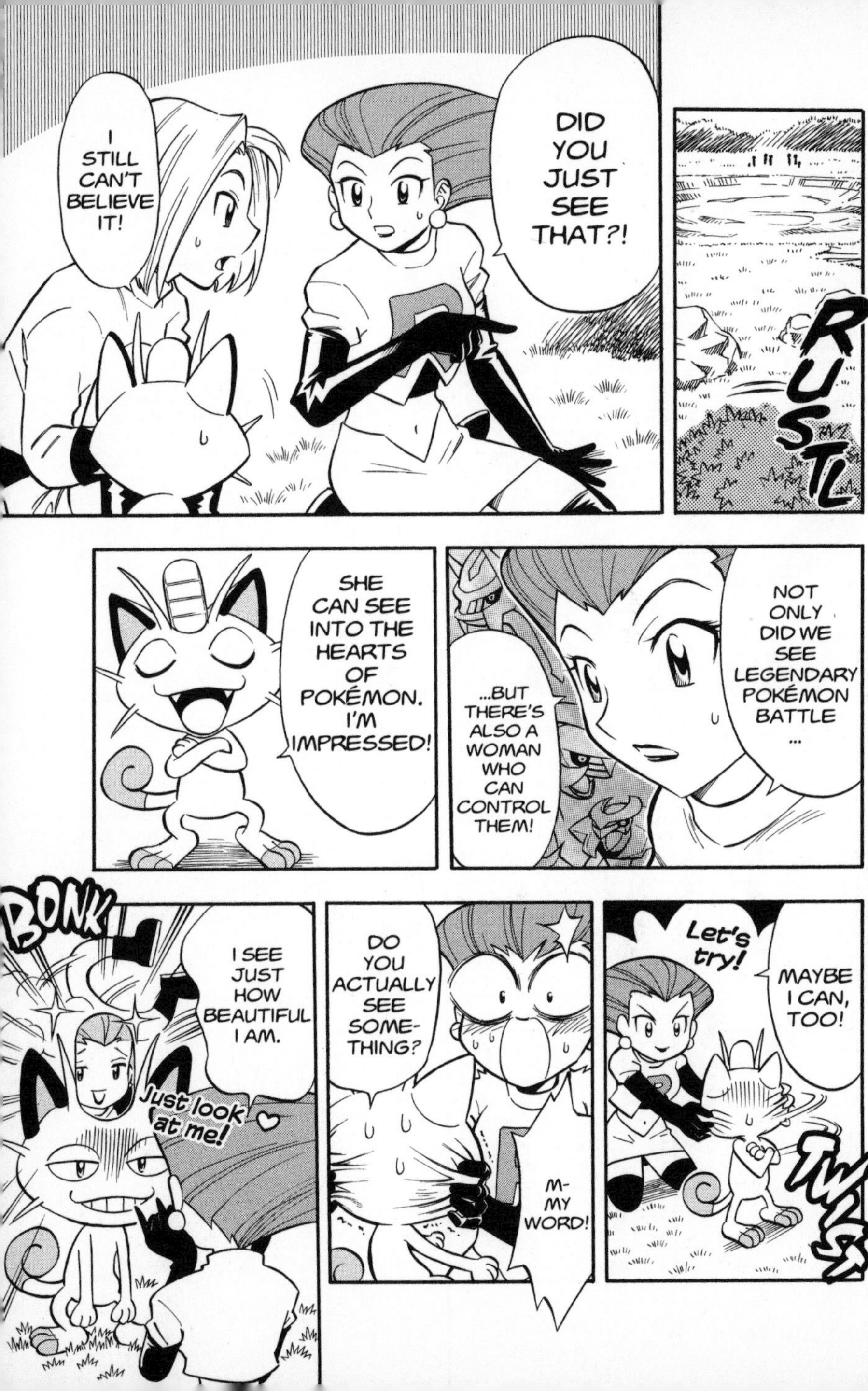
RUSTL
DID YOU JUST SEE THAT?!
I STILL CAN'T BELIEVE IT!
NOT ONLY DID WE SEE LEGENDARY POKÉMON BATTLE ...
...BUT THERE'S ALSO A WOMAN WHO CAN CONTROL THEM!
SHE CAN SEE INTO THE HEARTS OF POKÉMON. I'M IMPRESSED!
Let's try!
MAYBE I CAN, TOO!
TWIST
DO YOU ACTUALLY SEE SOME-THING?
M-MY WORD!
BONK
I SEE JUST HOW BEAUTIFUL I AM.
Just look at me!

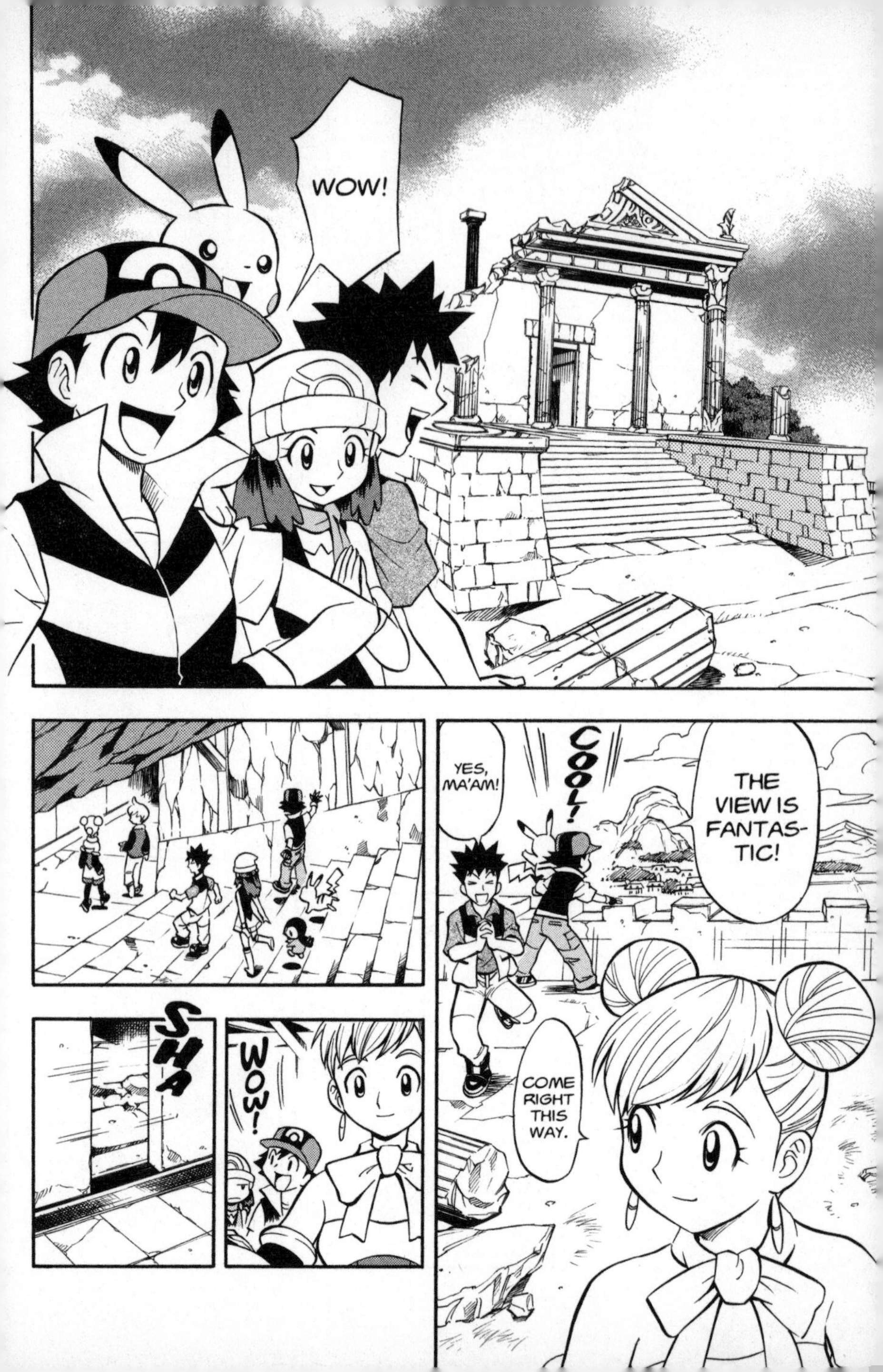
WOW!
THE VIEW IS FANTAS-TIC!
COOL!
YES, MA'AM!
COME RIGHT THIS WAY.
WOW!
SHA

WHOA!

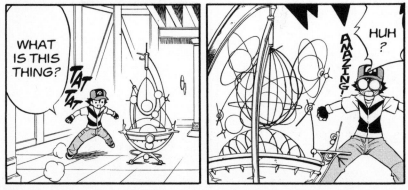

WHAT IS THIS THING?

TAT TAT

HUH ?

AMAZING!

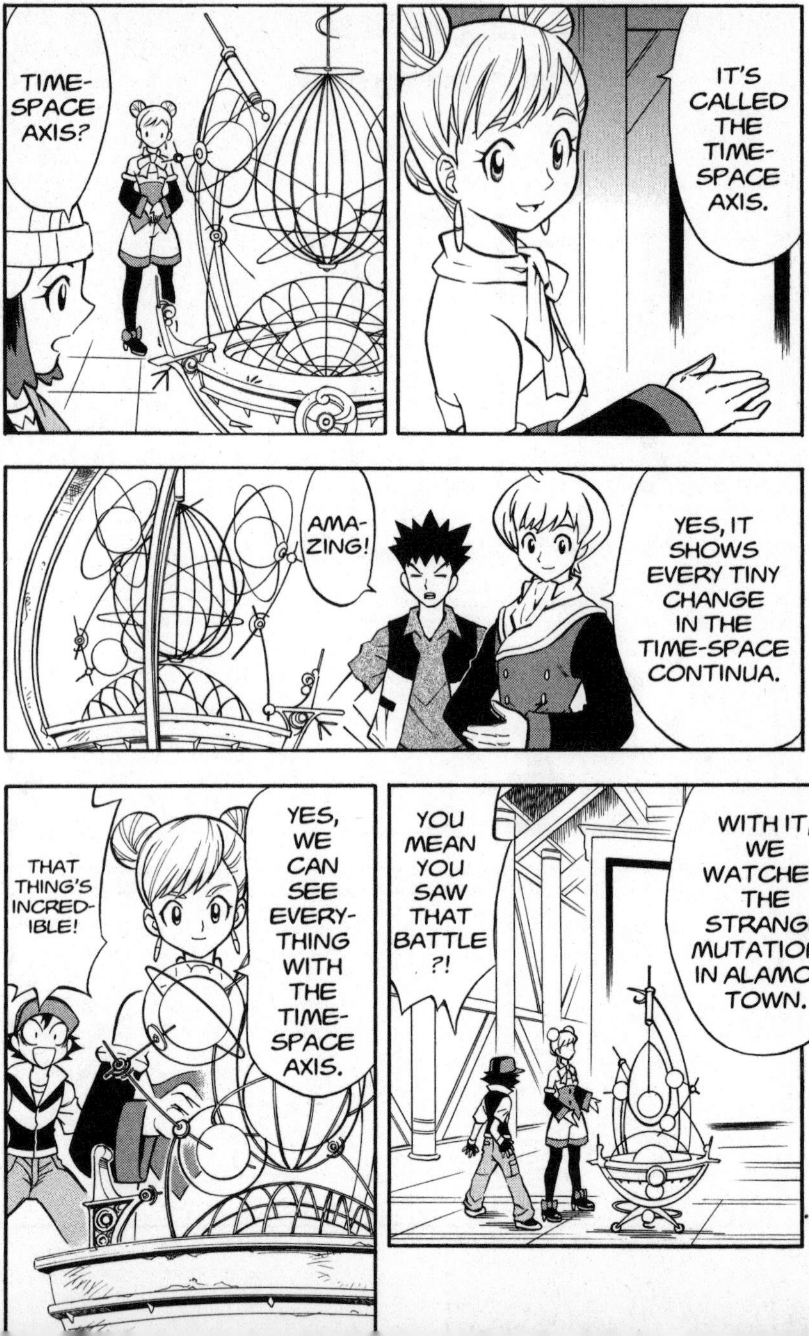
IT'S CALLED THE TIME-SPACE AXIS.
TIME-SPACE AXIS?
YES, IT SHOWS EVERY TINY CHANGE IN THE TIME-SPACE CONTINUA.
AMAZING!
WITH IT, WE WATCHED THE STRANGE MUTATIONS IN ALAMOS TOWN.
YOU MEAN YOU SAW THAT BATTLE?!
YES, WE CAN SEE EVERYTHING WITH THE TIME-SPACE AXIS.
THAT THING'S INCREDIBLE!

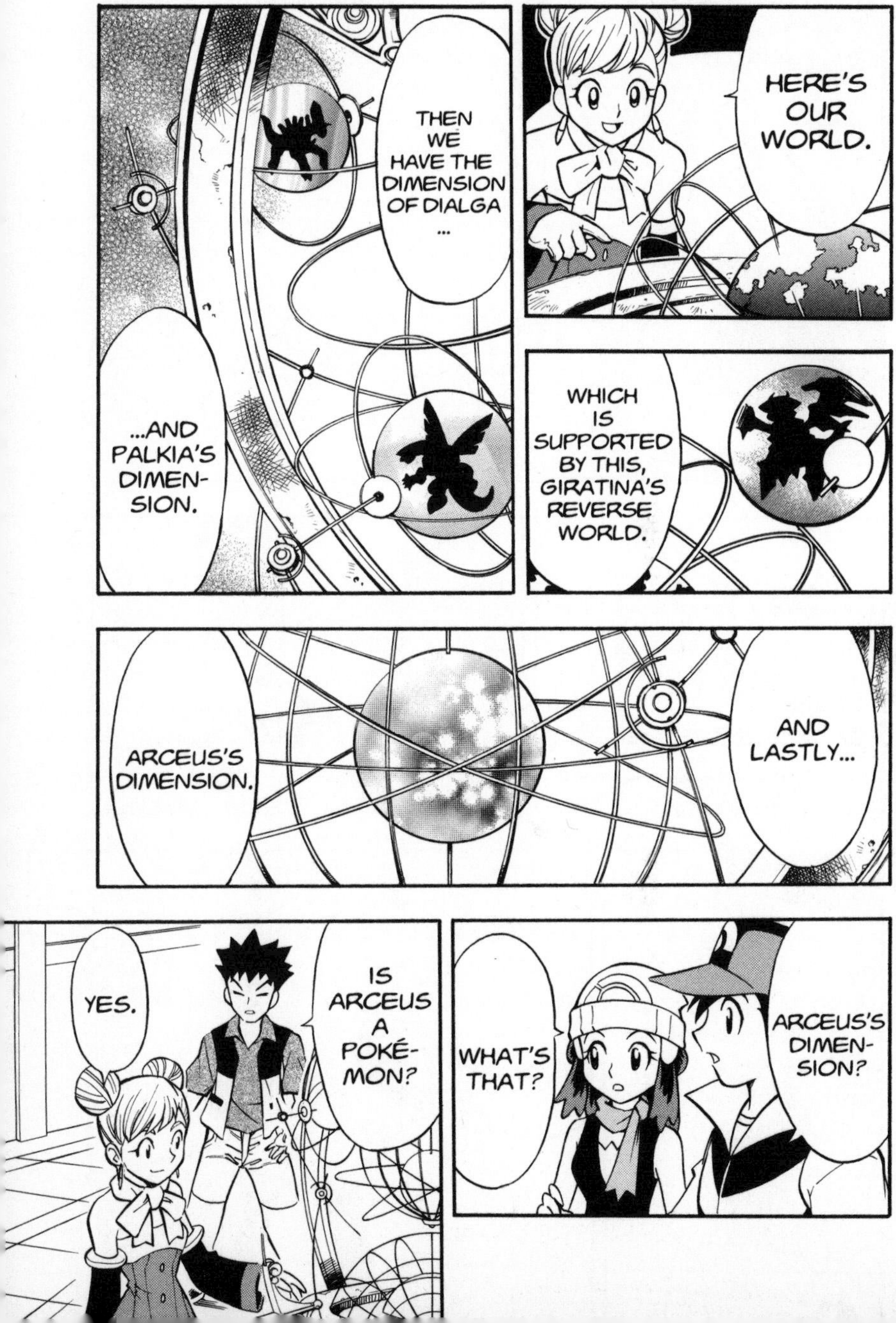
HERE'S OUR WORLD.
WHICH IS SUPPORTED BY THIS, GIRATINA'S REVERSE WORLD.
THEN WE HAVE THE DIMENSION OF DIALGA...
...AND PALKIA'S DIMEN-SION.
AND LASTLY...
ARCEUS'S DIMENSION.
ARCEUS'S DIMEN-SION?
WHAT'S THAT?
IS ARCEUS A POKÉ-MON?
YES.

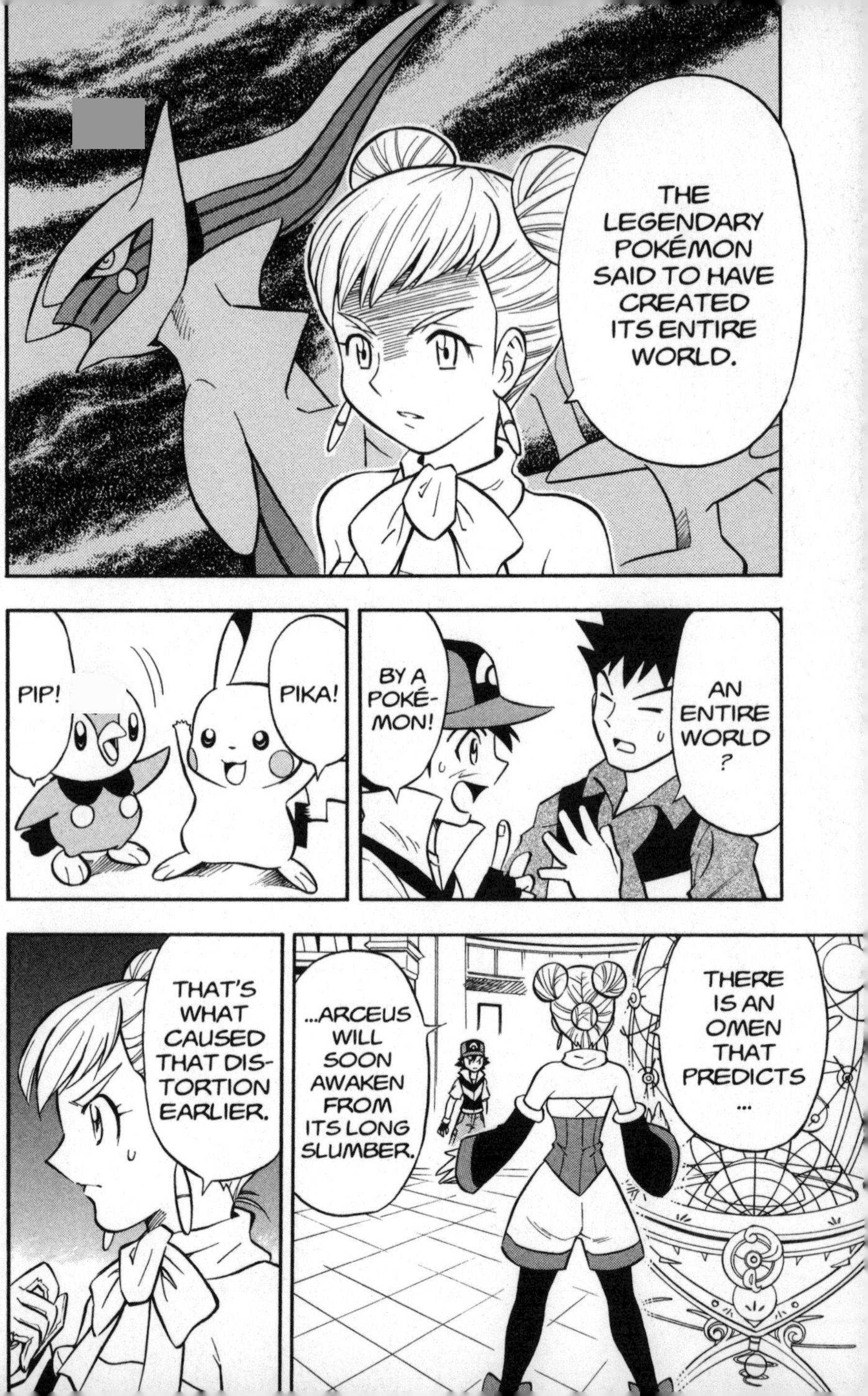
THE LEGENDARY POKÉMON SAID TO HAVE CREATED ITS ENTIRE WORLD.
AN ENTIRE WORLD?
BY A POKÉ-MON!
PIKA!
PIP!
THERE IS AN OMEN THAT PREDICTS...
...ARCEUS WILL SOON AWAKEN FROM ITS LONG SLUMBER.
THAT'S WHAT CAUSED THAT DIS-TORTION EARLIER.

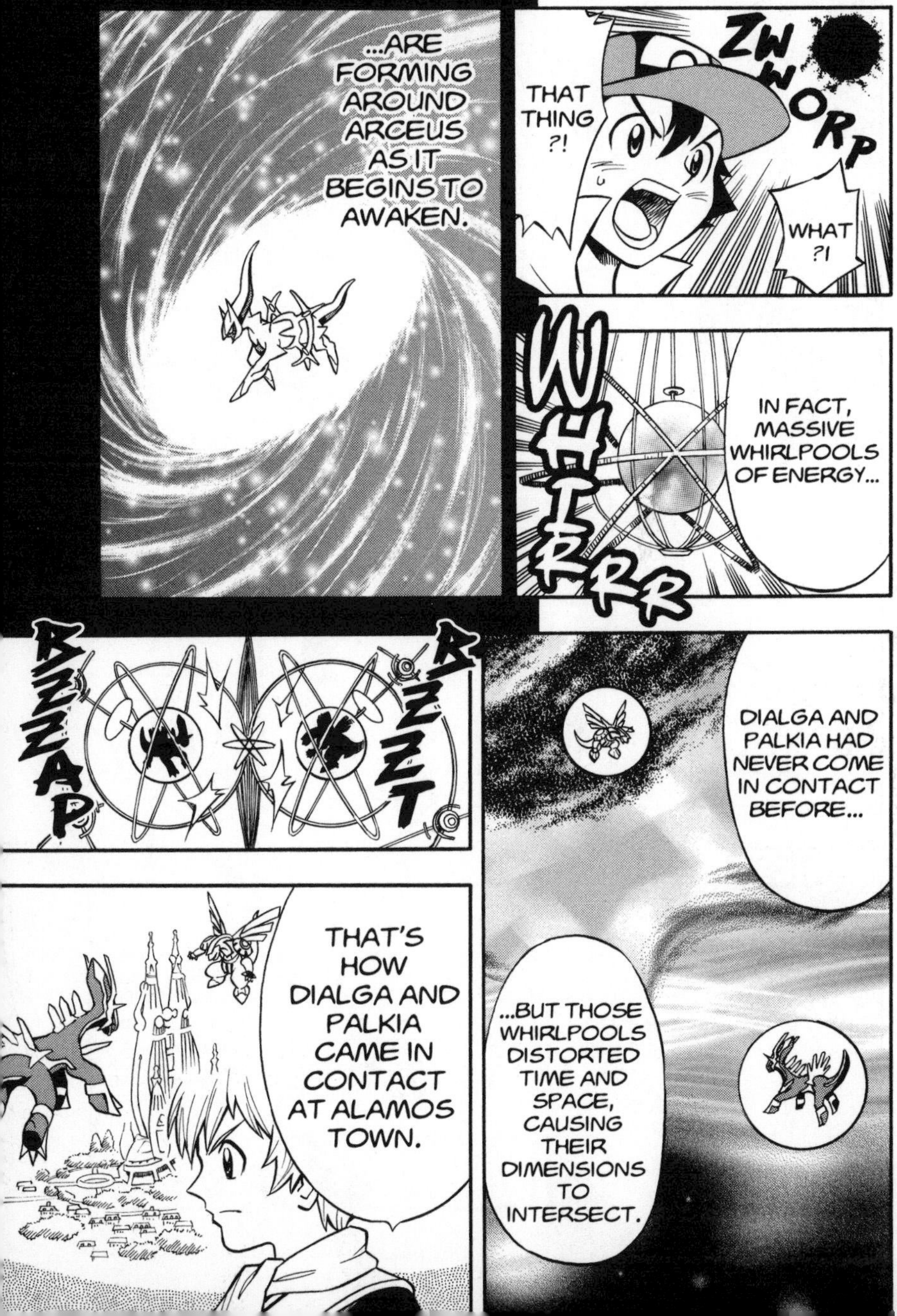
ZWWORP
WHAT?!
THAT THING?!
WHIRRR
IN FACT, MASSIVE WHIRLPOOLS OF ENERGY...
...ARE FORMING AROUND ARCEUS AS IT BEGINS TO AWAKEN.
DIALGA AND PALKIA HAD NEVER COME IN CONTACT BEFORE...
...BUT THOSE WHIRLPOOLS DISTORTED TIME AND SPACE, CAUSING THEIR DIMENSIONS TO INTERSECT.
BZZZZT
BZZZAP
THAT'S HOW DIALGA AND PALKIA CAME IN CONTACT AT ALAMOS TOWN.

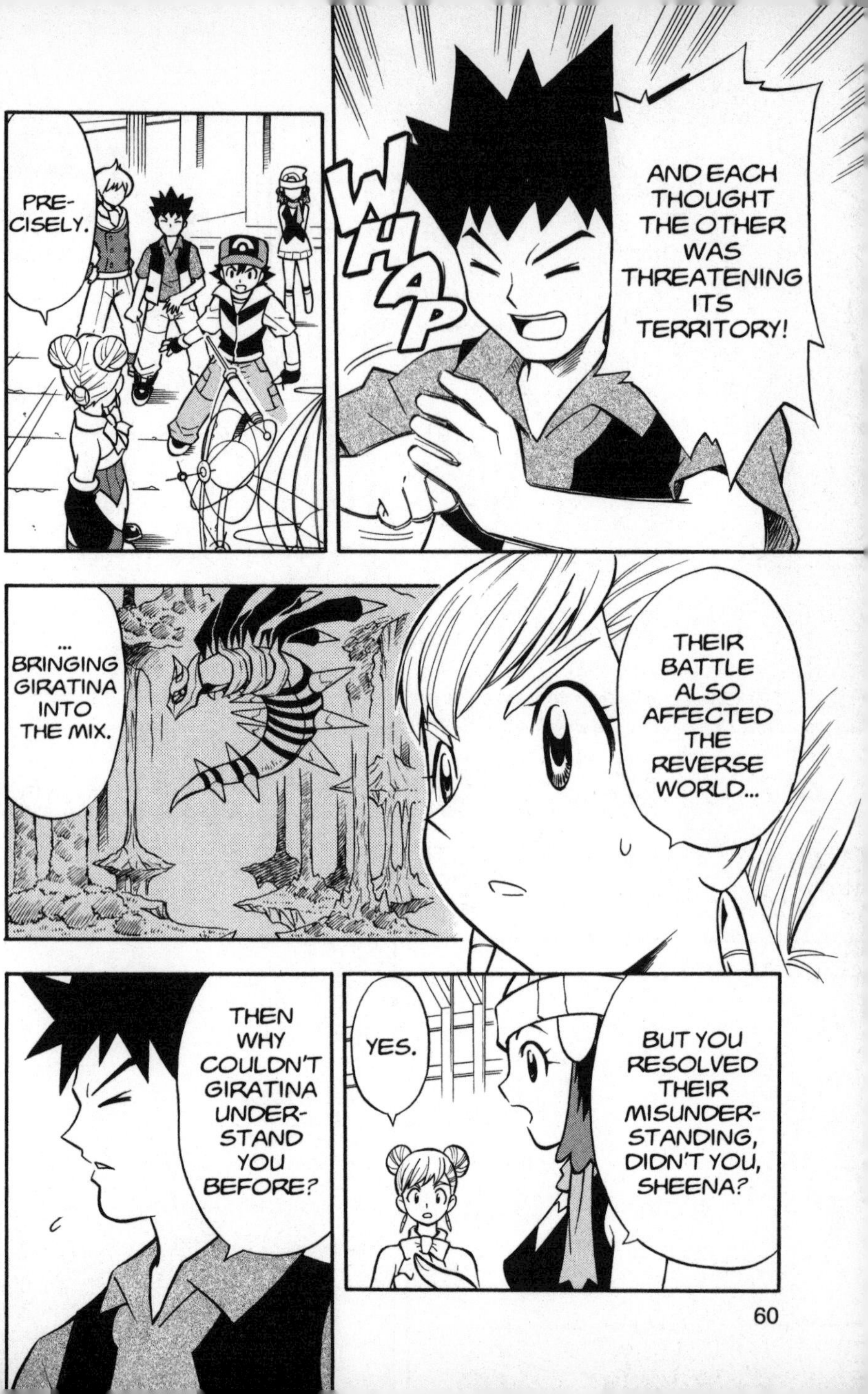
WHAP
AND EACH THOUGHT THE OTHER WAS THREATENING ITS TERRITORY!
PRE-CISELY.
THEIR BATTLE ALSO AFFECTED THE REVERSE WORLD...
...BRINGING GIRATINA INTO THE MIX.
BUT YOU RESOLVED THEIR MISUNDER-STANDING, DIDN'T YOU, SHEENA?
YES.
THEN WHY COULDN'T GIRATINA UNDER-STAND YOU BEFORE?

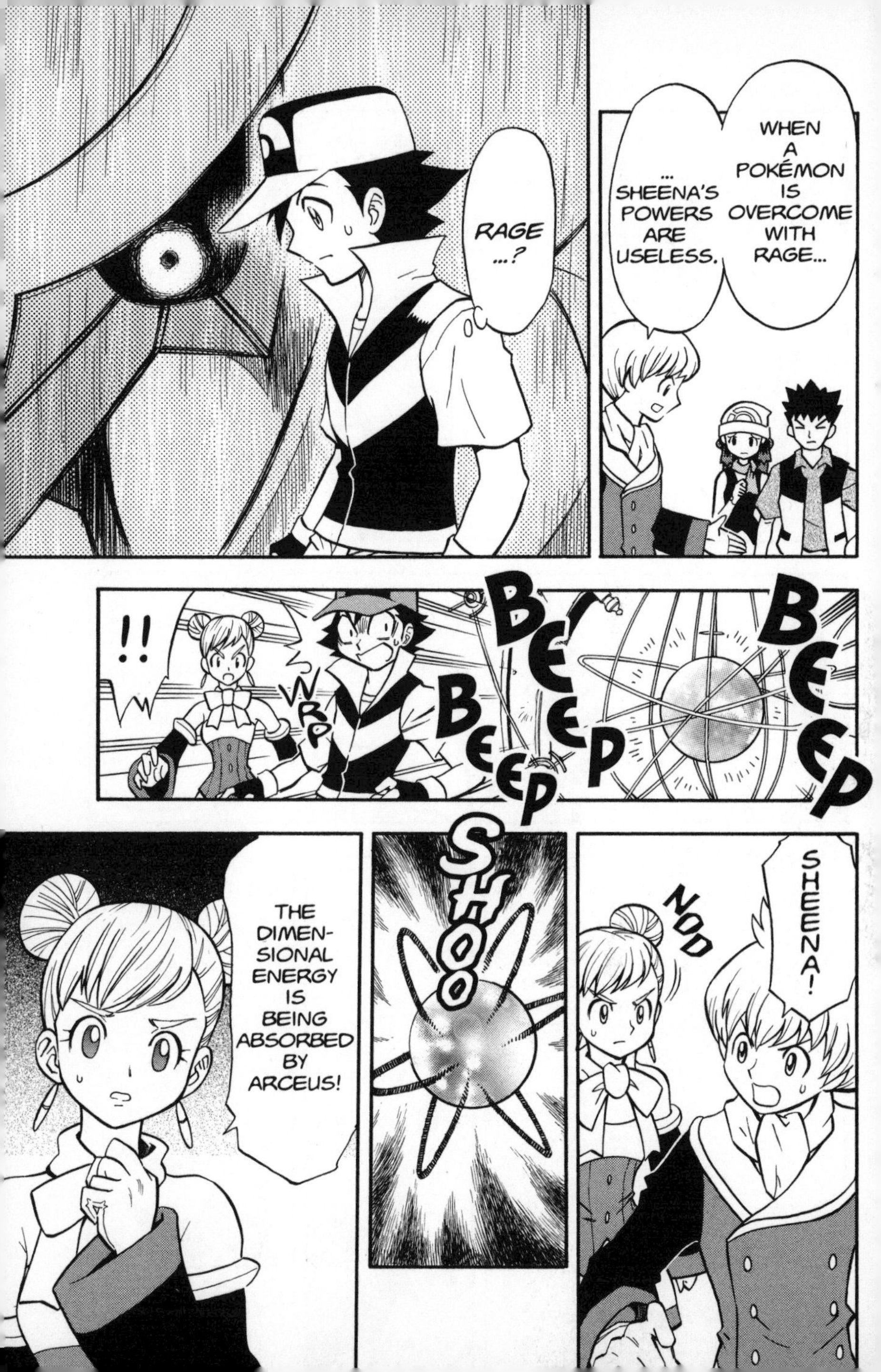
WHEN A POKÉMON IS OVERCOME WITH RAGE...
...SHEENA'S POWERS ARE USELESS.
RAGE ...?
BEEP
BEEP
BEEP
WRP
!!
SHEENA!
NOD
SHOOO
THE DIMENSIONAL ENERGY IS BEING ABSORBED BY ARCEUS!

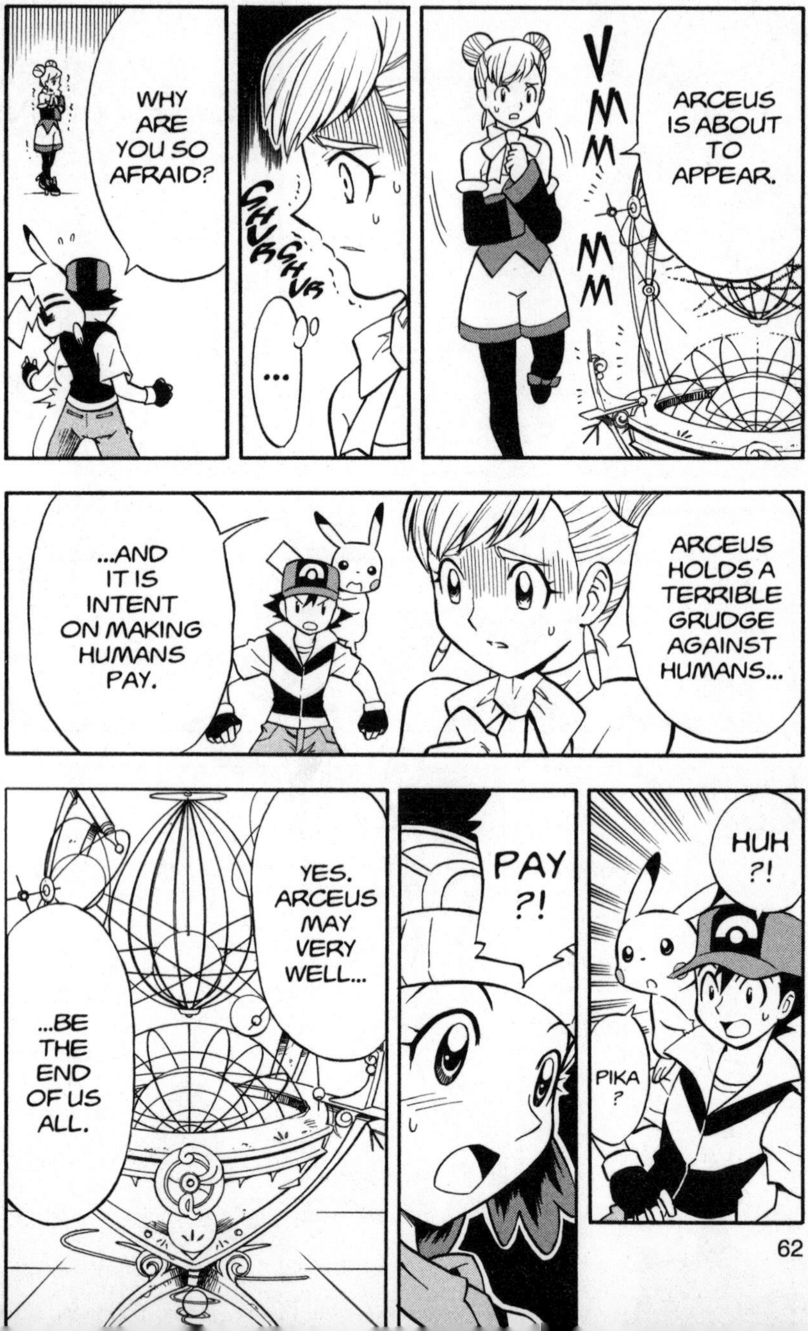
VMMM
MM
ARCEUS IS ABOUT TO APPEAR.
SHUR SHUR
...
WHY ARE YOU SO AFRAID?
ARCEUS HOLDS A TERRIBLE GRUDGE AGAINST HUMANS...
...AND IT IS INTENT ON MAKING HUMANS PAY.
HUH ?!
PIKA ?
PAY ?!
YES. ARCEUS MAY VERY WELL...
...BE THE END OF US ALL.

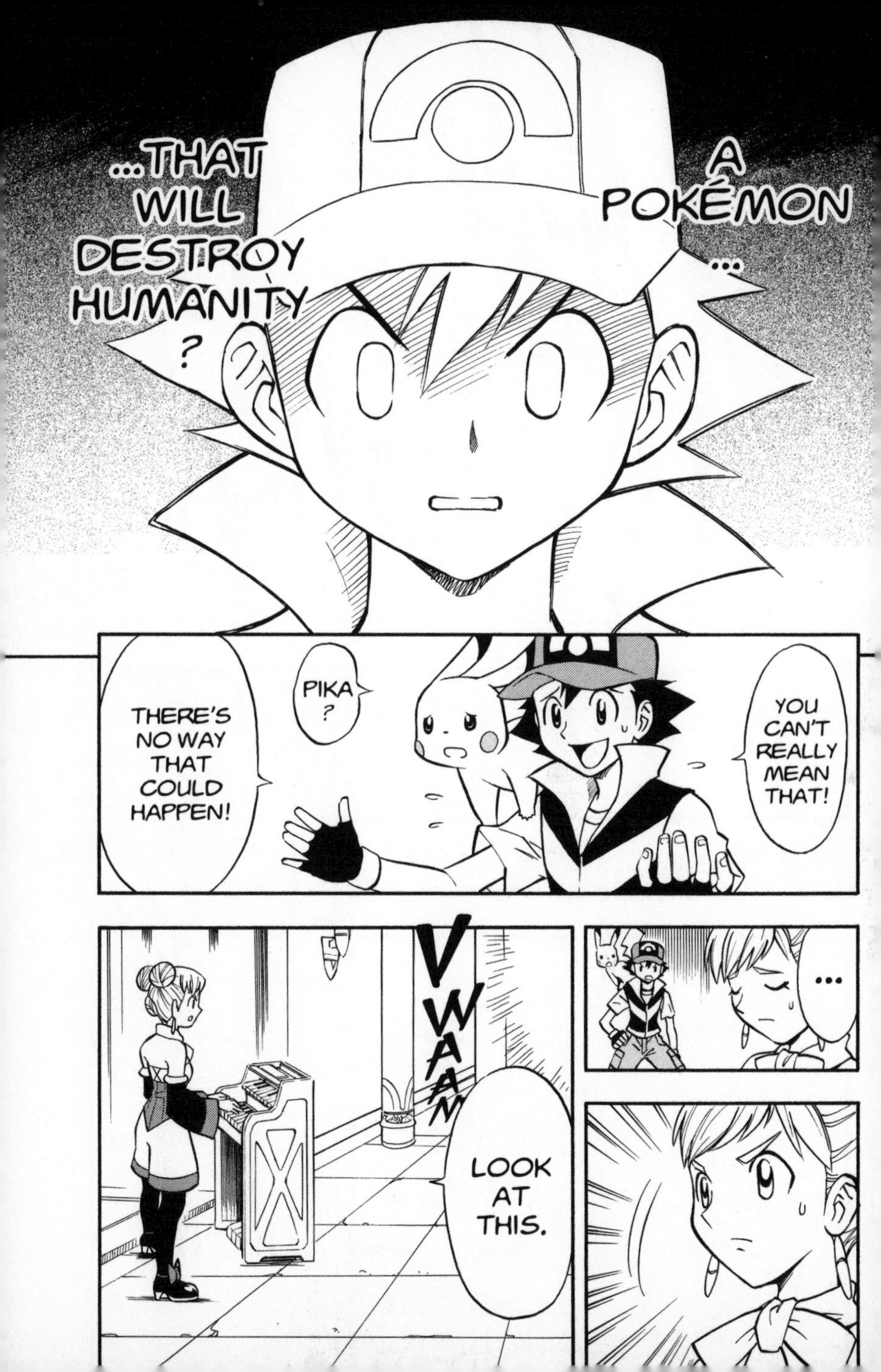
A POKÉMON ...
...THAT WILL DESTROY HUMANITY?
YOU CAN'T REALLY MEAN THAT!
PIKA?
THERE'S NO WAY THAT COULD HAPPEN!
...
VWAAN
LOOK AT THIS.

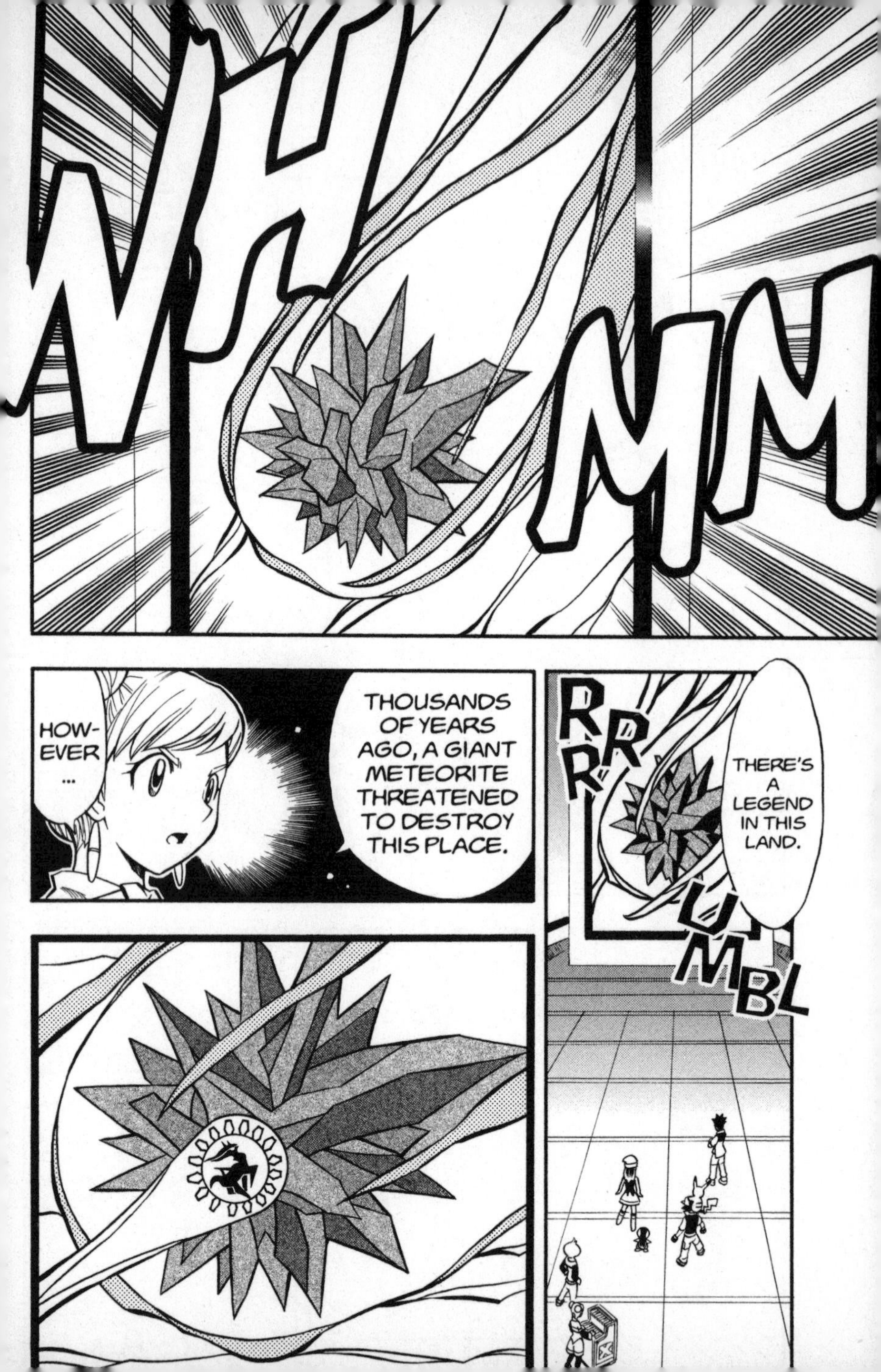
WHMMM
RRR
THERE'S A LEGEND IN THIS LAND.
UMBL
THOUSANDS OF YEARS AGO, A GIANT METEORITE THREATENED TO DESTROY THIS PLACE.
HOW-EVER ...

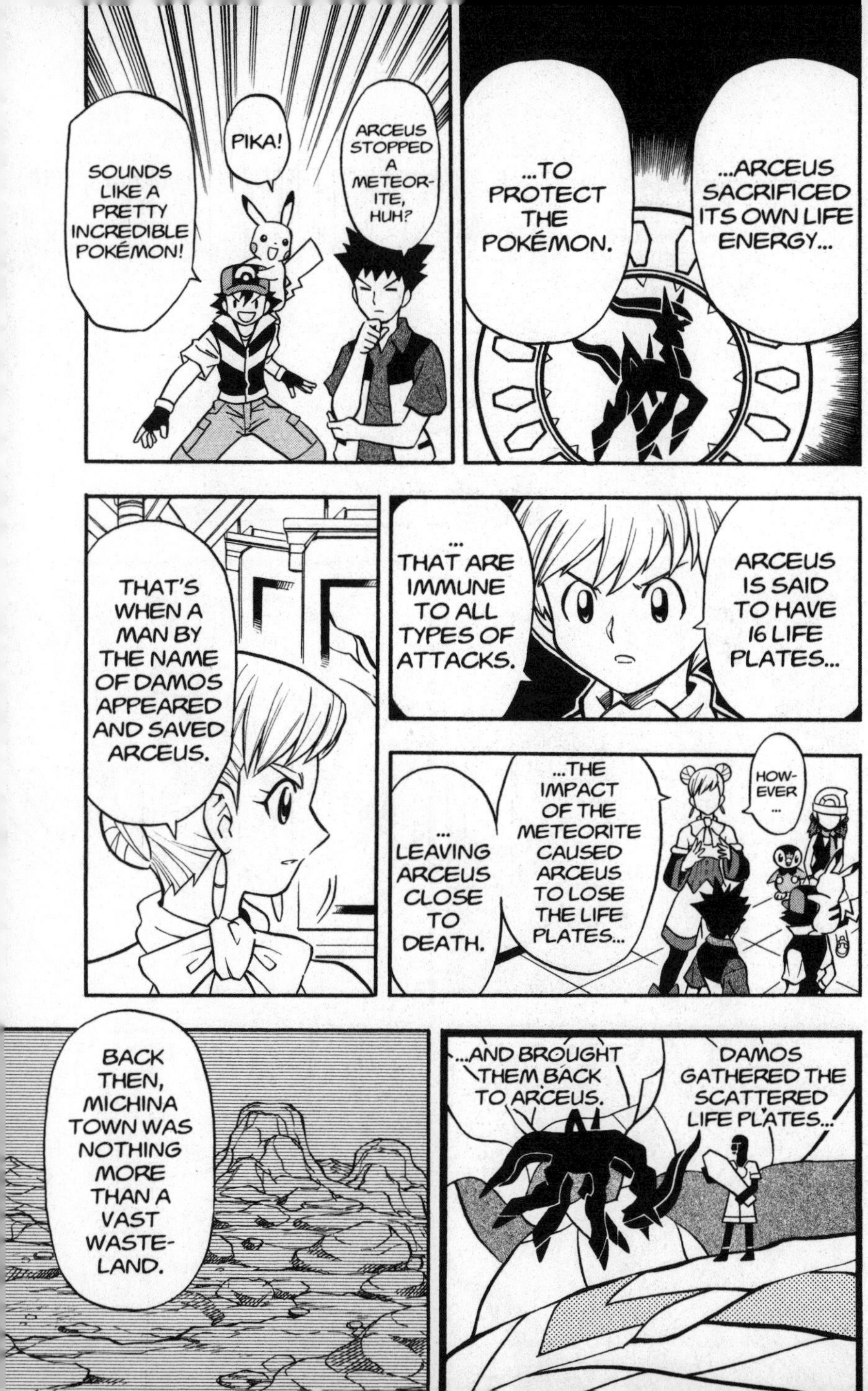
...ARCEUS SACRIFICED ITS OWN LIFE ENERGY...
...TO PROTECT THE POKÉMON.
ARCEUS STOPPED A METEORITE, HUH?
PIKA!
SOUNDS LIKE A PRETTY INCREDIBLE POKÉMON!
ARCEUS IS SAID TO HAVE 16 LIFE PLATES...
...THAT ARE IMMUNE TO ALL TYPES OF ATTACKS.
HOWEVER...
...THE IMPACT OF THE METEORITE CAUSED ARCEUS TO LOSE THE LIFE PLATES...
...LEAVING ARCEUS CLOSE TO DEATH.
THAT'S WHEN A MAN BY THE NAME OF DAMOS APPEARED AND SAVED ARCEUS.
DAMOS GATHERED THE SCATTERED LIFE PLATES...
...AND BROUGHT THEM BACK TO ARCEUS.
BACK THEN, MICHINA TOWN WAS NOTHING MORE THAN A VAST WASTELAND.

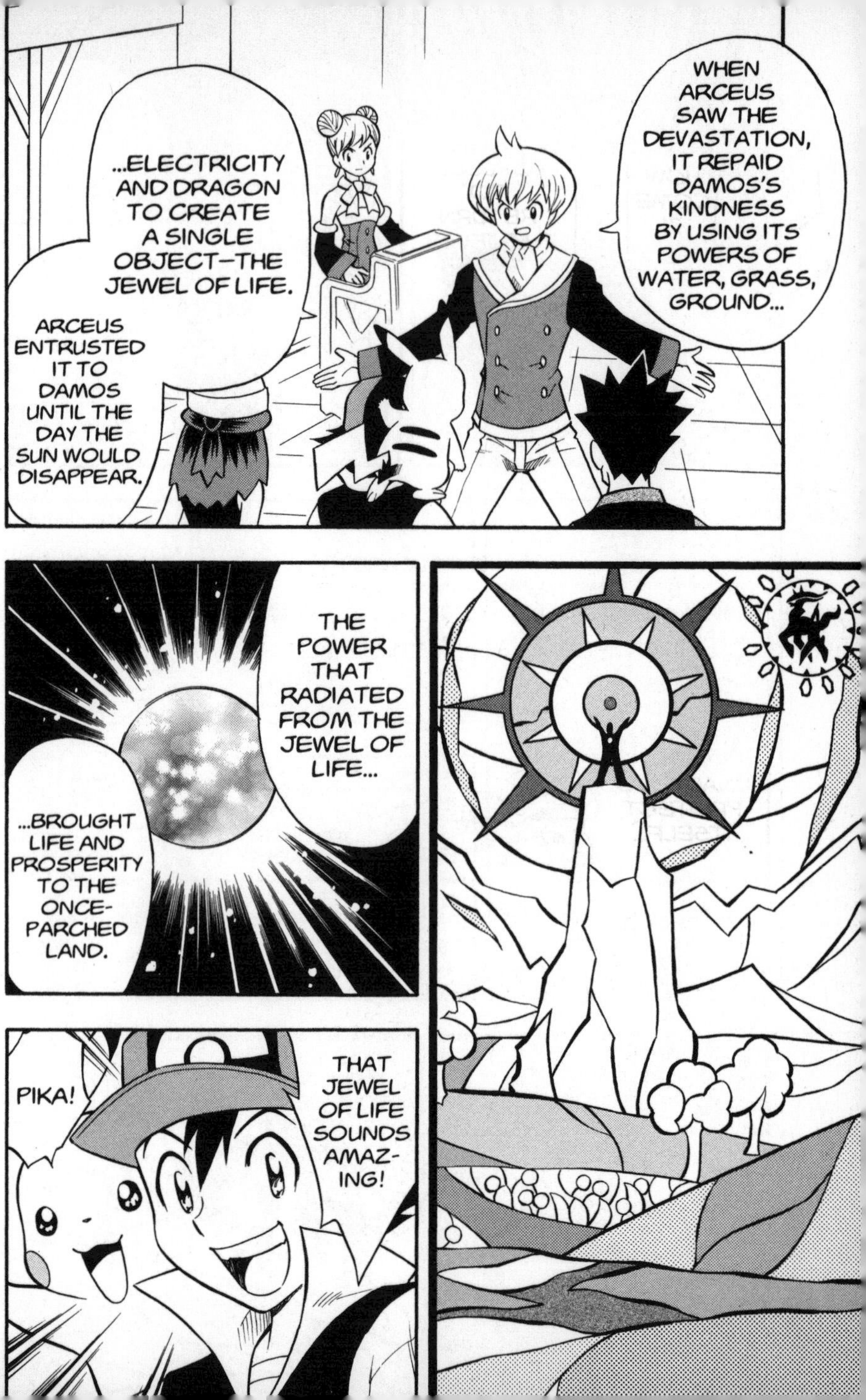
WHEN ARCEUS SAW THE DEVASTATION, IT REPAID DAMOS'S KINDNESS BY USING ITS POWERS OF WATER, GRASS, GROUND...
...ELECTRICITY AND DRAGON TO CREATE A SINGLE OBJECT—THE JEWEL OF LIFE.
ARCEUS ENTRUSTED IT TO DAMOS UNTIL THE DAY THE SUN WOULD DISAPPEAR.
THE POWER THAT RADIATED FROM THE JEWEL OF LIFE...
...BROUGHT LIFE AND PROSPERITY TO THE ONCE-PARCHED LAND.
THAT JEWEL OF LIFE SOUNDS AMAZ-ING!
PIKA!

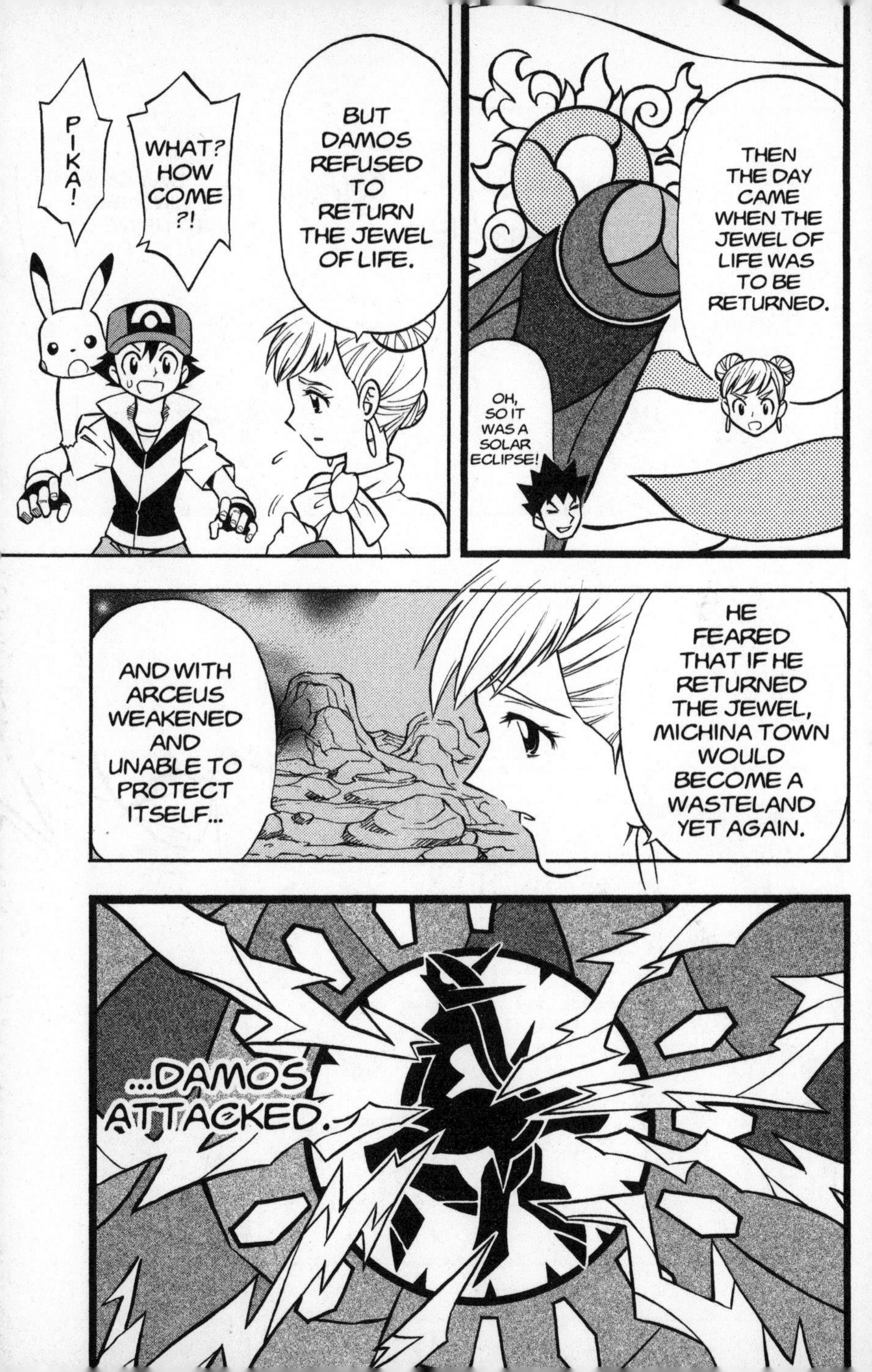
THEN THE DAY CAME WHEN THE JEWEL OF LIFE WAS TO BE RETURNED.
OH, SO IT WAS A SOLAR ECLIPSE!
BUT DAMOS REFUSED TO RETURN THE JEWEL OF LIFE.
WHAT? HOW COME ?!
PIKA!
HE FEARED THAT IF HE RETURNED THE JEWEL, MICHINA TOWN WOULD BECOME A WASTELAND YET AGAIN.
AND WITH ARCEUS WEAKENED AND UNABLE TO PROTECT ITSELF...
...DAMOS ATTACKED.

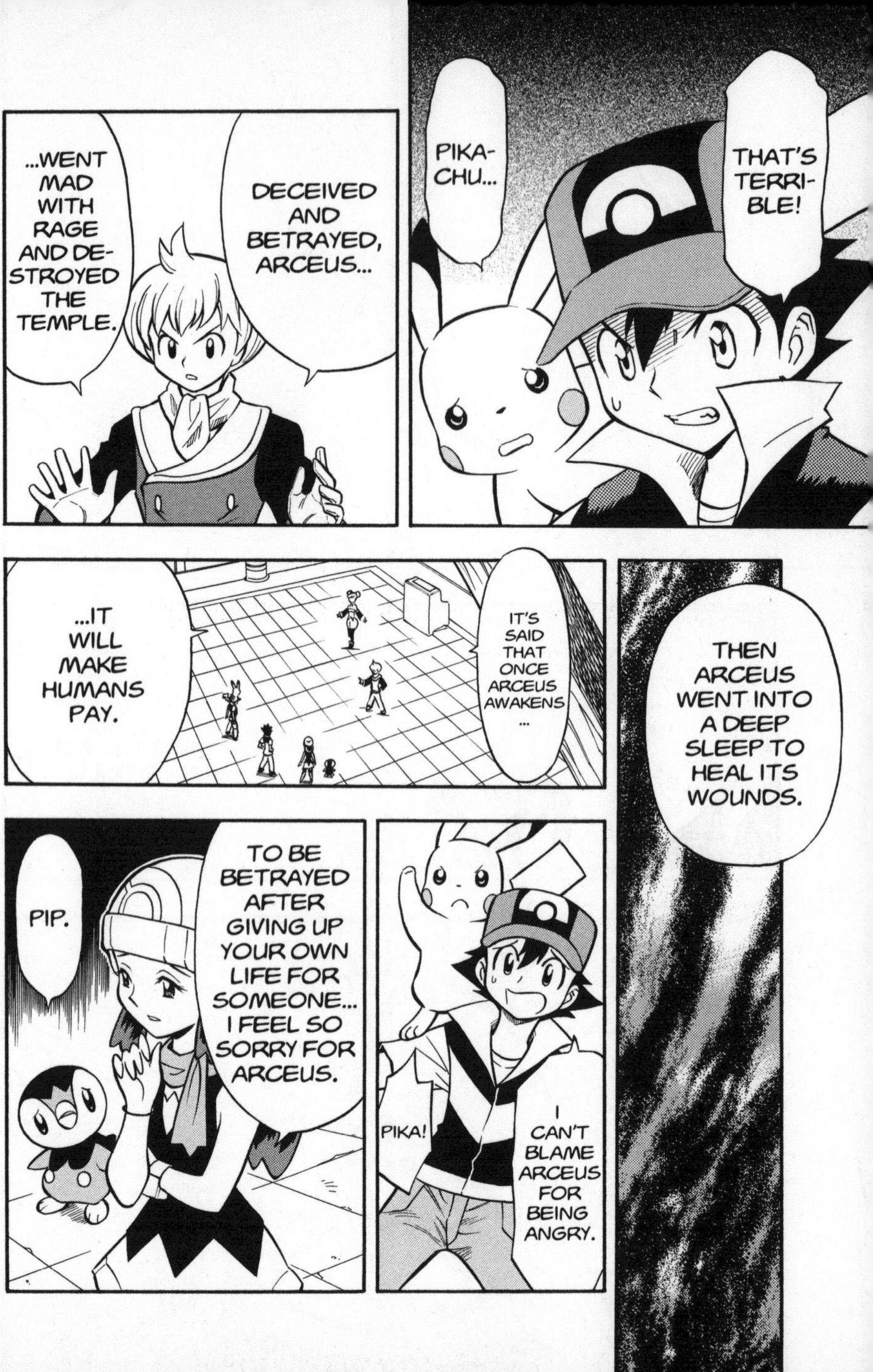
THAT'S TERRI-BLE!
PIKA-CHU...
DECEIVED AND BETRAYED, ARCEUS...
...WENT MAD WITH RAGE AND DE-STROYED THE TEMPLE.
THEN ARCEUS WENT INTO A DEEP SLEEP TO HEAL ITS WOUNDS.
IT'S SAID THAT ONCE ARCEUS AWAKENS...
...IT WILL MAKE HUMANS PAY.
I CAN'T BLAME ARCEUS FOR BEING ANGRY.
PIKA!
TO BE BETRAYED AFTER GIVING UP YOUR OWN LIFE FOR SOMEONE... I FEEL SO SORRY FOR ARCEUS.
PIP.

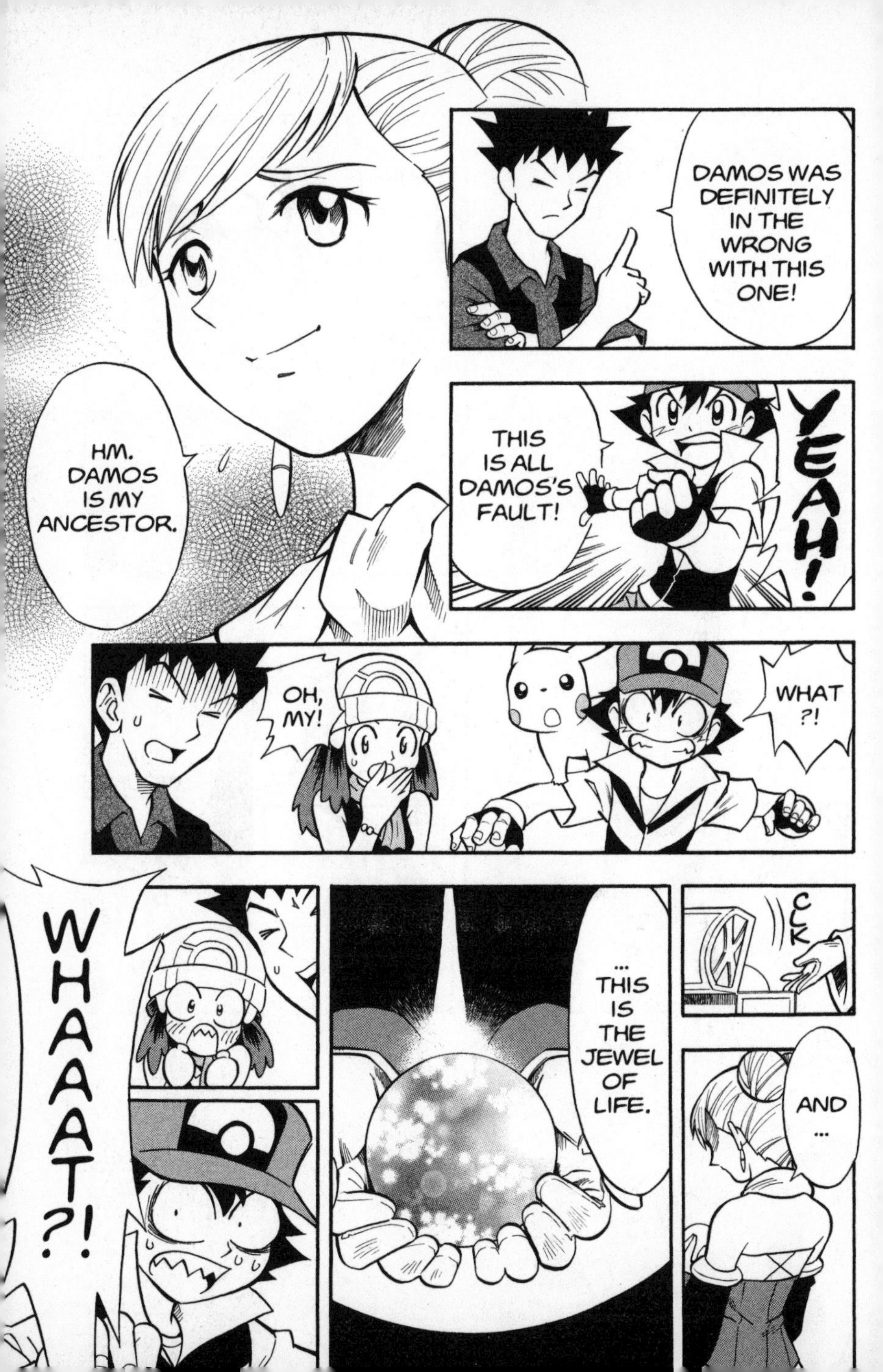
DAMOS WAS DEFINITELY IN THE WRONG WITH THIS ONE!
THIS IS ALL DAMOS'S FAULT!
YEAH!
HM. DAMOS IS MY ANCESTOR.
WHAT?!
OH, MY!
CLK
AND ...
... THIS IS THE JEWEL OF LIFE.
WHAAAT?!

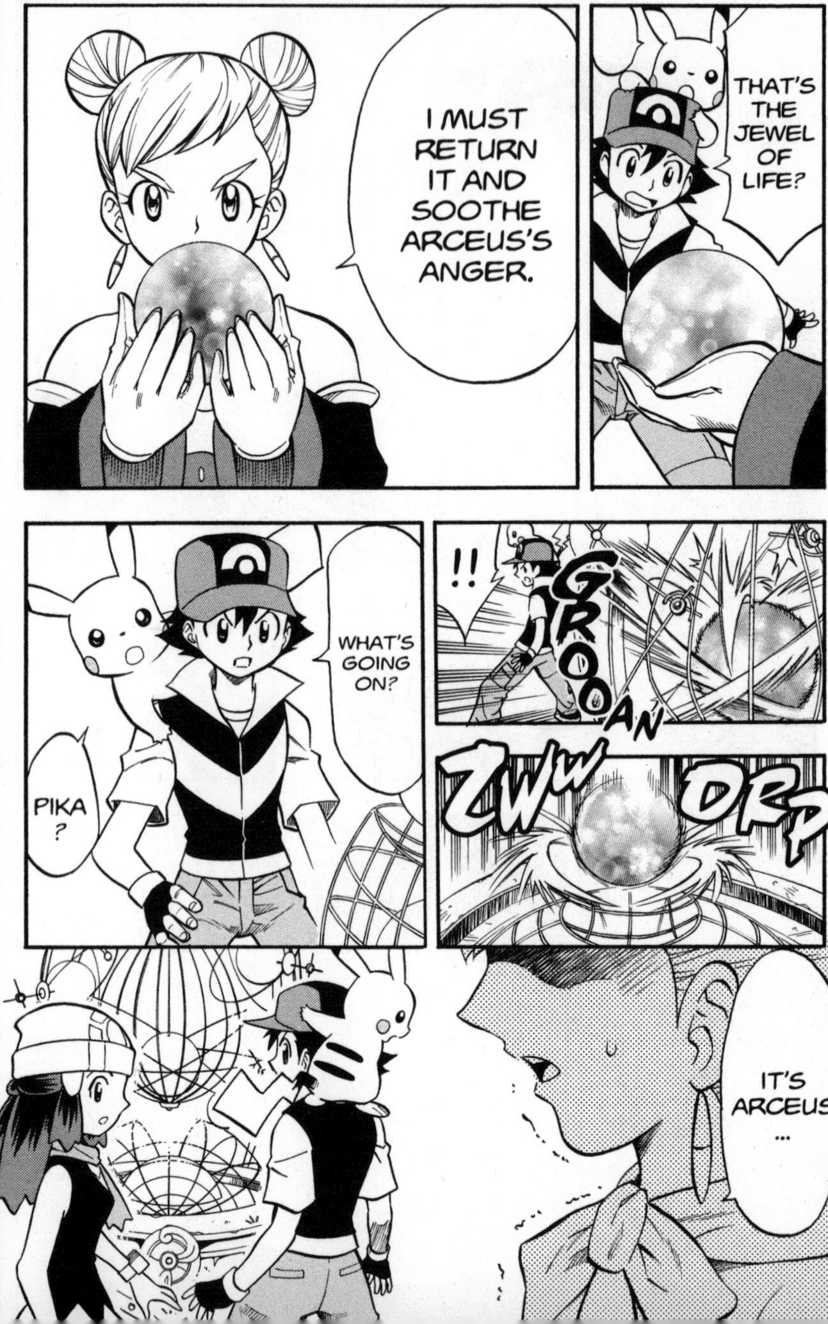
THAT'S THE JEWEL OF LIFE?
I MUST RETURN IT AND SOOTHE ARCEUS'S ANGER.
!!
GROOAN
ZWW
DRP
WHAT'S GOING ON?
PIKA?
IT'S ARCEUS ...

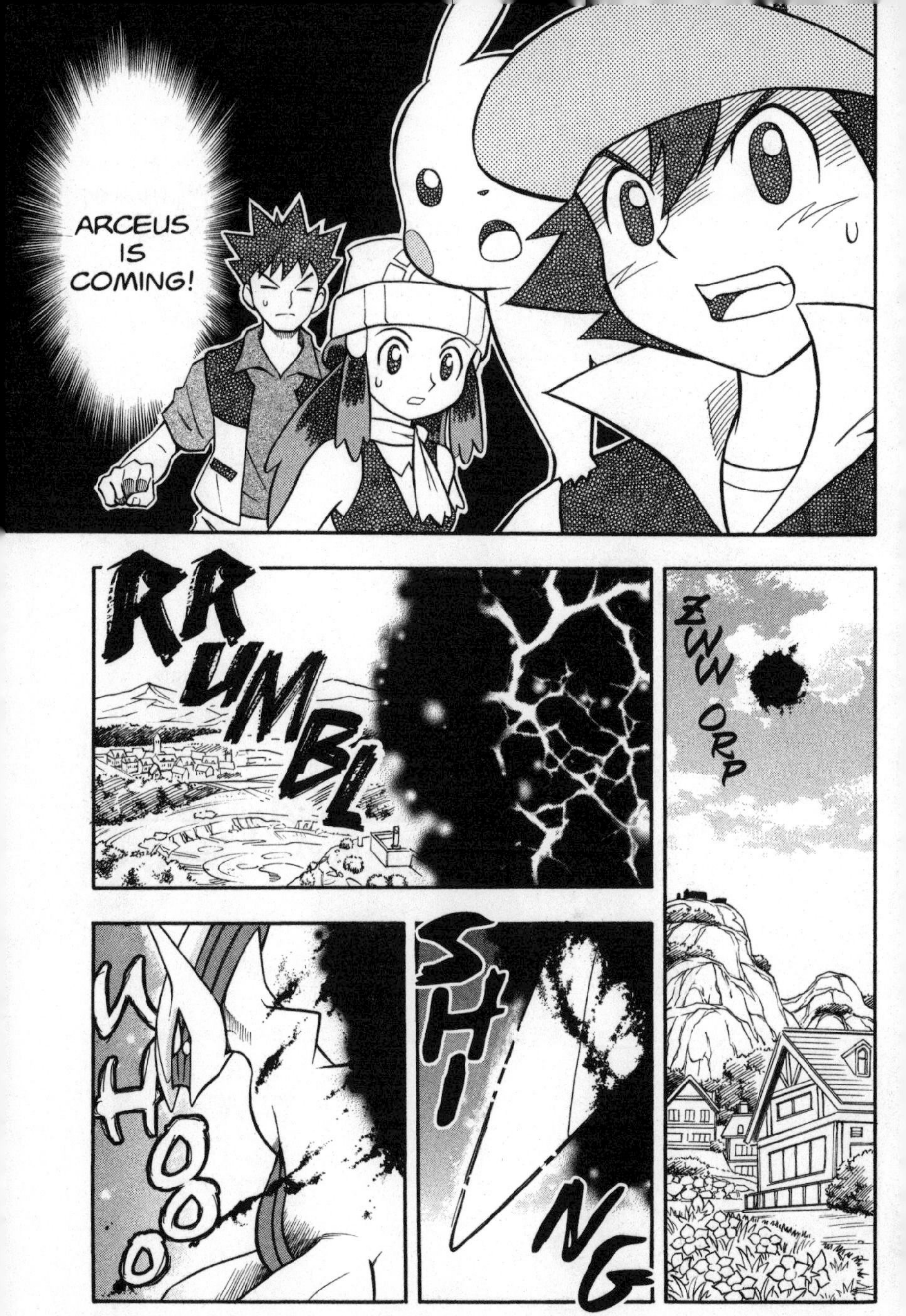
ARCEUS IS COMING!
ZWWORA
RRUMBL
SHING
WHOOO

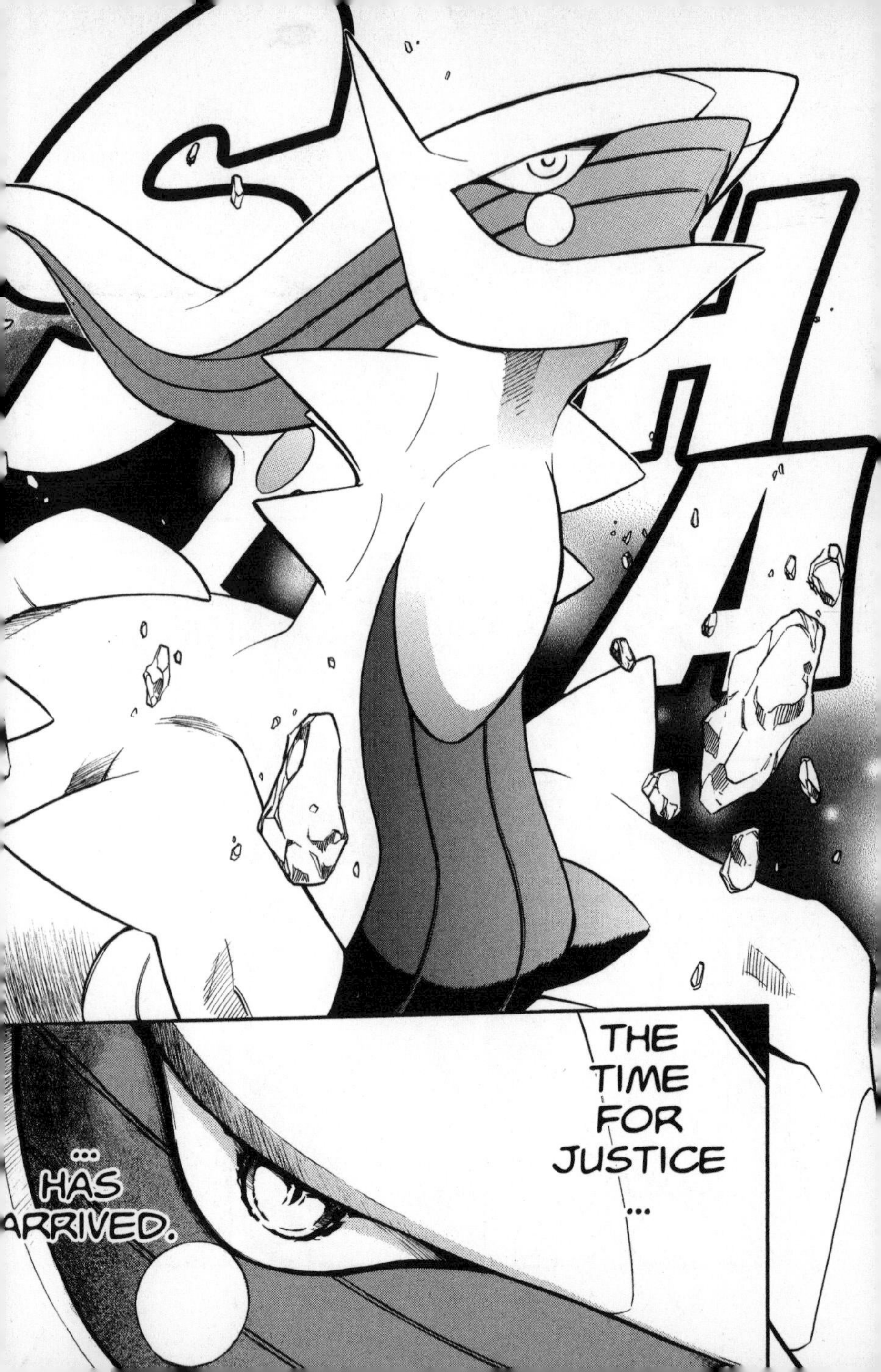
THE TIME FOR JUSTICE ...
... HAS ARRIVED.

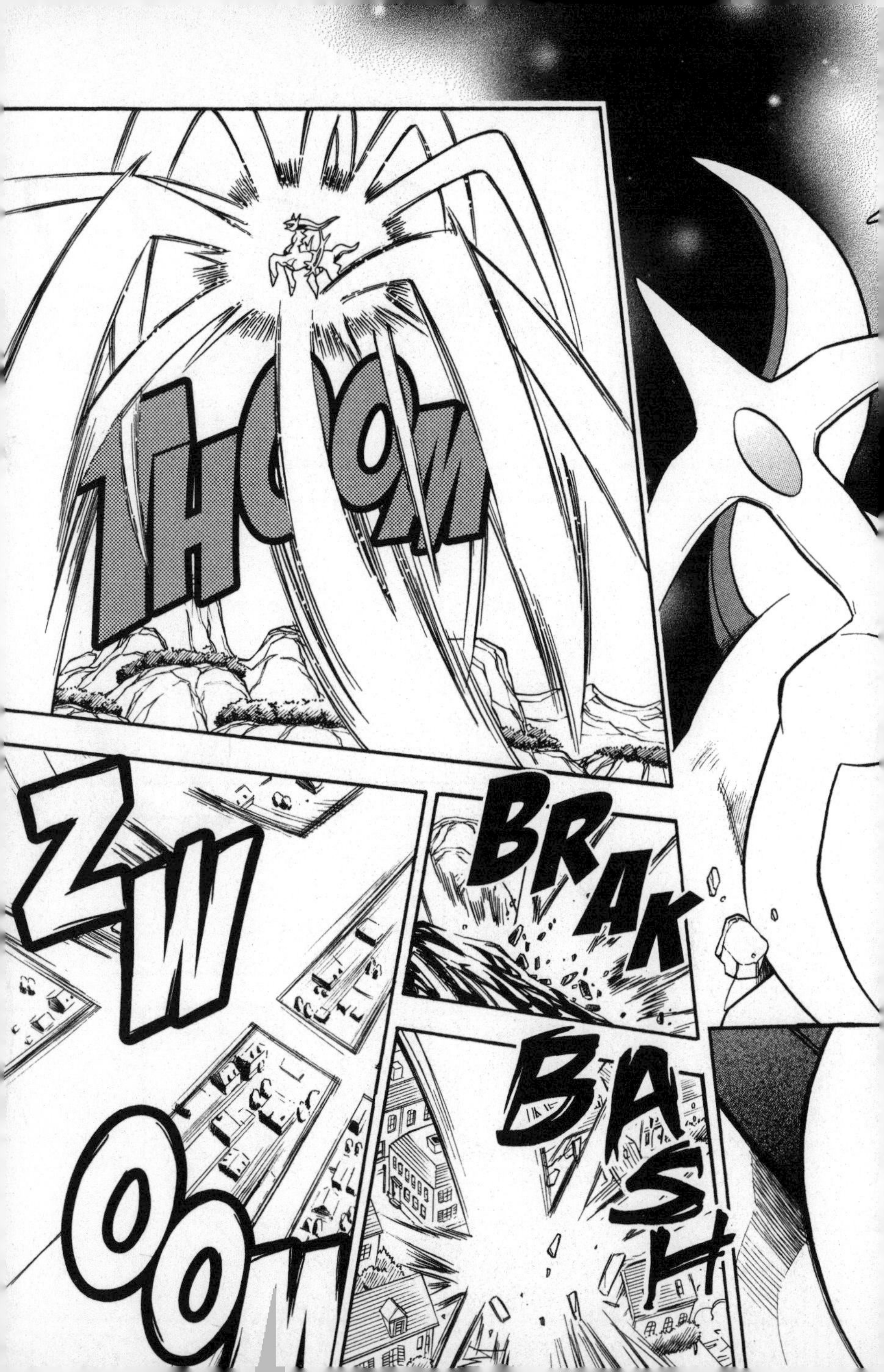
THOOM
BRAK
BASH
ZWOOM

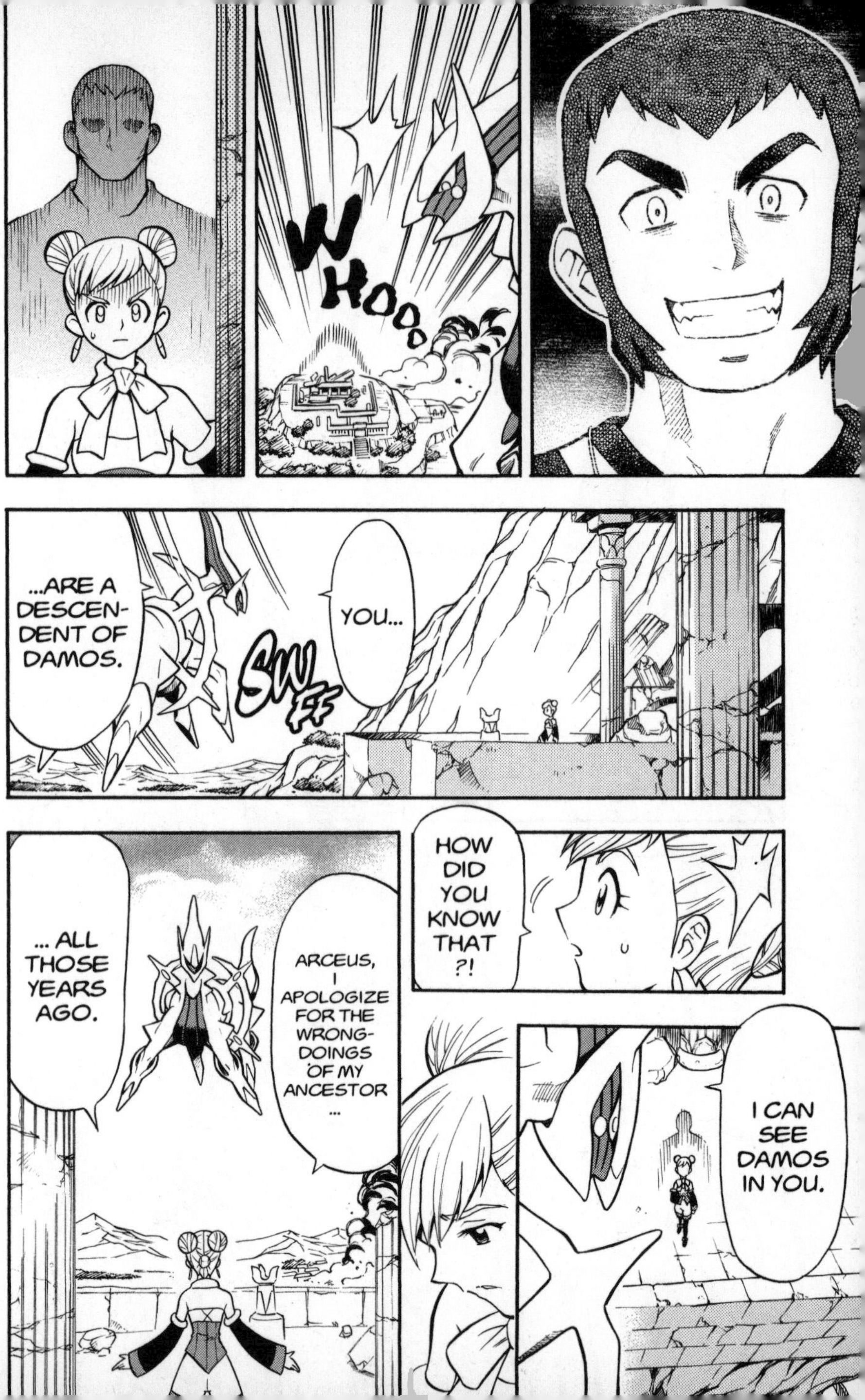
WHOOO
YOU...
SWFF
...ARE A DESCENDENT OF DAMOS.
HOW DID YOU KNOW THAT?!
I CAN SEE DAMOS IN YOU.
ARCEUS, I APOLOGIZE FOR THE WRONGDOINGS OF MY ANCESTOR...
... ALL THOSE YEARS AGO.

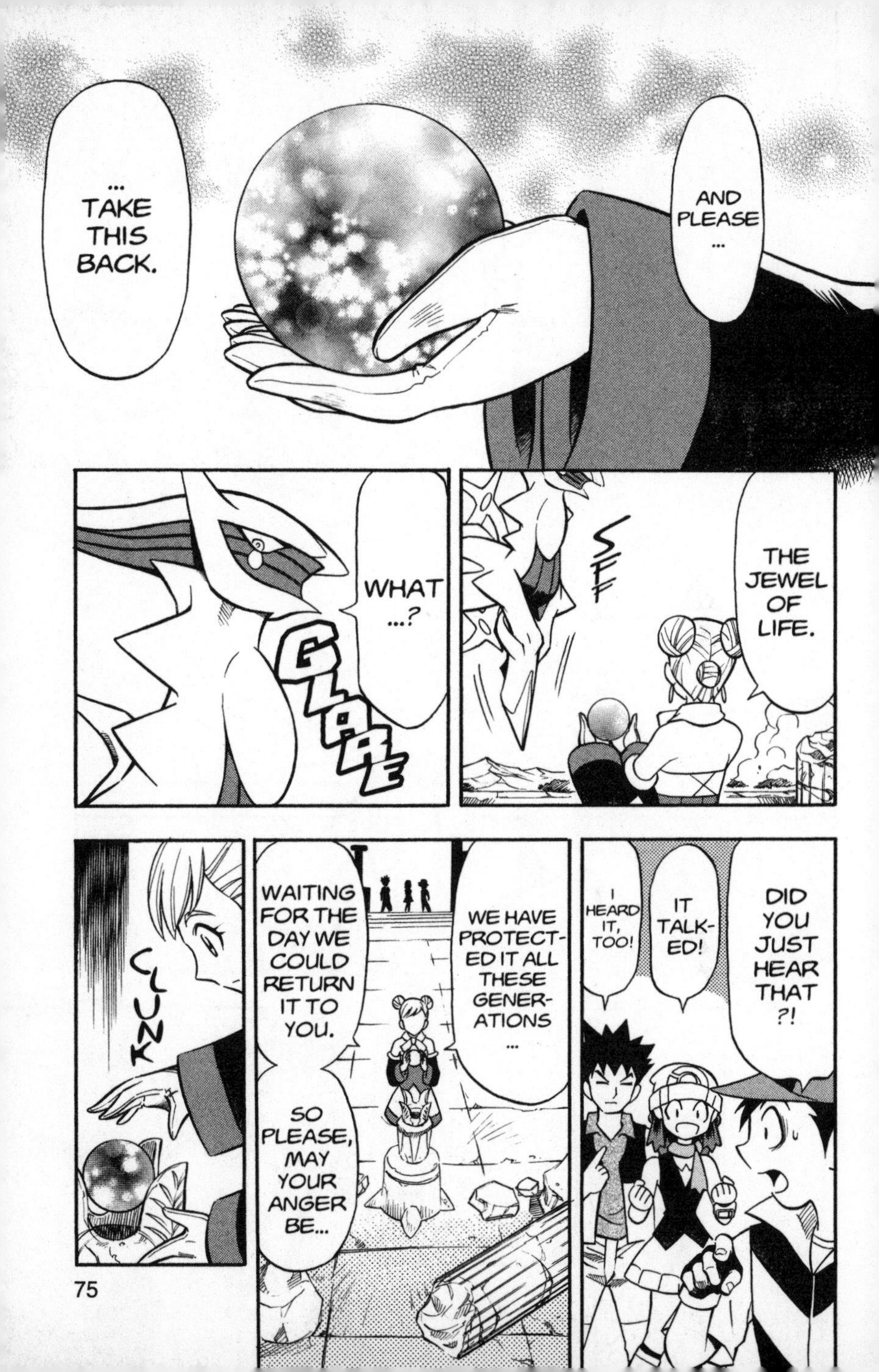
AND PLEASE ...
... TAKE THIS BACK.
THE JEWEL OF LIFE.
SFF
WHAT ...?
GLARE
DID YOU JUST HEAR THAT?!
IT TALK-ED!
I HEARD IT, TOO!
WE HAVE PROTECT-ED IT ALL THESE GENER-ATIONS ...
WAITING FOR THE DAY WE COULD RETURN IT TO YOU.
SO PLEASE, MAY YOUR ANGER BE...
CLUNK

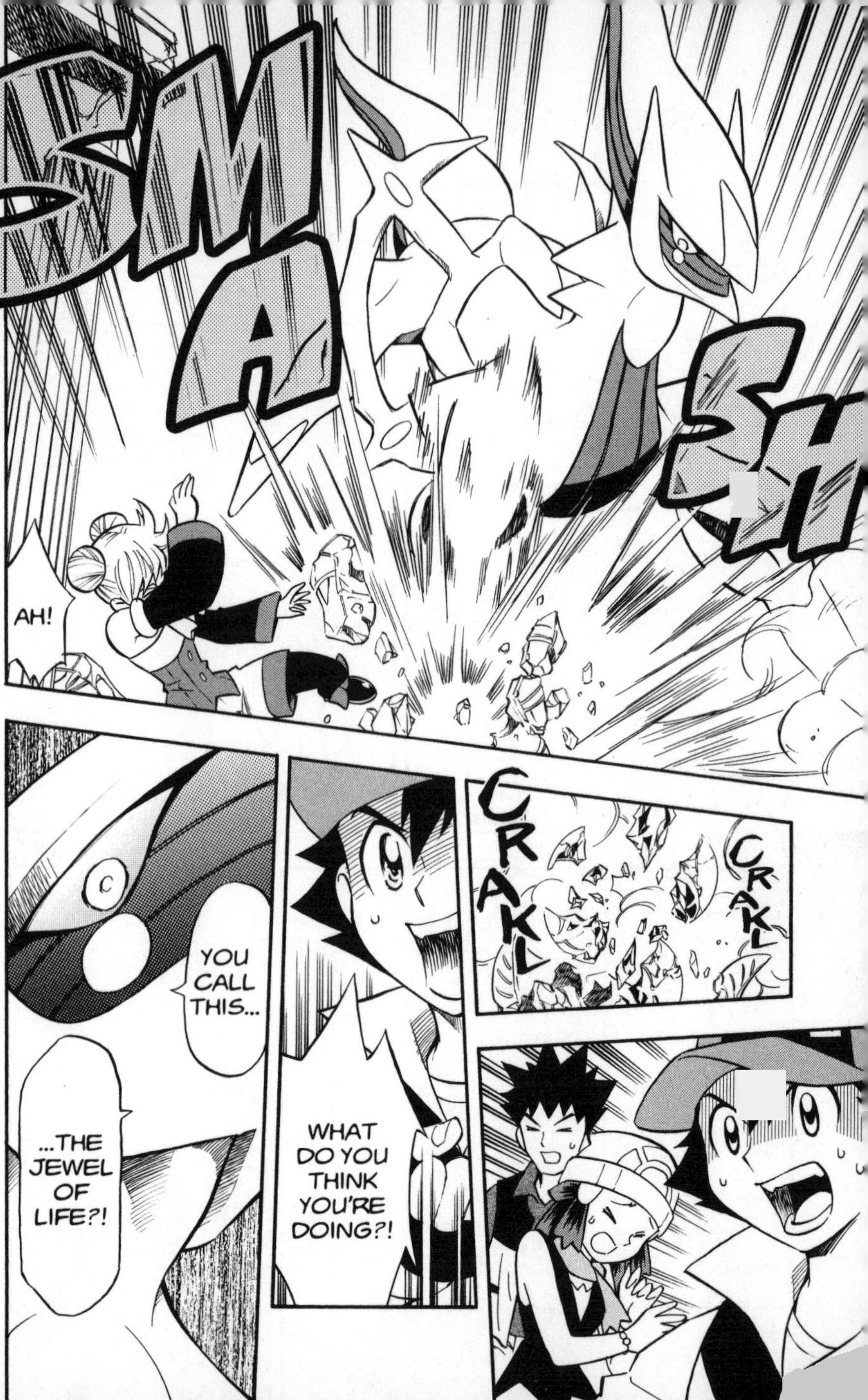
SMASH
AH!
CRAKL
CRAKL
WHAT DO YOU THINK YOU'RE DOING?!
YOU CALL THIS...
...THE JEWEL OF LIFE?!

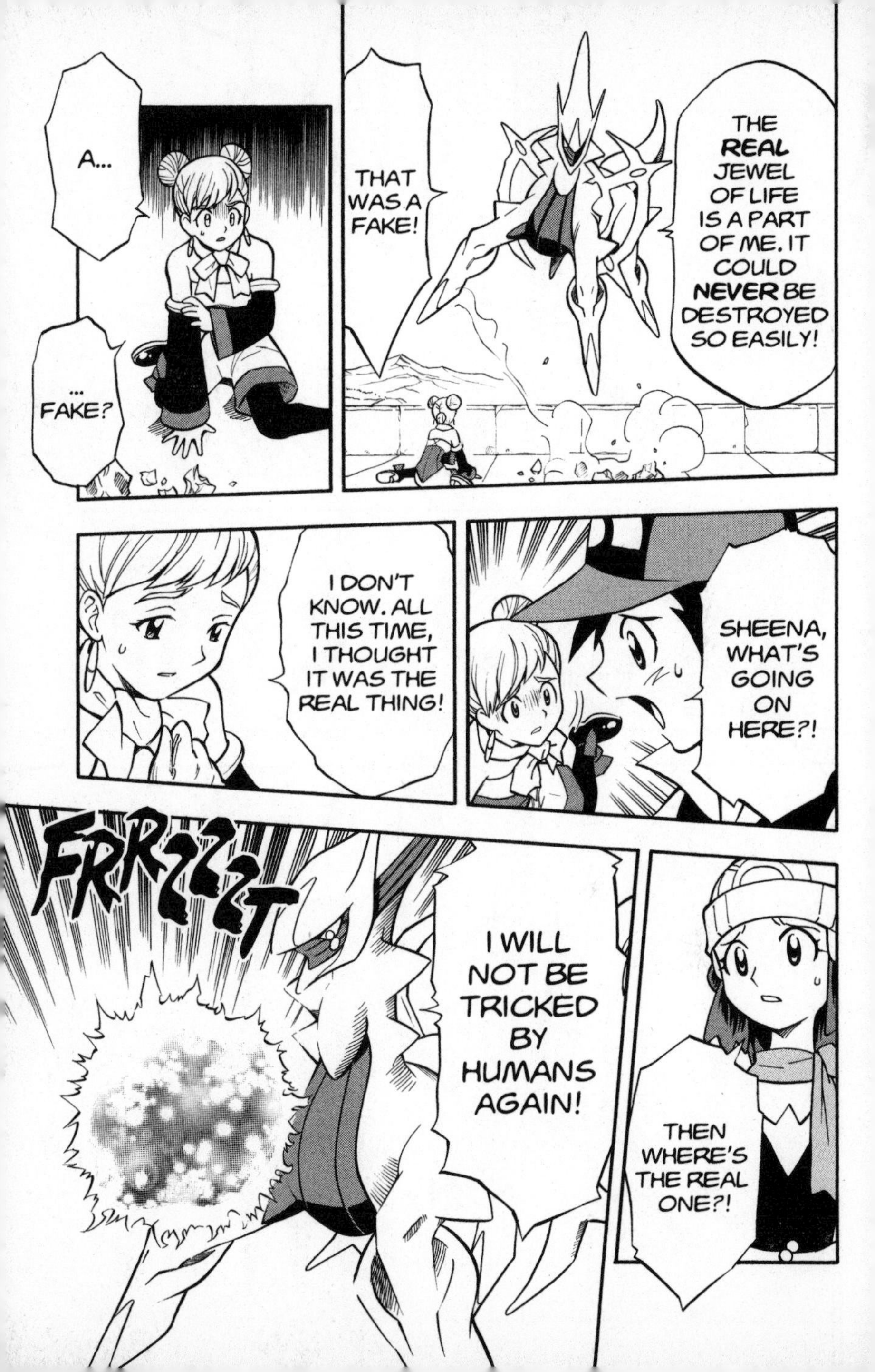
THAT WAS A FAKE!
THE REAL JEWEL OF LIFE IS A PART OF ME. IT COULD NEVER BE DESTROYED SO EASILY!
A...
... FAKE?
SHEENA, WHAT'S GOING ON HERE?!
I DON'T KNOW. ALL THIS TIME, I THOUGHT IT WAS THE REAL THING!
THEN WHERE'S THE REAL ONE?!
I WILL NOT BE TRICKED BY HUMANS AGAIN!
FRZZZT

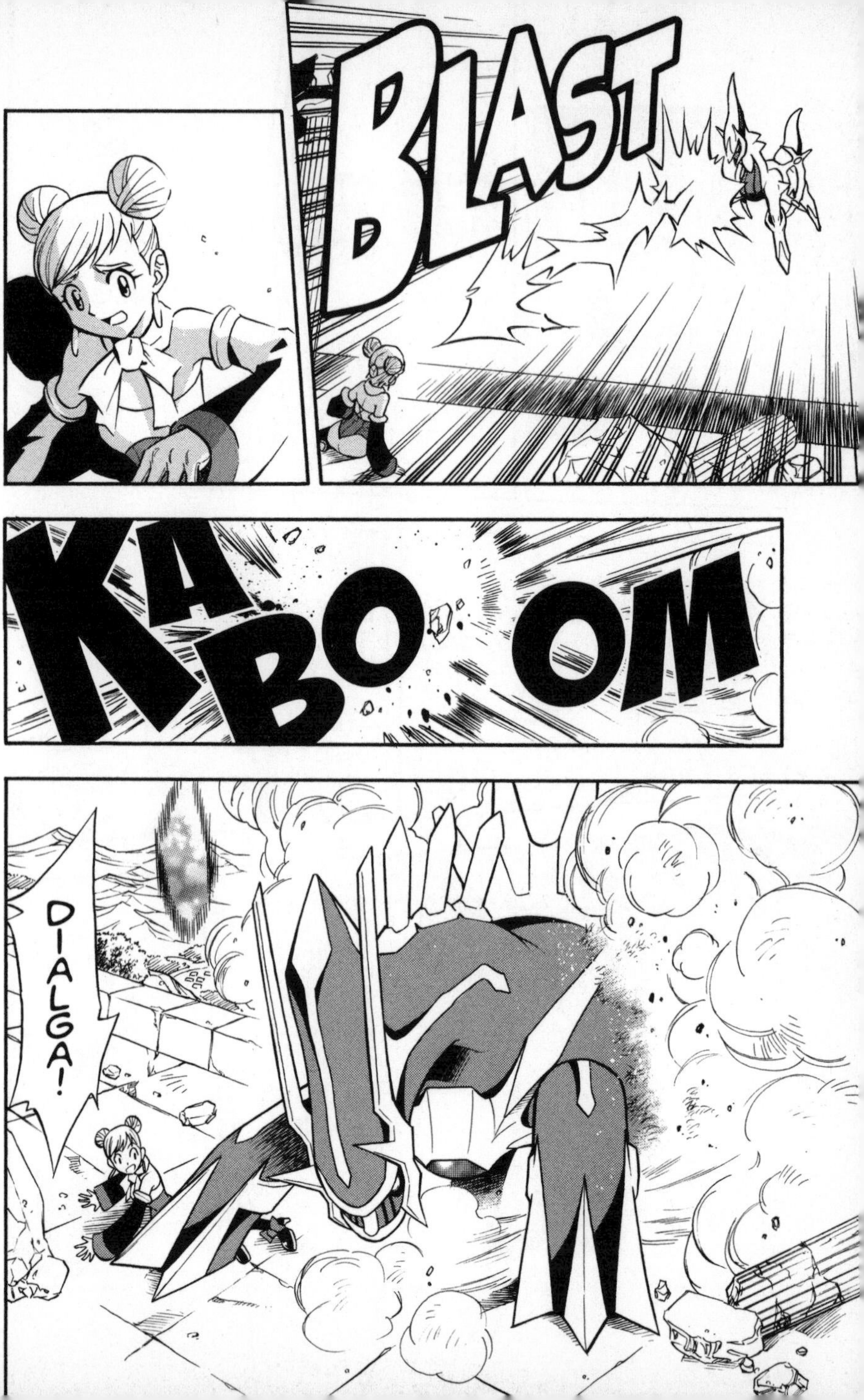
BLAST
KABOOM
DIALGA!

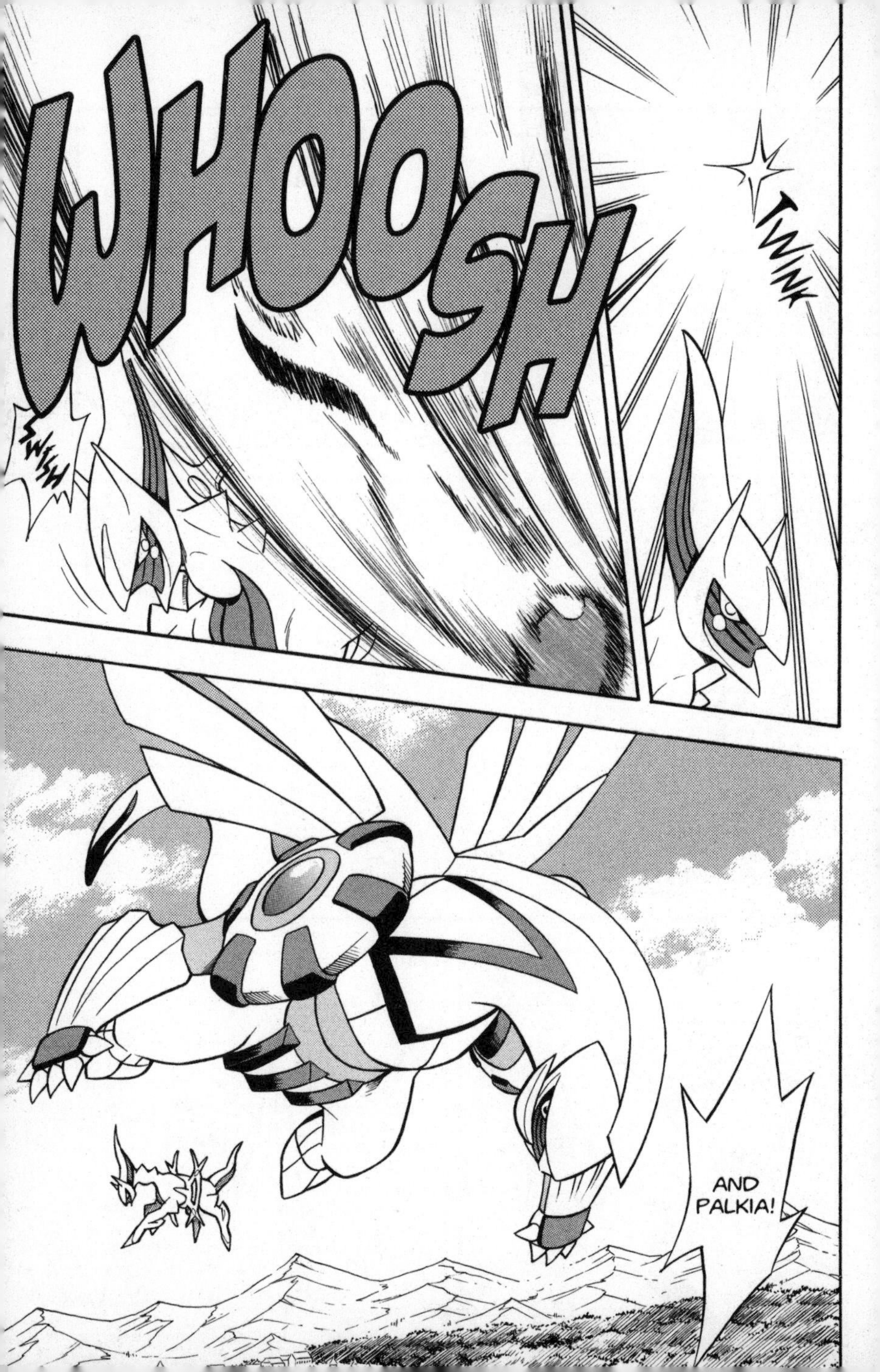
TWINK
WHOOSH
SWISH
AND PALKIA!

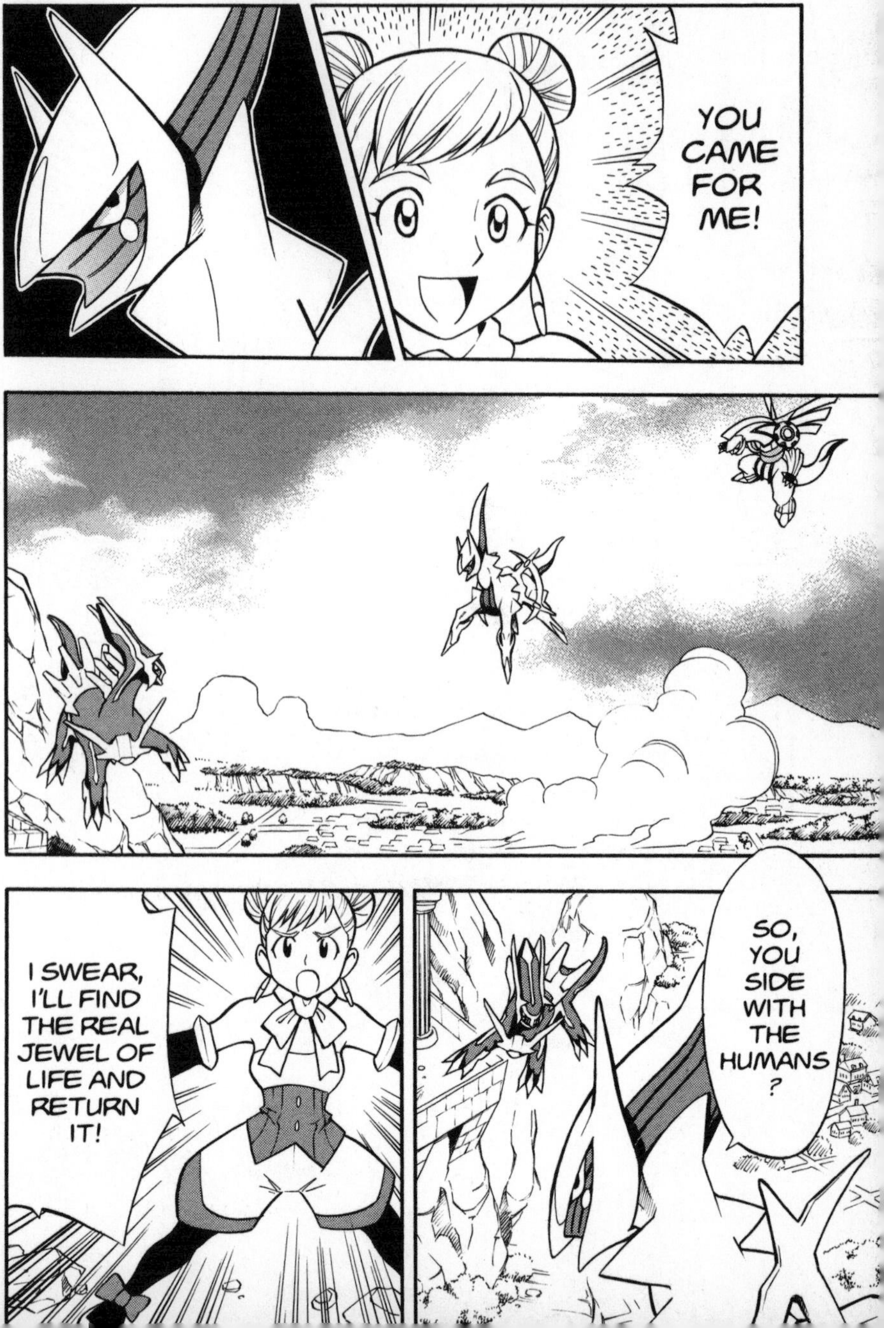
YOU CAME FOR ME!
SO, YOU SIDE WITH THE HUMANS?
I SWEAR, I'LL FIND THE REAL JEWEL OF LIFE AND RETURN IT!

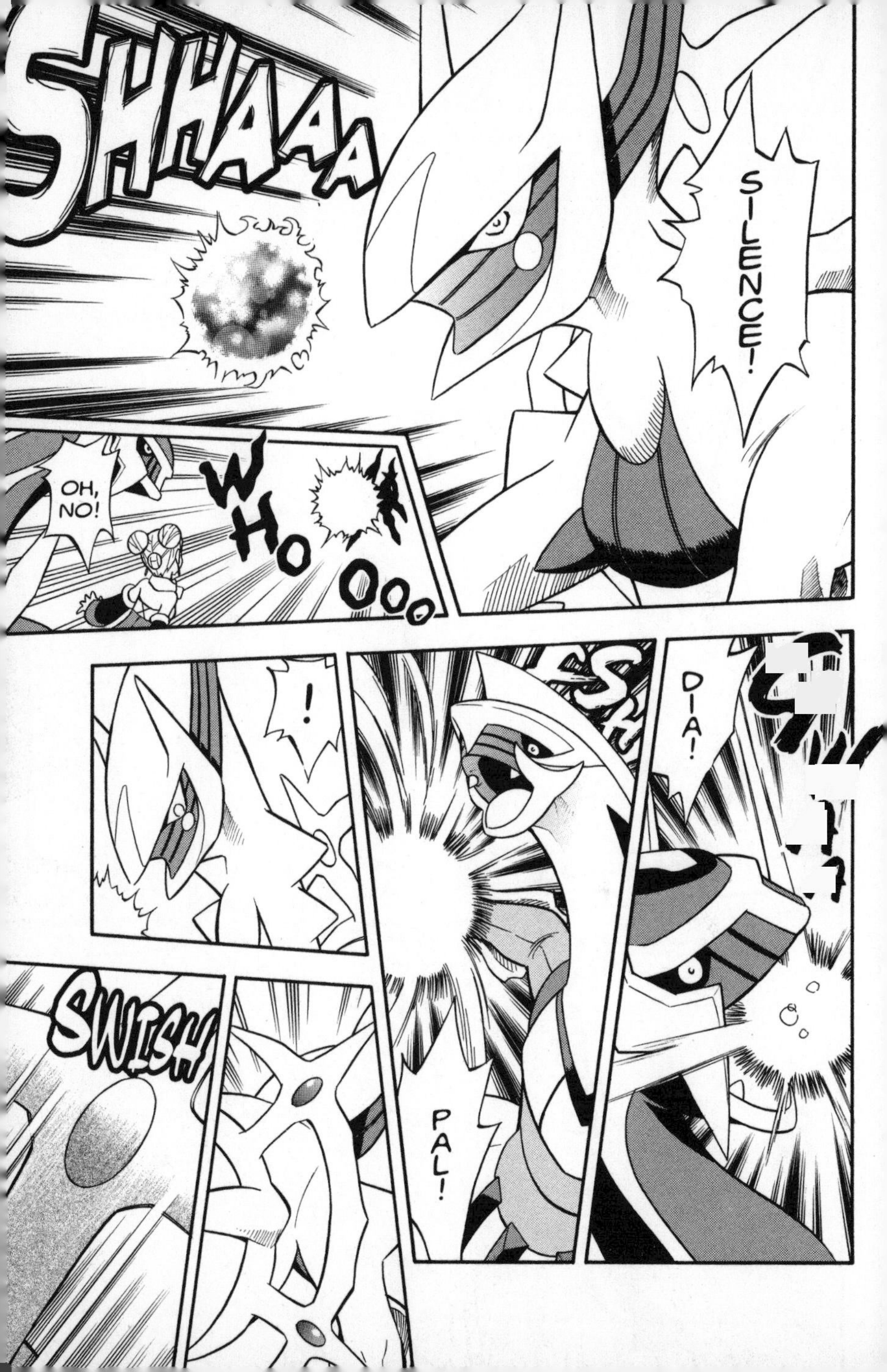
SILENCE!
SHHAAA
WHOOOO
OH, NO!
DIA!
SH
PAL!
!
SWISH

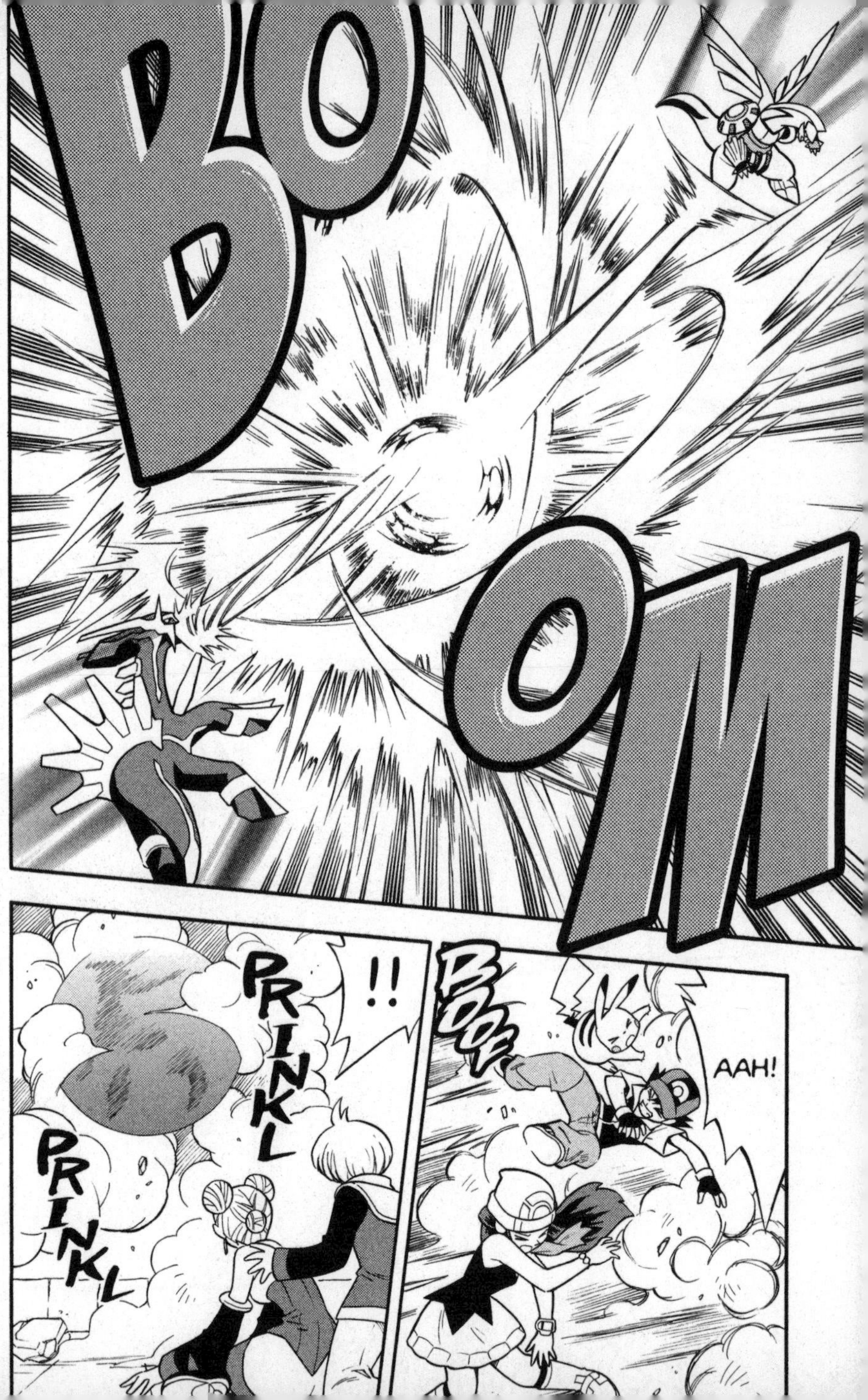
BOOM
BOOM
AAH!
PRINKL
!!
PRINKL

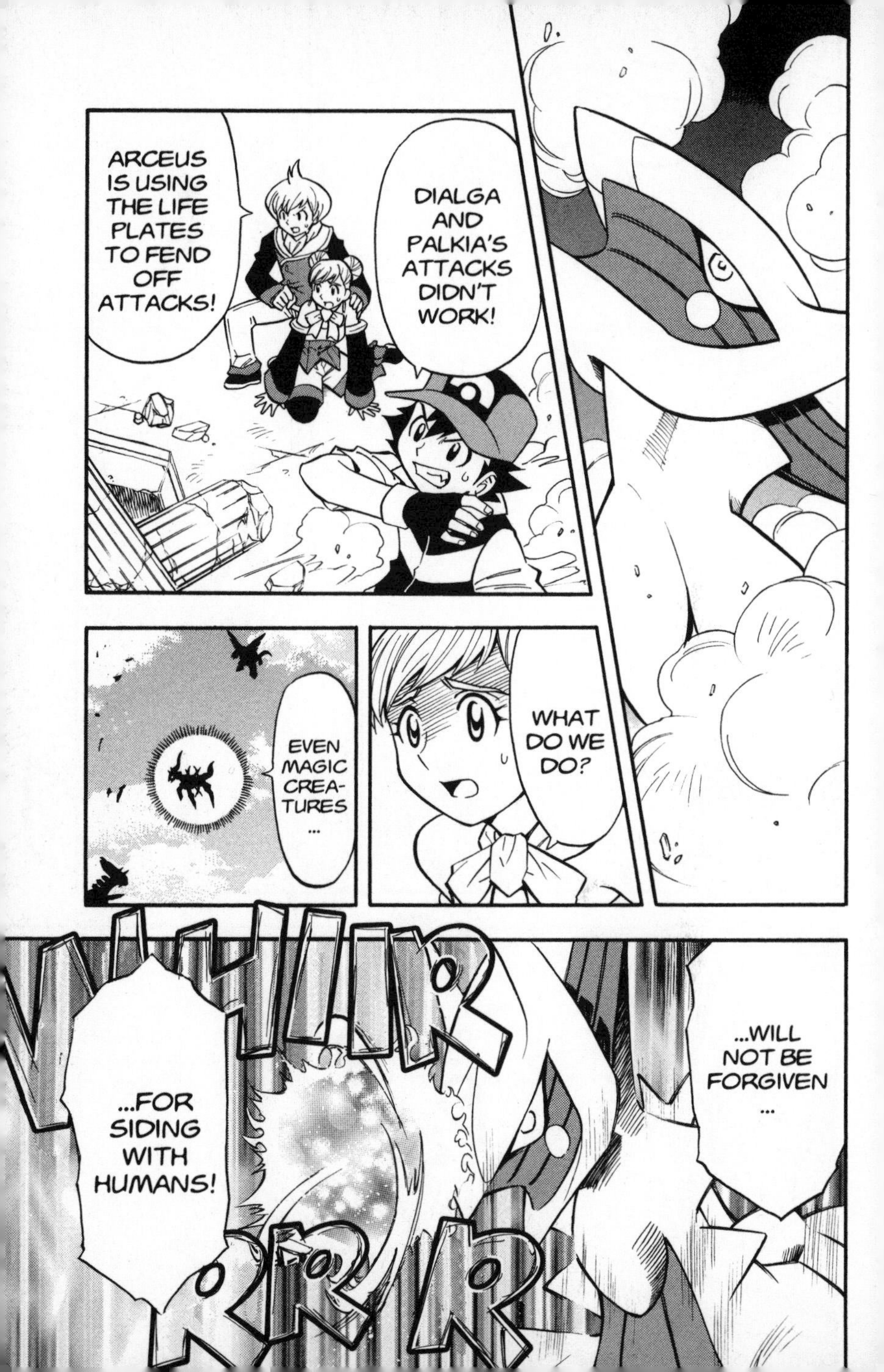
DIALGA AND PALKIA'S ATTACKS DIDN'T WORK!
ARCEUS IS USING THE LIFE PLATES TO FEND OFF ATTACKS!
WHAT DO WE DO?
EVEN MAGIC CREATURES ...
...WILL NOT BE FORGIVEN ...
...FOR SIDING WITH HUMANS!

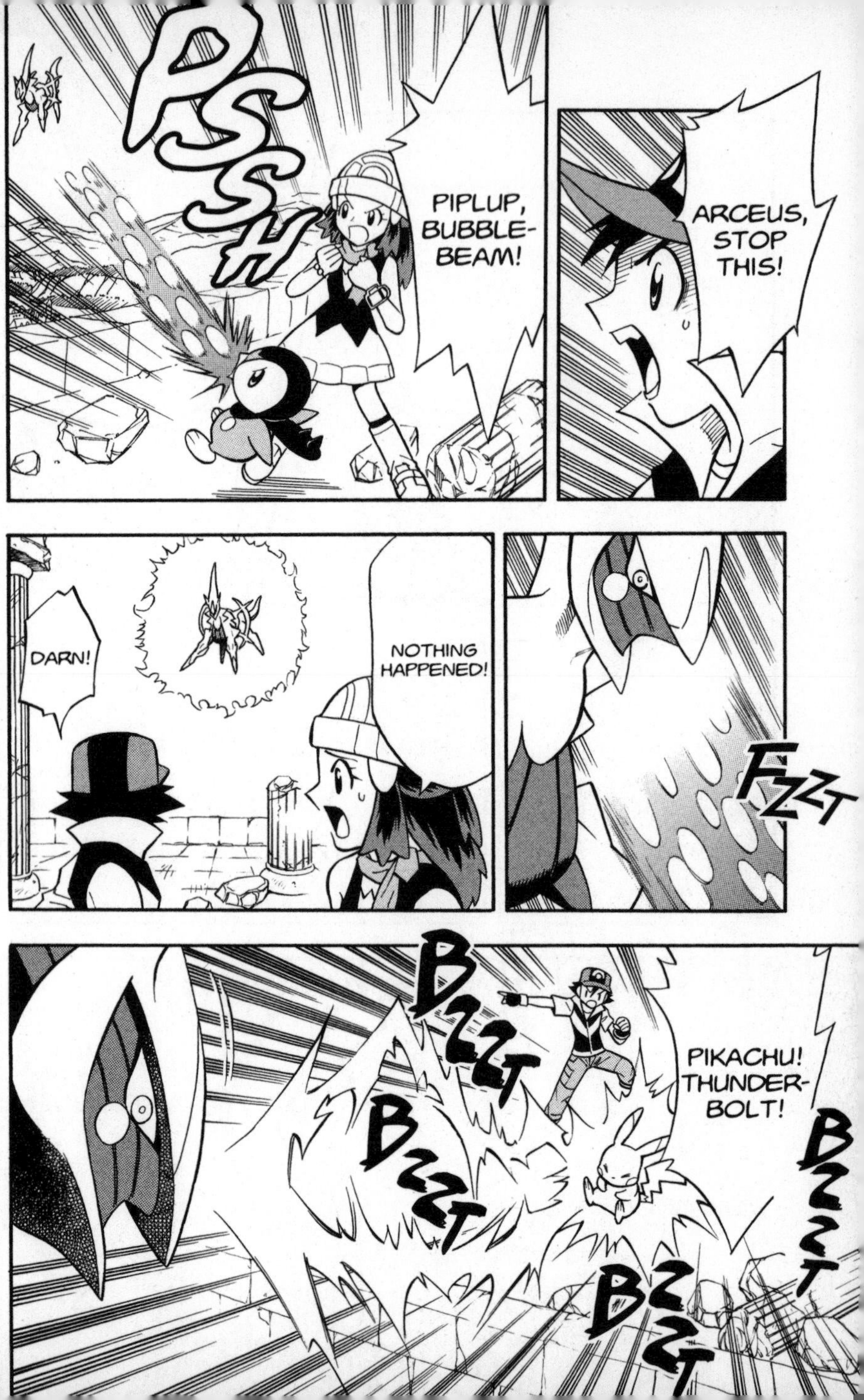
ARCEUS, STOP THIS!
PSSH
PIPLUP, BUBBLE-BEAM!
FZZT
NOTHING HAPPENED!
DARN!
PIKACHU! THUNDER-BOLT!
BZZT
BZZT
BZZT
BZZT

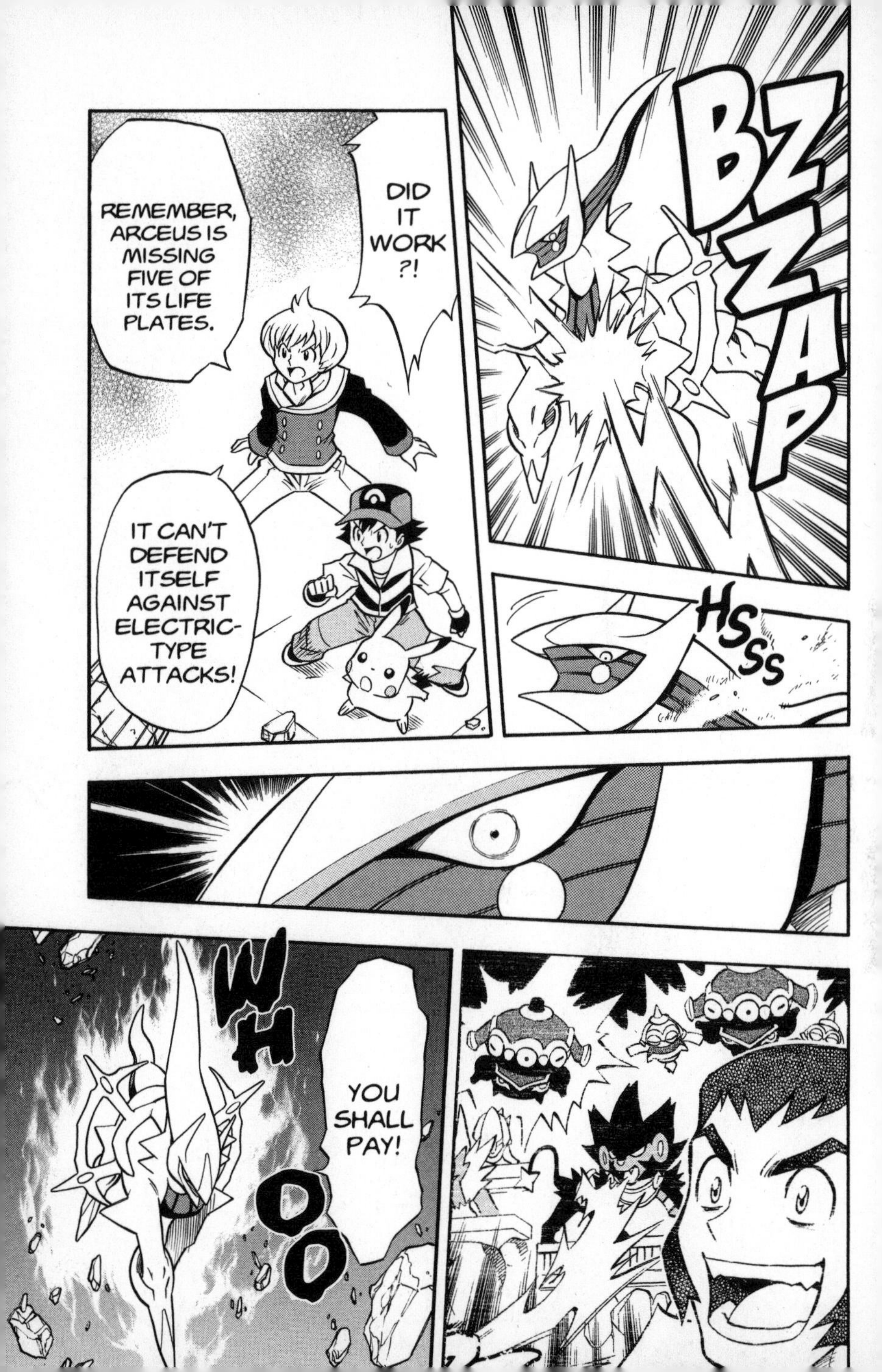
BZZAP
HSSS
DID IT WORK?!
REMEMBER, ARCEUS IS MISSING FIVE OF ITS LIFE PLATES.
IT CAN'T DEFEND ITSELF AGAINST ELECTRIC-TYPE ATTACKS!
WHOO
YOU SHALL PAY!

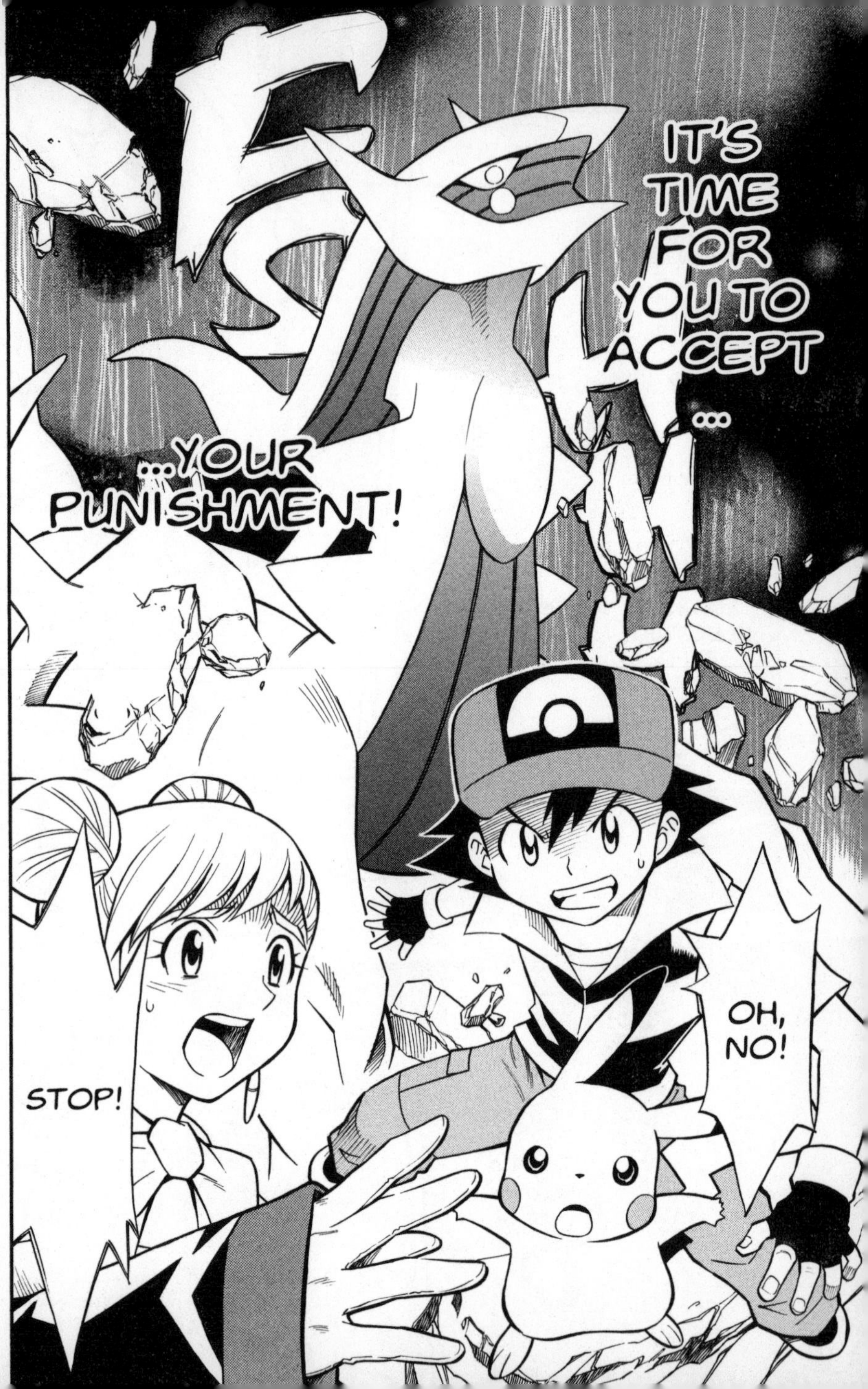
IT'S TIME FOR YOU TO ACCEPT ...
...YOUR PUNISHMENT!
OH, NO!
STOP!

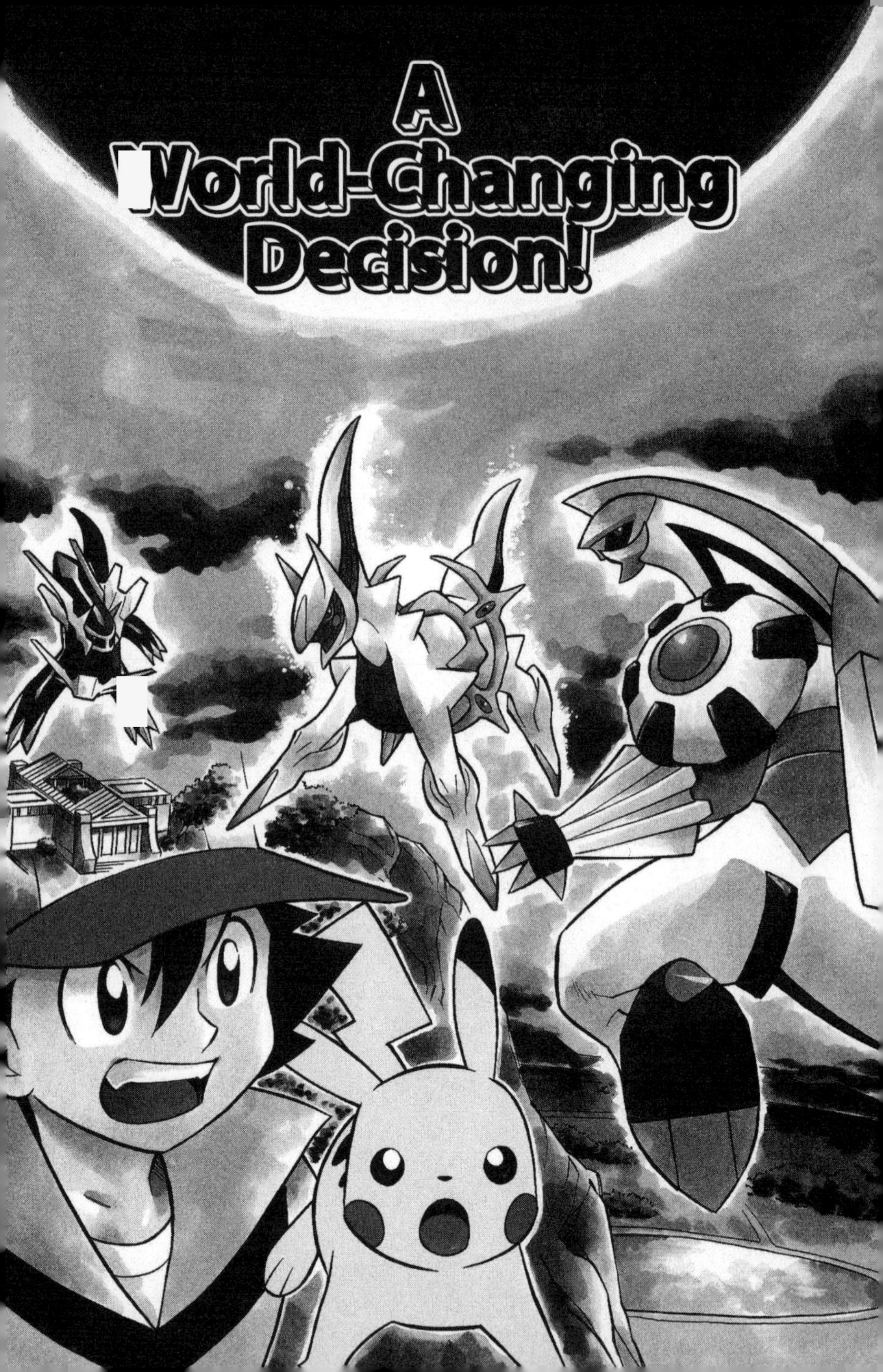
A World-Changing Decision!

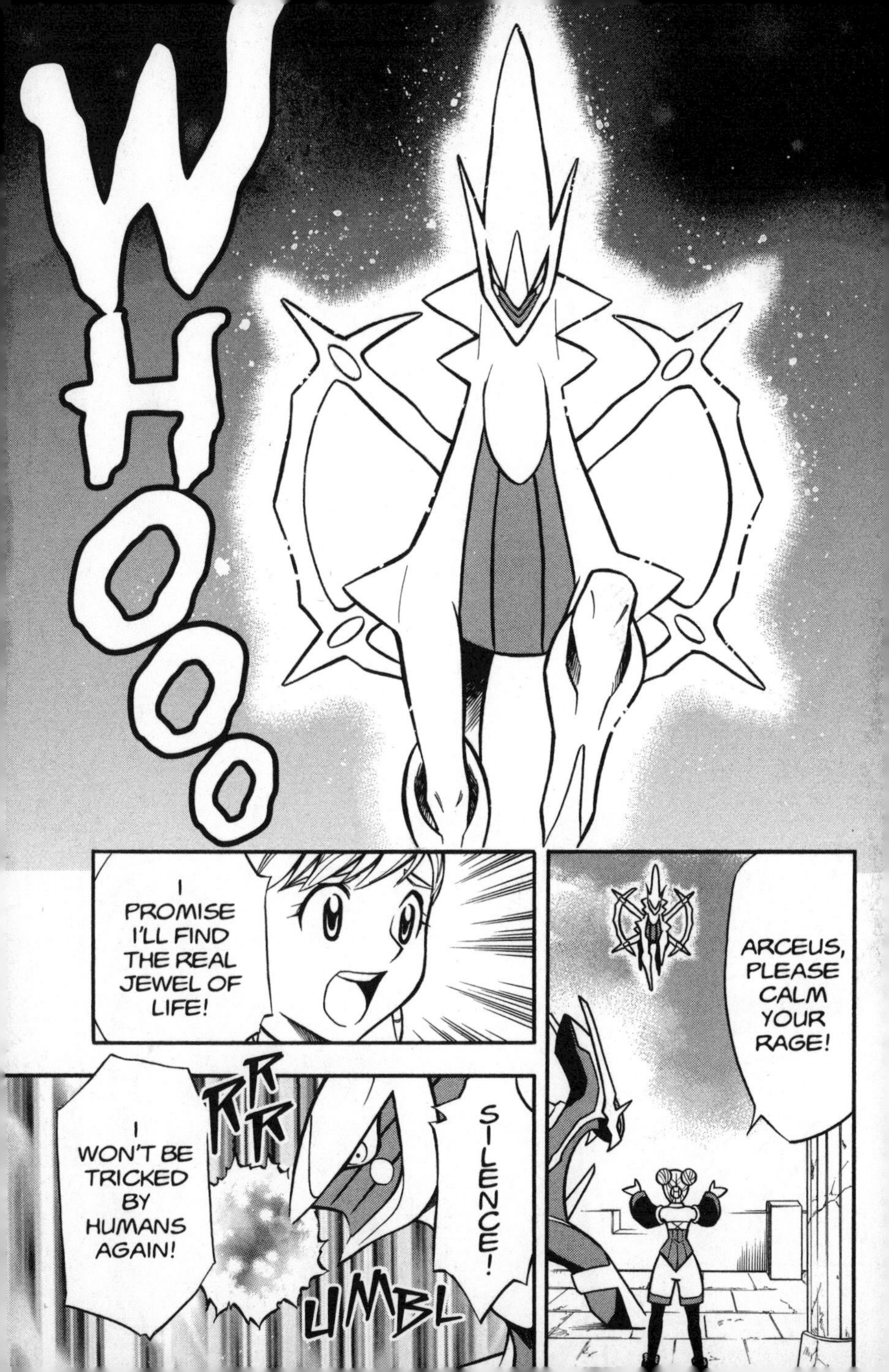
WHOOOO
ARCEUS, PLEASE CALM YOUR RAGE!
I PROMISE I'LL FIND THE REAL JEWEL OF LIFE!
SILENCE!
RRRR
I WON'T BE TRICKED BY HUMANS AGAIN!
UMBL

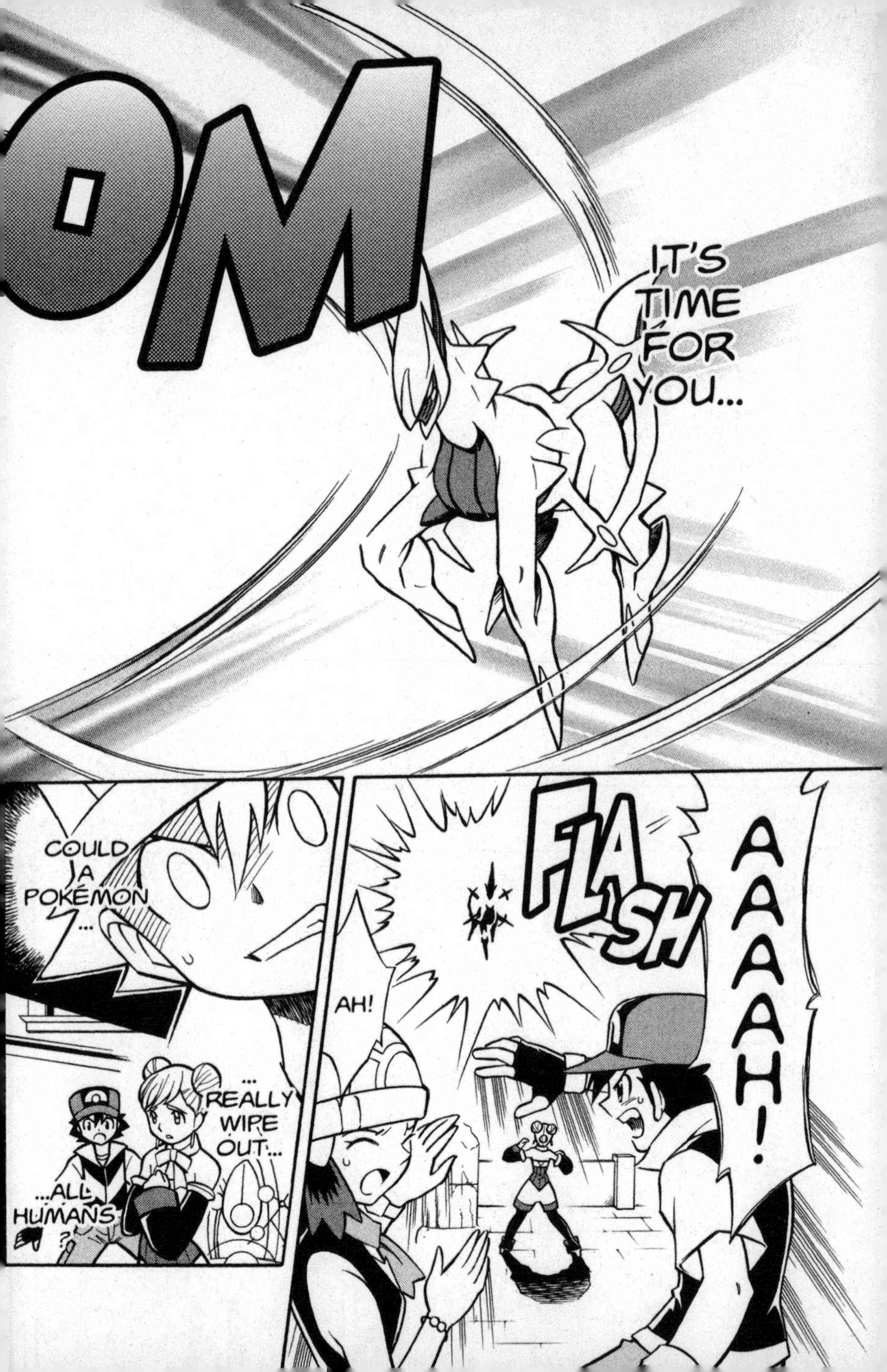
OM
IT'S TIME FOR YOU...
AAAAH!
FLASH
AH!
COULD A POKÉMON ...
...REALLY WIPE OUT...
...ALL HUMANS ?

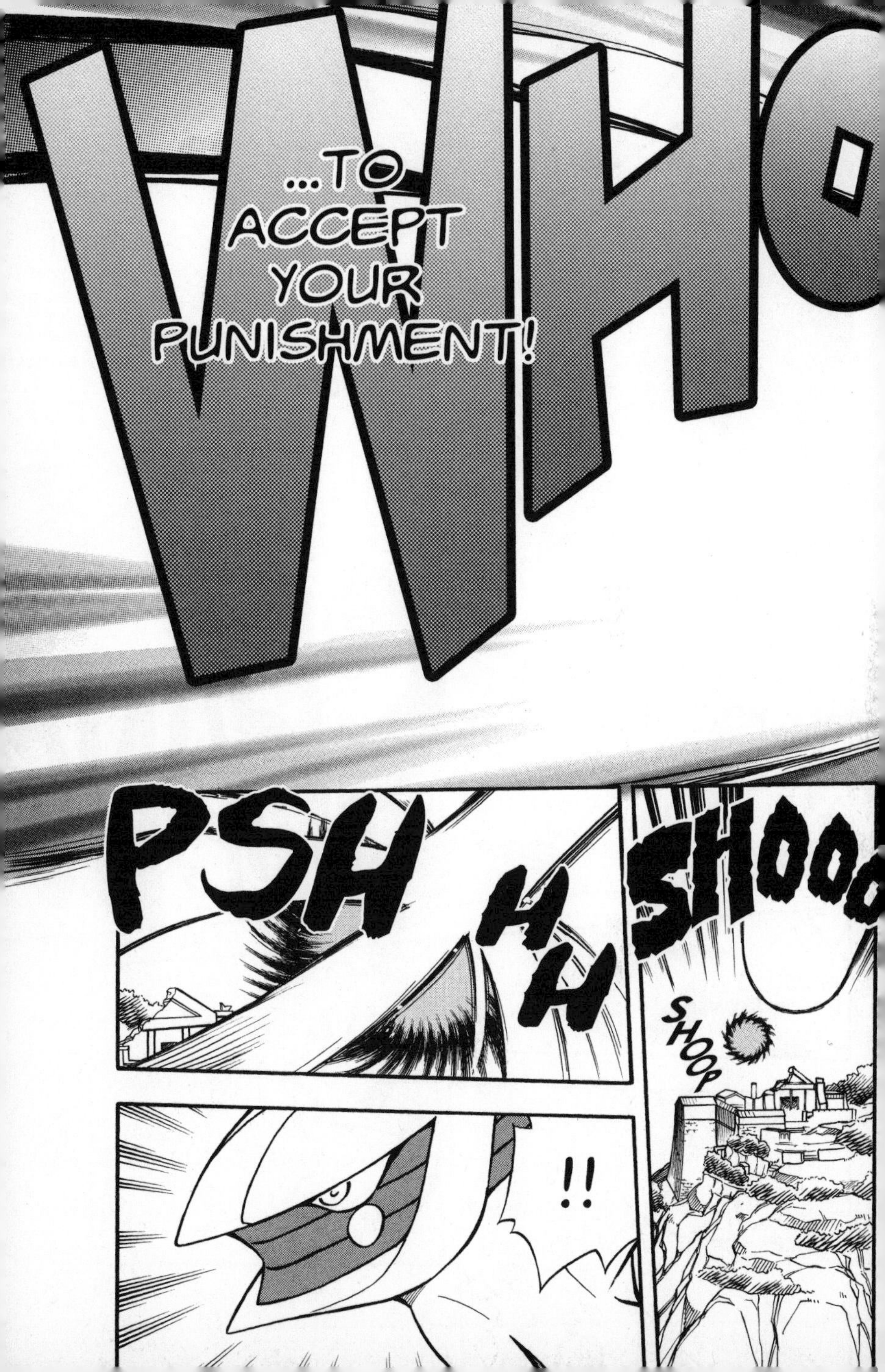
WHO
...TO ACCEPT YOUR PUNISHMENT!
SHOOO
SHOOP
PSHHH
!!

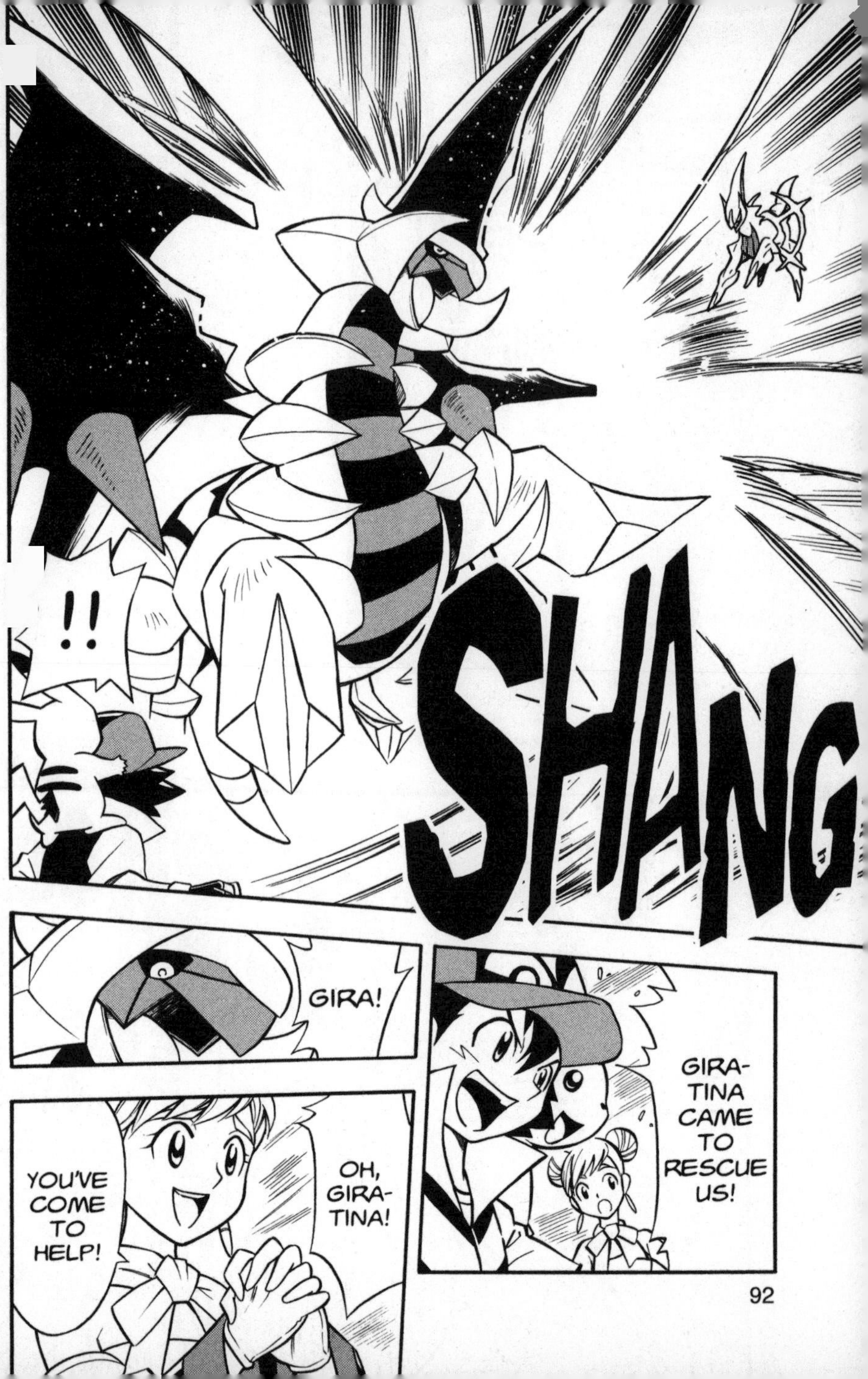
!!
SHANG
GIRA-TINA CAME TO RESCUE US!
GIRA!
OH, GIRA-TINA!
YOU'VE COME TO HELP!

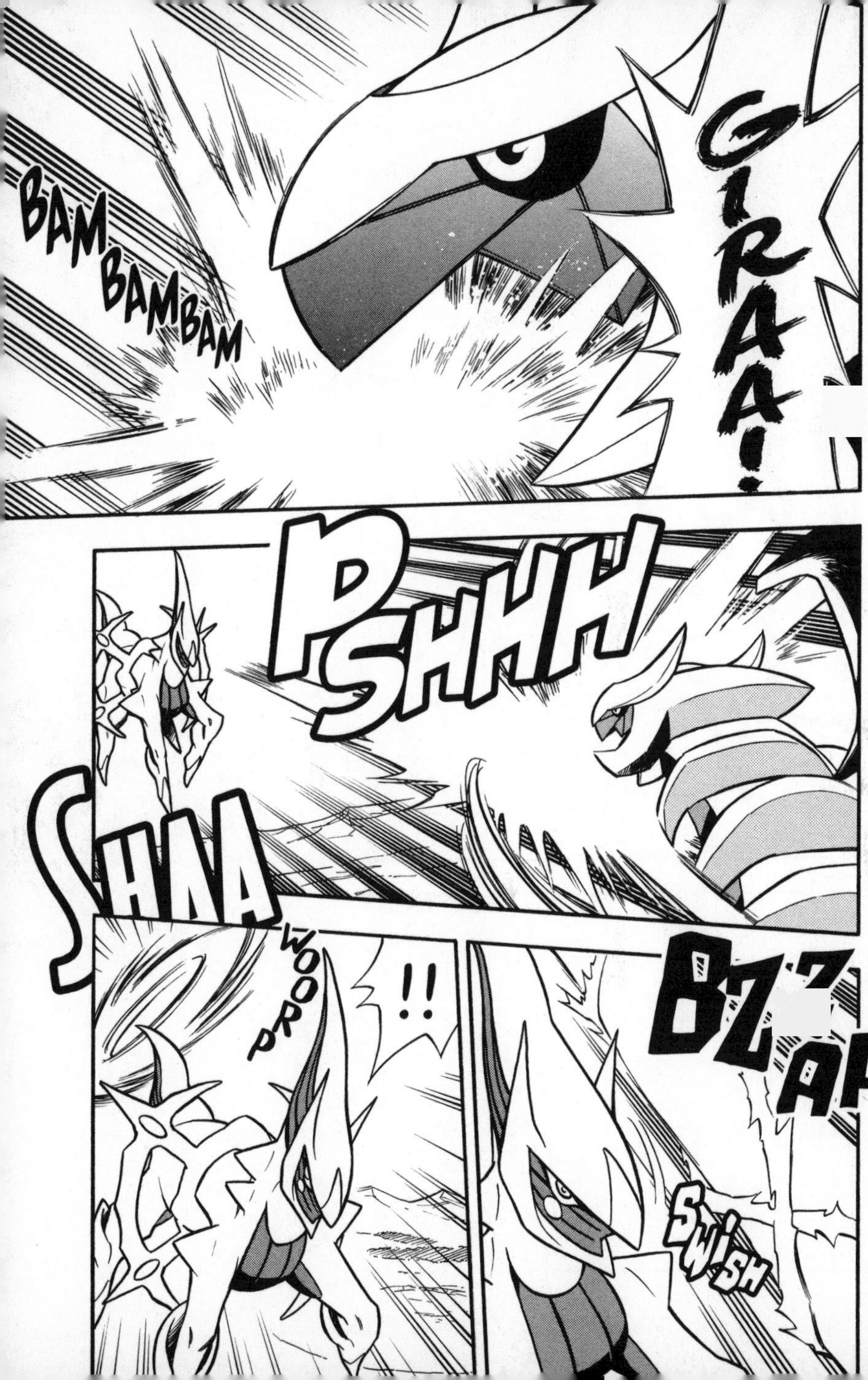
GIRAA!
BAM BAMBAMBAM
PSHHH
SHAA
BZ AP
SWISH
!!
WOORP

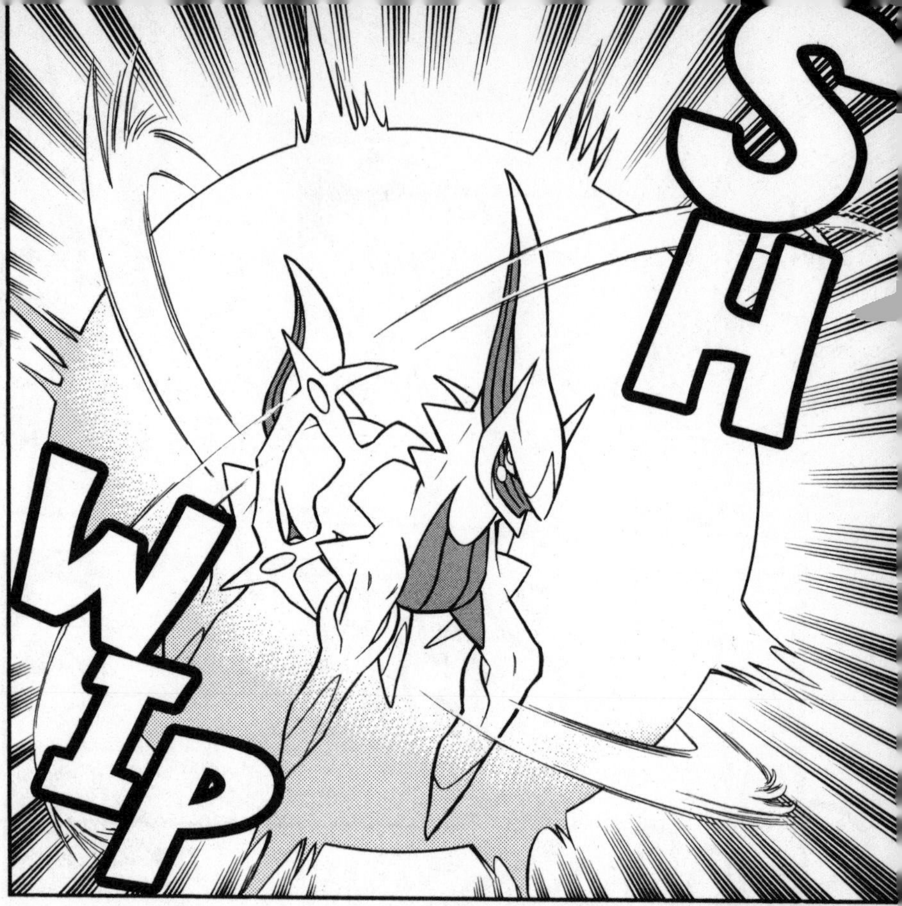
SH
WIP
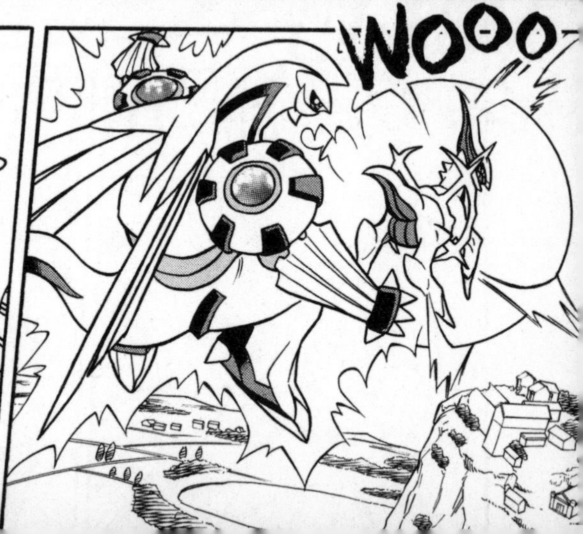
WOOO
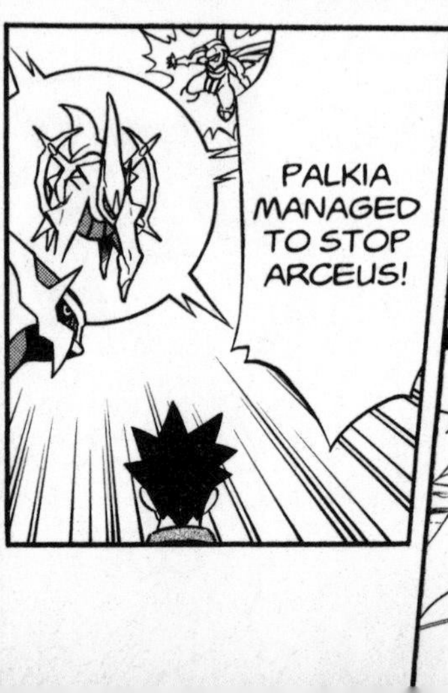
PALKIA MANAGED TO STOP ARCEUS!

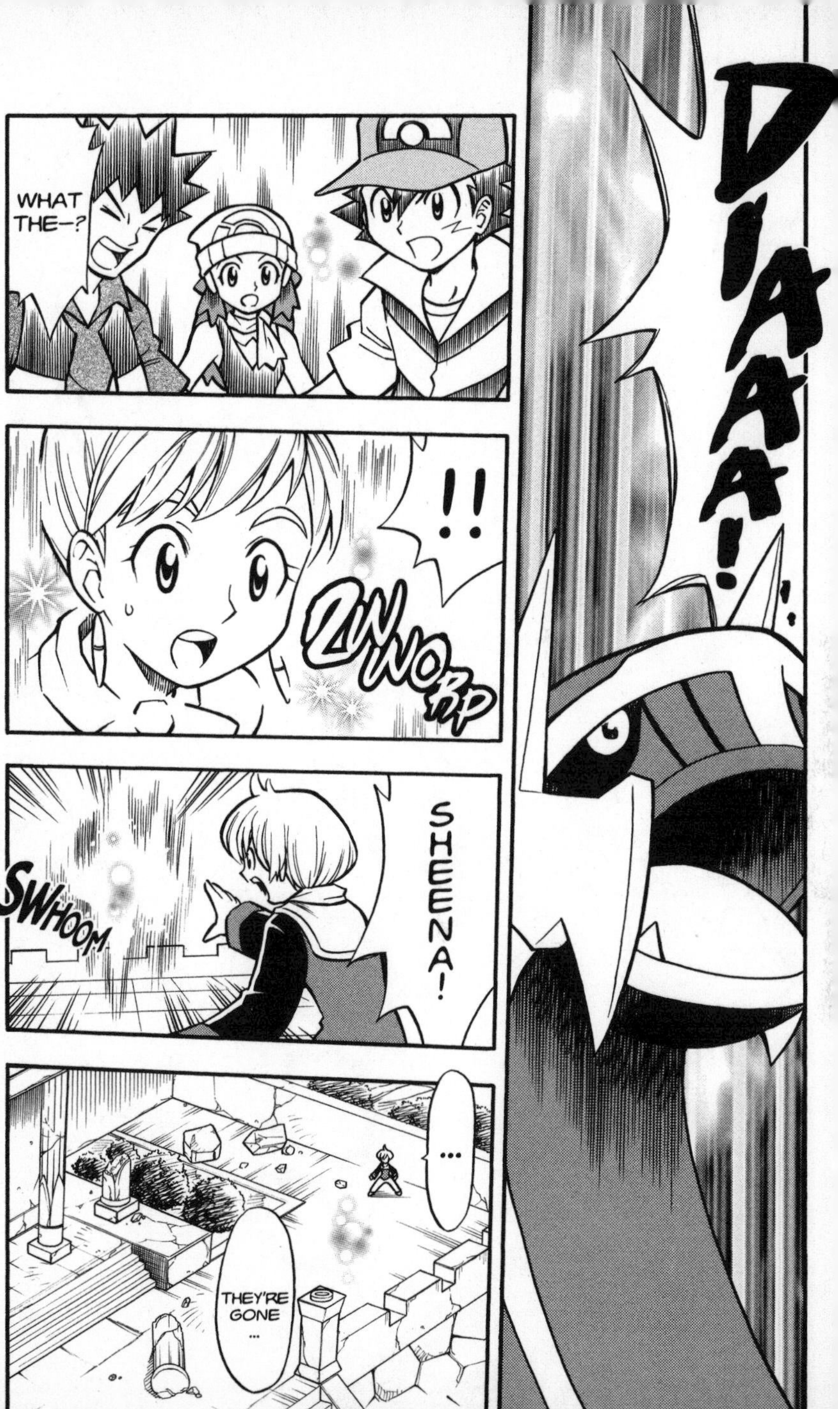
DIAAAAI!
WHAT THE--?
!!
ZWORP
SHEENA!
SWHOOM
...
THEY'RE GONE ...

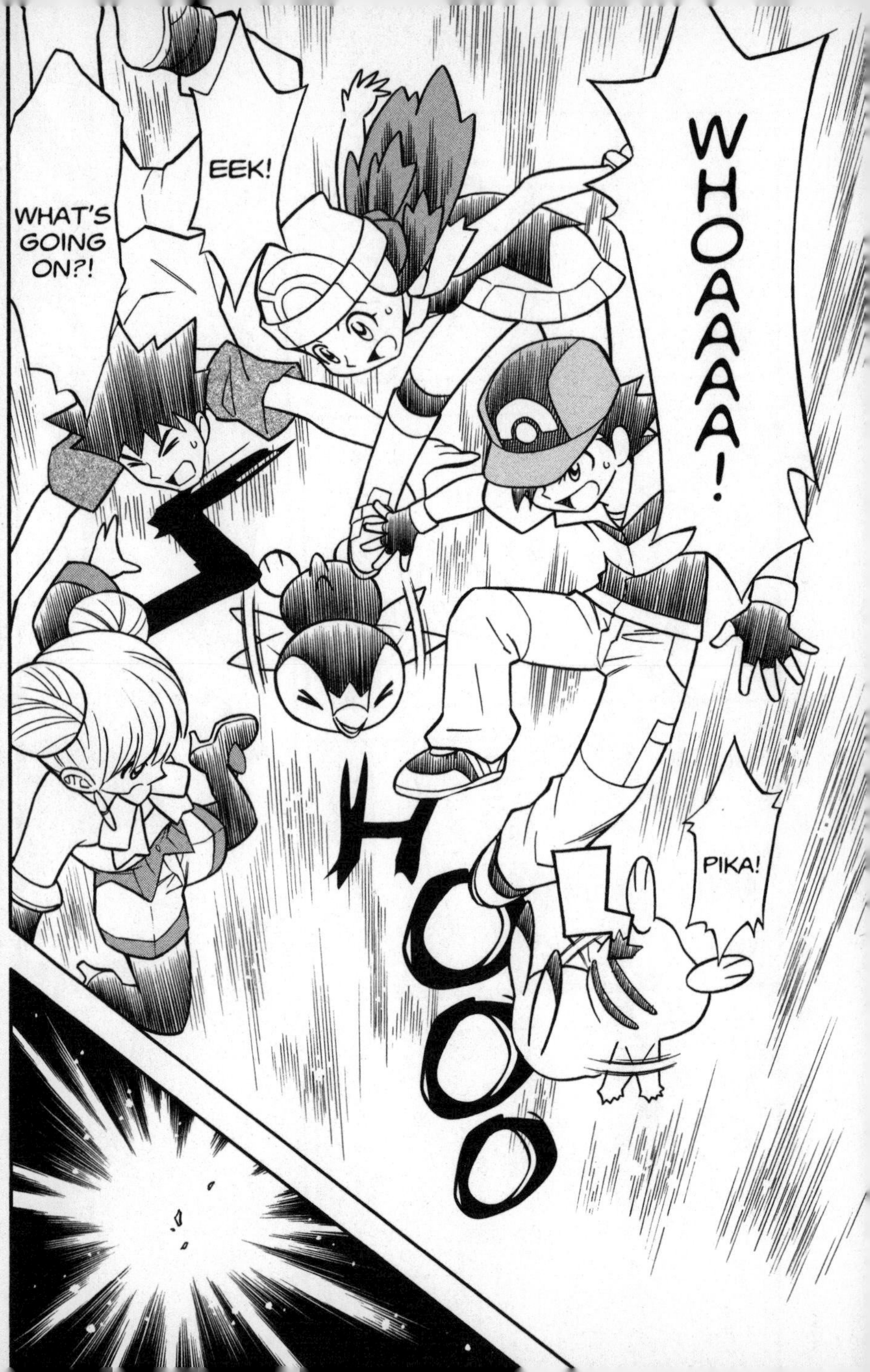
WHOAAAA!
EEK!
WHAT'S GOING ON?!
PIKA!
HOOOOO

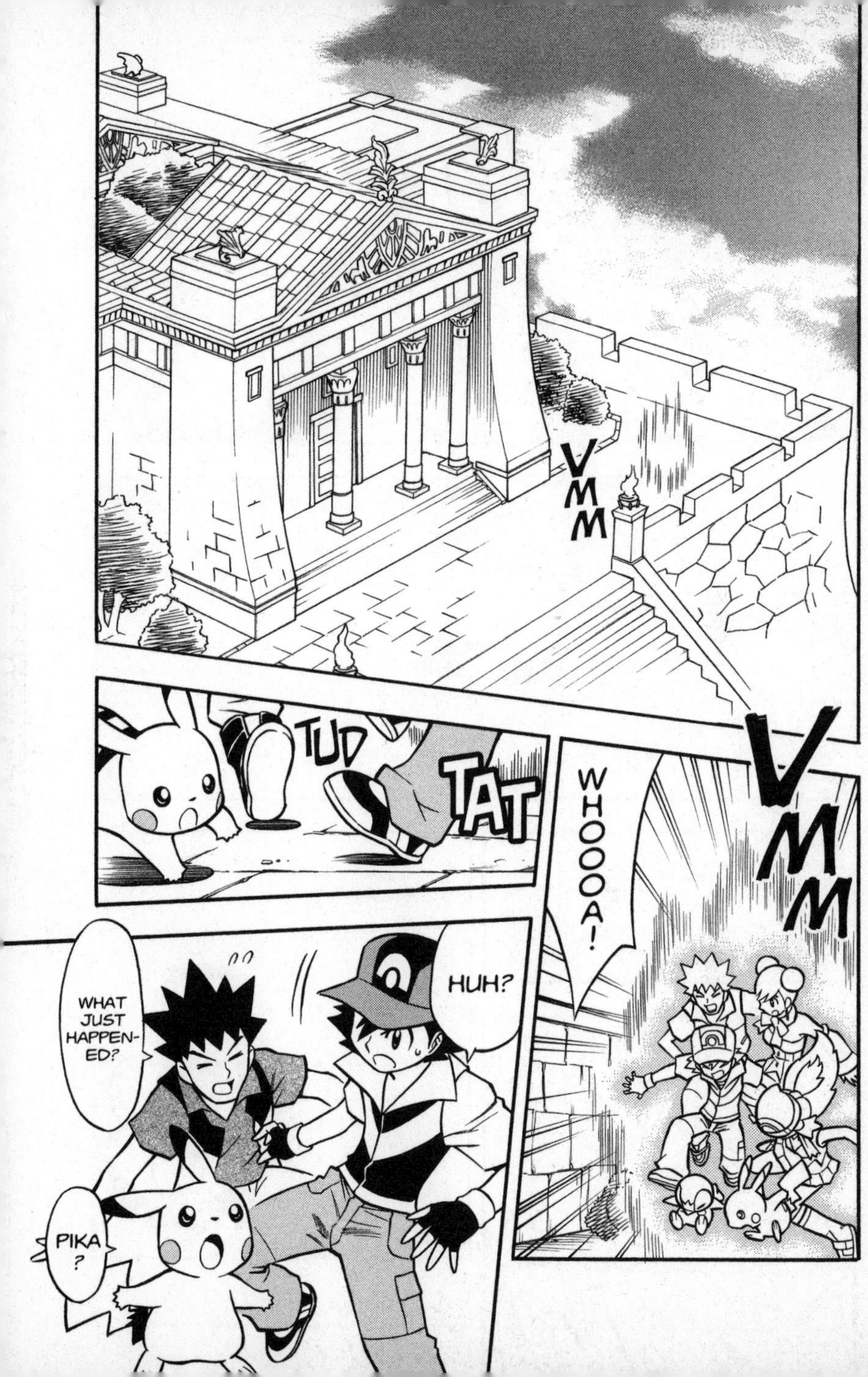
VMM
VMM
WHOOOOA!
TAT
TUD
HUH?
WHAT JUST HAPPEN-ED?
PIKA?

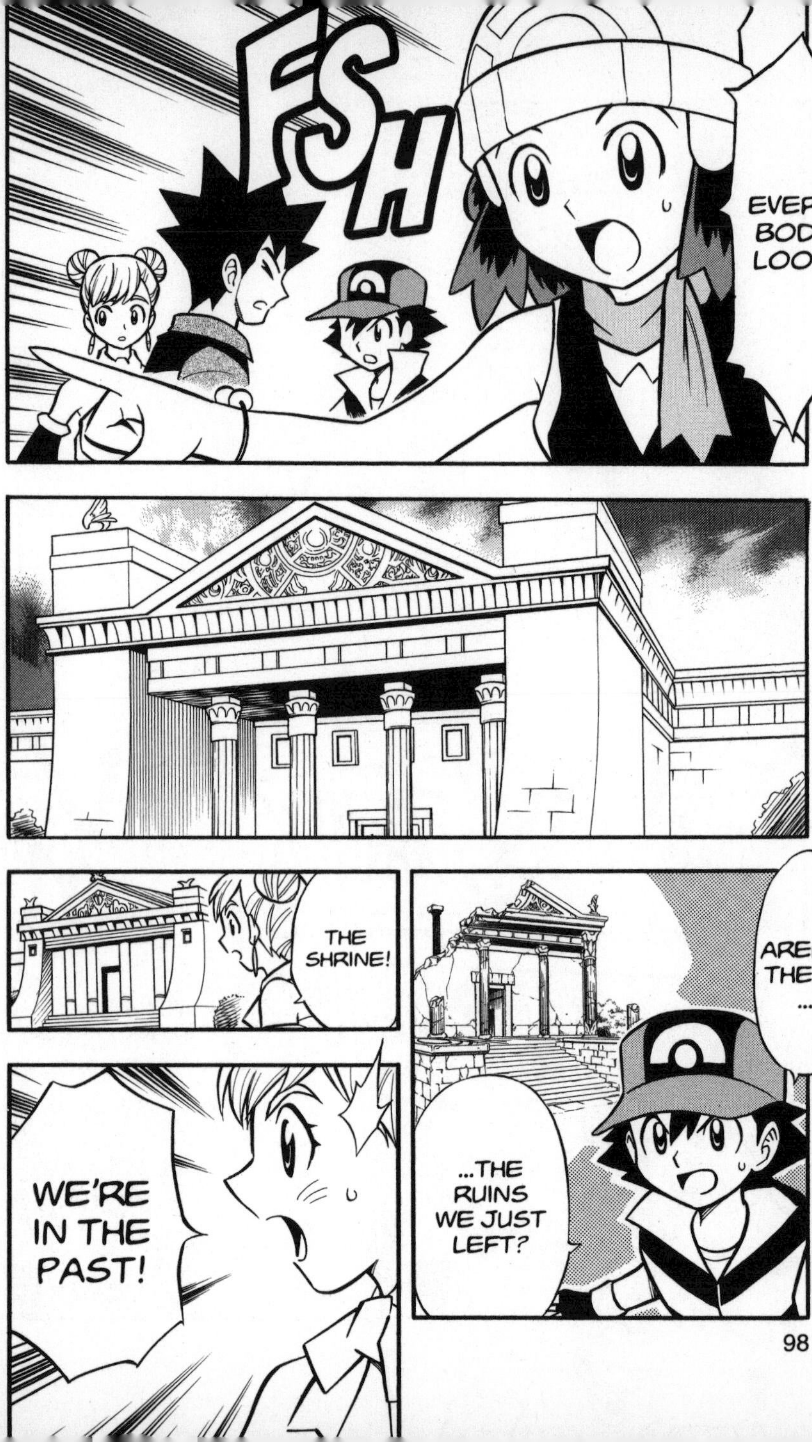
EVERY-BODY, LOOK!
FSH
AREN'T THESE ...
...THE RUINS WE JUST LEFT?
THE SHRINE!
WE'RE IN THE PAST!

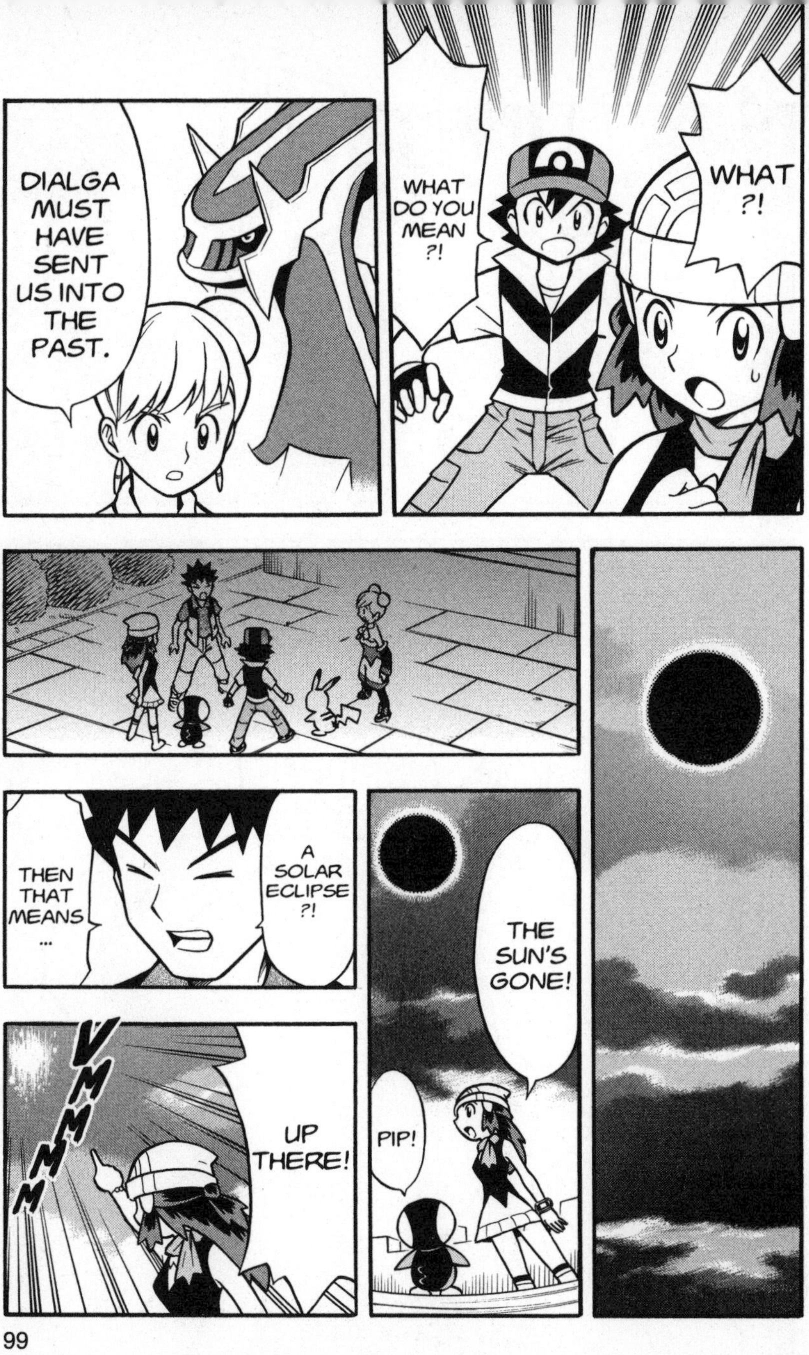
WHAT ?!
WHAT DO YOU MEAN ?!
DIALGA MUST HAVE SENT US INTO THE PAST.
THE SUN'S GONE!
PIP!
A SOLAR ECLIPSE ?!
THEN THAT MEANS ...
UP THERE!
VMMMMM

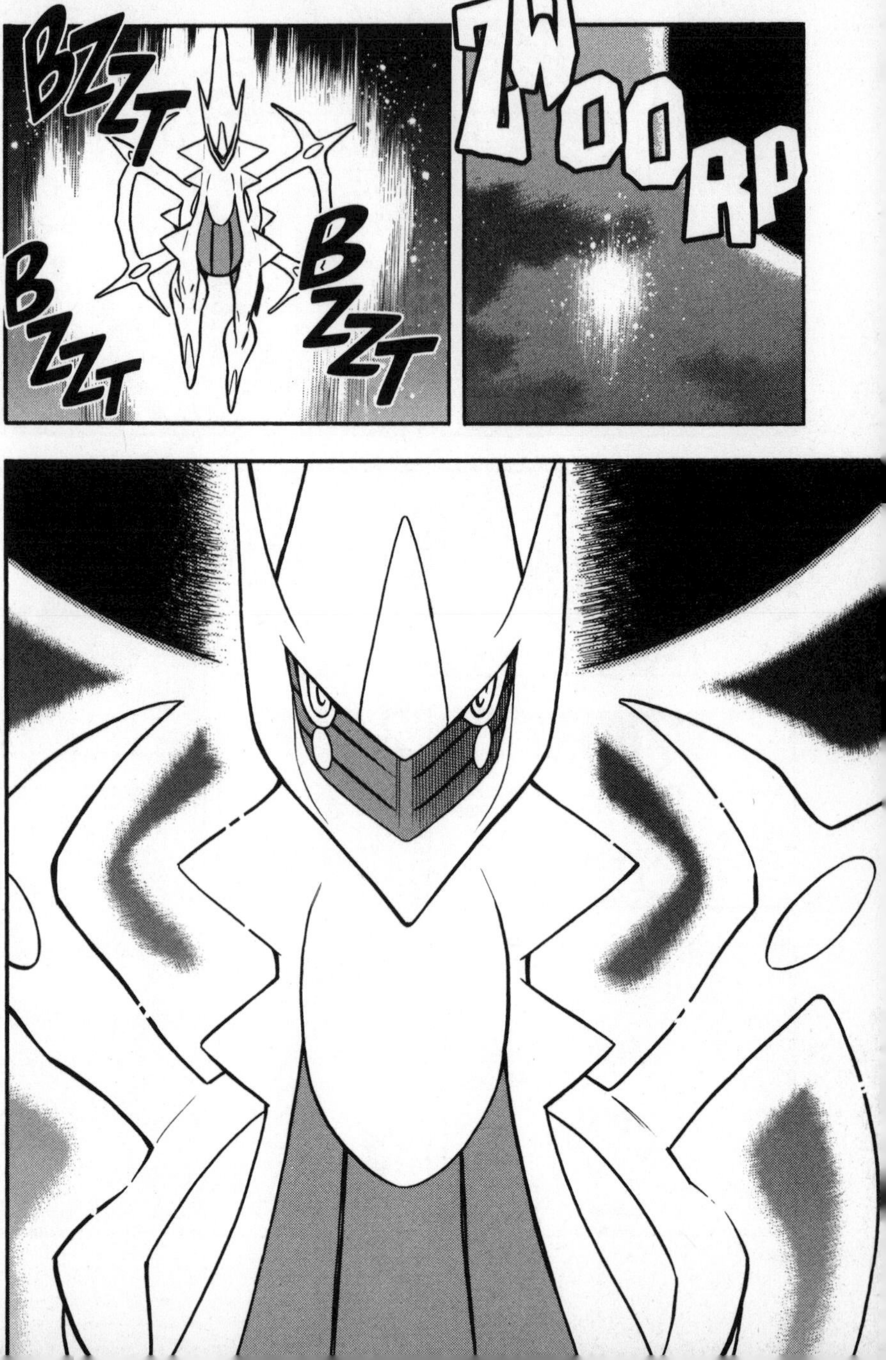
ZWOORP
BZZT
BZZT
BZZT

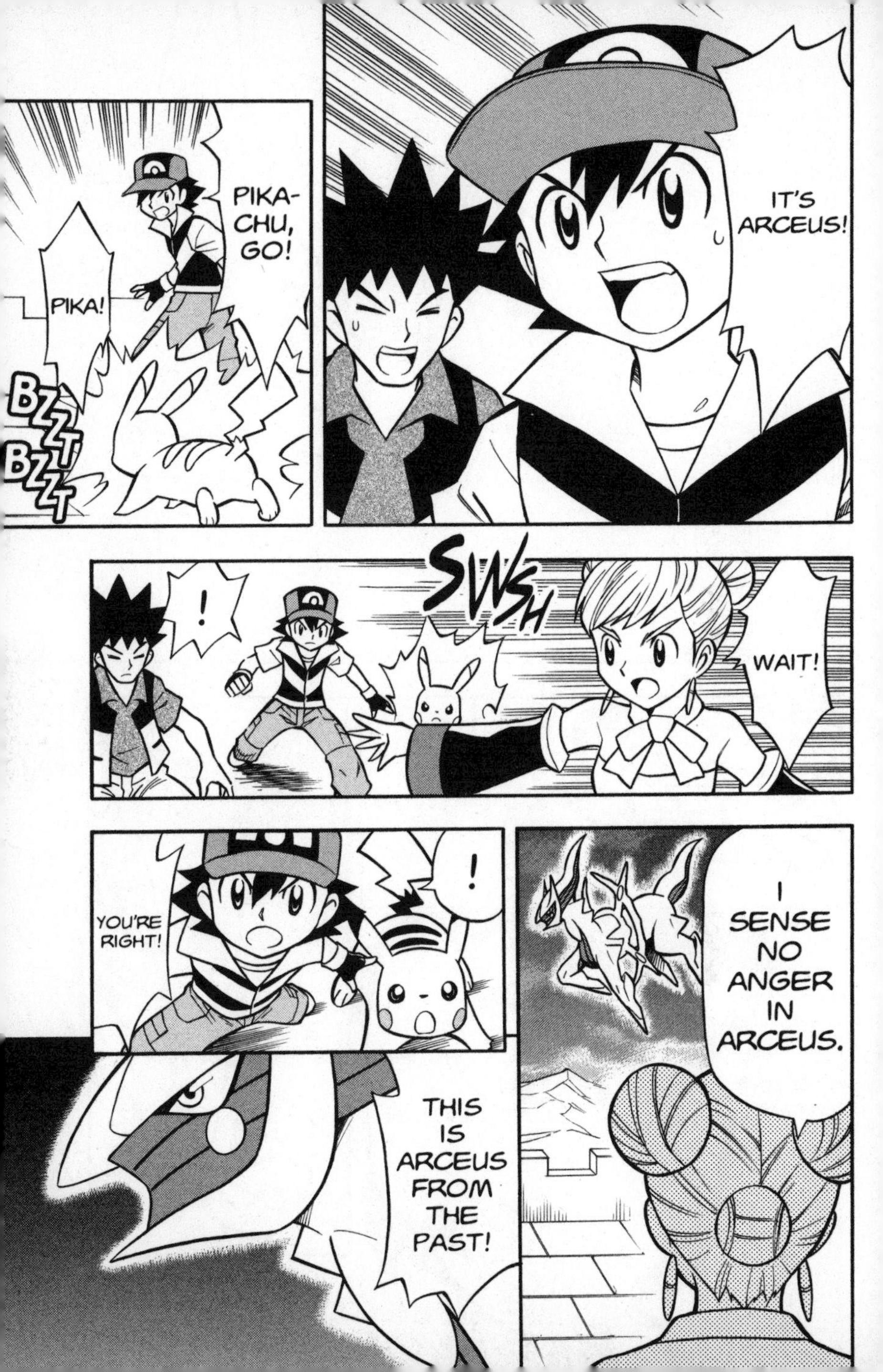
IT'S ARCEUS!
PIKA-CHU, GO!
PIKA!
BZZT BZZT
WAIT!
SWSH
!
I SENSE NO ANGER IN ARCEUS.
!
YOU'RE RIGHT!
THIS IS ARCEUS FROM THE PAST!

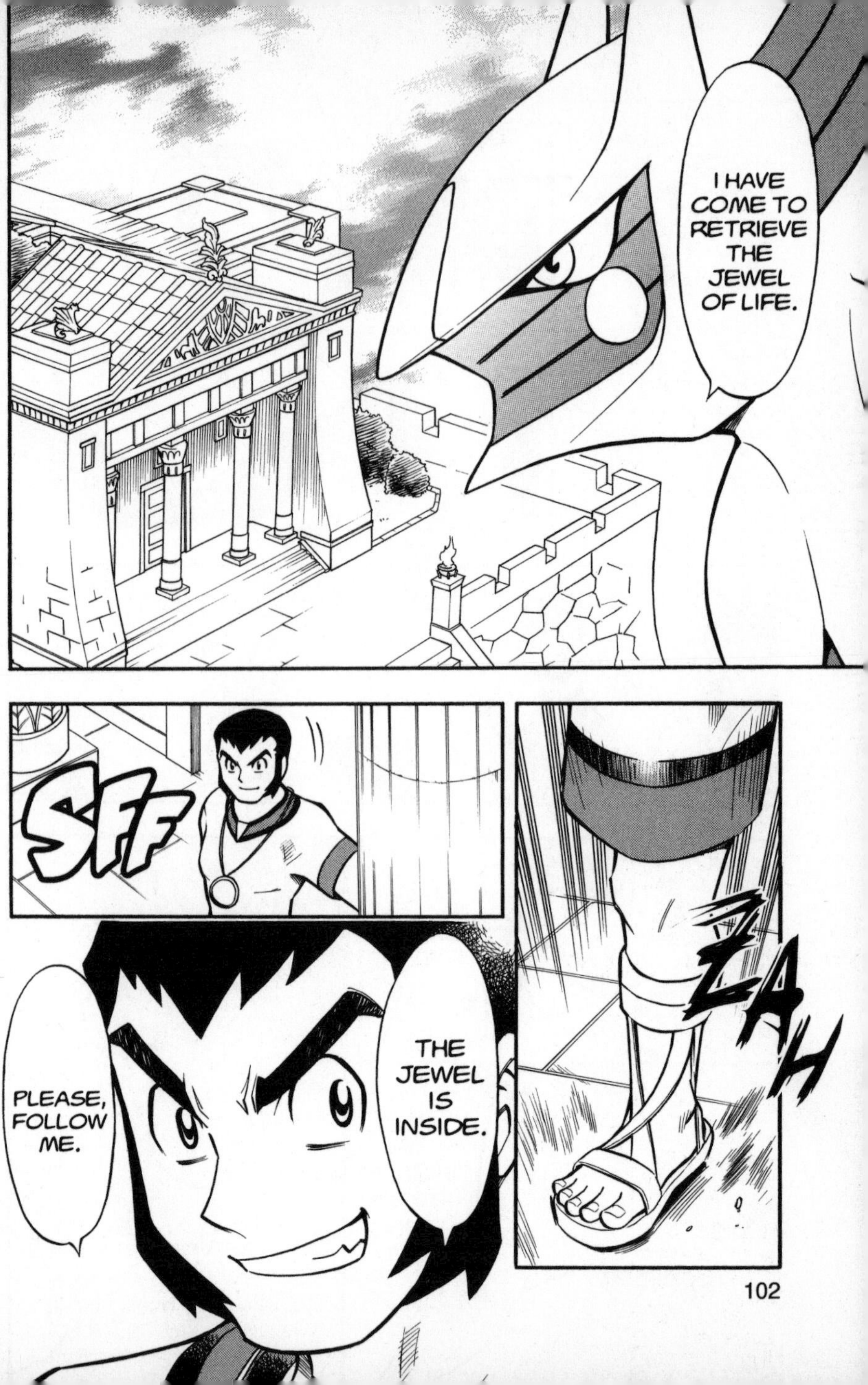
I HAVE COME TO RETRIEVE THE JEWEL OF LIFE.
ZZAH
SFF
THE JEWEL IS INSIDE.
PLEASE, FOLLOW ME.

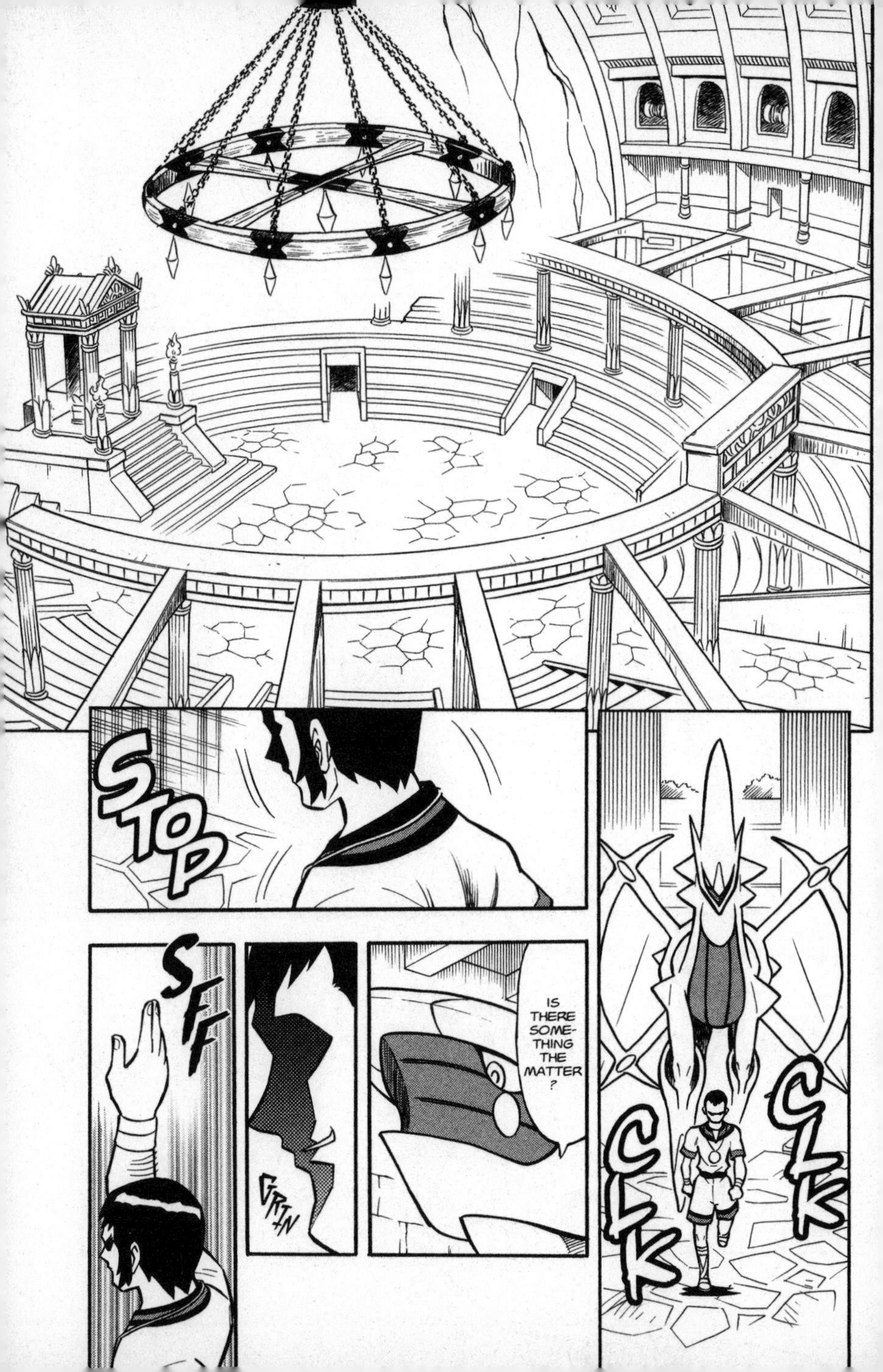

CLK
CLK
STOP
IS THERE SOMETHING THE MATTER?
GRIN
SFF

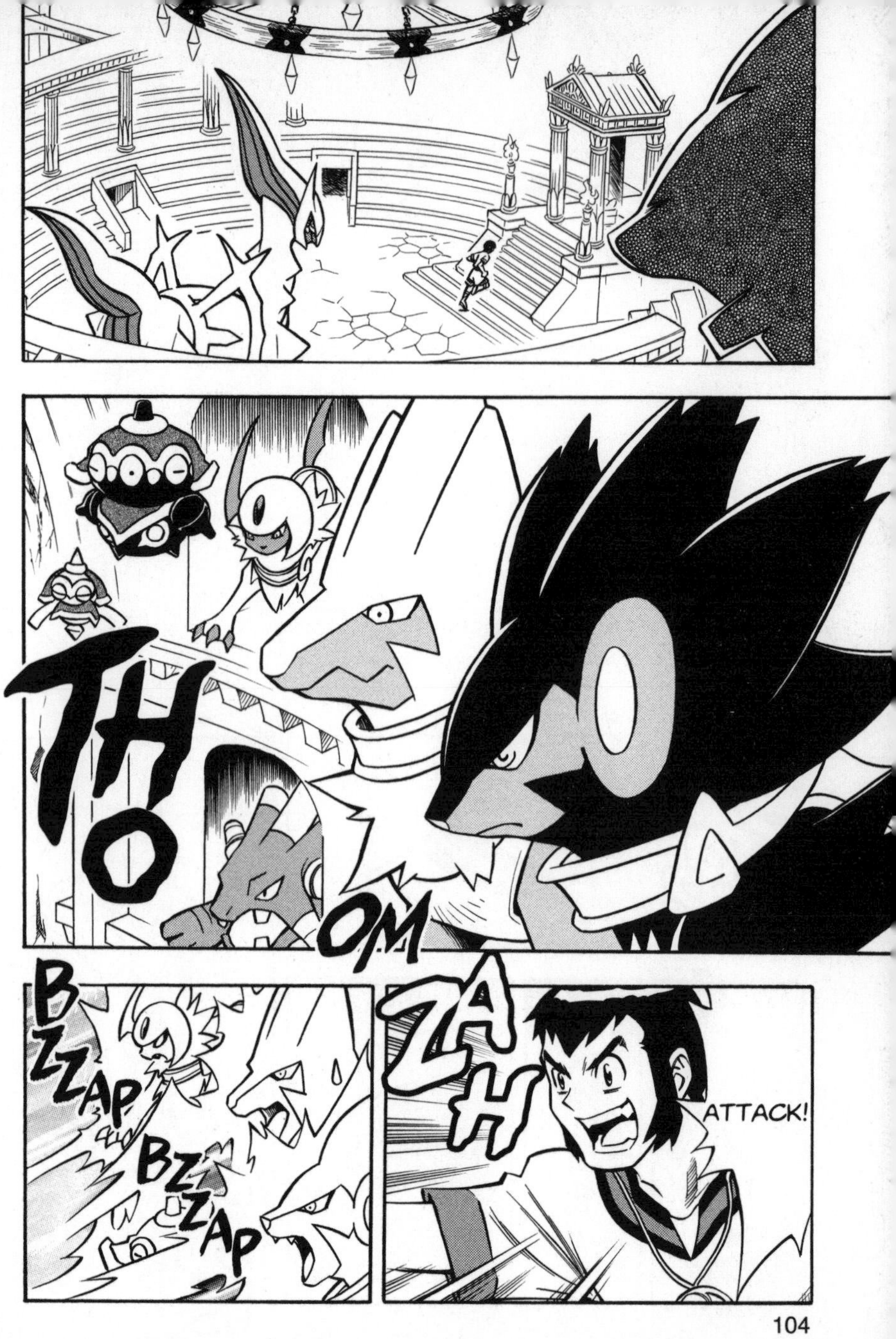
THOOM
ZAHH
ATTACK!
BZZZAP
BZZZAP

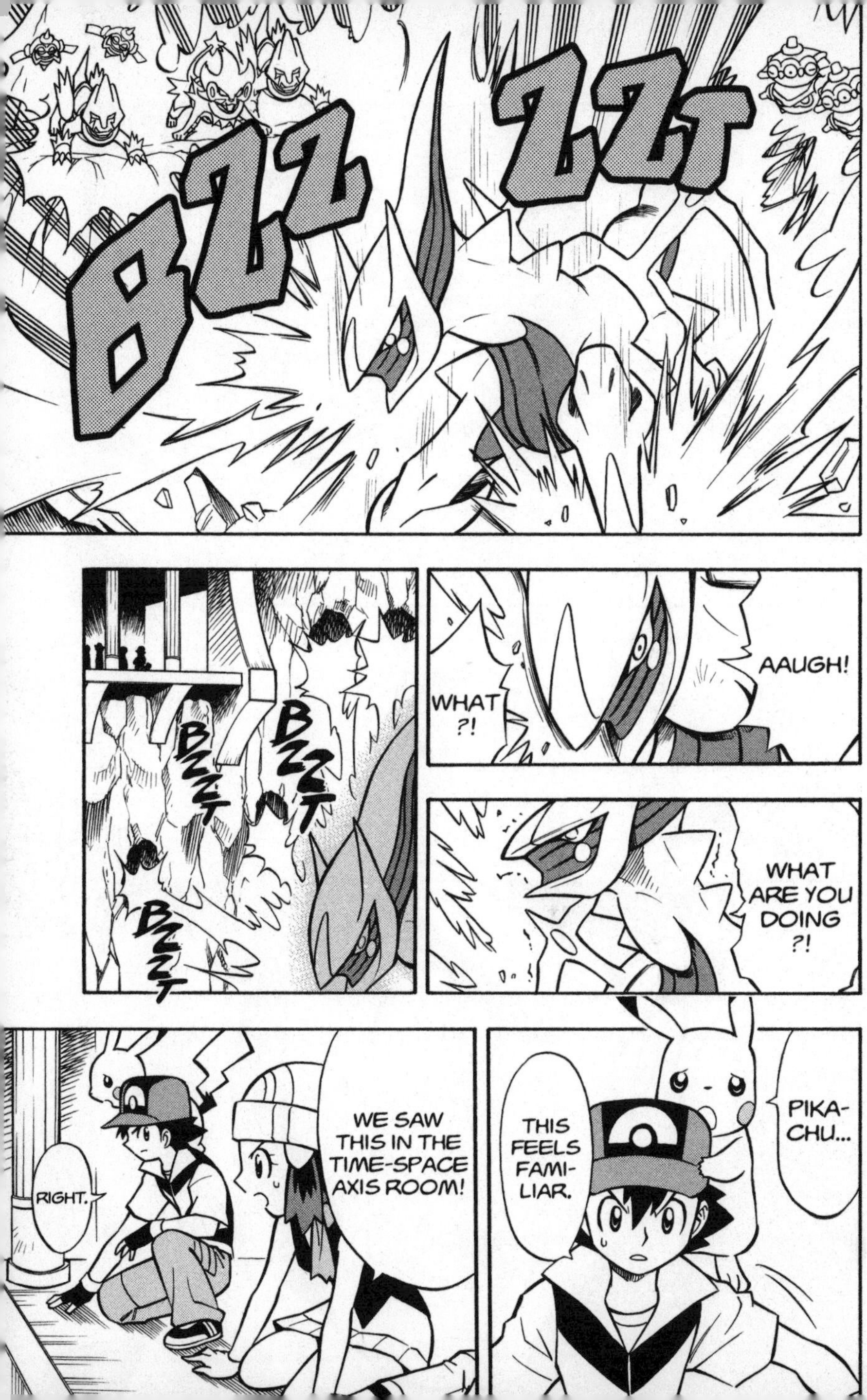
BZZZZT
AAUGH!
WHAT ?!
WHAT ARE YOU DOING ?!
BZZT
BZZT
BZZT
PIKA-CHU...
THIS FEELS FAMI-LIAR.
WE SAW THIS IN THE TIME-SPACE AXIS ROOM!
RIGHT.

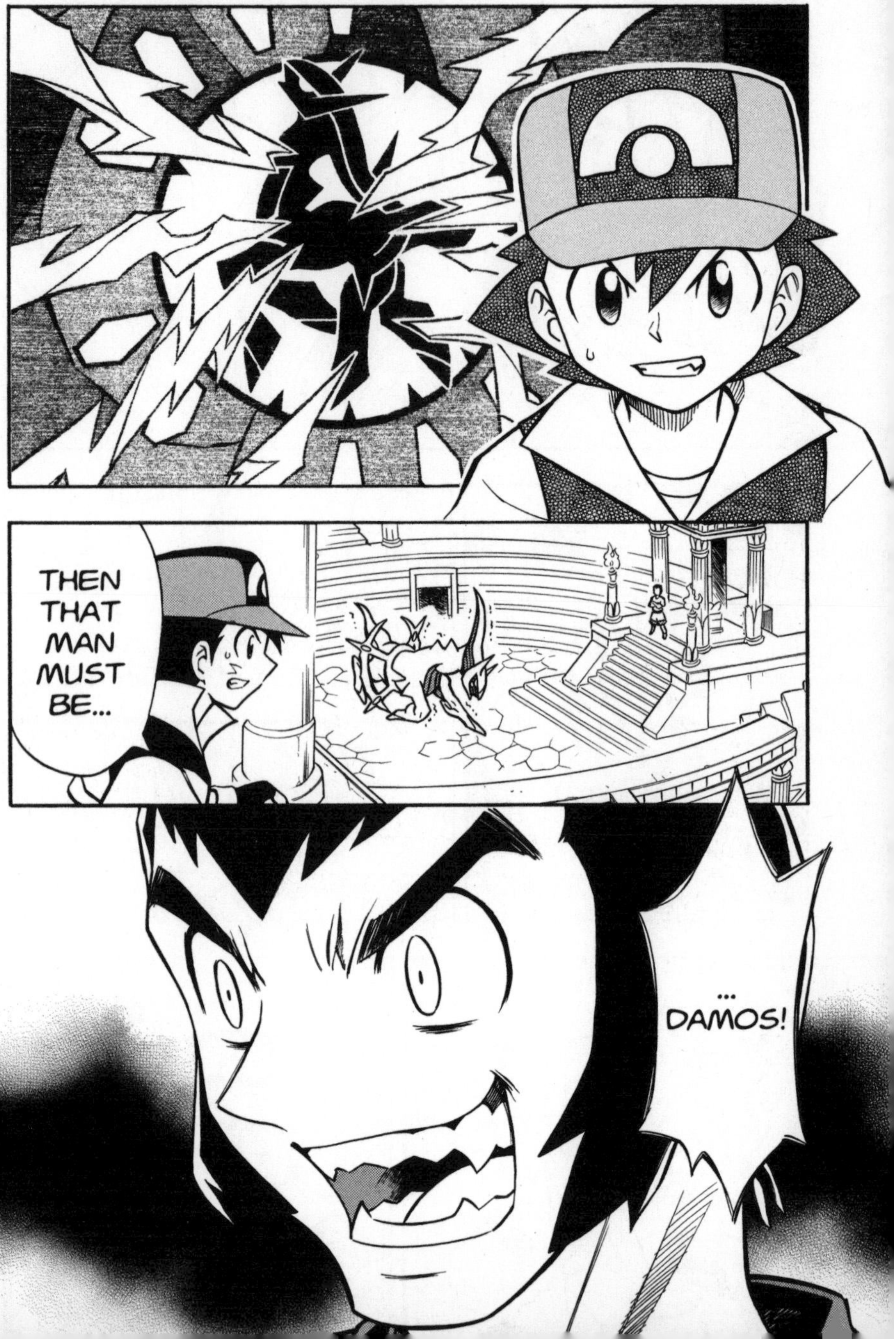
THEN THAT MAN MUST BE...
... DAMOS!

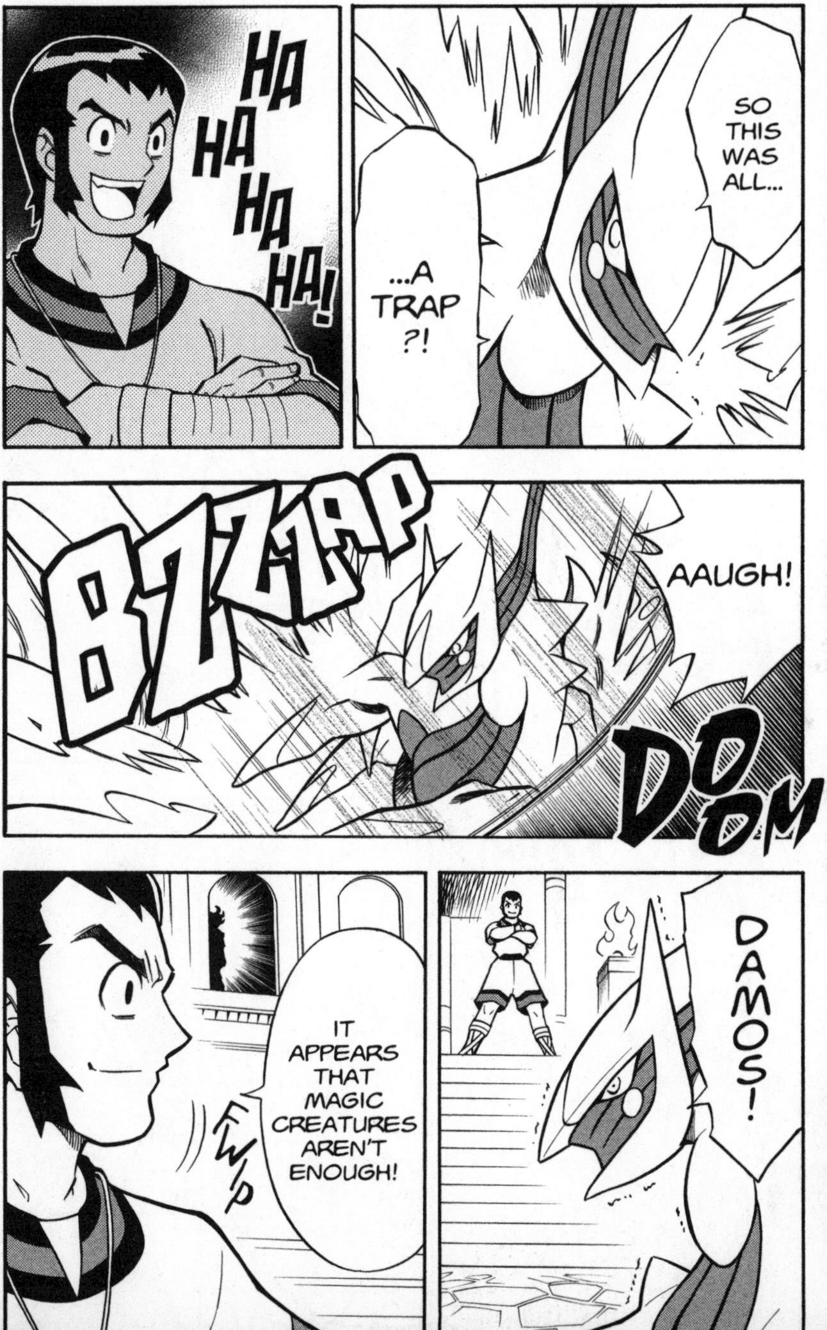
SO THIS WAS ALL...
...A TRAP ?!
HA HA HA HA!
AAUGH!
DOOM
BZZZAP
DAMOS!
IT APPEARS THAT MAGIC CREATURES AREN'T ENOUGH!
FWIP

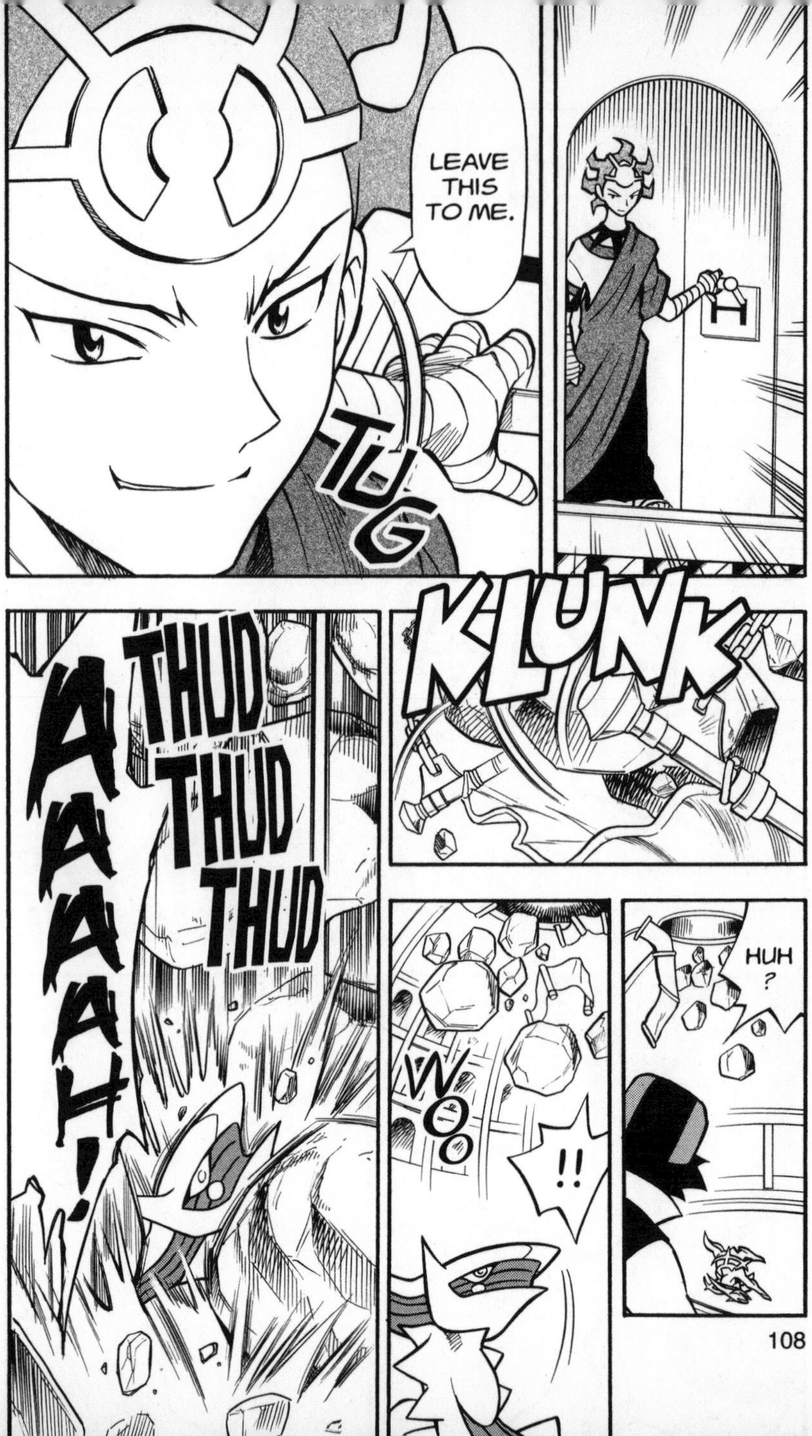
LEAVE THIS TO ME.
TUG
KLUNK
HUH ?
WOO
!!
THUD THUD THUD
AAAAH!!

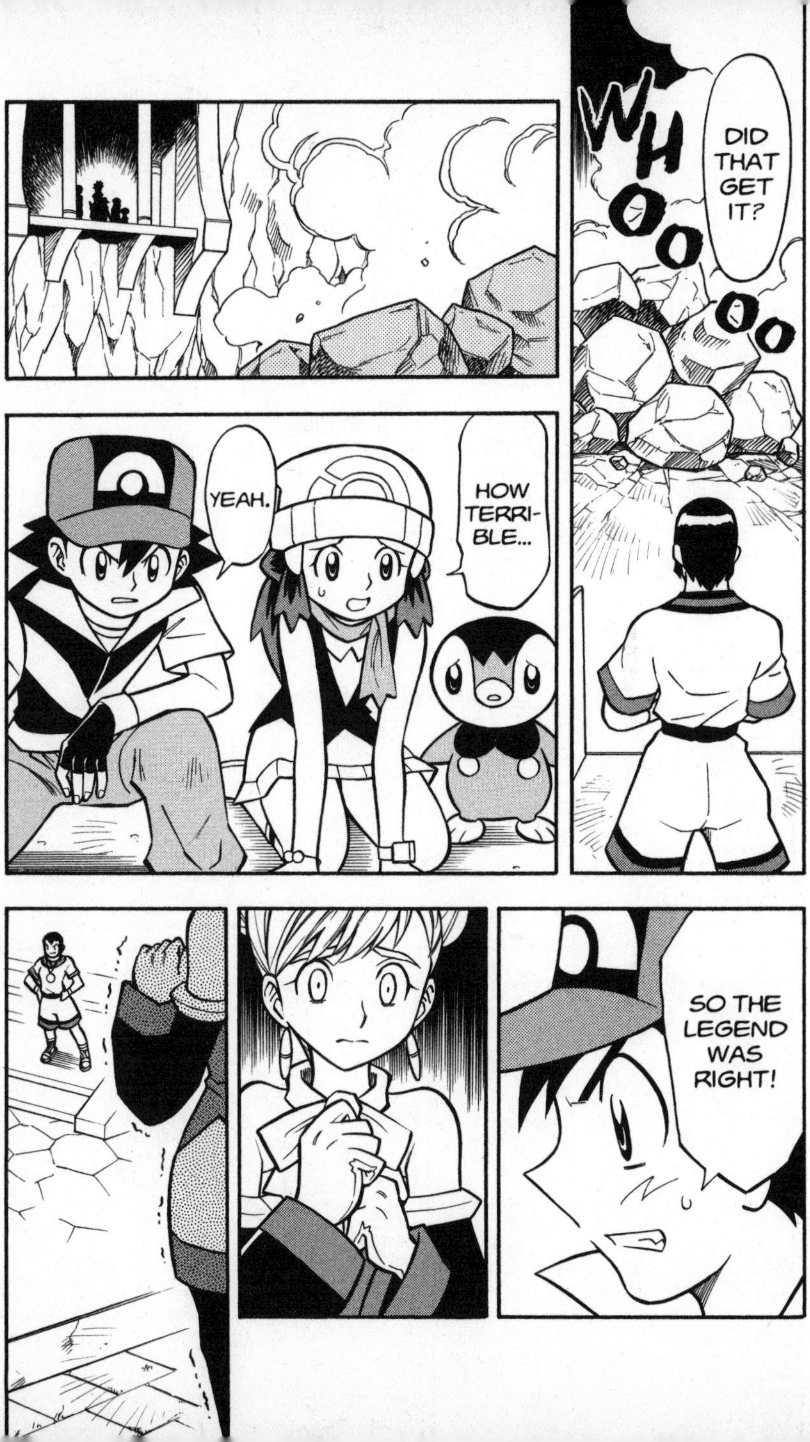

WHOOOOO
DID THAT GET IT?
HOW TERRI-BLE...
YEAH.
SO THE LEGEND WAS RIGHT!

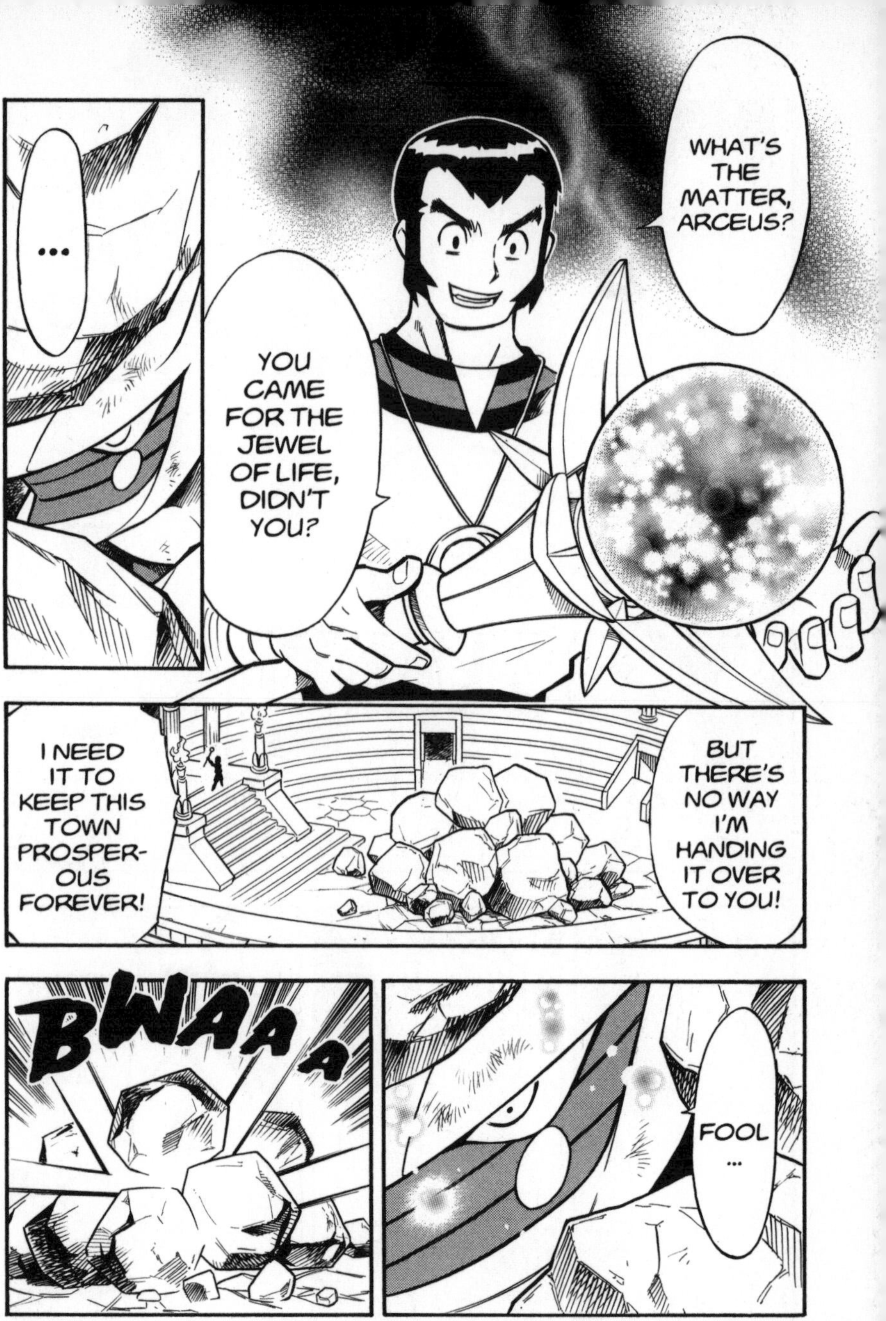
WHAT'S THE MATTER, ARCEUS?
YOU CAME FOR THE JEWEL OF LIFE, DIDN'T YOU?
...
I NEED IT TO KEEP THIS TOWN PROSPER-OUS FOREVER!
BUT THERE'S NO WAY I'M HANDING IT OVER TO YOU!
FOOL ...
BWAAAA

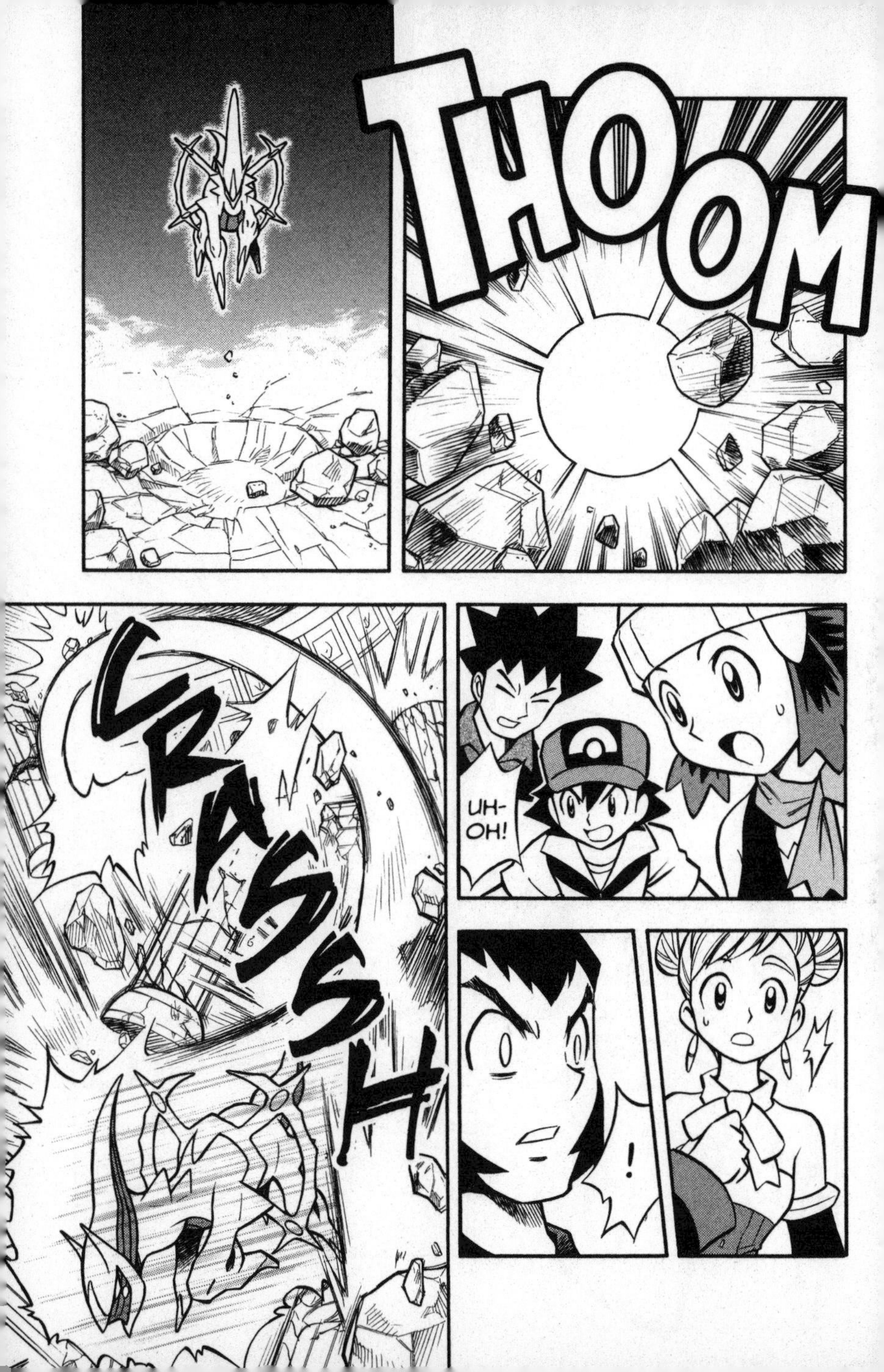
THOOM
UH-OH!
!
CRASH

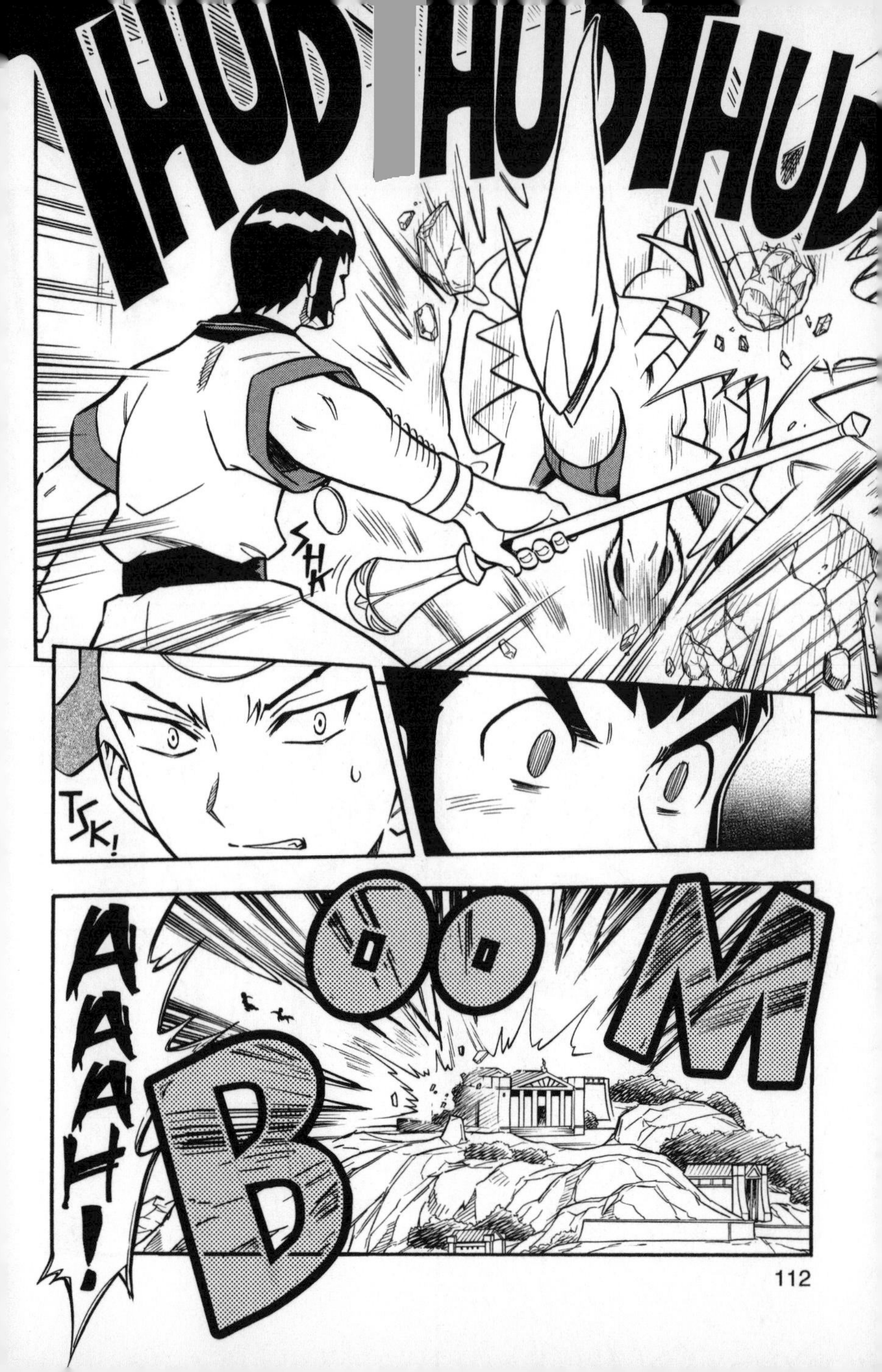
THUD THUD THUD
SHK
TSK!
BOOM
AAAH!

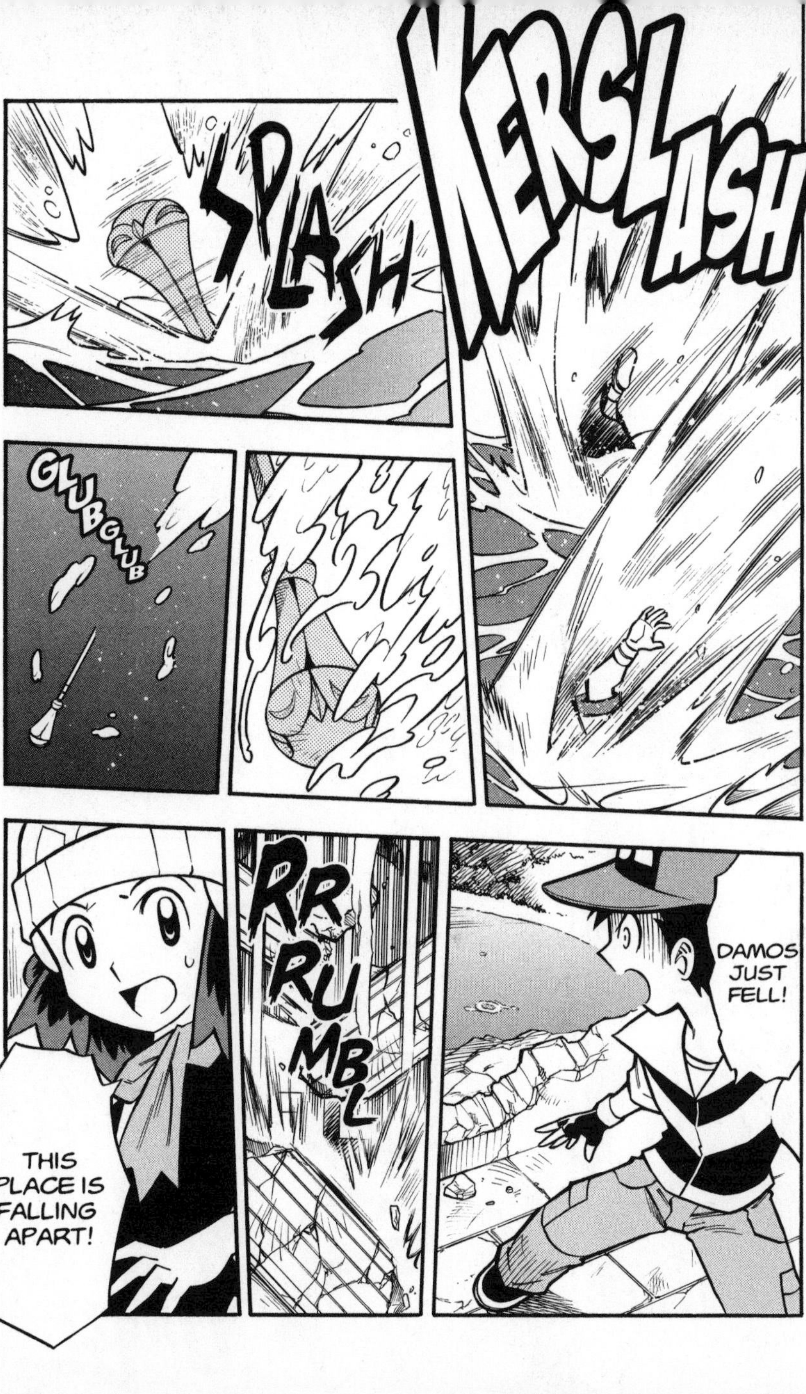
WATERSLASH
SPLASH
GLUBGLUB
DAMOS JUST FELL!
RRRUMBL
THIS PLACE IS FALLING APART!

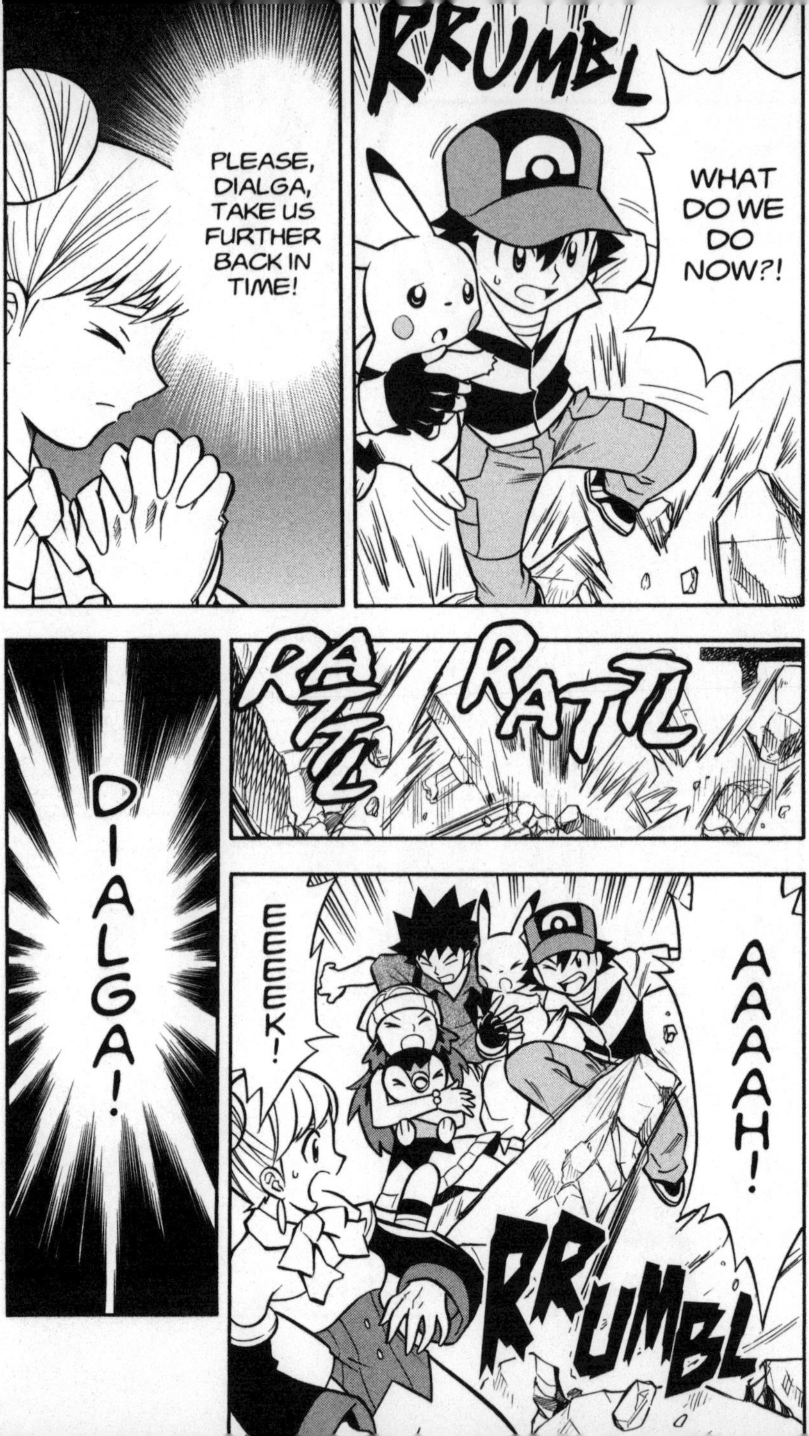
RRUMBL
WHAT DO WE DO NOW?!
PLEASE, DIALGA, TAKE US FURTHER BACK IN TIME!
RATTL RATTL
AAAAH!
EEEEK!
RRUMBL
DIALGA!

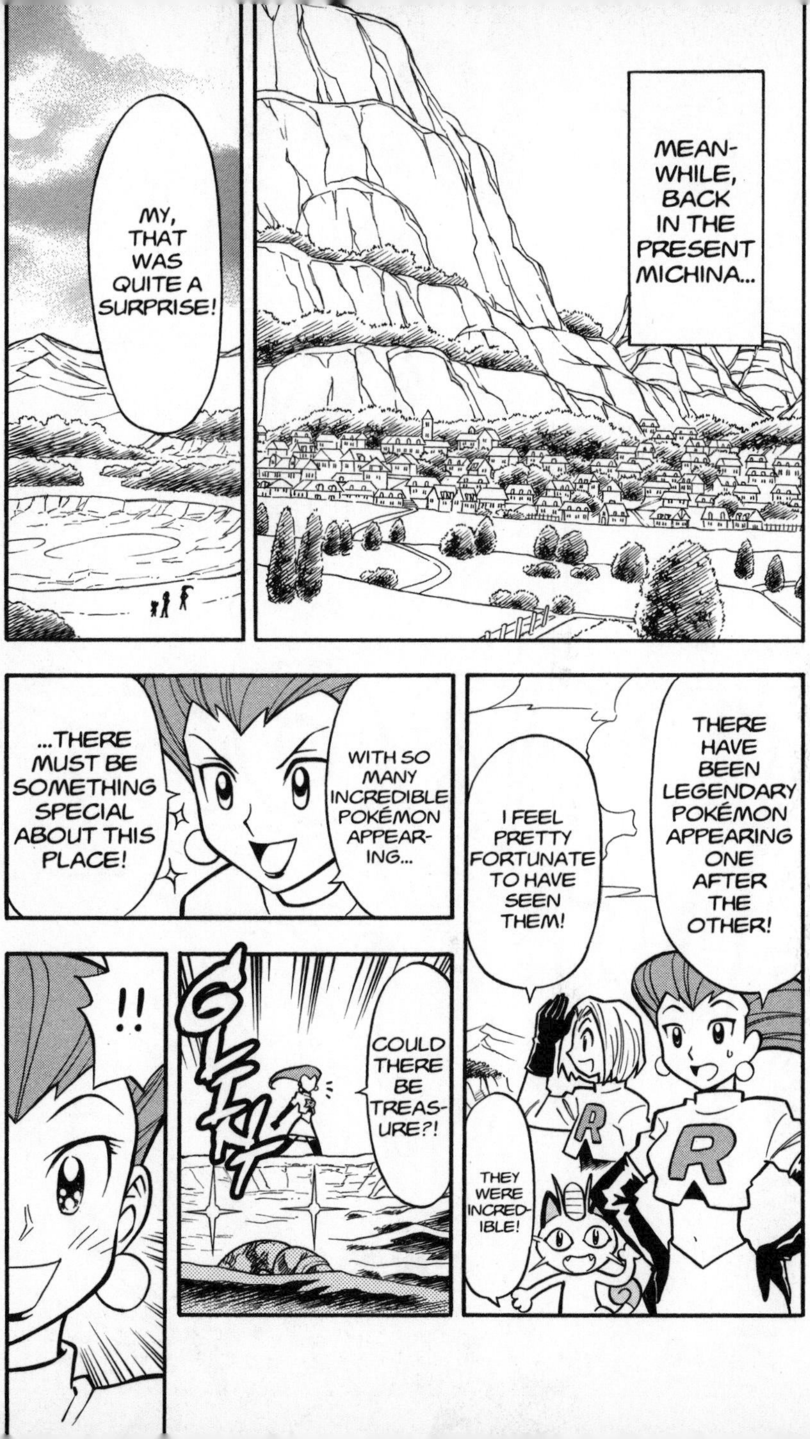
MEAN-WHILE, BACK IN THE PRESENT MICHINA...
MY, THAT WAS QUITE A SURPRISE!
THERE HAVE BEEN LEGENDARY POKÉMON APPEARING ONE AFTER THE OTHER!
I FEEL PRETTY FORTUNATE TO HAVE SEEN THEM!
THEY WERE INCREDIBLE!
WITH SO MANY INCREDIBLE POKÉMON APPEARING...
...THERE MUST BE SOMETHING SPECIAL ABOUT THIS PLACE!
COULD THERE BE TREASURE?!
!!

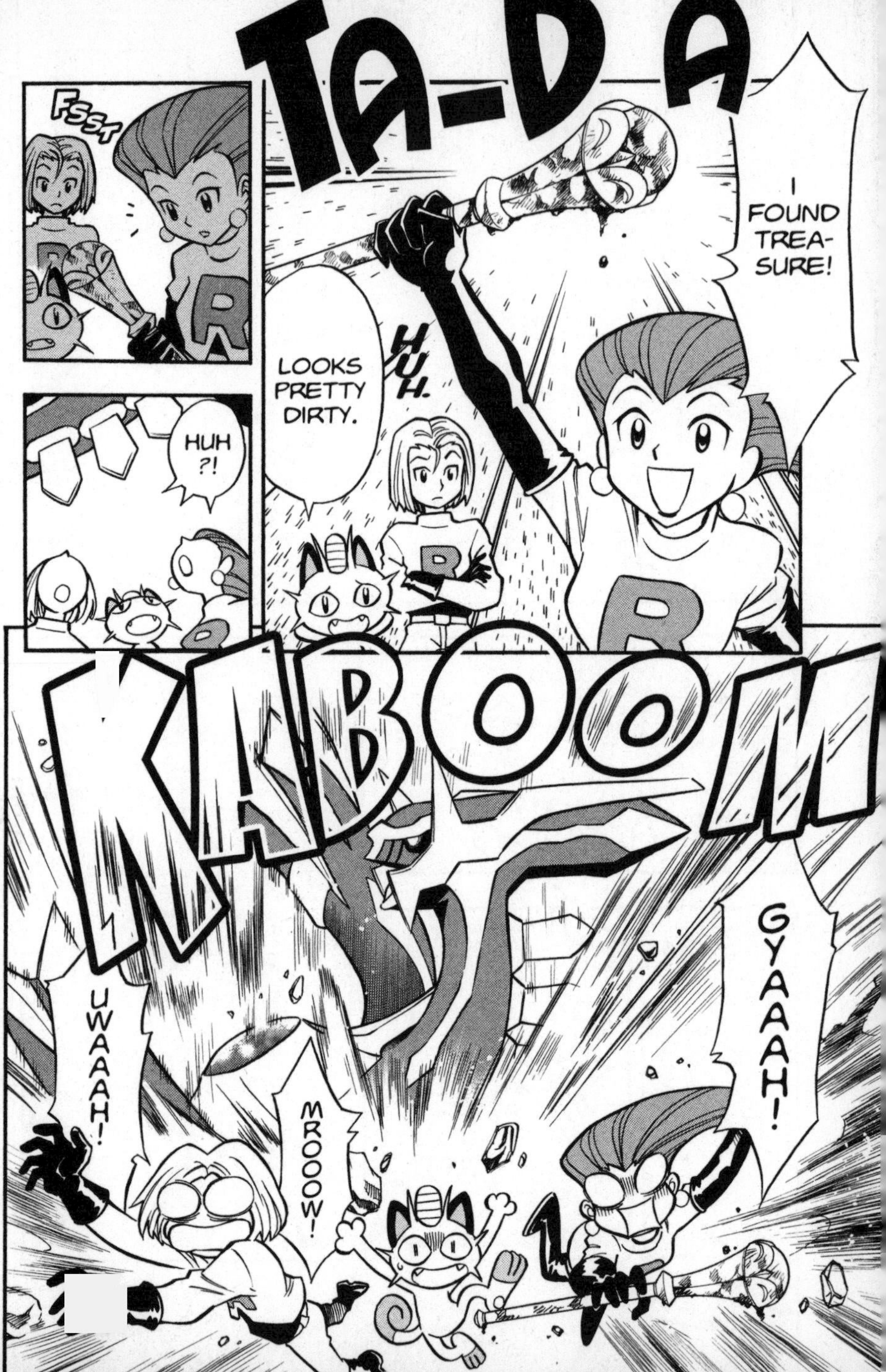
TA-DA
I FOUND TREASURE!
HUH.
LOOKS PRETTY DIRTY.
FSST
HUH ?!
KABOOM
GYAAAAH!
MROOOOW!
UWAAAAH!

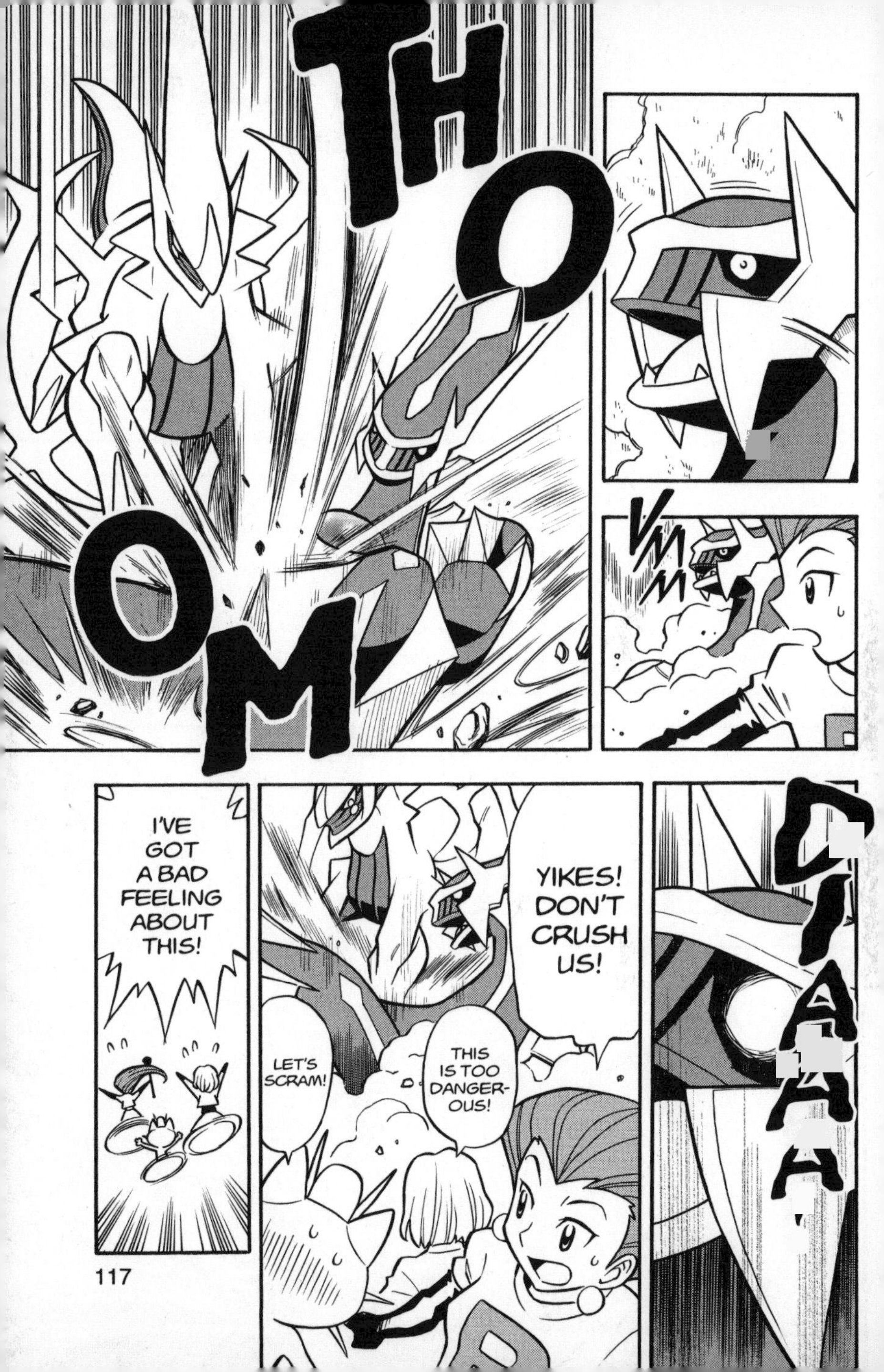
VMM
THOOM
YIKES! DON'T CRUSH US!
THIS IS TOO DANGER-OUS!
LET'S SCRAM!
I'VE GOT A BAD FEELING ABOUT THIS!

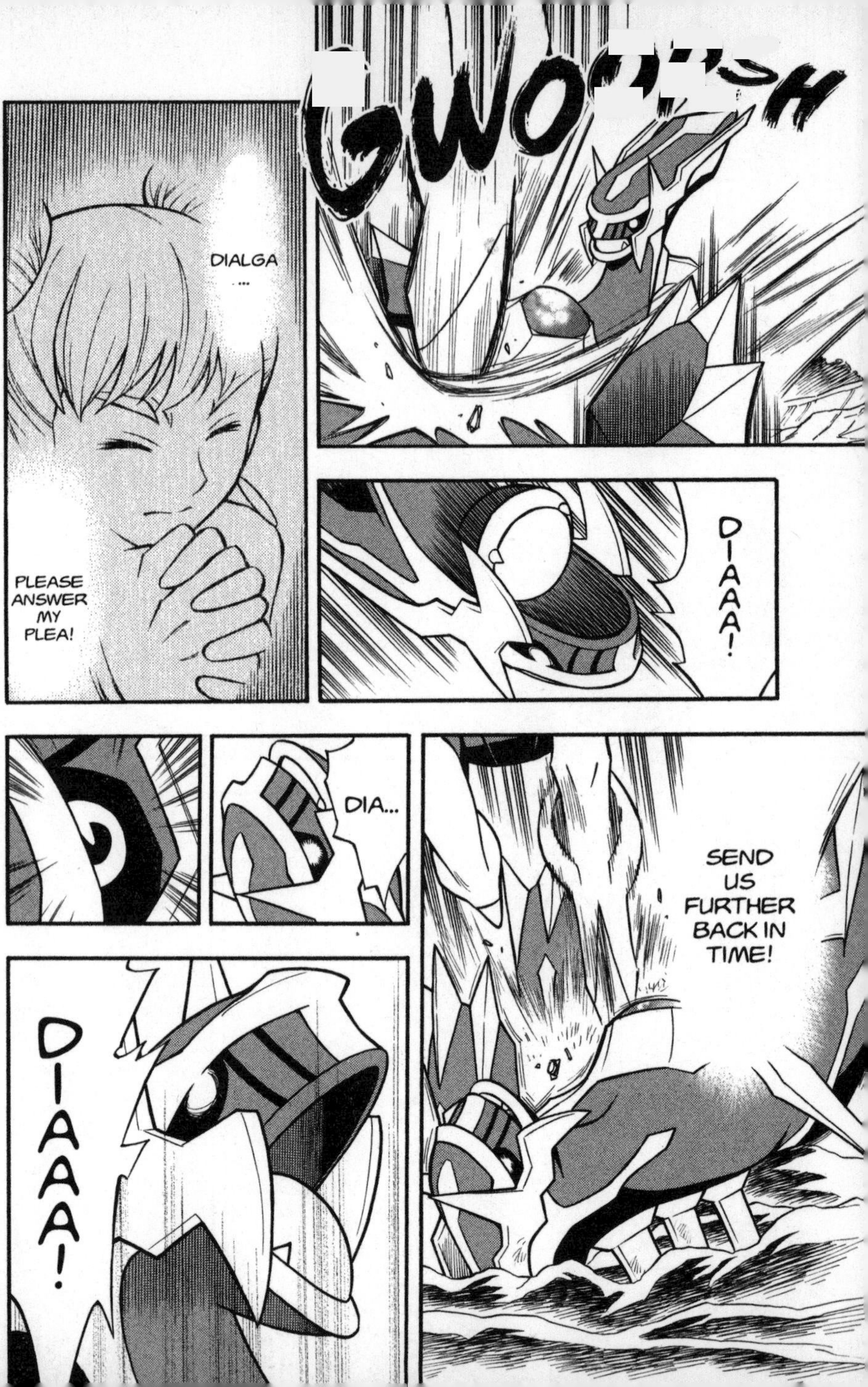
DIAAAA!
DIALGA...
PLEASE ANSWER MY PLEA!
SEND US FURTHER BACK IN TIME!
DIA...
DIAAAA!

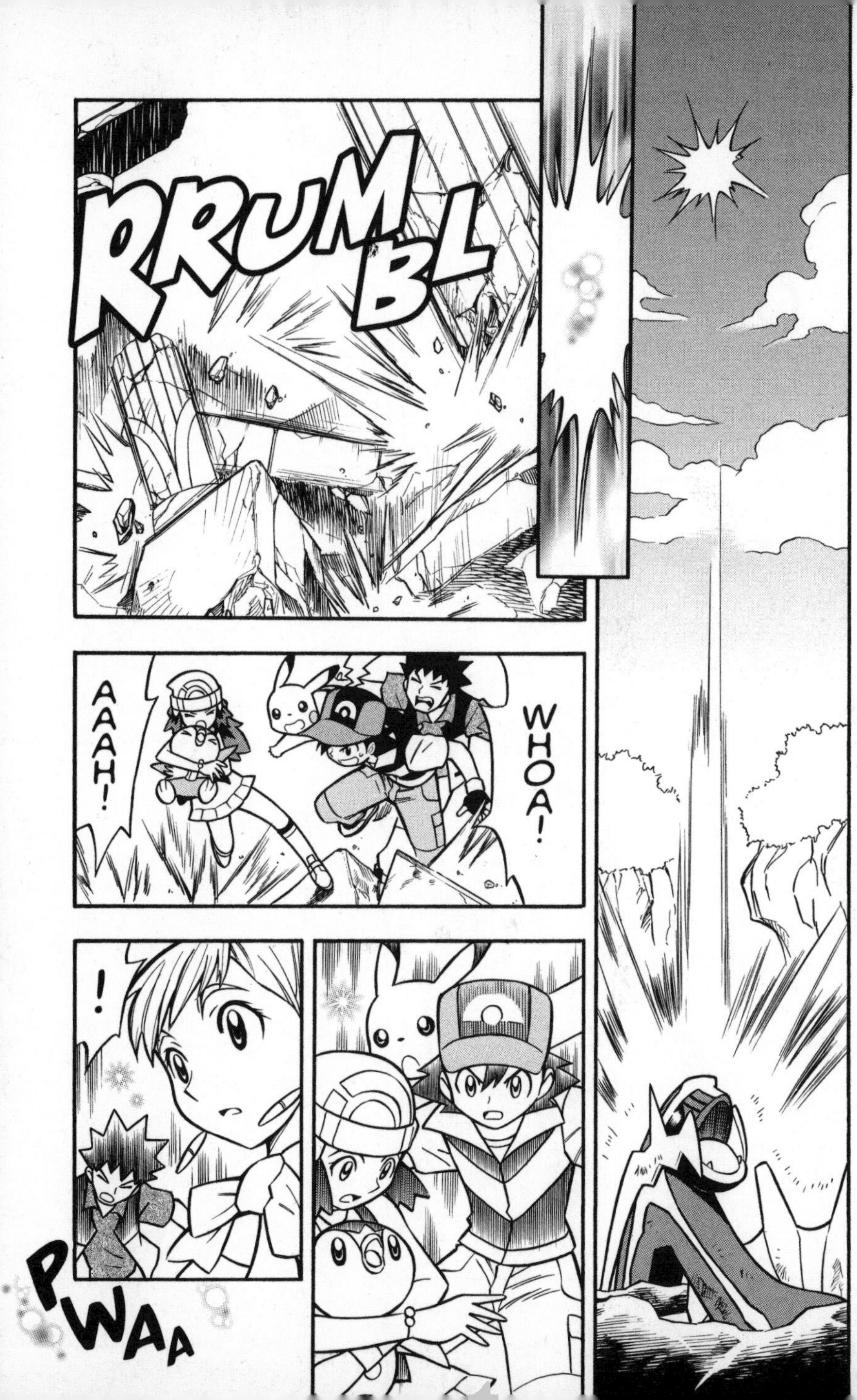
RRUMBL
WHOA!
AAAH!
!
PWAA

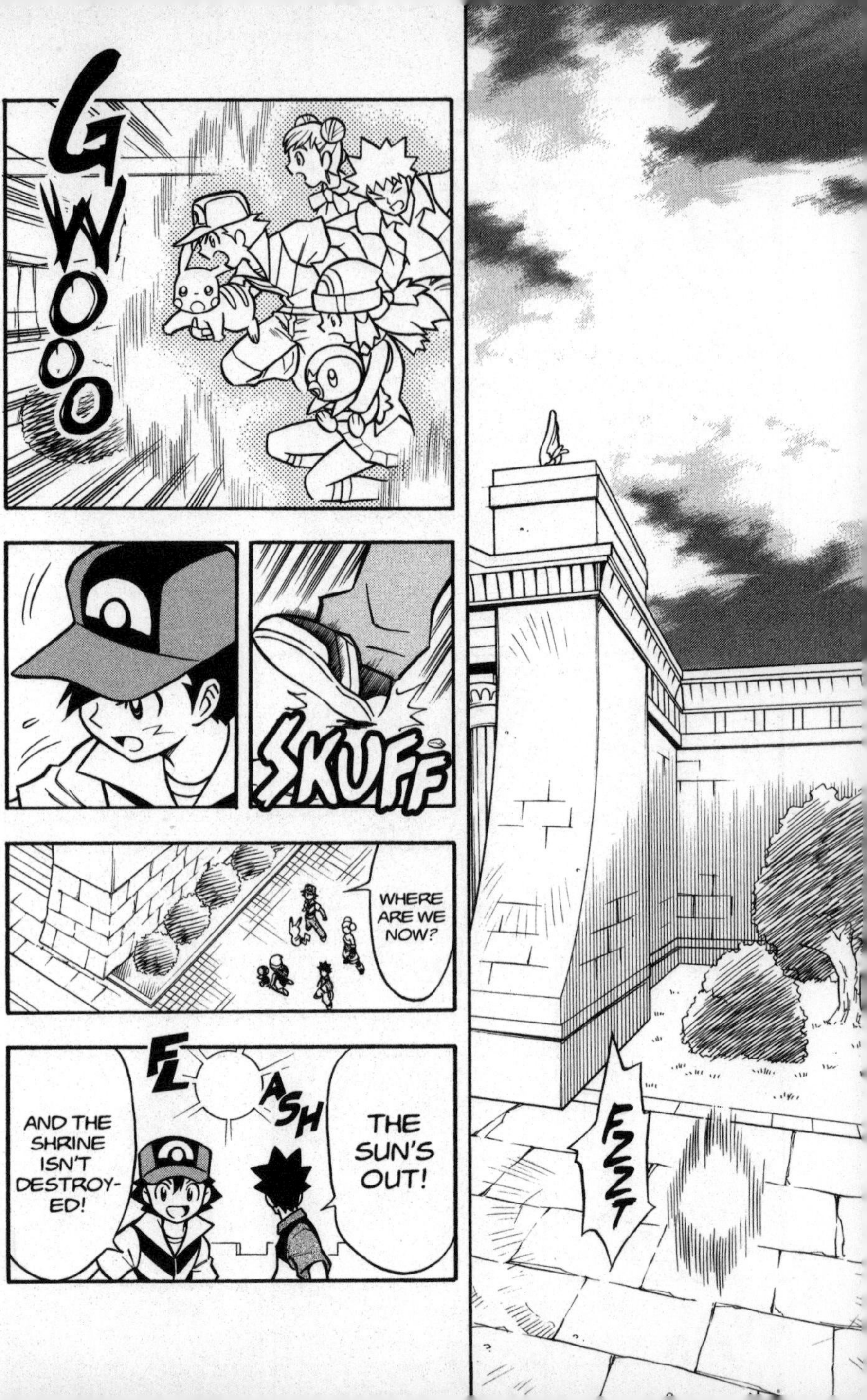
FZZT
GWOOOO
SKUFF
WHERE ARE WE NOW?
THE SUN'S OUT!
FLASH
AND THE SHRINE ISN'T DESTROYED!

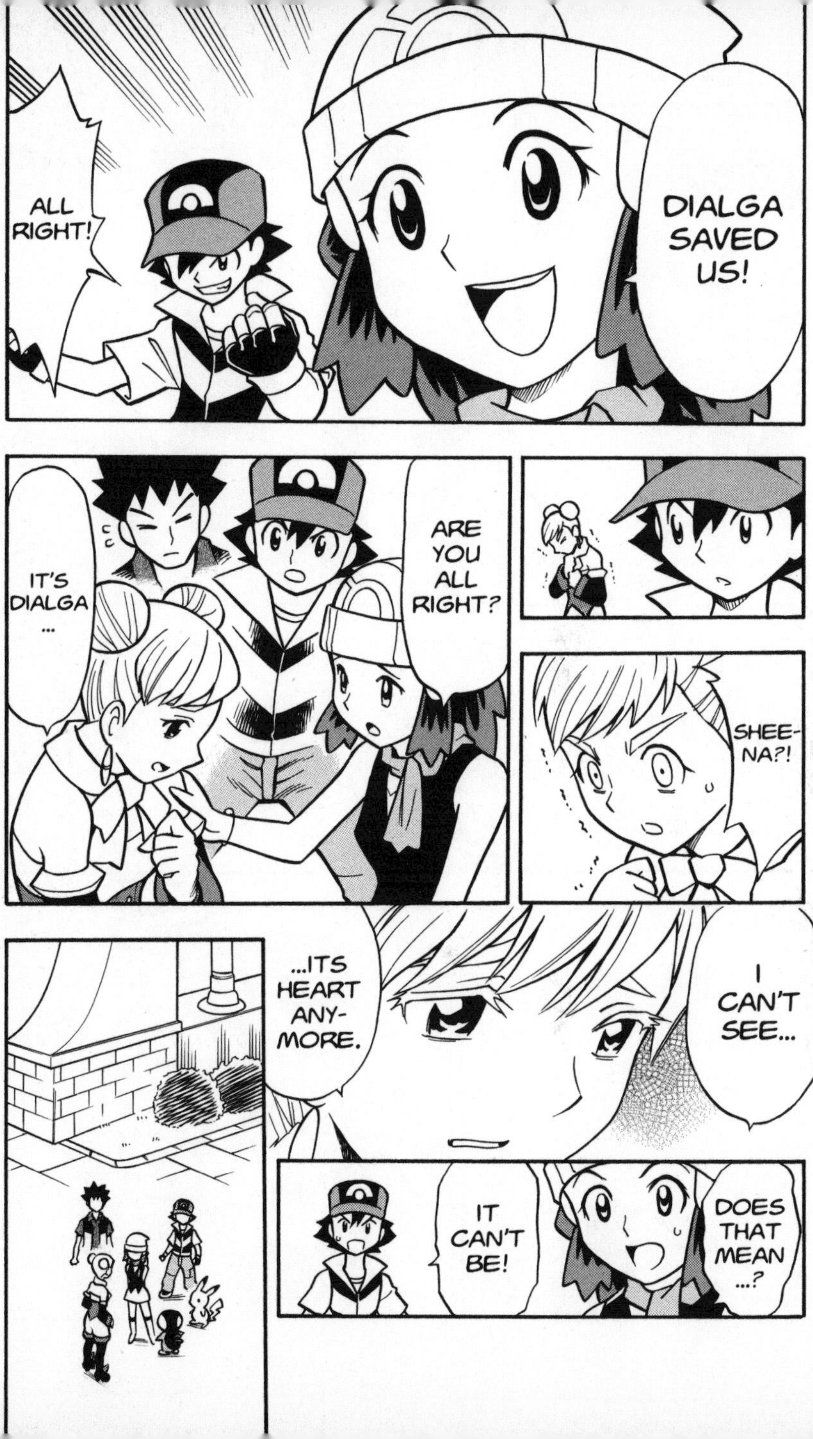
DIALGA SAVED US!
ALL RIGHT!
SHEE-NA?!
ARE YOU ALL RIGHT?
IT'S DIALGA ...
I CAN'T SEE...
...ITS HEART ANY-MORE.
DOES THAT MEAN ...?
IT CAN'T BE!

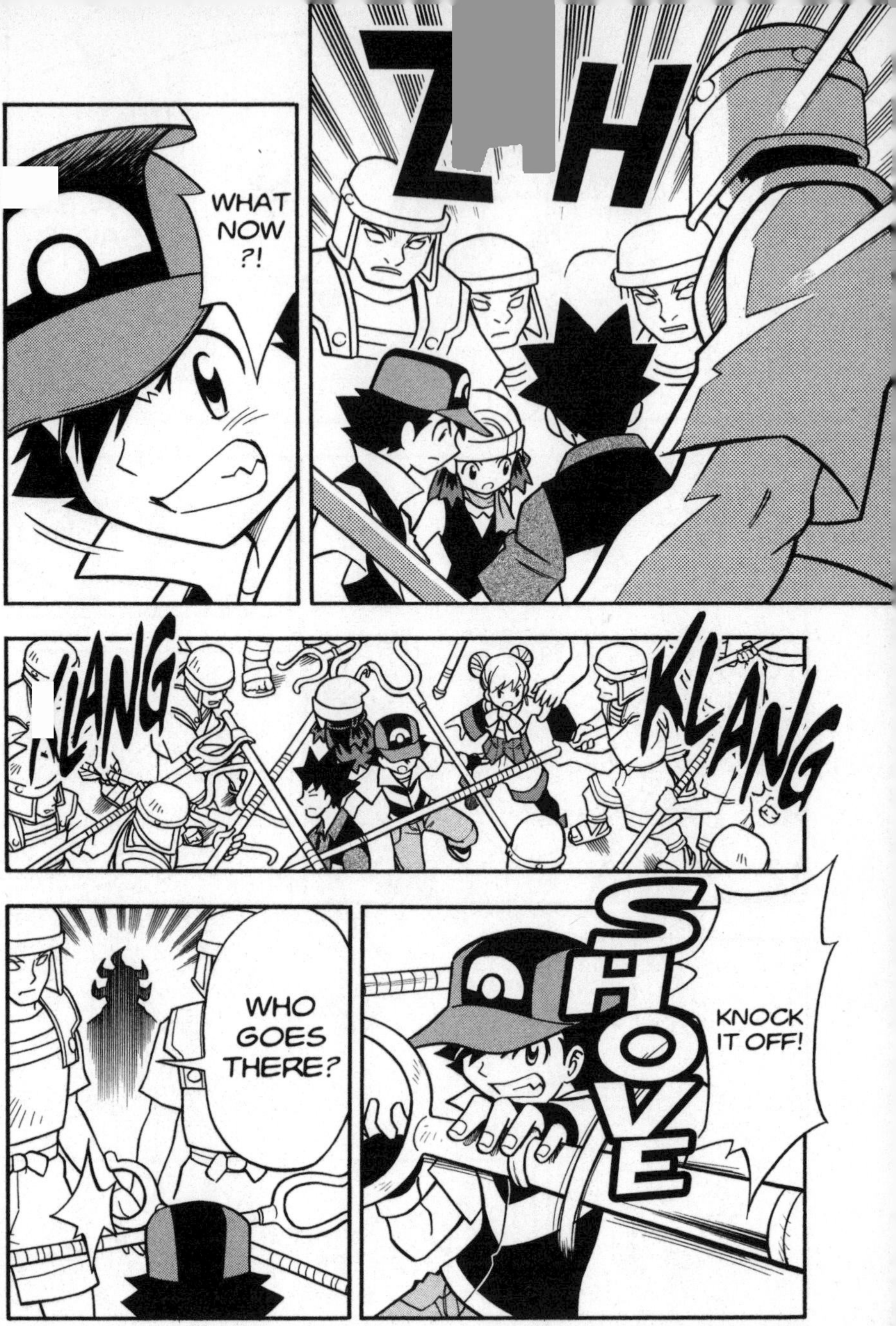
WHAT NOW ?!
KLANG
SHOVE
KNOCK IT OFF!
WHO GOES THERE?

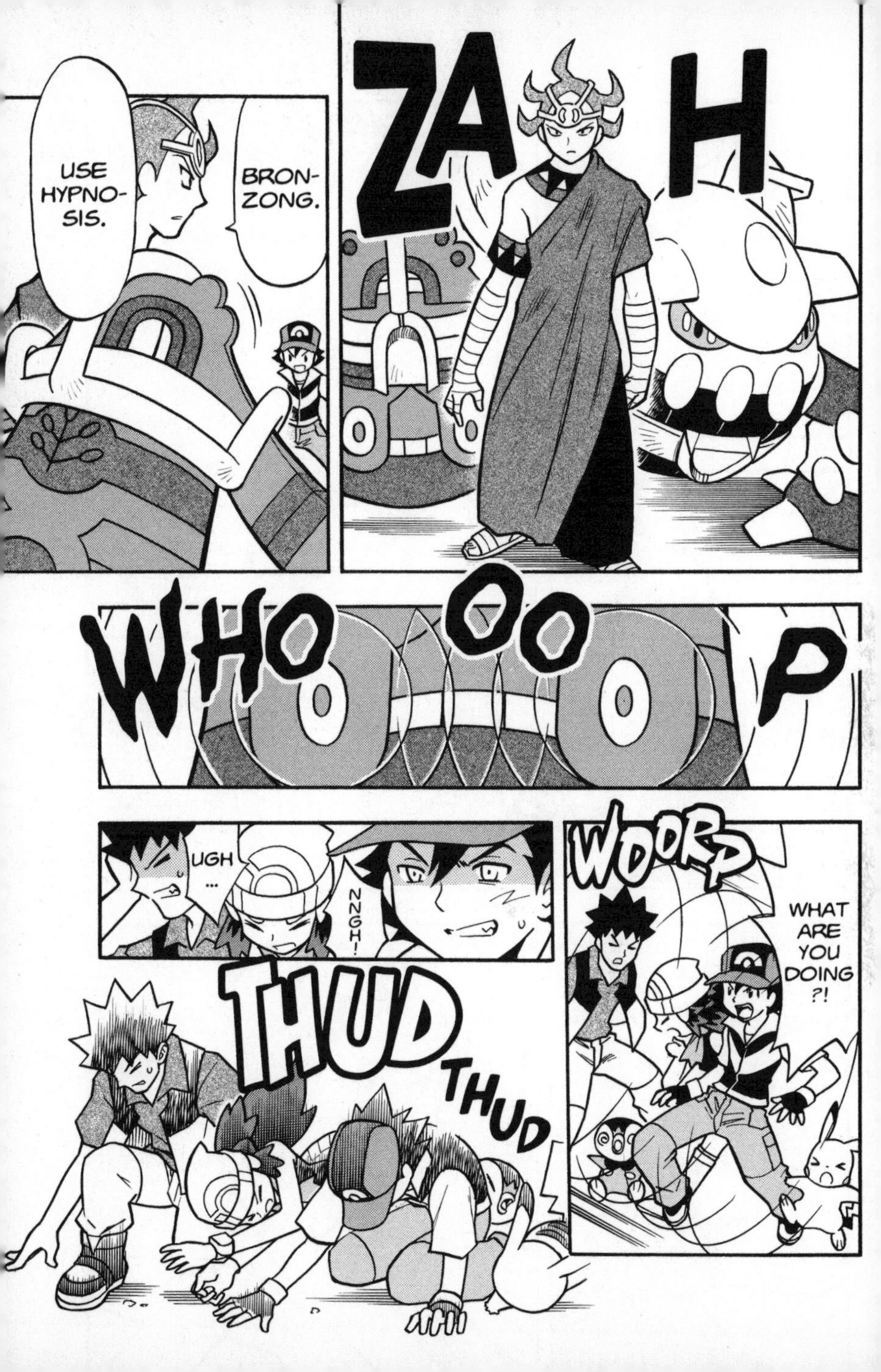
ZA H
BRON-ZONG.
USE HYPNO-SIS.
WHOOOOP
WOORP
WHAT ARE YOU DOING ?!
UGH ...
NNGH!
THUD
THUD

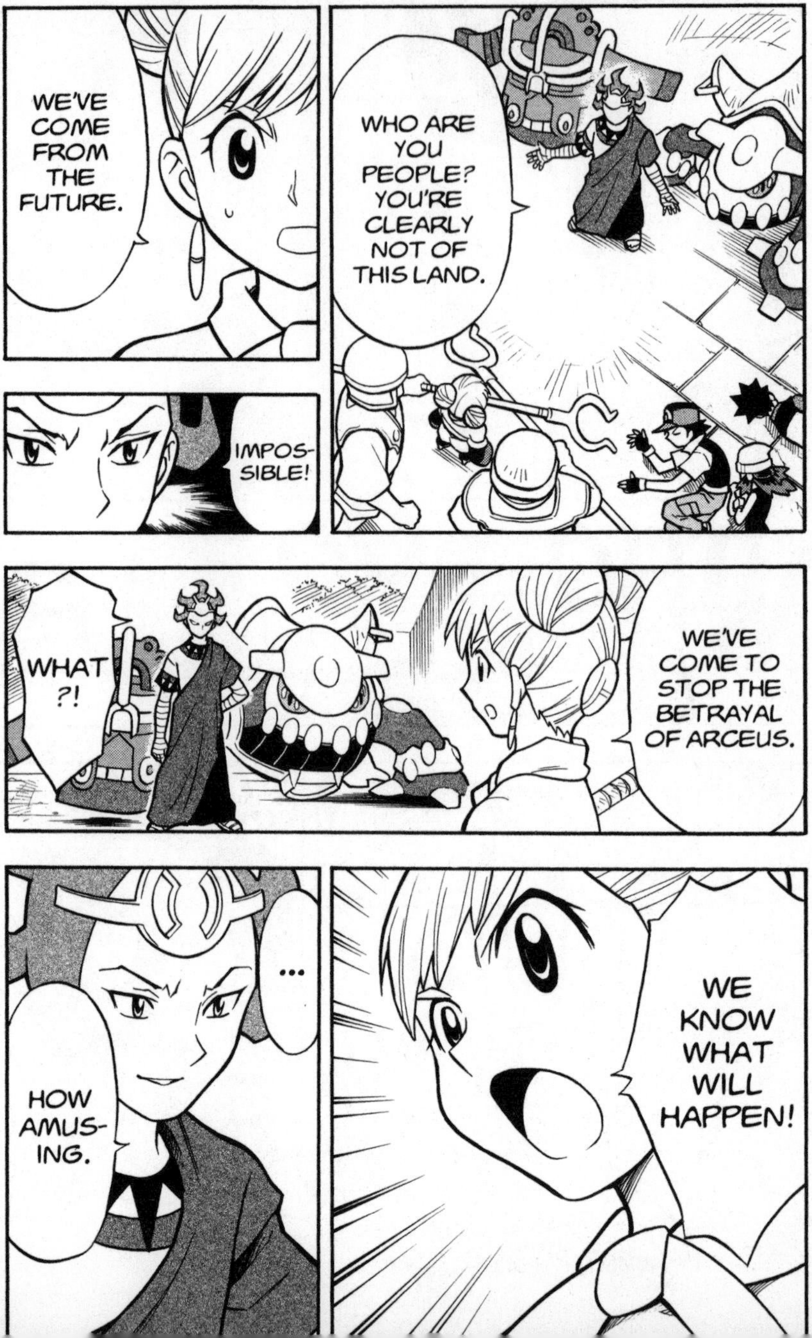
WHO ARE YOU PEOPLE? YOU'RE CLEARLY NOT OF THIS LAND.
WE'VE COME FROM THE FUTURE.
IMPOSSIBLE!
WE'VE COME TO STOP THE BETRAYAL OF ARCEUS.
WHAT?!
WE KNOW WHAT WILL HAPPEN!
...
HOW AMUSING.

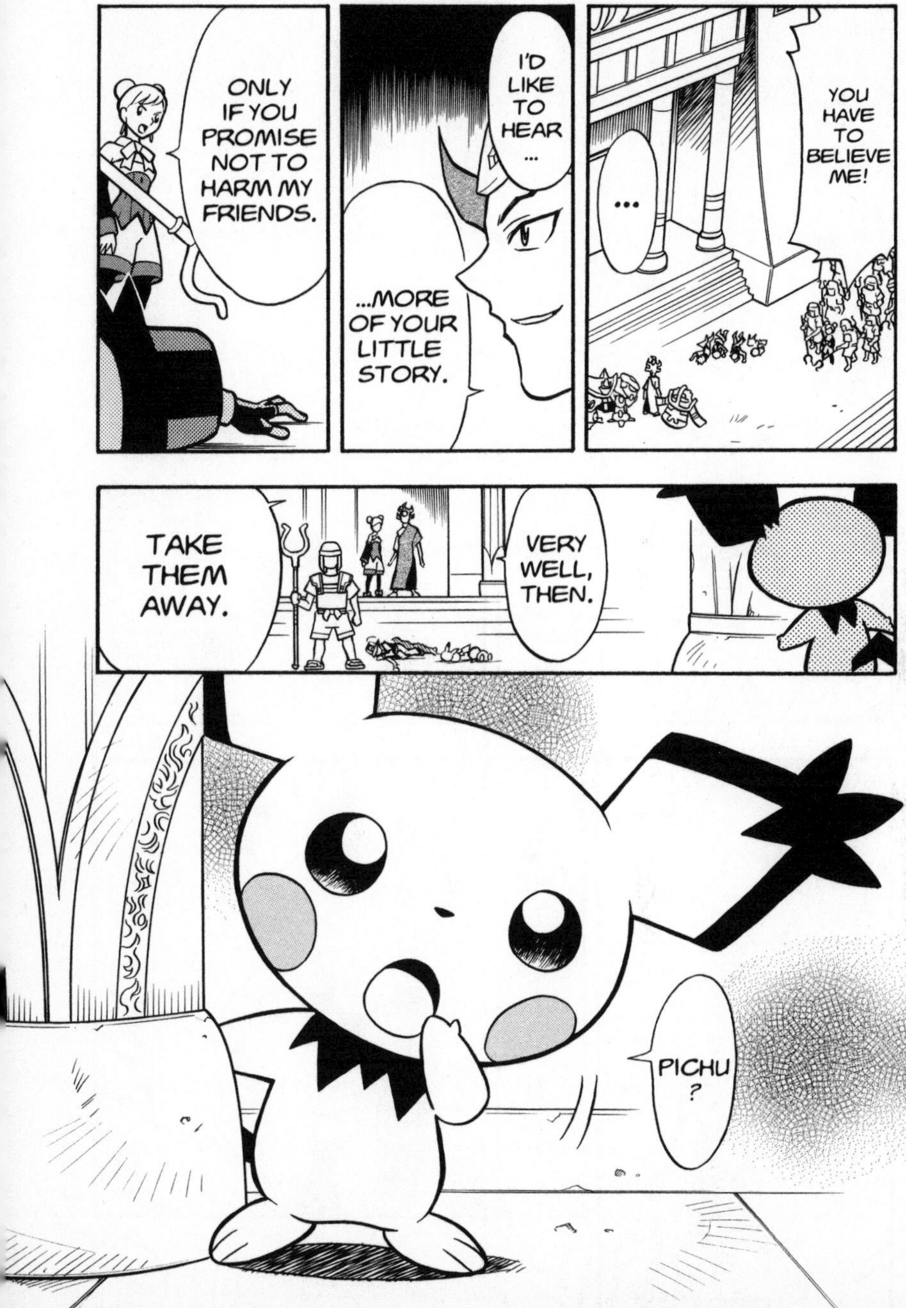
YOU HAVE TO BELIEVE ME!
...
I'D LIKE TO HEAR ...
...MORE OF YOUR LITTLE STORY.
ONLY IF YOU PROMISE NOT TO HARM MY FRIENDS.
VERY WELL, THEN.
TAKE THEM AWAY.
PICHU ?

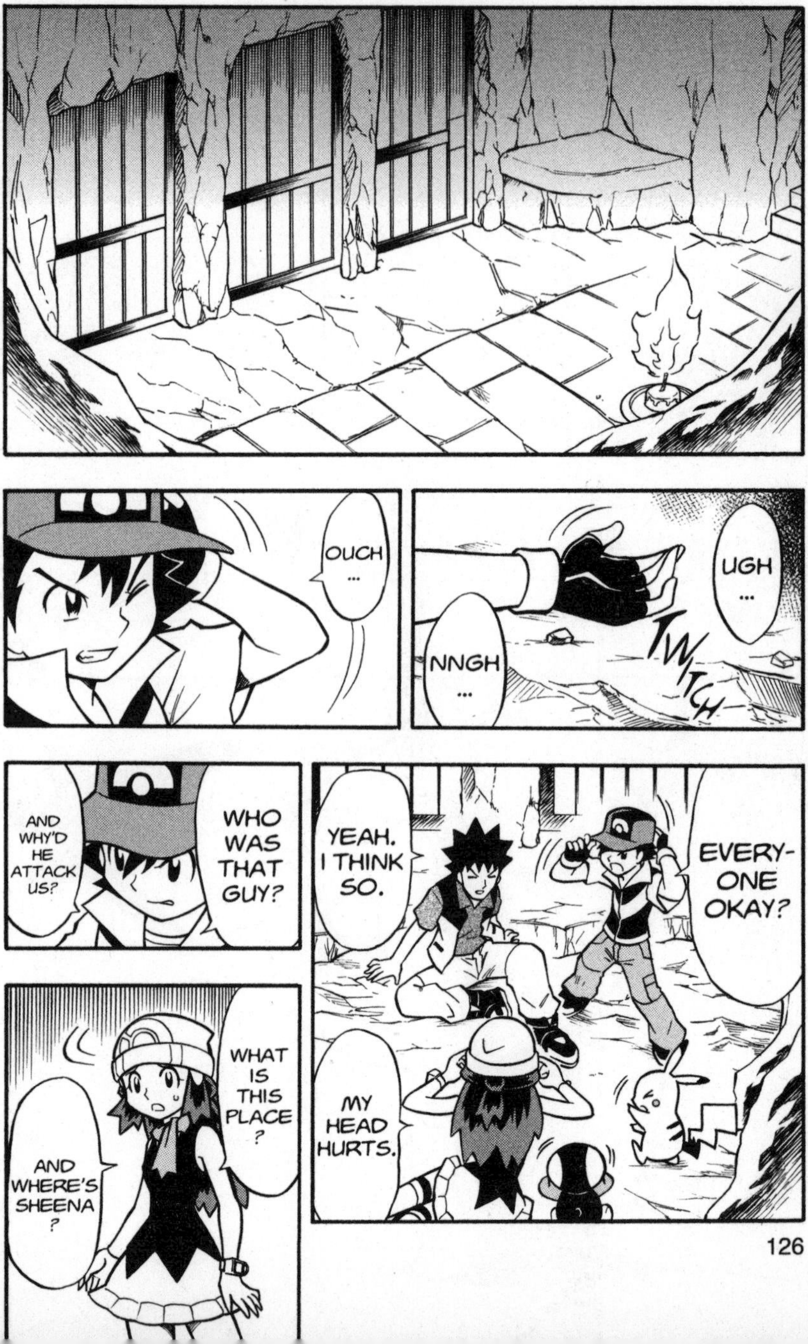
UGH ...
NNGH ...
TWITCH
OUCH ...
EVERY-ONE OKAY?
YEAH. I THINK SO.
MY HEAD HURTS.
WHO WAS THAT GUY?
AND WHY'D HE ATTACK US?
WHAT IS THIS PLACE?
AND WHERE'S SHEENA?

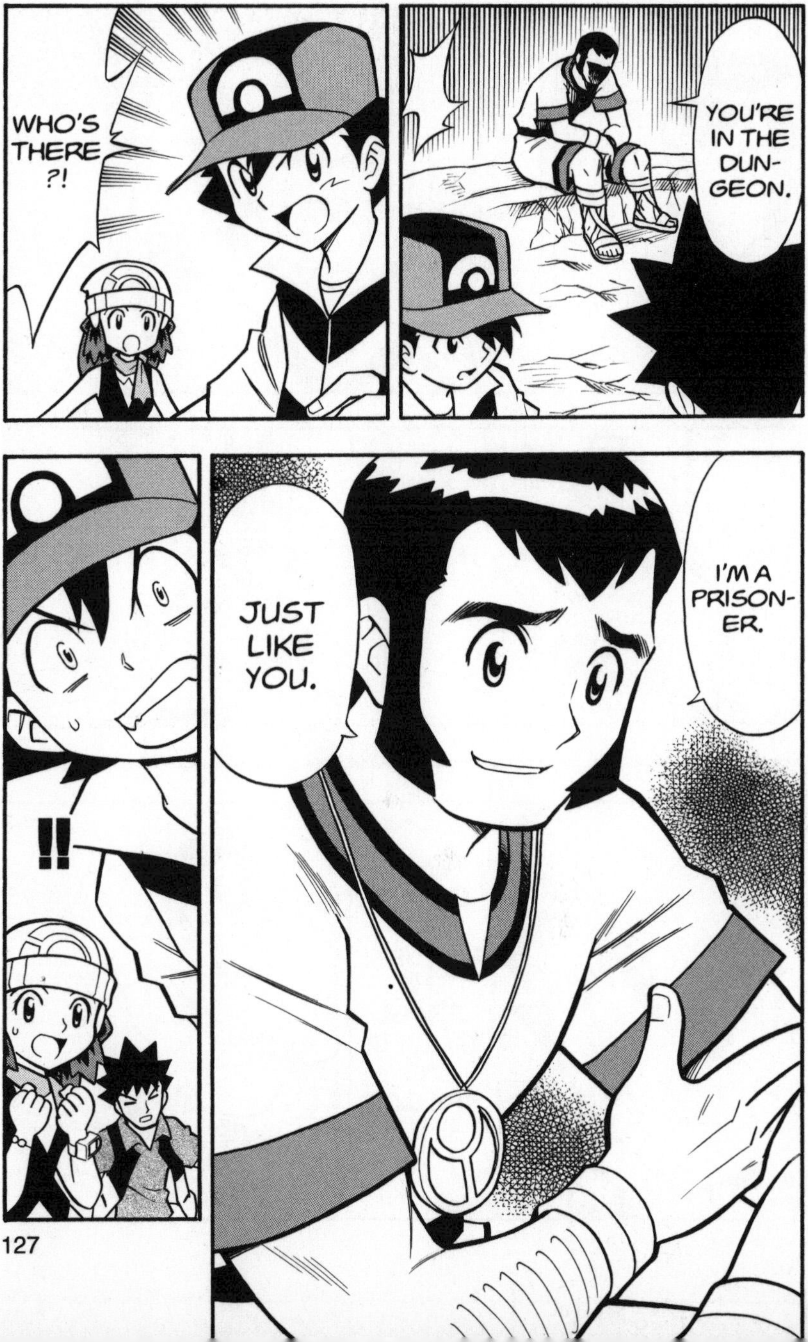
YOU'RE IN THE DUN-GEON.
WHO'S THERE ?!
I'M A PRISON-ER.
JUST LIKE YOU.
!!

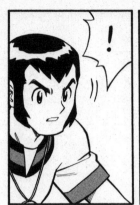

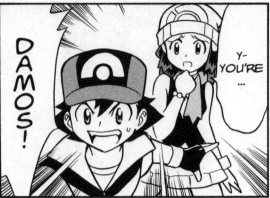

Y-YOU'RE ...
DAMOS!
!
YOU KNOW ME?
OF COURSE WE DO!
SORRY, BUT YOU'RE UN-FAMILIAR TO ME. HAVE WE MET?
WHY DIDN'T YOU RETURN THE JEWEL OF LIFE TO ARCEUS?!

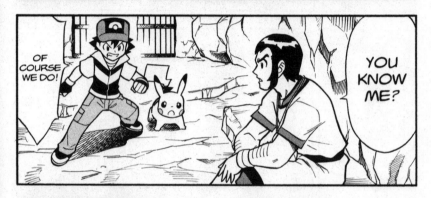

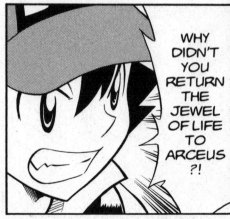

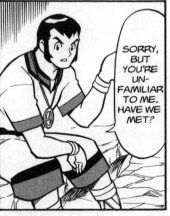

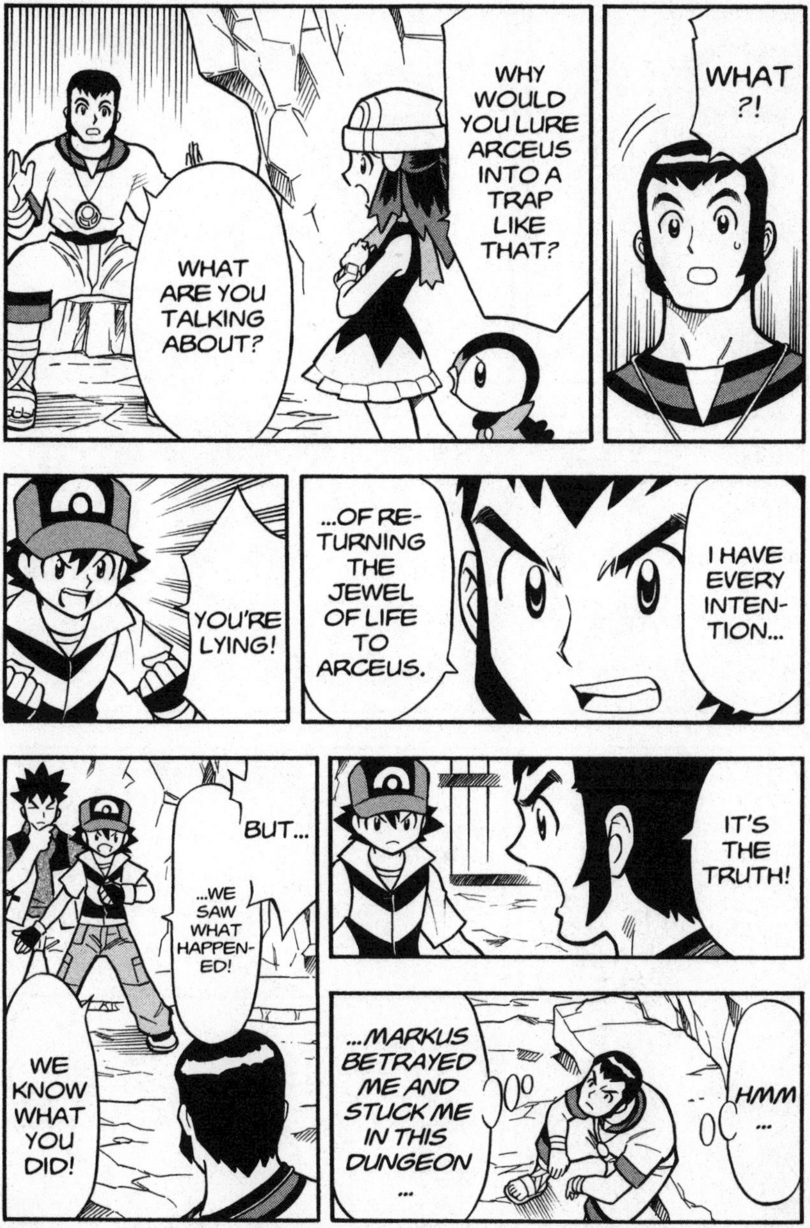
WHAT ?!
WHY WOULD YOU LURE ARCEUS INTO A TRAP LIKE THAT?
WHAT ARE YOU TALKING ABOUT?
I HAVE EVERY INTEN-TION...
...OF RE-TURNING THE JEWEL OF LIFE TO ARCEUS.
YOU'RE LYING!
IT'S THE TRUTH!
HMM ...
...MARKUS BETRAYED ME AND STUCK ME IN THIS DUNGEON ...
BUT...
...WE SAW WHAT HAPPEN-ED!
WE KNOW WHAT YOU DID!

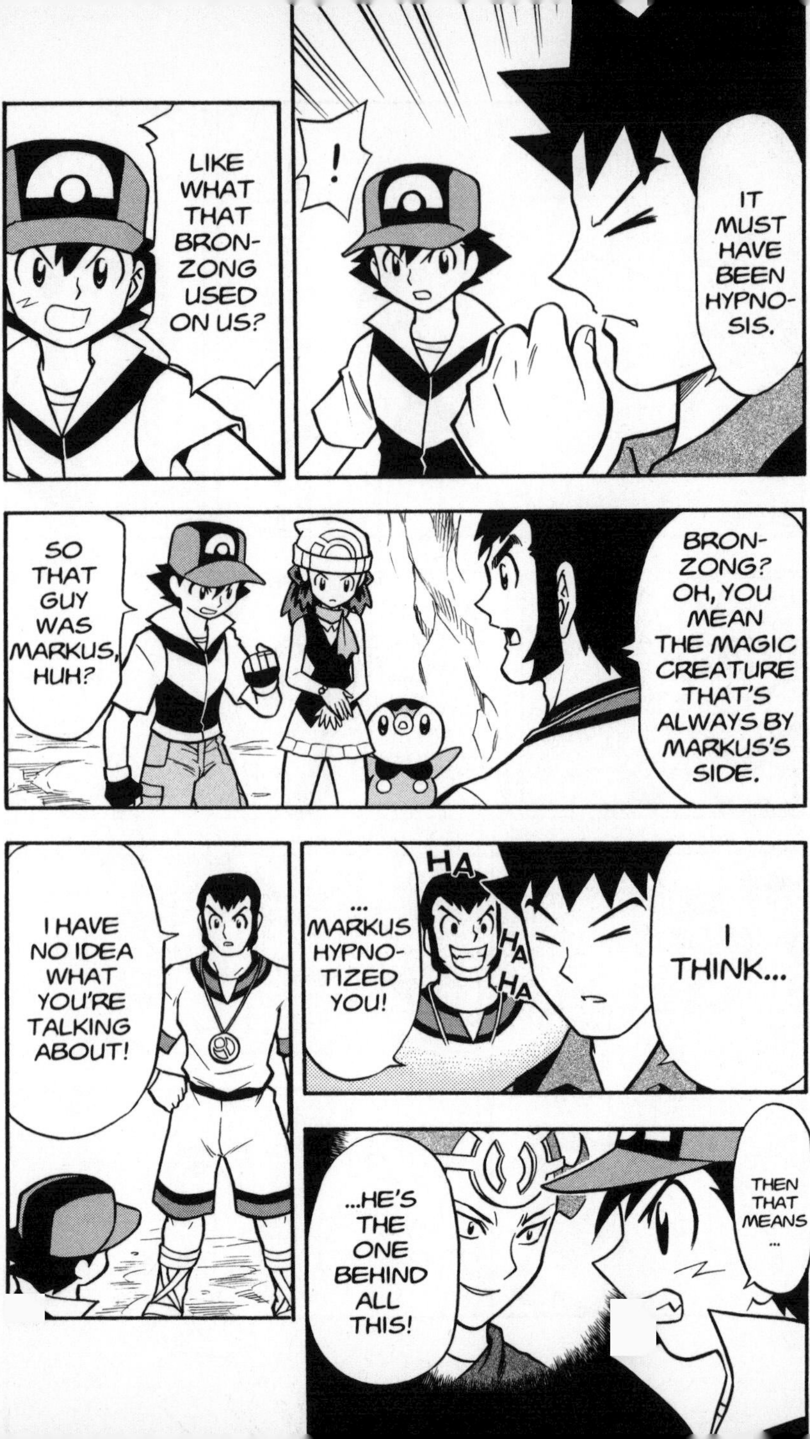
!
IT MUST HAVE BEEN HYPNOSIS.
LIKE WHAT THAT BRONZONG USED ON US?
BRONZONG? OH, YOU MEAN THE MAGIC CREATURE THAT'S ALWAYS BY MARKUS'S SIDE.
SO THAT GUY WAS MARKUS, HUH?
I THINK...
...MARKUS HYPNOTIZED YOU!
HA HA HA HA
THEN THAT MEANS...
...HE'S THE ONE BEHIND ALL THIS!
I HAVE NO IDEA WHAT YOU'RE TALKING ABOUT!

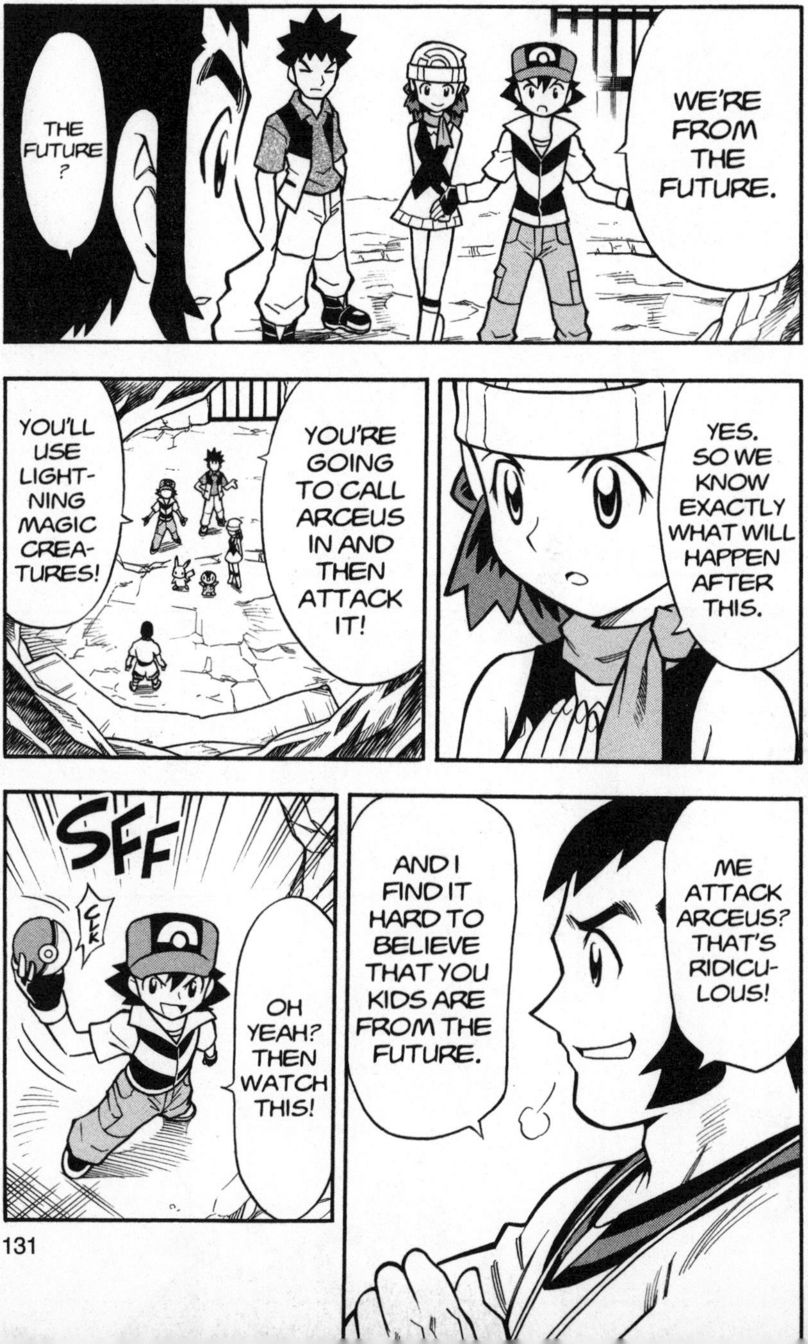
WE'RE FROM THE FUTURE.
THE FUTURE?
YES. SO WE KNOW EXACTLY WHAT WILL HAPPEN AFTER THIS.
YOU'RE GOING TO CALL ARCEUS IN AND THEN ATTACK IT!
YOU'LL USE LIGHT-NING MAGIC CREA-TURES!
ME ATTACK ARCEUS? THAT'S RIDICU-LOUS!
AND I FIND IT HARD TO BELIEVE THAT YOU KIDS ARE FROM THE FUTURE.
SFF
CLK
OH YEAH? THEN WATCH THIS!

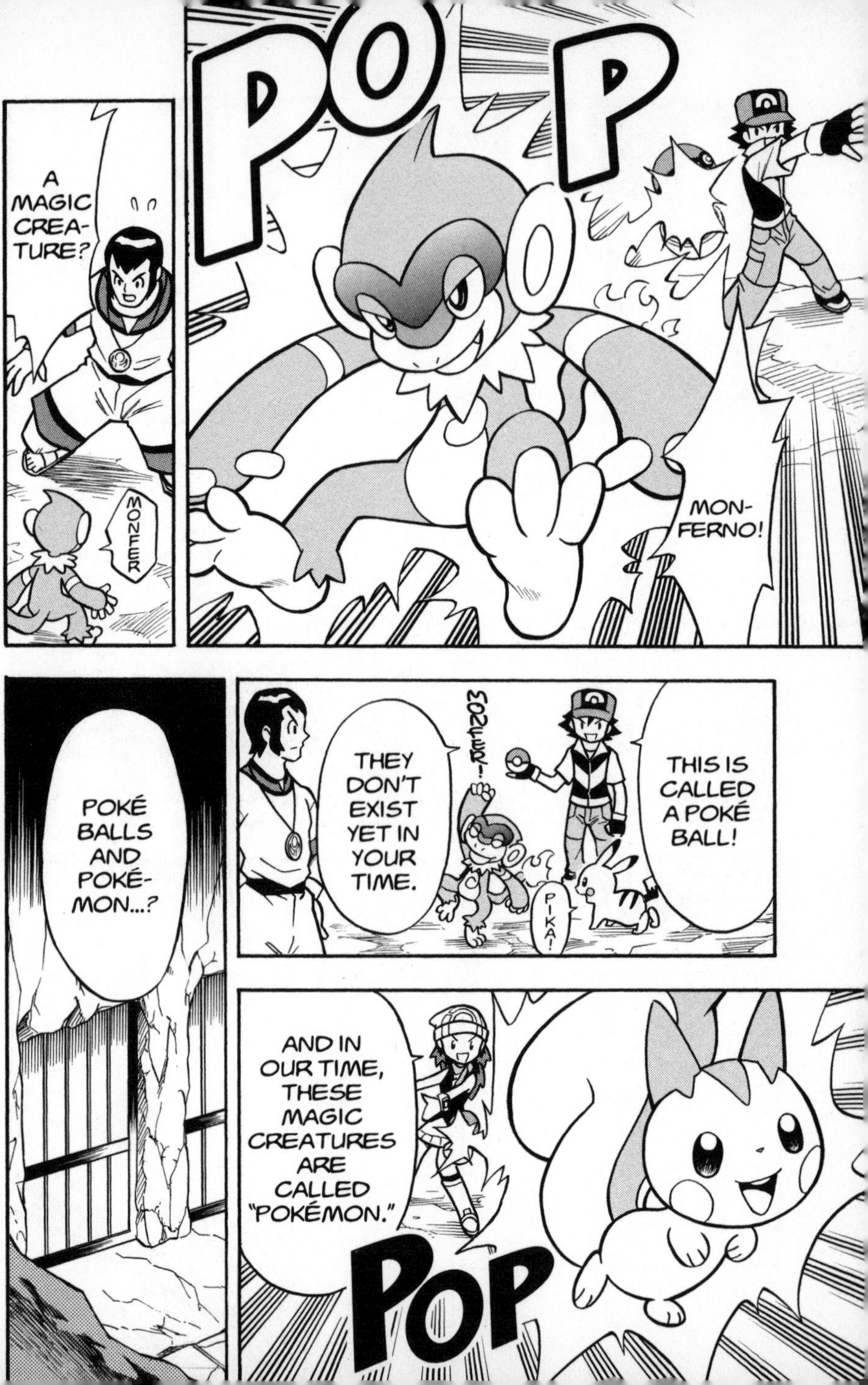
POP
MON-FERNO!
A MAGIC CREATURE?
MONFER
THIS IS CALLED A POKÉ BALL!
MONFER!
THEY DON'T EXIST YET IN YOUR TIME.
PIKA!
AND IN OUR TIME, THESE MAGIC CREATURES ARE CALLED "POKÉMON."
POP
POKÉ BALLS AND POKÉMON...?

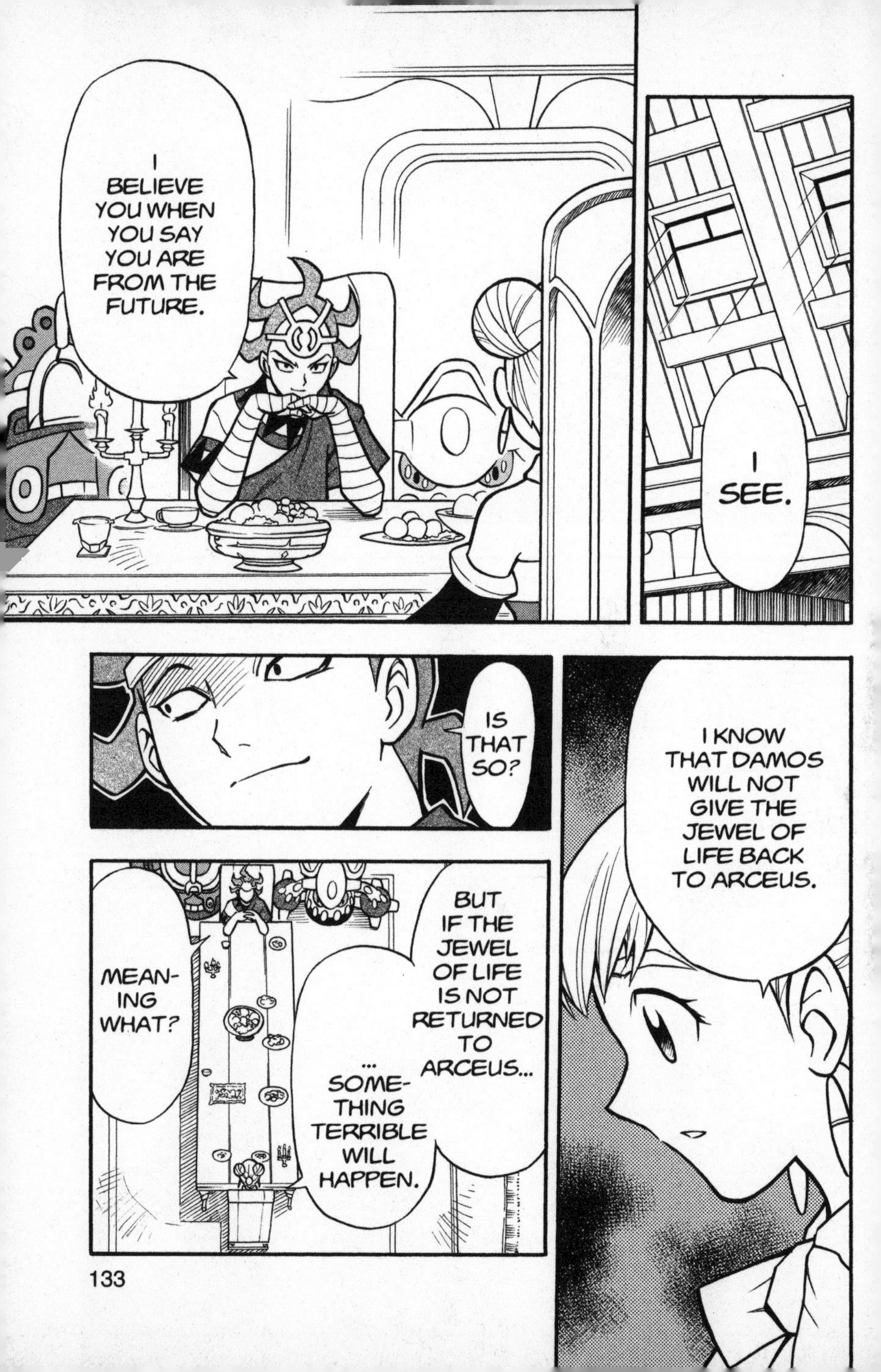
I SEE.
I BELIEVE YOU WHEN YOU SAY YOU ARE FROM THE FUTURE.
I KNOW THAT DAMOS WILL NOT GIVE THE JEWEL OF LIFE BACK TO ARCEUS.
IS THAT SO?
BUT IF THE JEWEL OF LIFE IS NOT RETURNED TO ARCEUS...
... SOME-THING TERRIBLE WILL HAPPEN.
MEAN-ING WHAT?

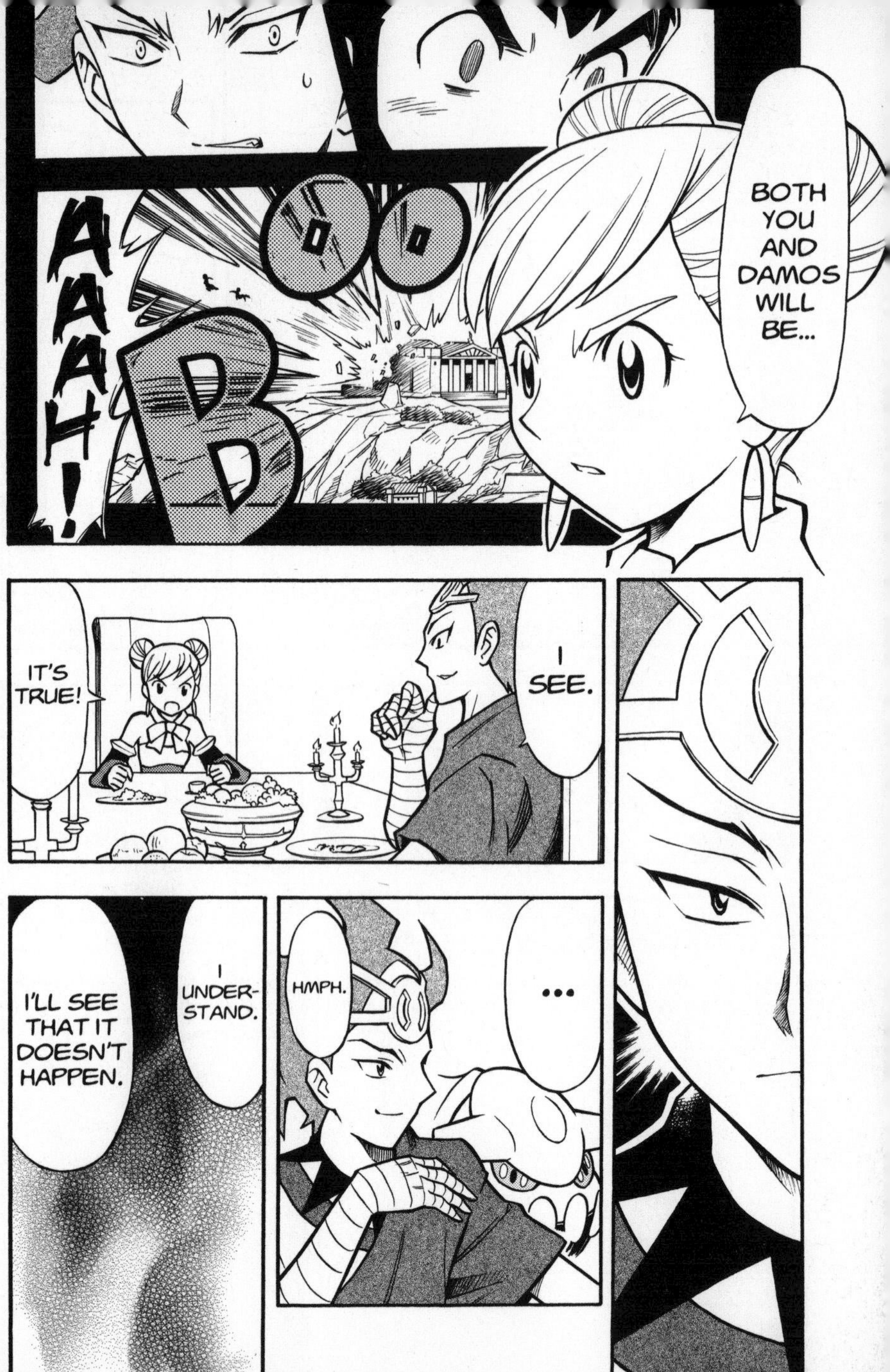
BOTH YOU AND DAMOS WILL BE...
AAAH!
BOO
I SEE.
IT'S TRUE!
...
HMPH.
I UNDER-STAND.
I'LL SEE THAT IT DOESN'T HAPPEN.

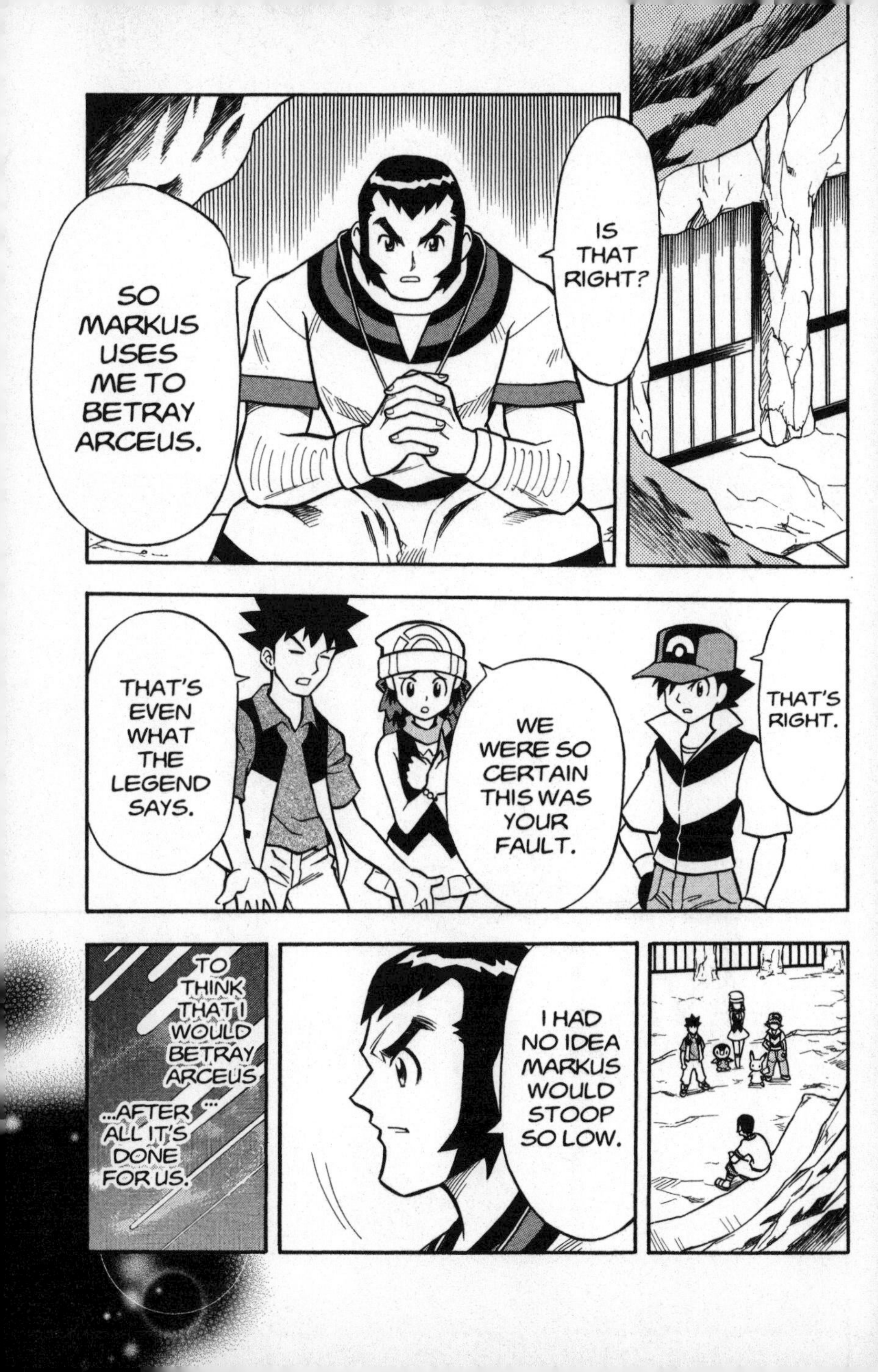
IS THAT RIGHT?
SO MARKUS USES ME TO BETRAY ARCEUS.
THAT'S RIGHT.
WE WERE SO CERTAIN THIS WAS YOUR FAULT.
THAT'S EVEN WHAT THE LEGEND SAYS.
I HAD NO IDEA MARKUS WOULD STOOP SO LOW.
TO THINK THAT I WOULD BETRAY ARCEUS...
...AFTER ALL IT'S DONE FOR US.

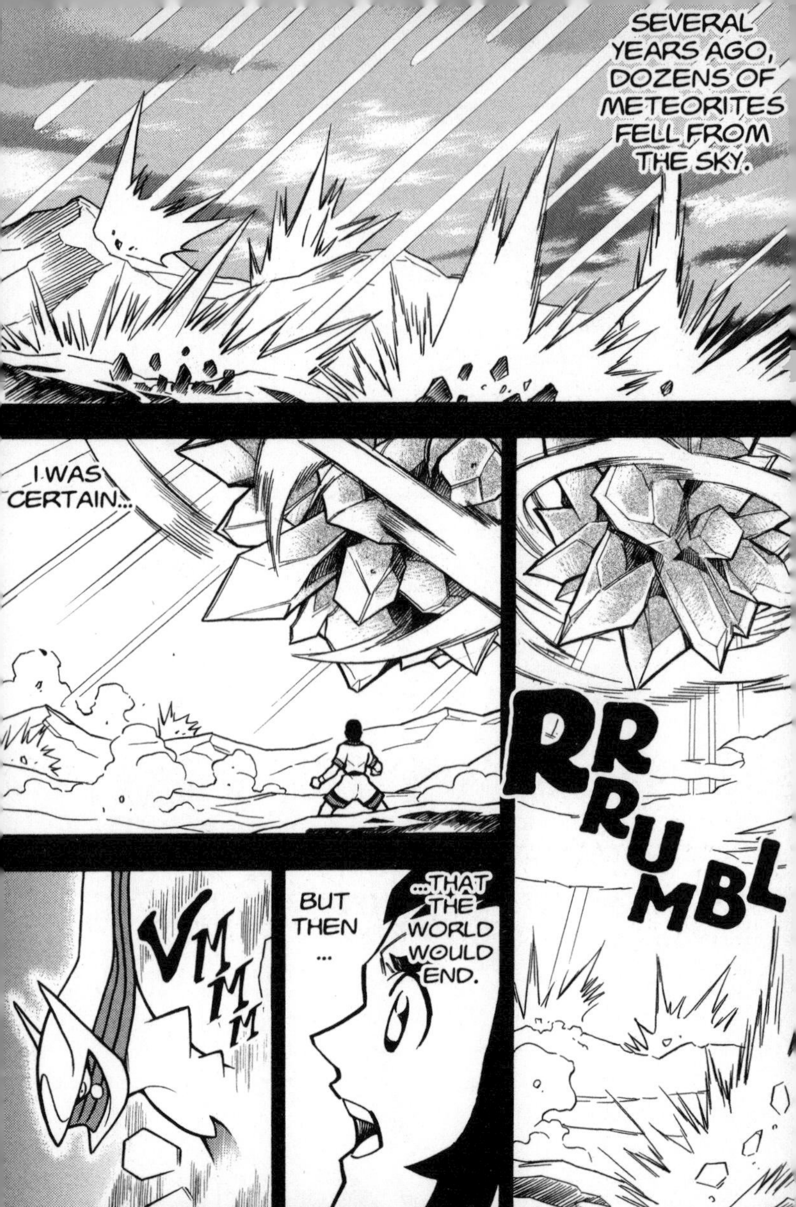
SEVERAL YEARS AGO, DOZENS OF METEORITES FELL FROM THE SKY.
RRRUMBL
I WAS CERTAIN...
...THAT THE WORLD WOULD END.
BUT THEN ...
VMMM

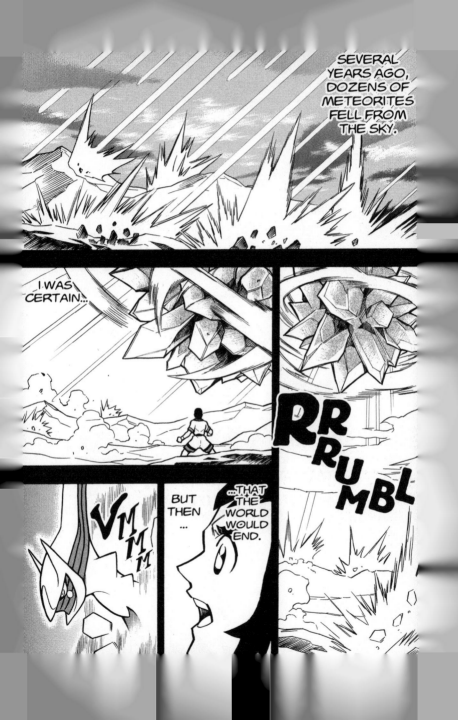

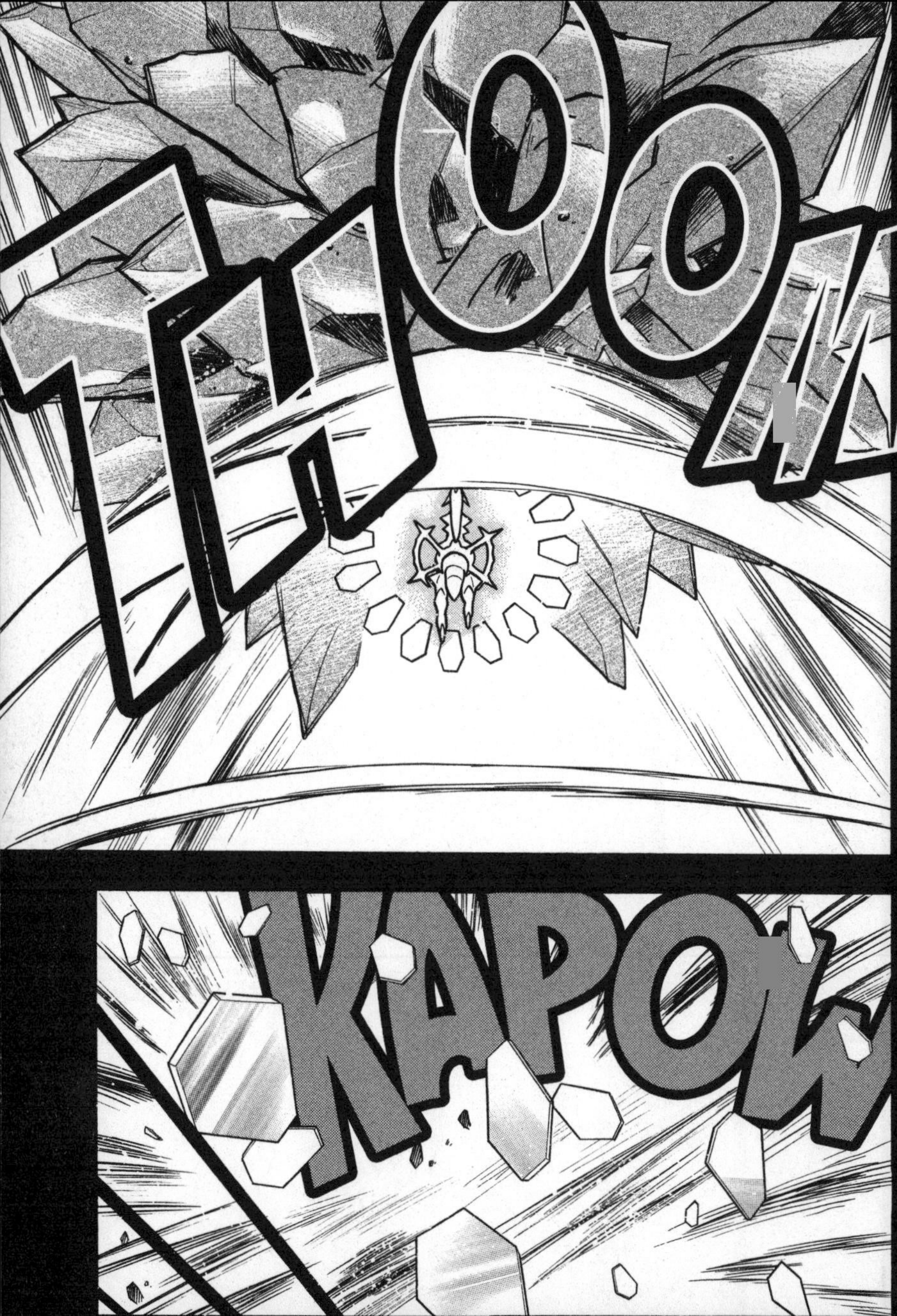
THOOM
KAPOW

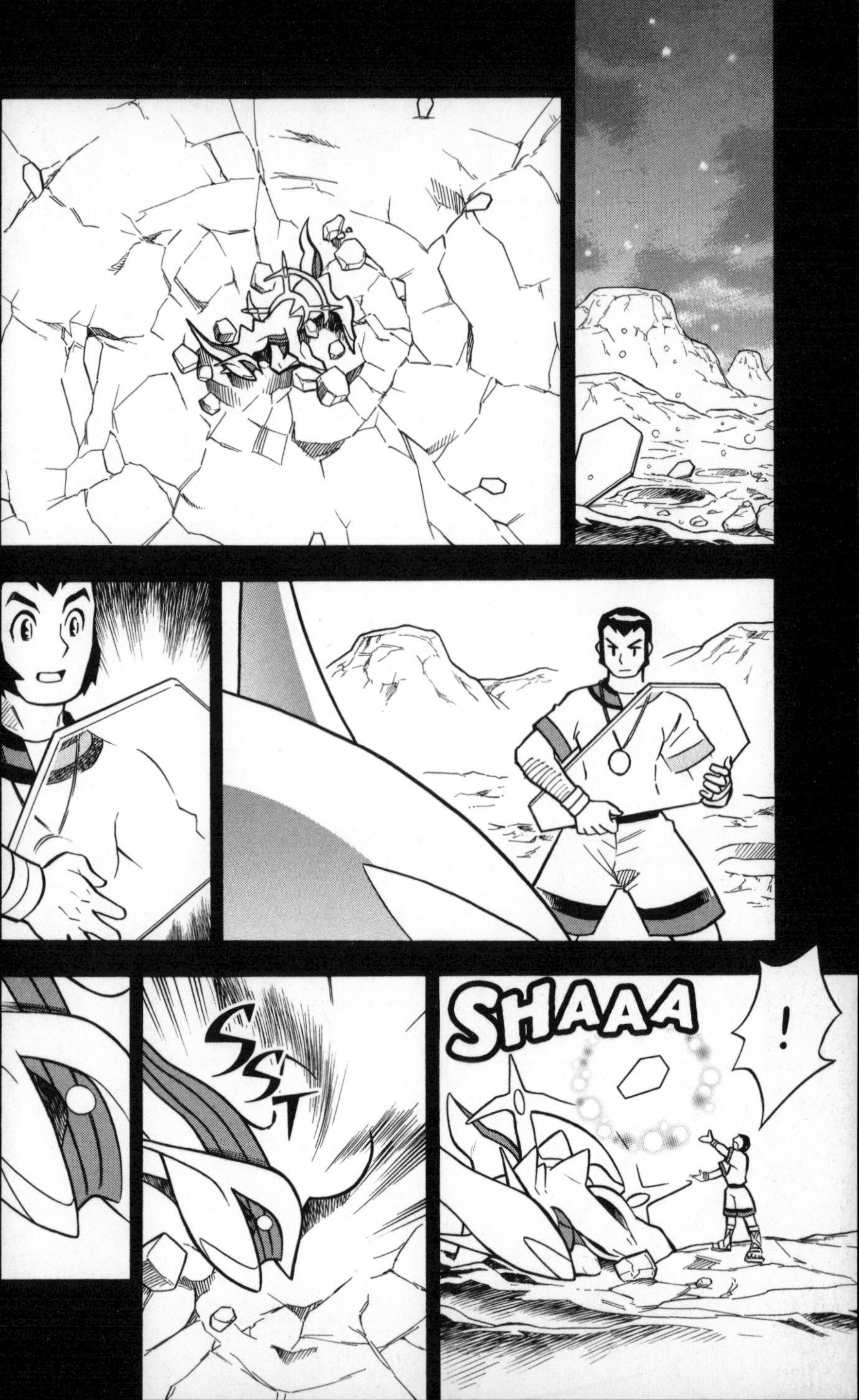
!
SHAAA
SST

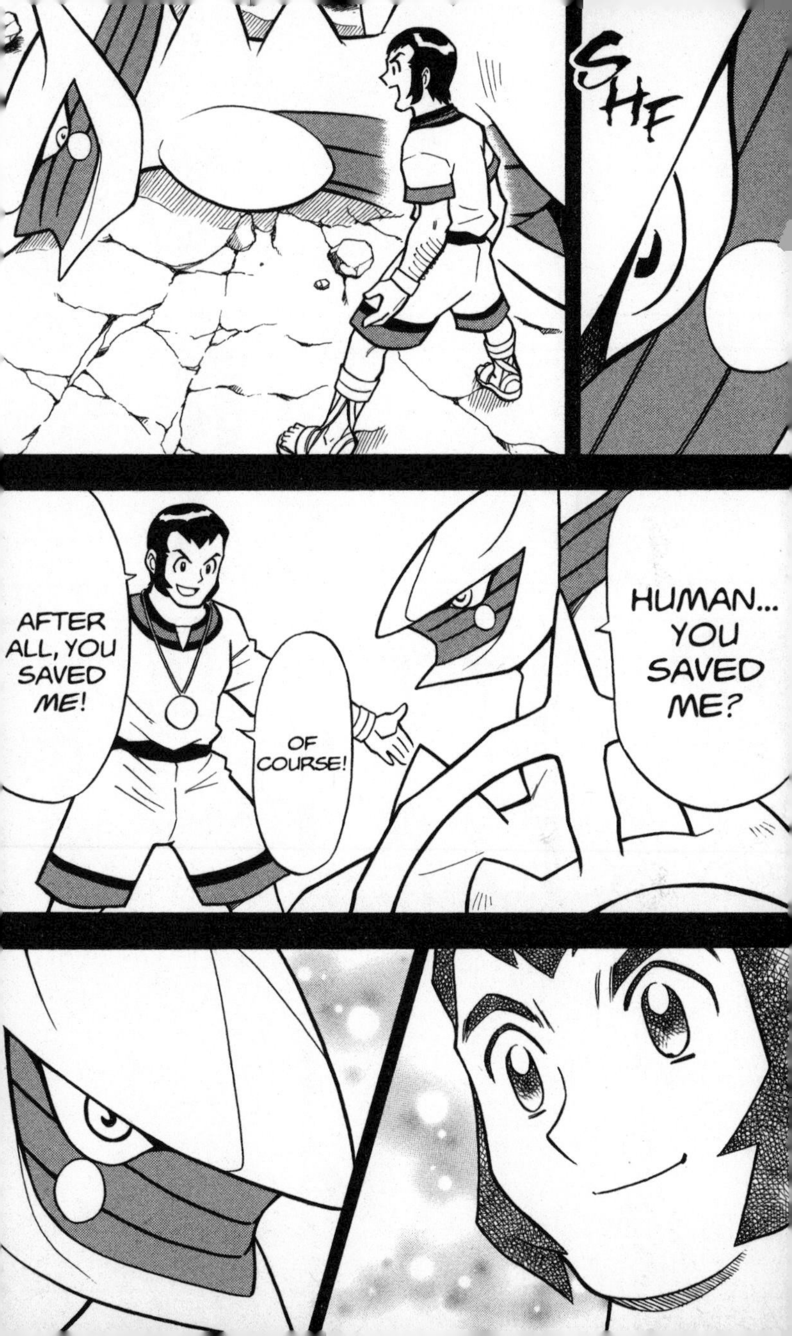
SHF
HUMAN... YOU SAVED ME?
OF COURSE!
AFTER ALL, YOU SAVED ME!

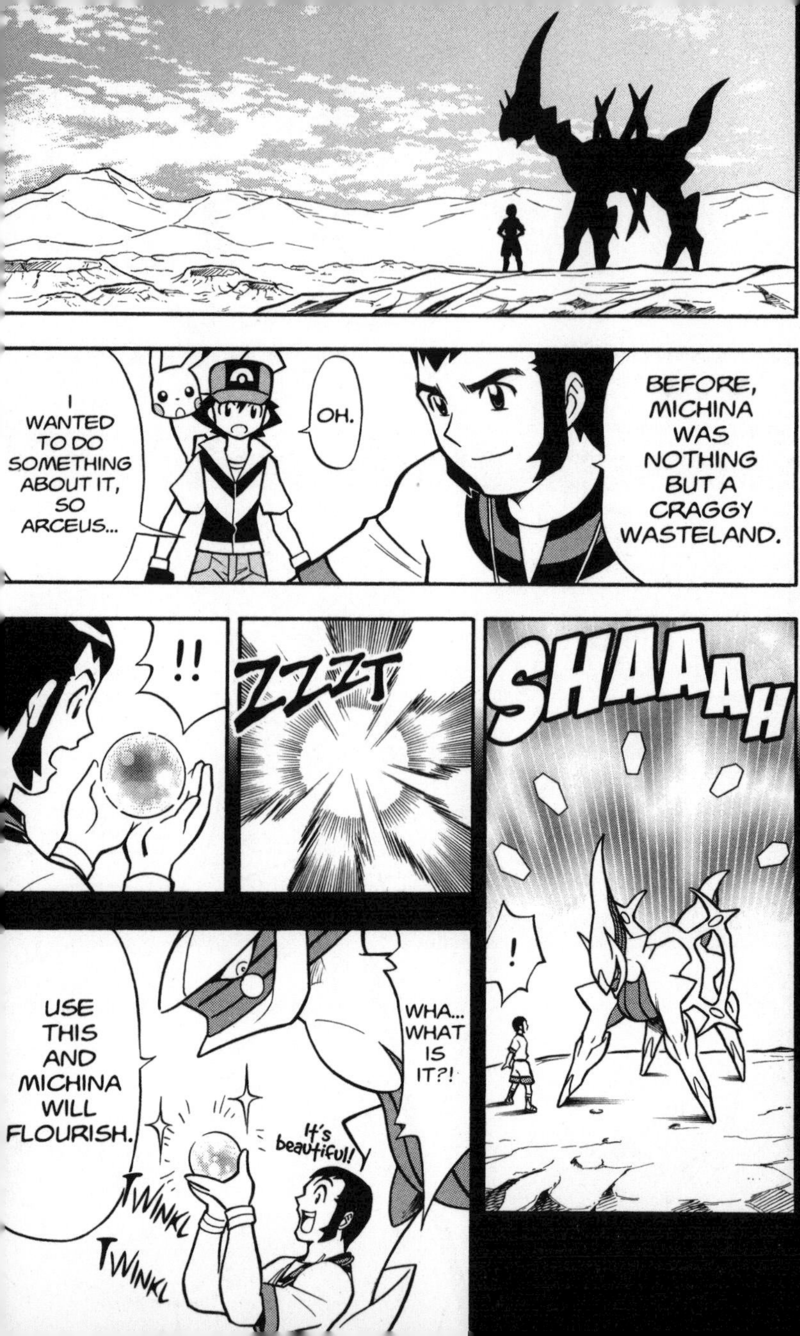
BEFORE, MICHINA WAS NOTHING BUT A CRAGGY WASTELAND.
OH.
I WANTED TO DO SOMETHING ABOUT IT, SO ARCEUS...
SHAAAAH
!
ZZZT
!!
WHA... WHAT IS IT?!
USE THIS AND MICHINA WILL FLOURISH.
It's beautiful!
TWINKL
TWINKL

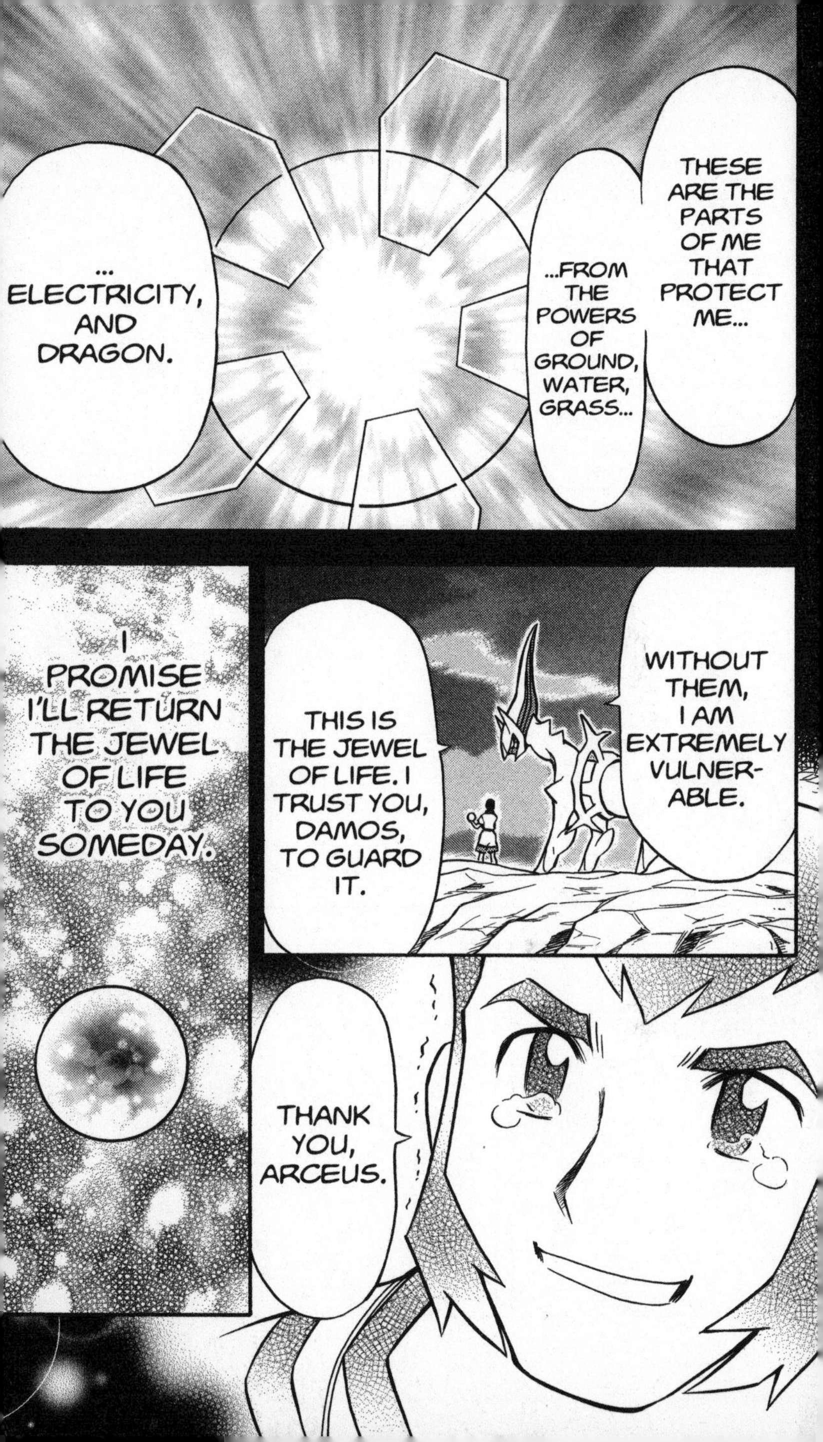
THESE ARE THE PARTS OF ME THAT PROTECT ME...
...FROM THE POWERS OF GROUND, WATER, GRASS...
...ELECTRICITY, AND DRAGON.
WITHOUT THEM, I AM EXTREMELY VULNER-ABLE.
THIS IS THE JEWEL OF LIFE. I TRUST YOU, DAMOS, TO GUARD IT.
THANK YOU, ARCEUS.
I PROMISE I'LL RETURN THE JEWEL OF LIFE TO YOU SOMEDAY.

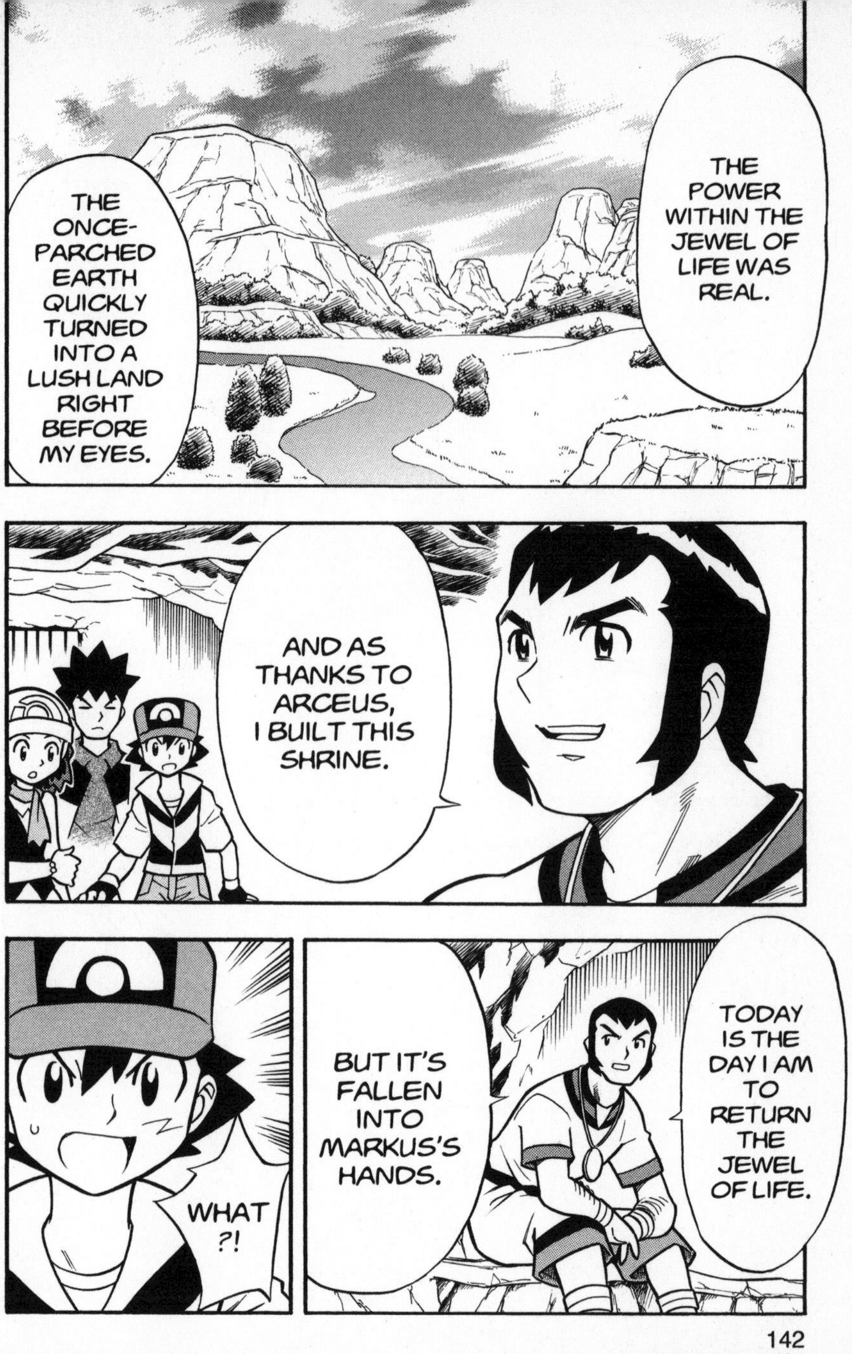
THE POWER WITHIN THE JEWEL OF LIFE WAS REAL.
THE ONCE-PARCHED EARTH QUICKLY TURNED INTO A LUSH LAND RIGHT BEFORE MY EYES.
AND AS THANKS TO ARCEUS, I BUILT THIS SHRINE.
TODAY IS THE DAY I AM TO RETURN THE JEWEL OF LIFE.
BUT IT'S FALLEN INTO MARKUS'S HANDS.
WHAT?!

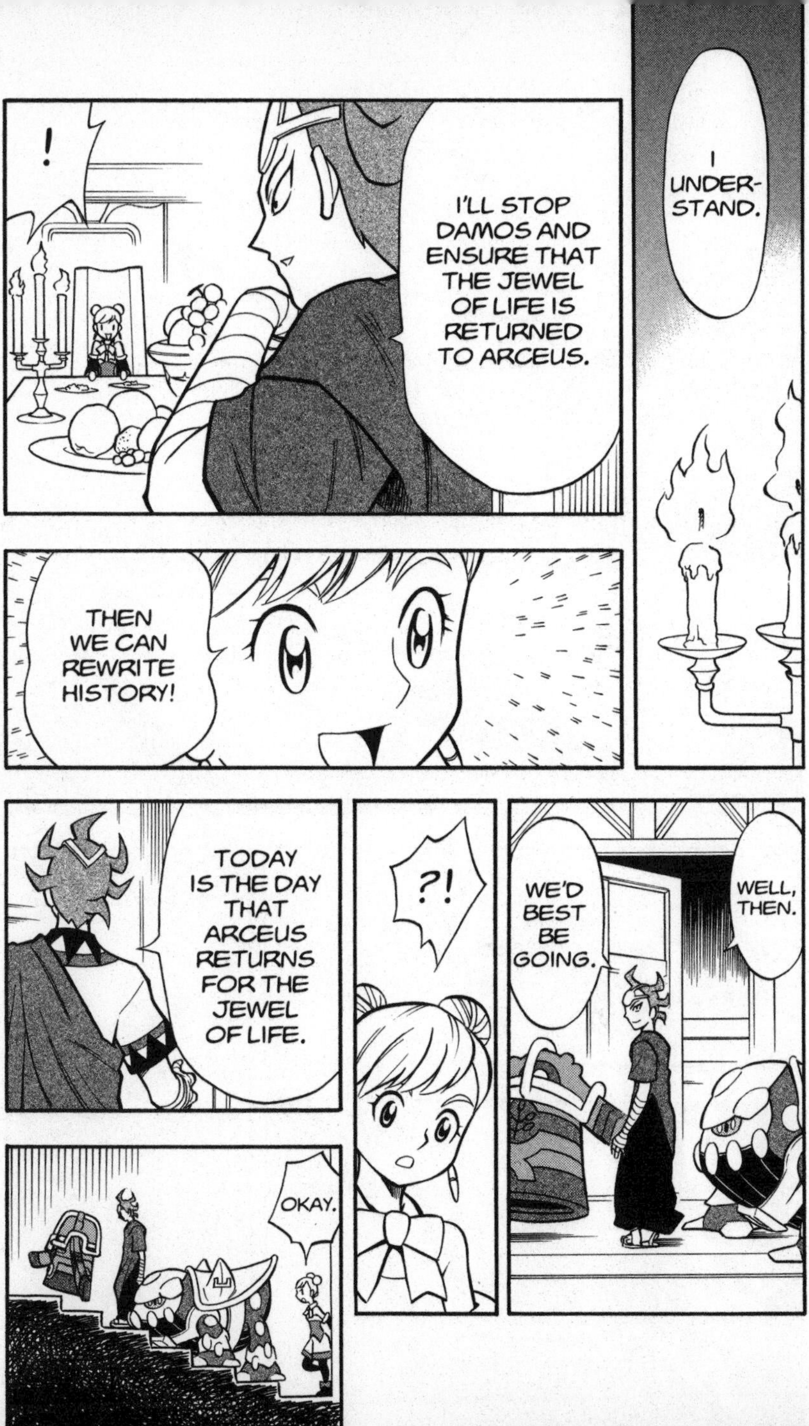
I UNDERSTAND.
!
I'LL STOP DAMOS AND ENSURE THAT THE JEWEL OF LIFE IS RETURNED TO ARCEUS.
THEN WE CAN REWRITE HISTORY!
WELL, THEN.
WE'D BEST BE GOING.
?!
TODAY IS THE DAY THAT ARCEUS RETURNS FOR THE JEWEL OF LIFE.
OKAY.

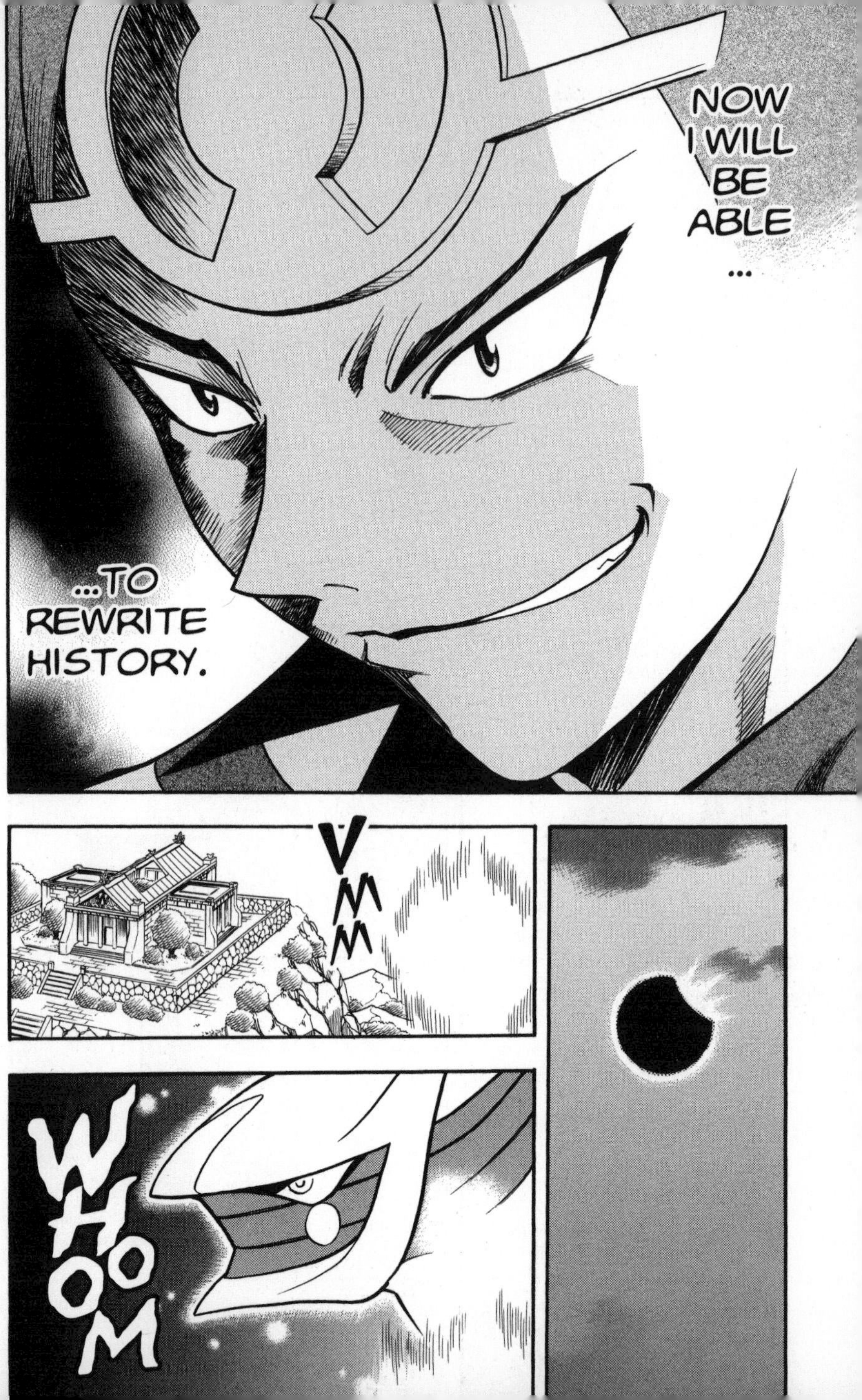
NOW I WILL BE ABLE ...
...TO REWRITE HISTORY.
VMM
WHOOM

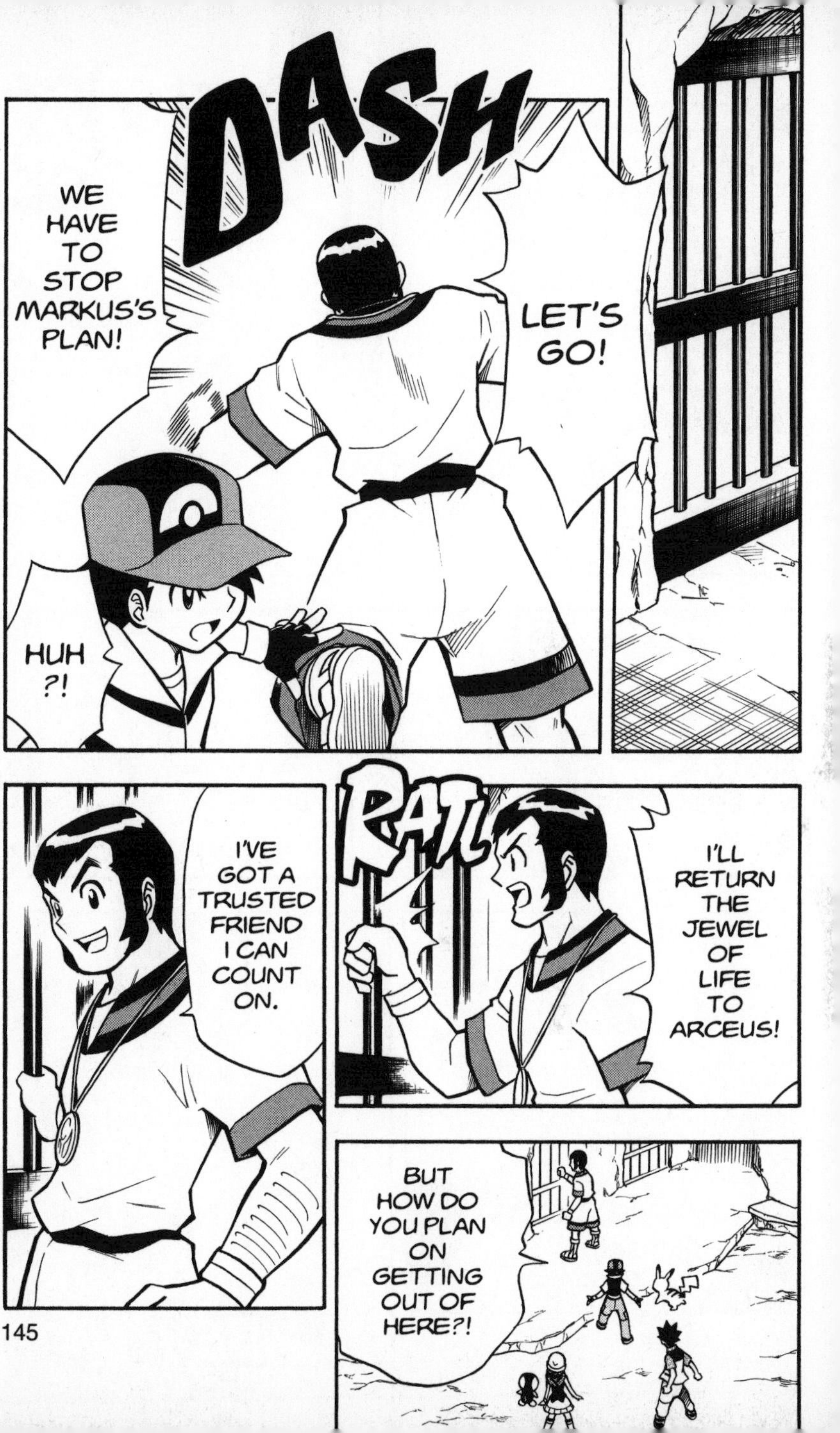
DASH
LET'S GO!
WE HAVE TO STOP MARKUS'S PLAN!
HUH ?!
RATL
I'LL RETURN THE JEWEL OF LIFE TO ARCEUS!
I'VE GOT A TRUSTED FRIEND I CAN COUNT ON.
BUT HOW DO YOU PLAN ON GETTING OUT OF HERE?!

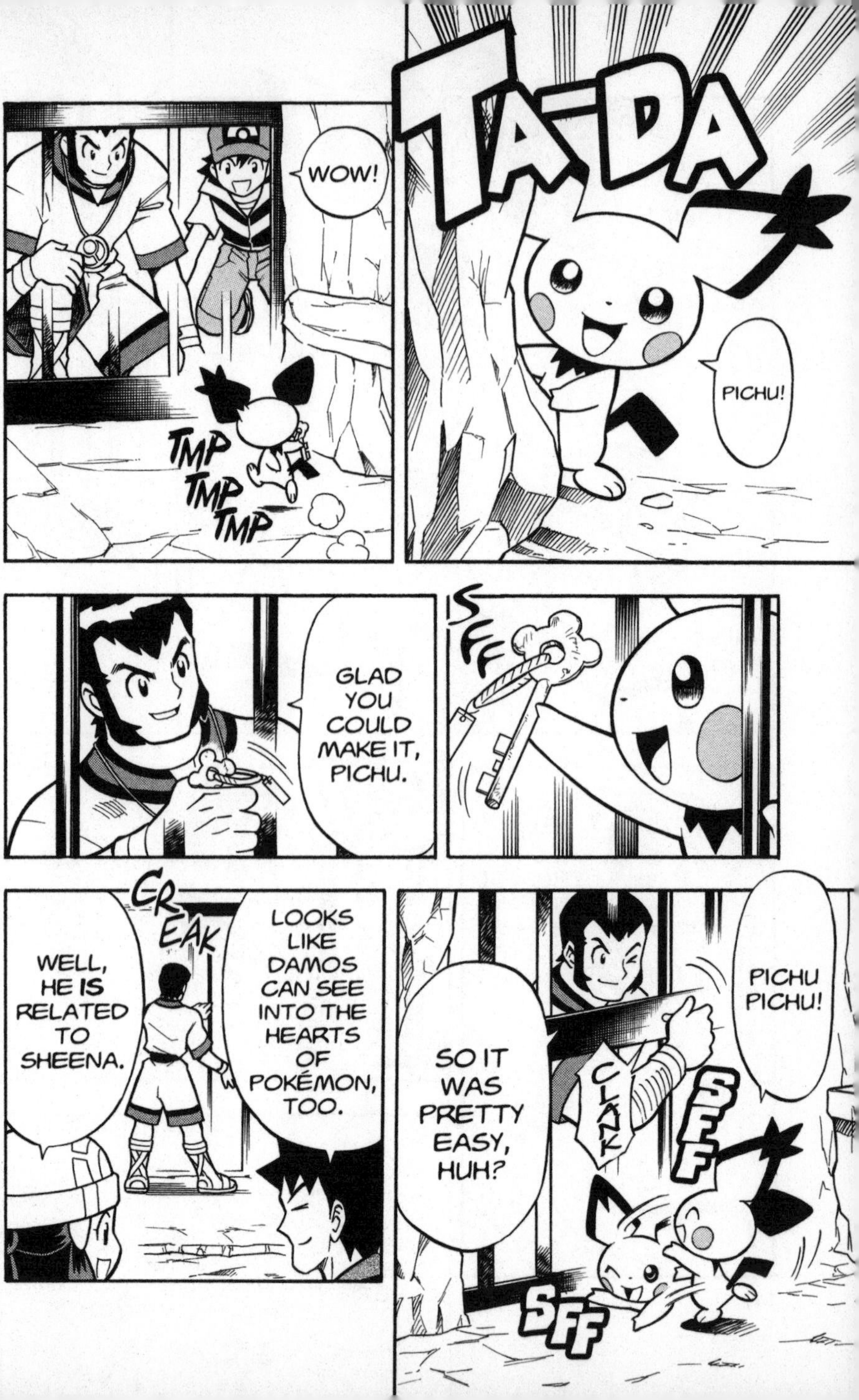
TA-DA
PICHU!
WOW!
TMP TMP TMP
SFF
GLAD YOU COULD MAKE IT, PICHU.
PICHU PICHU!
SO IT WAS PRETTY EASY, HUH?
CLANK
SFF
SFF
LOOKS LIKE DAMOS CAN SEE INTO THE HEARTS OF POKÉMON, TOO.
CREAK
WELL, HE **IS** RELATED TO SHEENA.

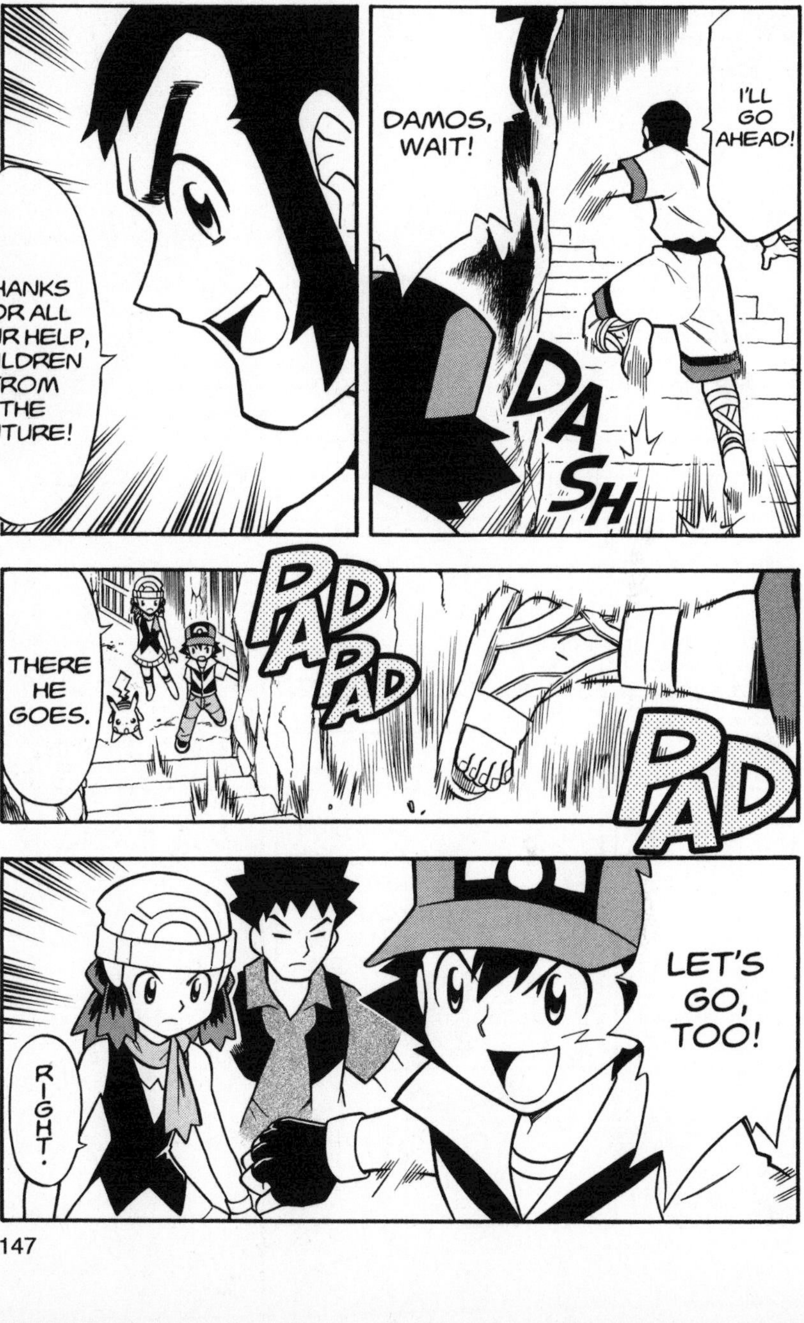
I'LL GO AHEAD!
DAMOS, WAIT!
DASH
THANKS FOR ALL YOUR HELP, CHILDREN FROM THE FUTURE!
PAD
PAPAD
PAD
THERE HE GOES.
LET'S GO, TOO!
RIGHT.

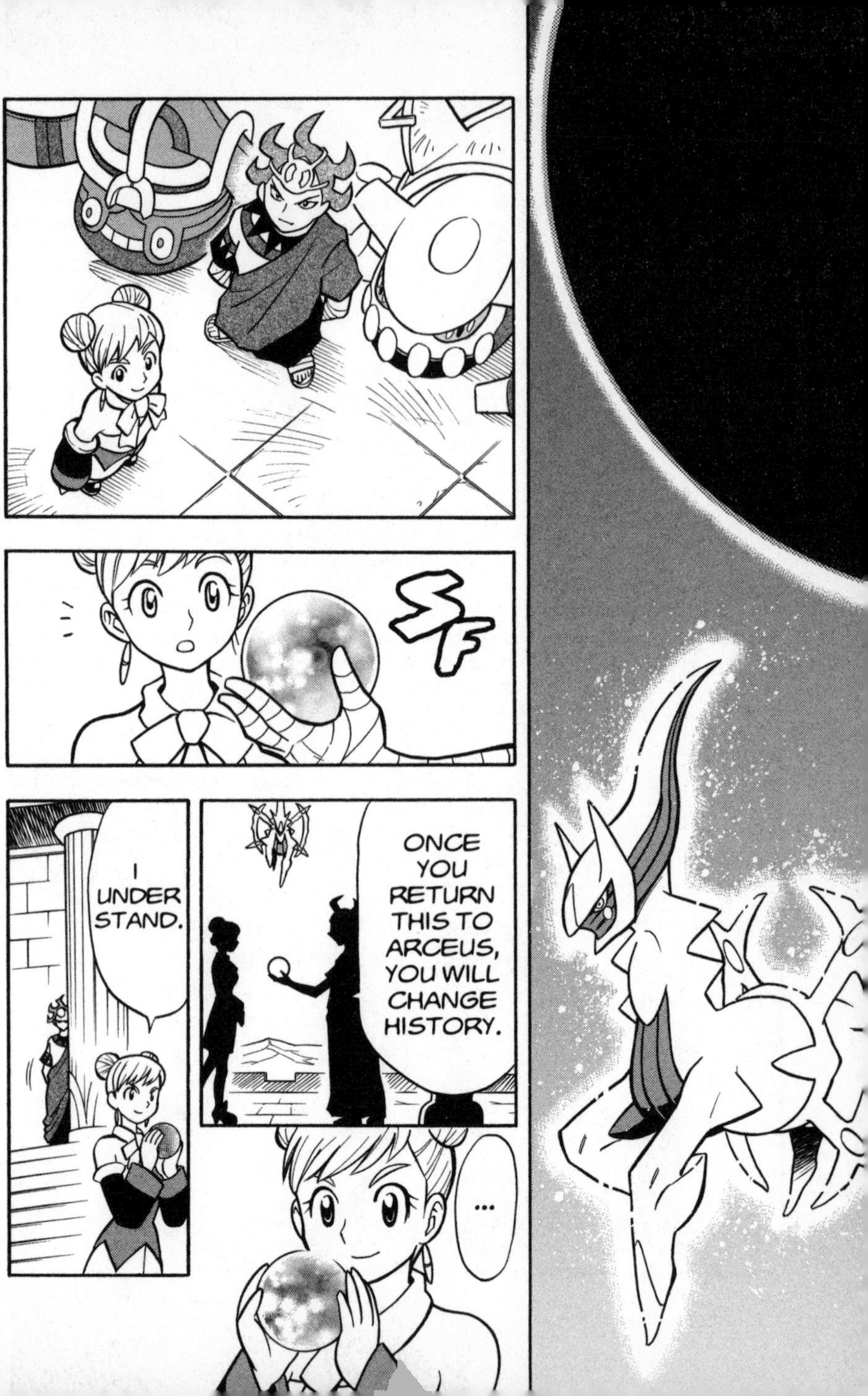
SF
ONCE YOU RETURN THIS TO ARCEUS, YOU WILL CHANGE HISTORY.
I UNDERSTAND.
...

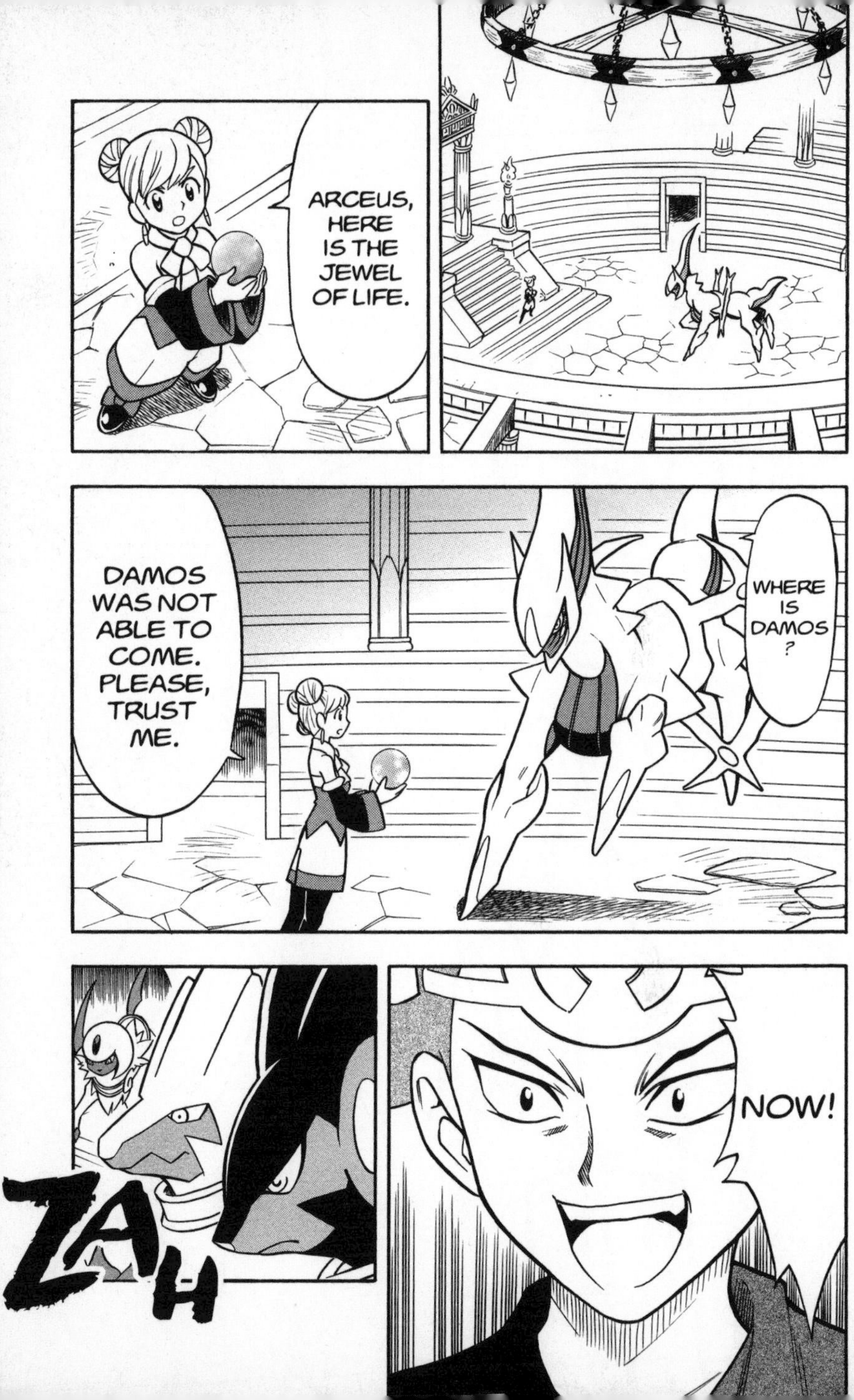
ARCEUS, HERE IS THE JEWEL OF LIFE.
WHERE IS DAMOS?
DAMOS WAS NOT ABLE TO COME. PLEASE, TRUST ME.
NOW!
ZAH

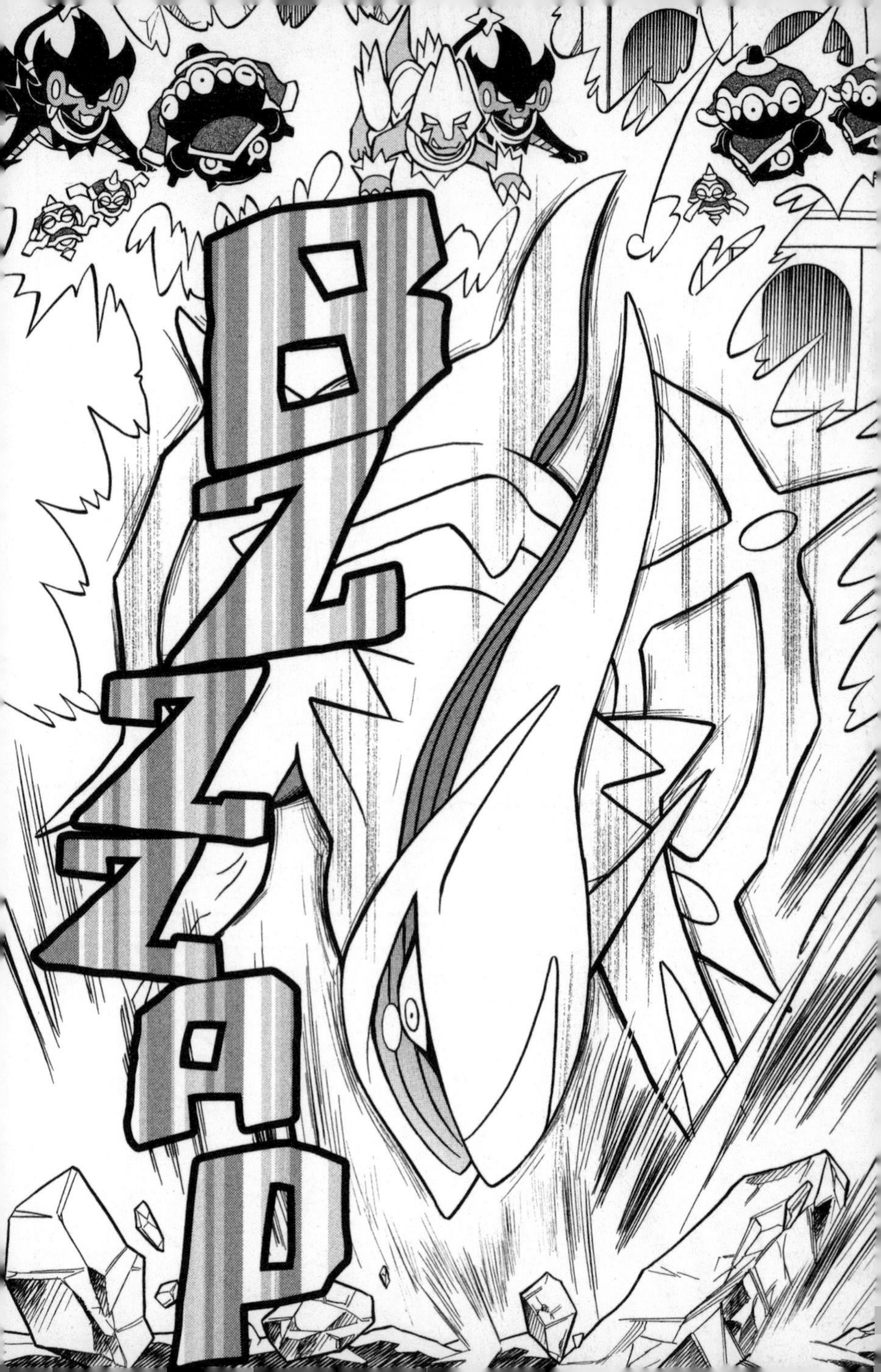
BZZZAP

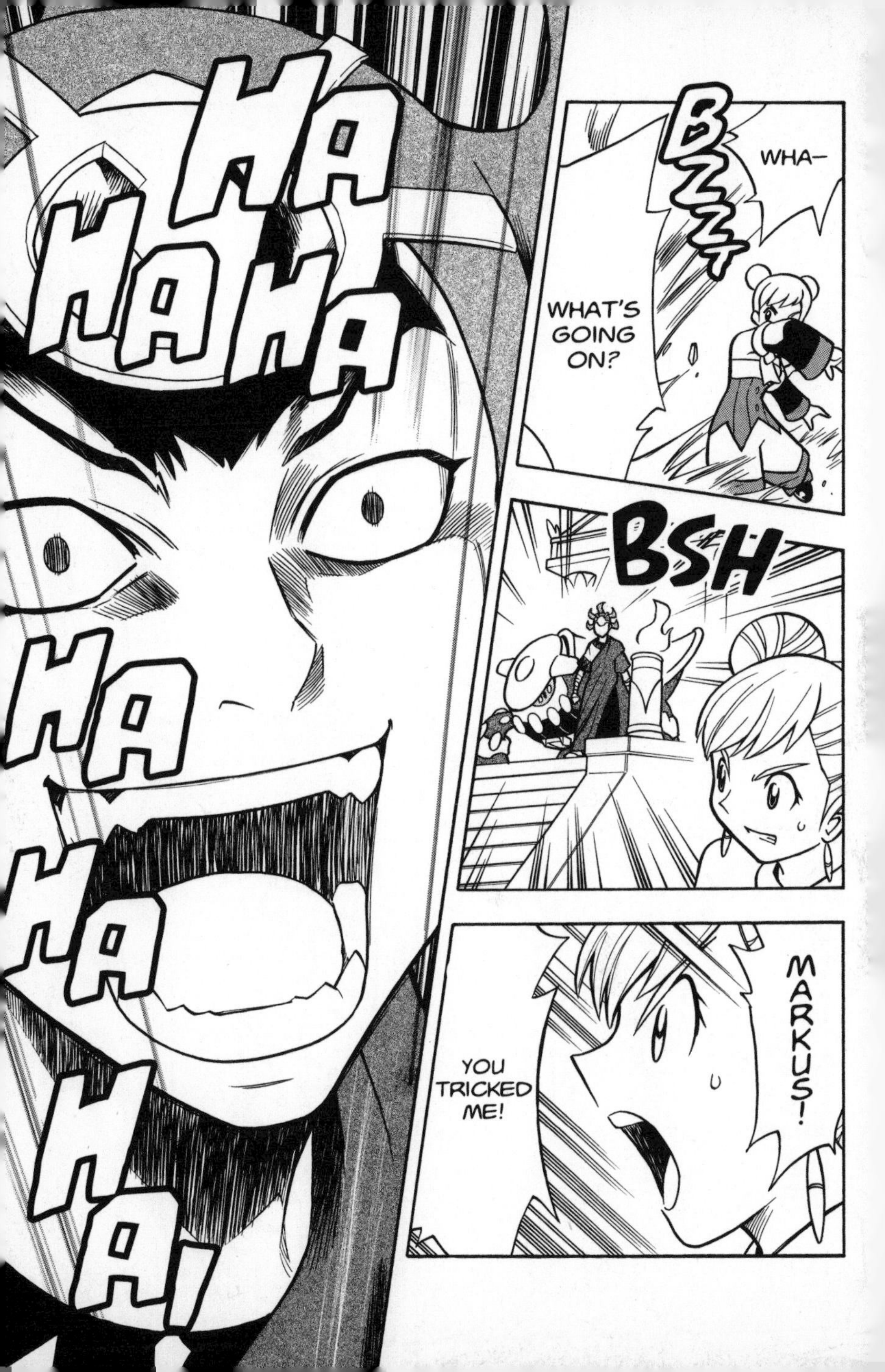
BZZT
WHA—
WHAT'S GOING ON?
BSH
MARKUS!
YOU TRICKED ME!
HA HAHA
HA HA HA HA!

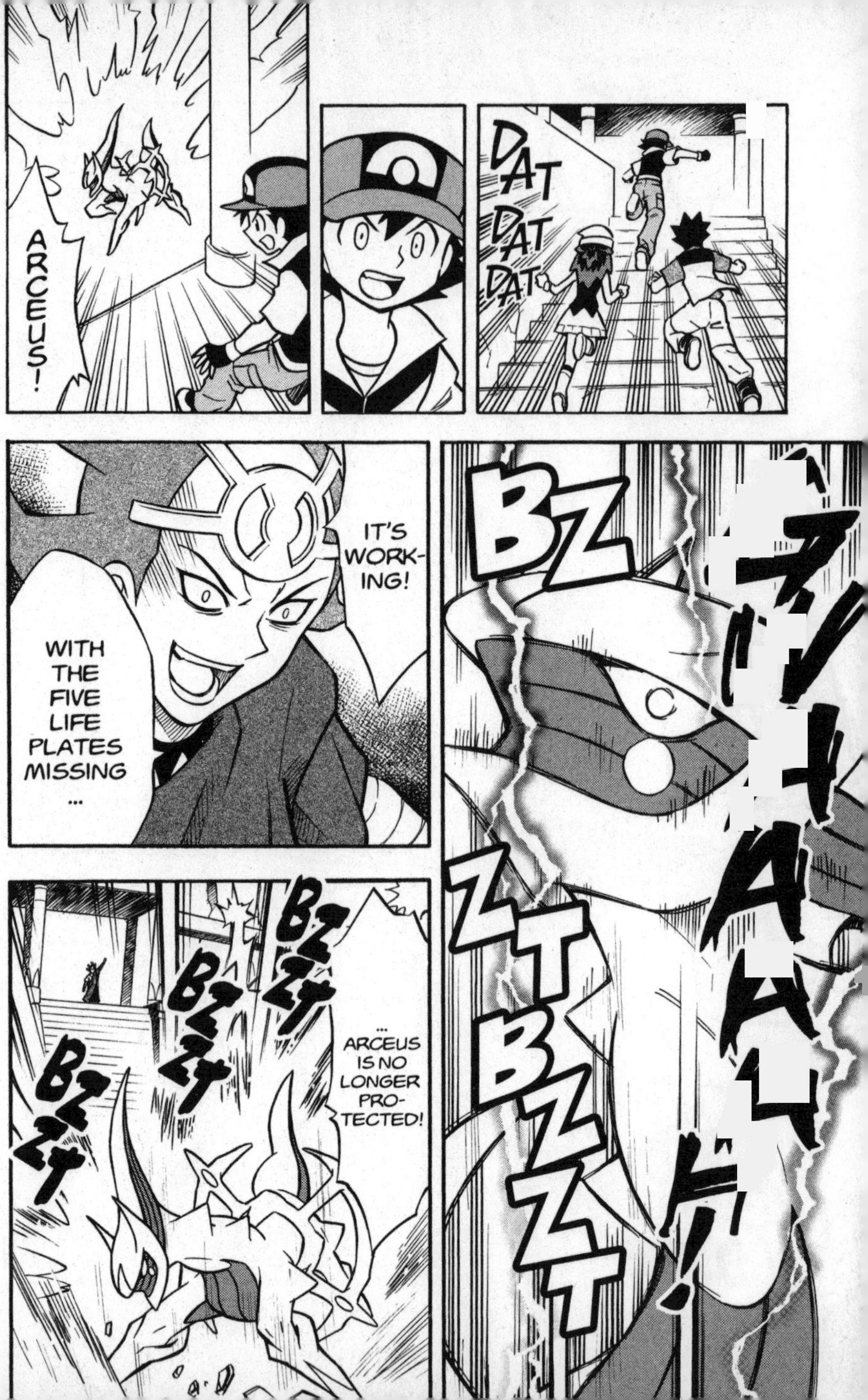
DAT DAT DAT
ARCEUS!
BZZT BZZZT
IT'S WORKING!
WITH THE FIVE LIFE PLATES MISSING...
BZZT BZZT BZZT
...ARCEUS IS NO LONGER PROTECTED!

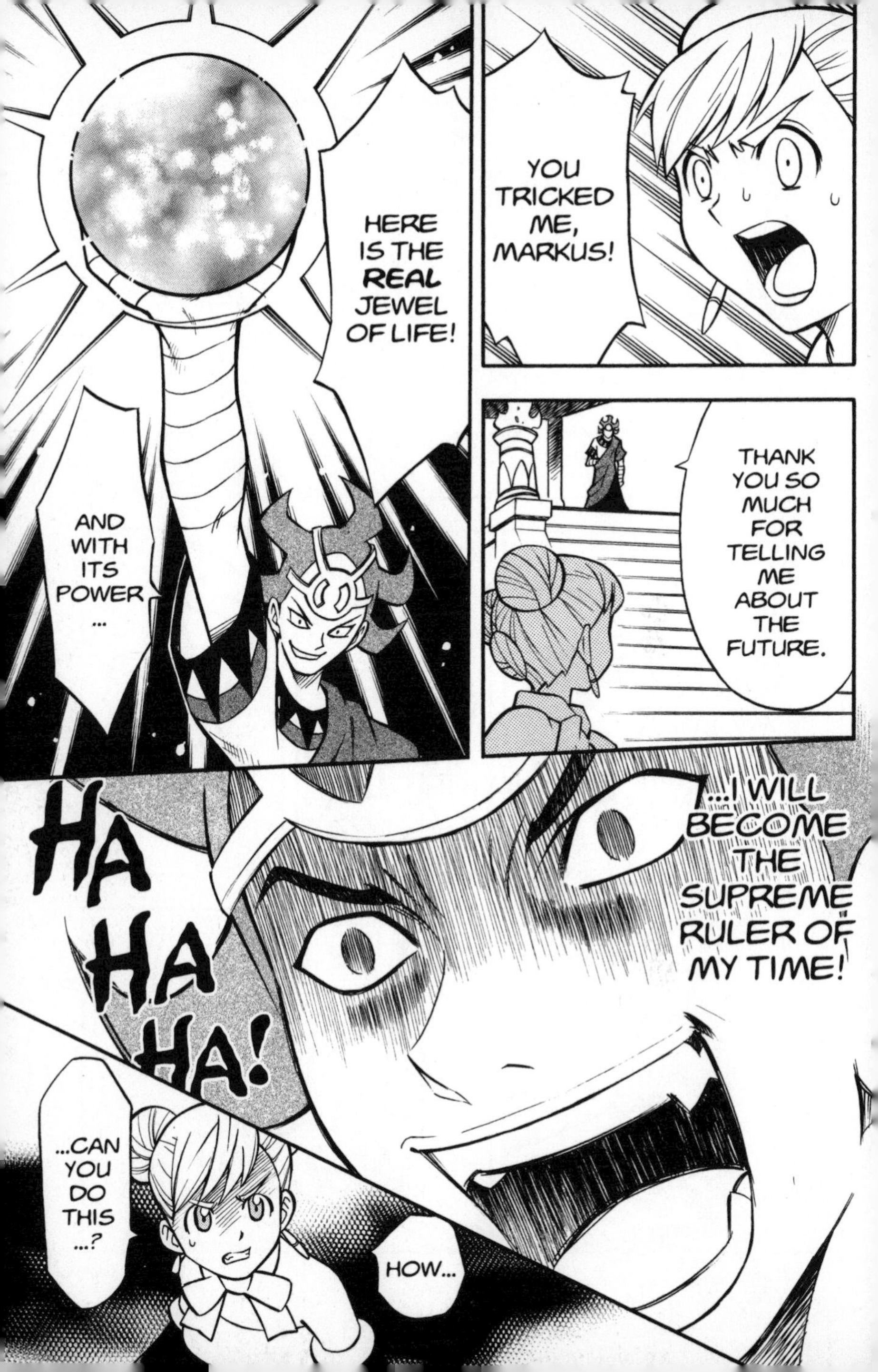
YOU TRICKED ME, MARKUS!
THANK YOU SO MUCH FOR TELLING ME ABOUT THE FUTURE.
HERE IS THE REAL JEWEL OF LIFE!
AND WITH ITS POWER ...
...I WILL BECOME THE SUPREME RULER OF MY TIME!
HA HA HA HA!
HOW...
...CAN YOU DO THIS ...?

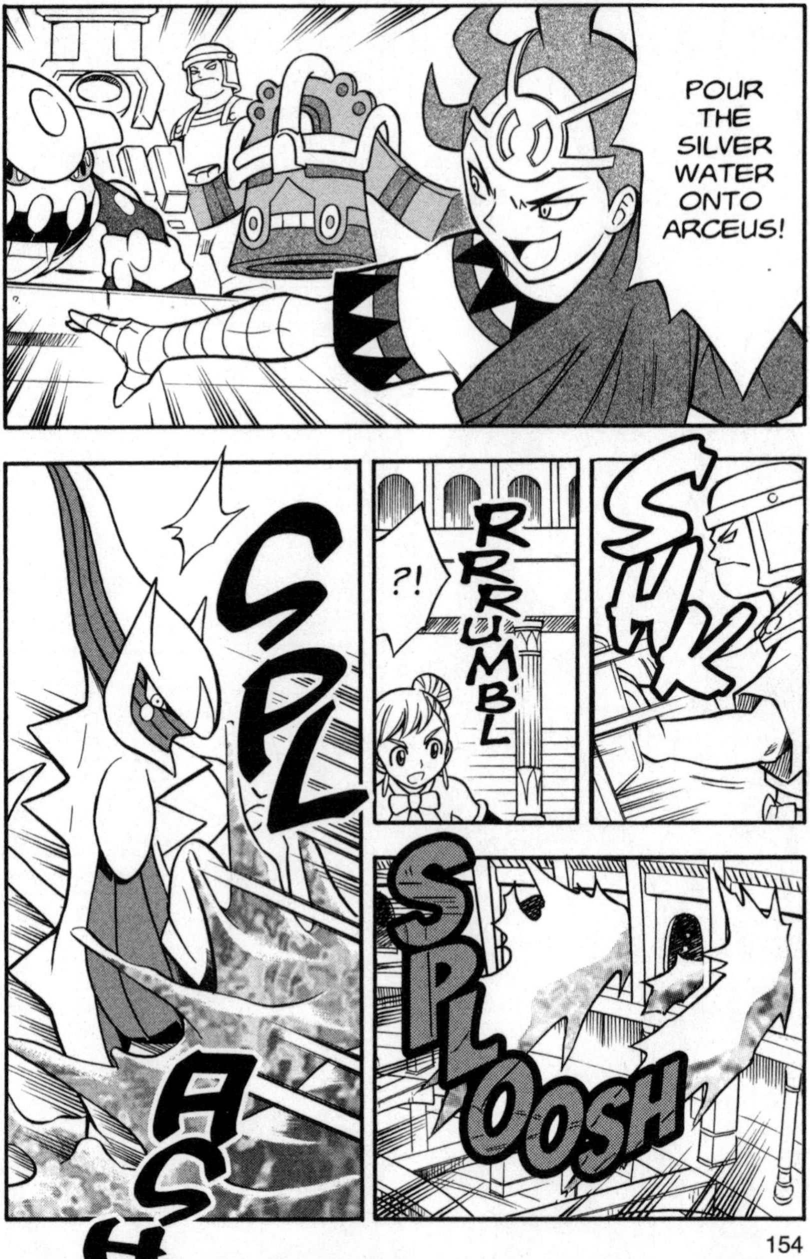
POUR THE SILVER WATER ONTO ARCEUS!
SHUK
?!
RRRUMBL
SPLOOSH
SPLASH

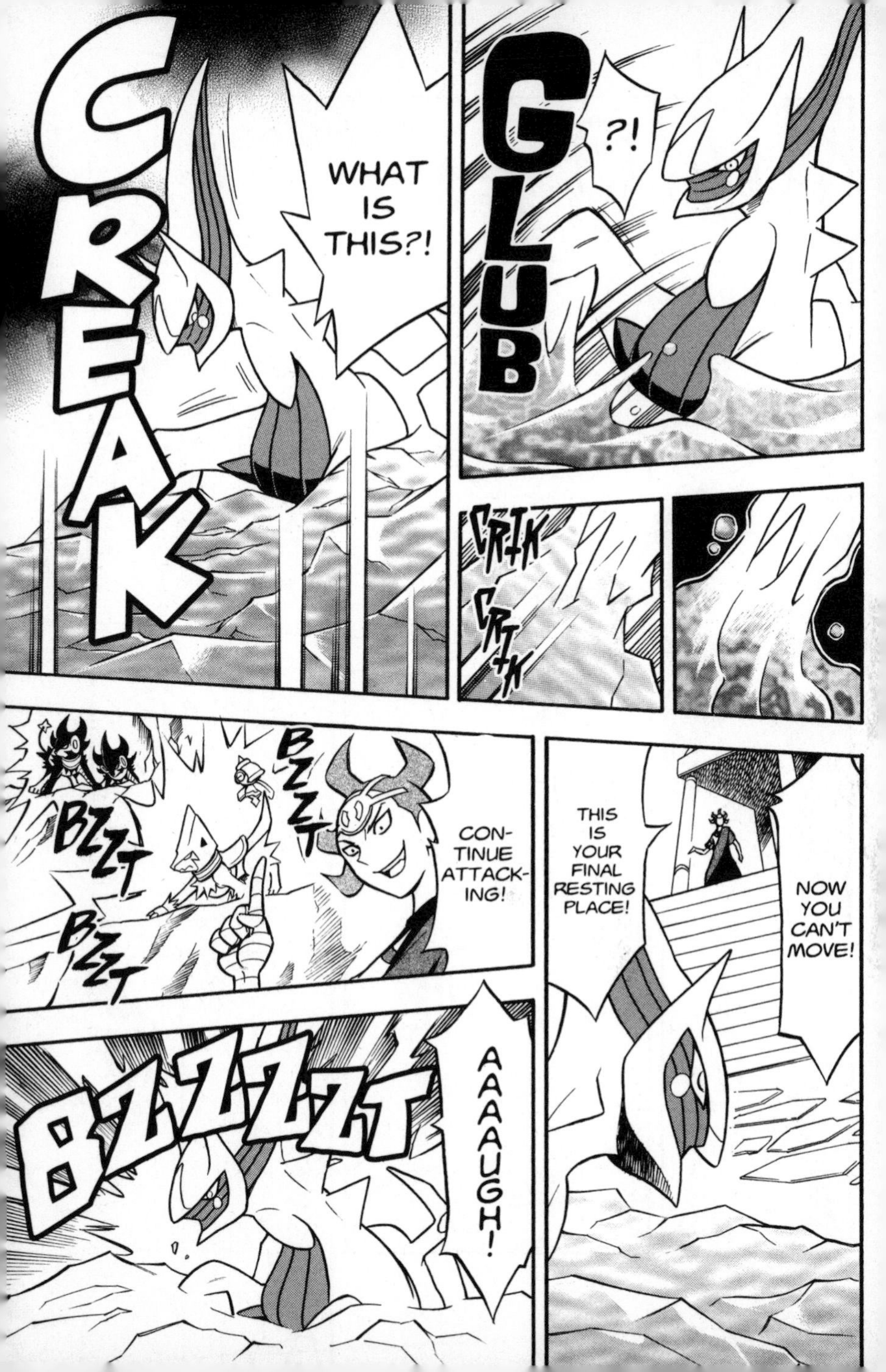
GLUB
?!
CRIK
CRIK
CRIK
CREAK
WHAT IS THIS?!
NOW YOU CAN'T MOVE!
THIS IS YOUR FINAL RESTING PLACE!
BZZT
CONTINUE ATTACKING!
BZZT
BZZT
AAAAUGH!
BZZZZT

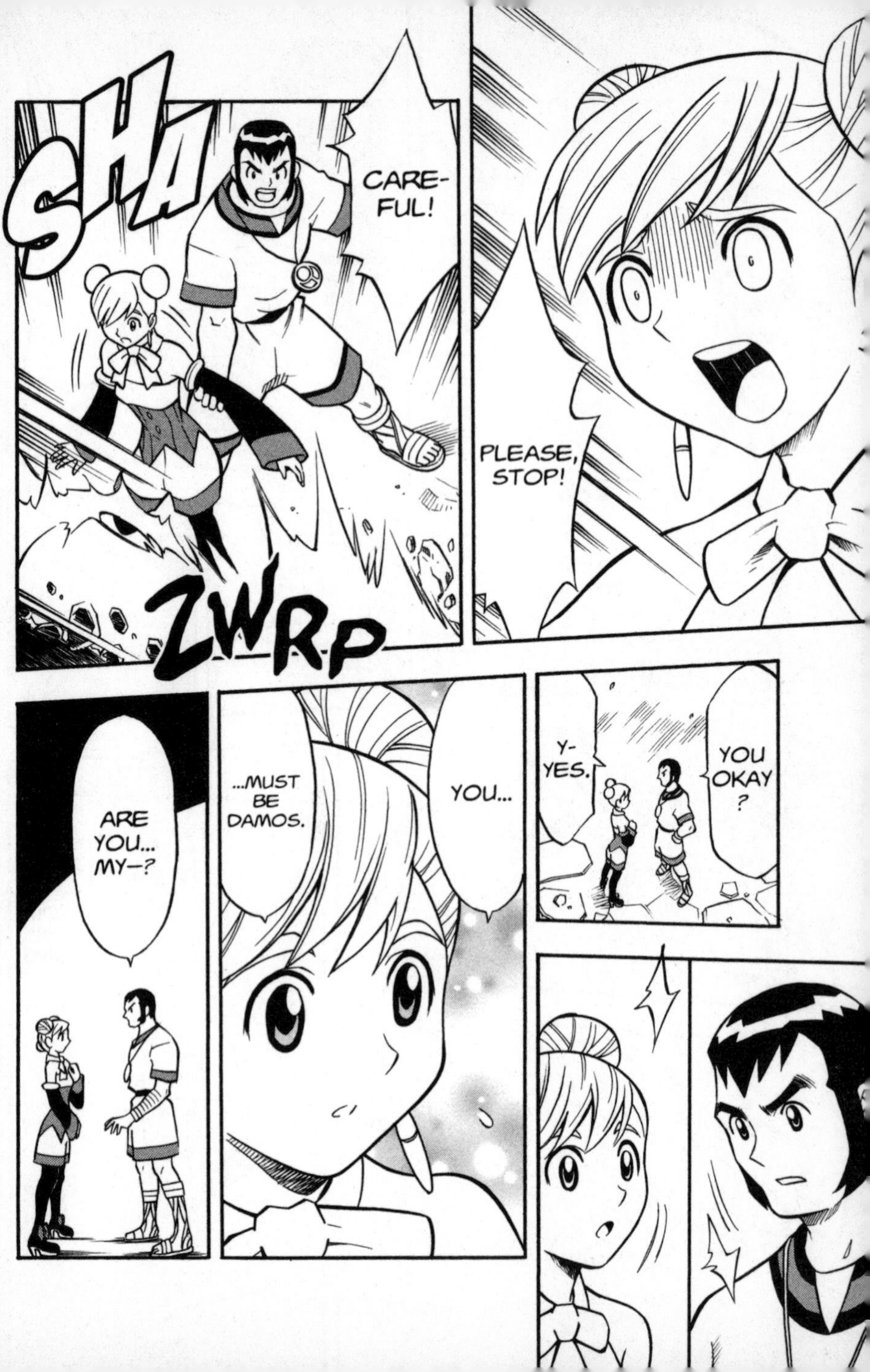
PLEASE, STOP!
CARE-FUL!
SHA
ZWRP
YOU OKAY?
Y-YES.
YOU...
...MUST BE DAMOS.
ARE YOU... MY-?

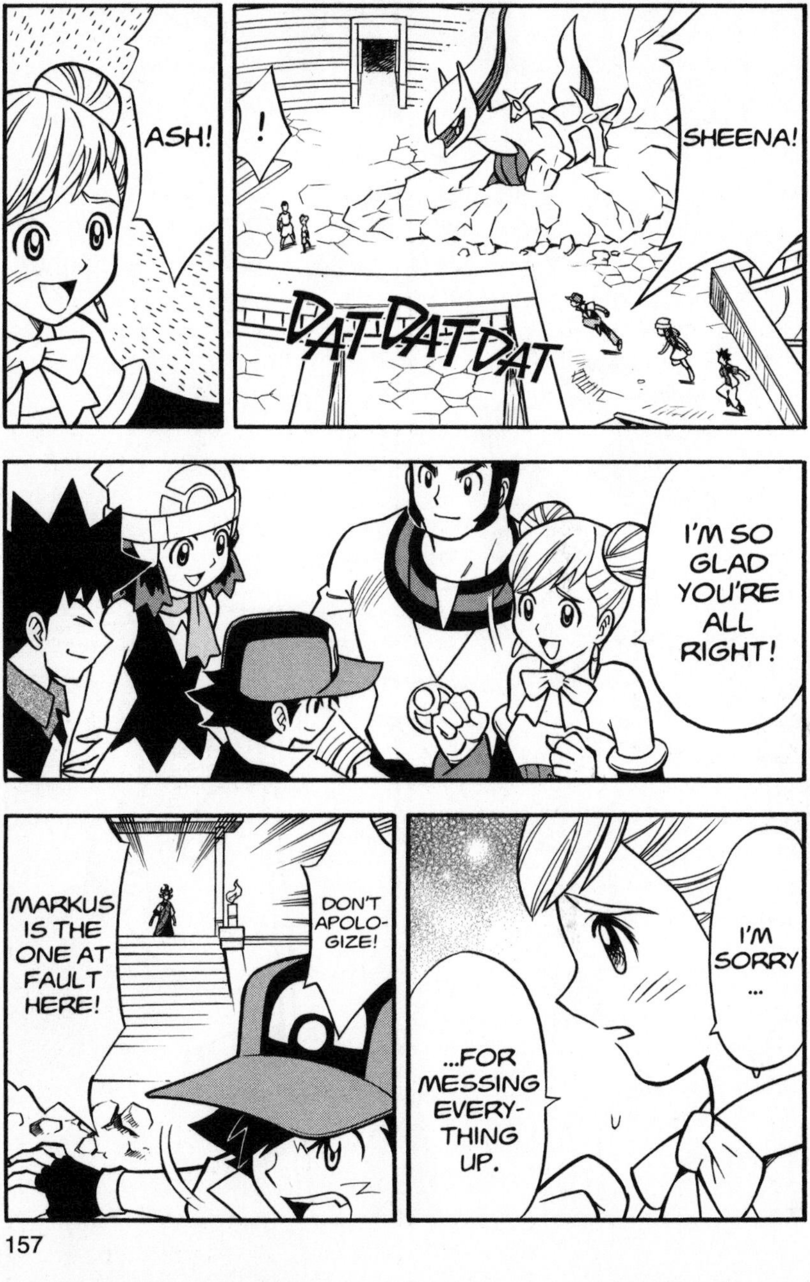
SHEENA!
!
DAT DAT DAT
ASH!
I'M SO GLAD YOU'RE ALL RIGHT!
I'M SORRY...
...FOR MESSING EVERYTHING UP.
DON'T APOLOGIZE!
MARKUS IS THE ONE AT FAULT HERE!

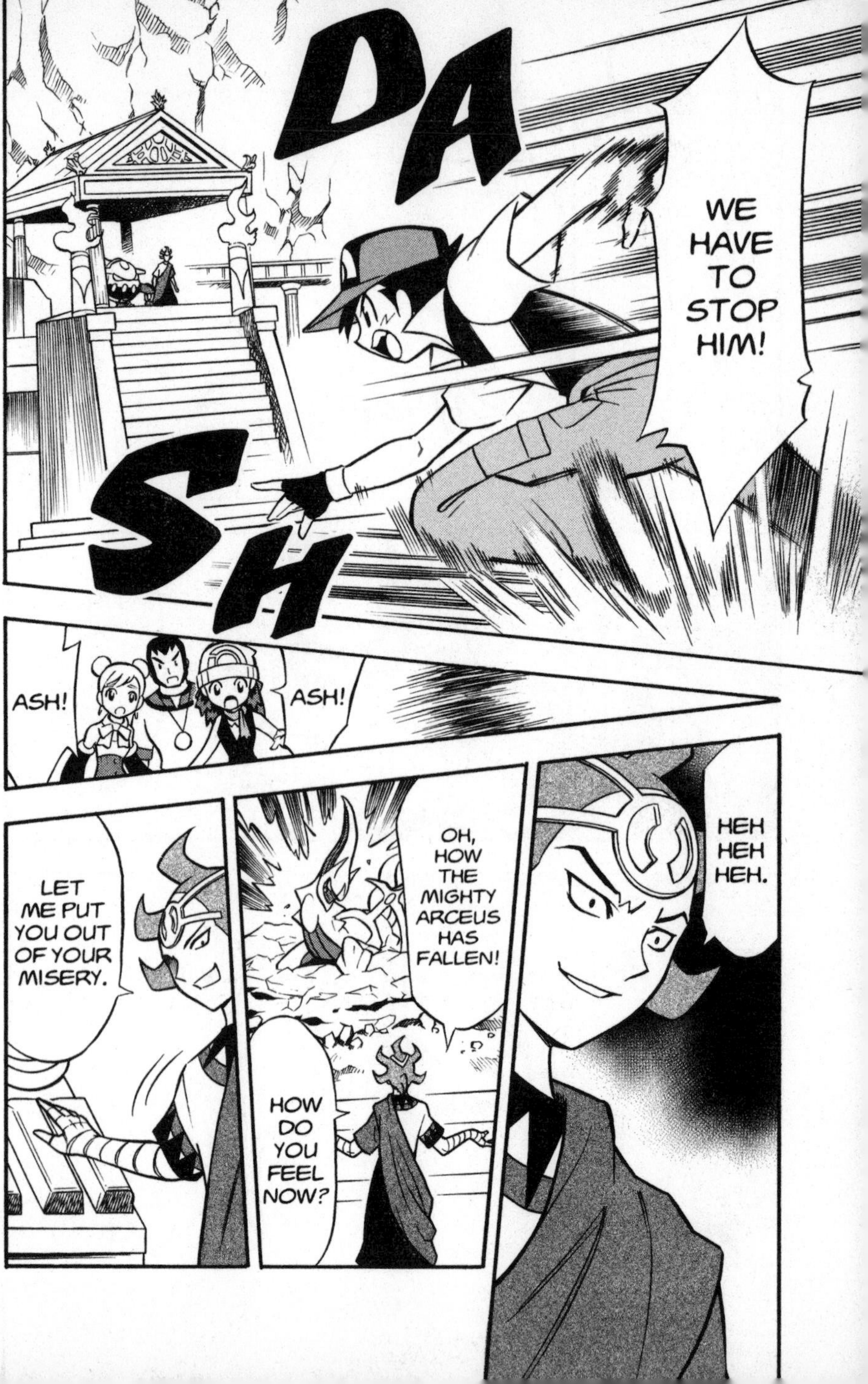
WE HAVE TO STOP HIM!
DA
SH
ASH!
ASH!
HEH HEH HEH.
OH, HOW THE MIGHTY ARCEUS HAS FALLEN!
HOW DO YOU FEEL NOW?
LET ME PUT YOU OUT OF YOUR MISERY.

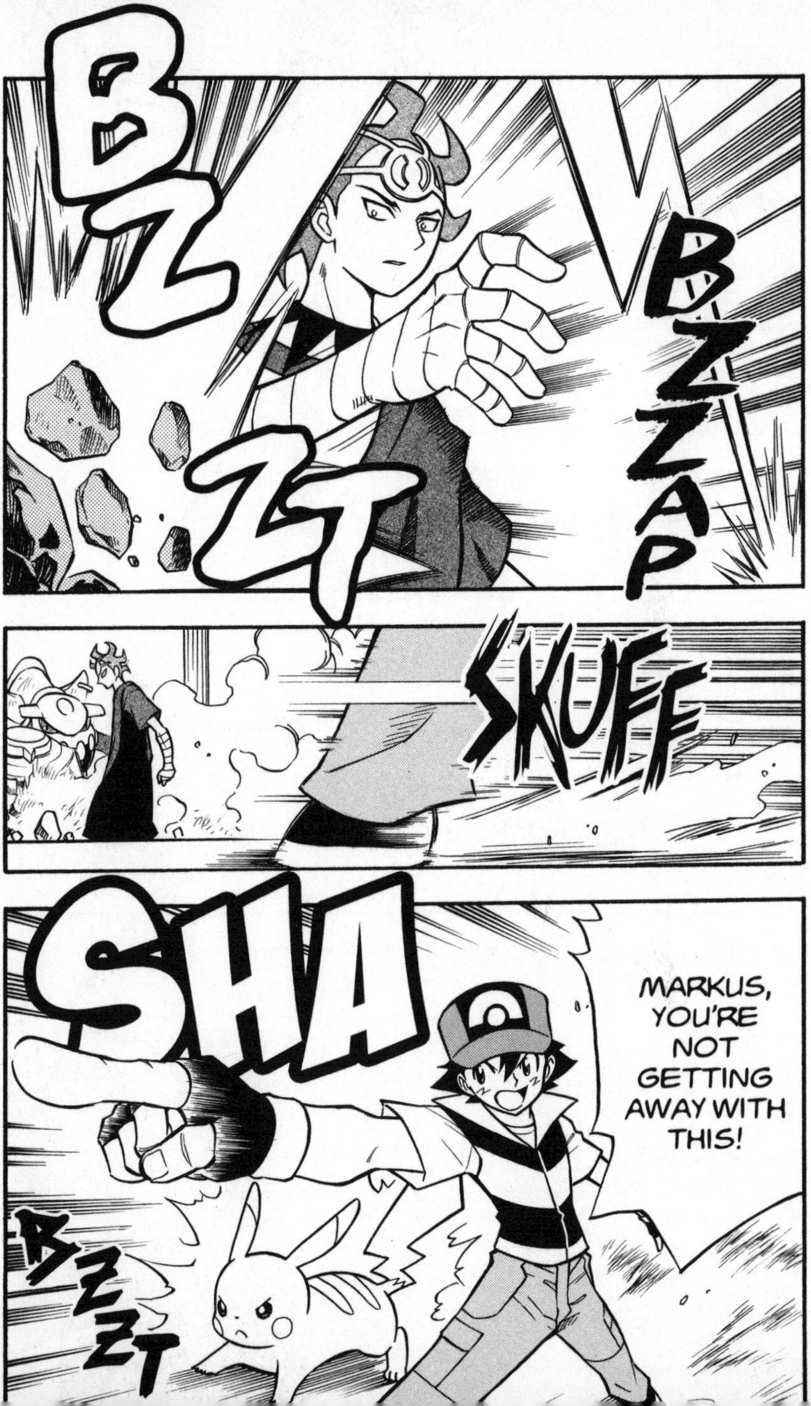
BZZAP
BZZT
SKUFF
MARKUS, YOU'RE NOT GETTING AWAY WITH THIS!
SHA
BZZZT

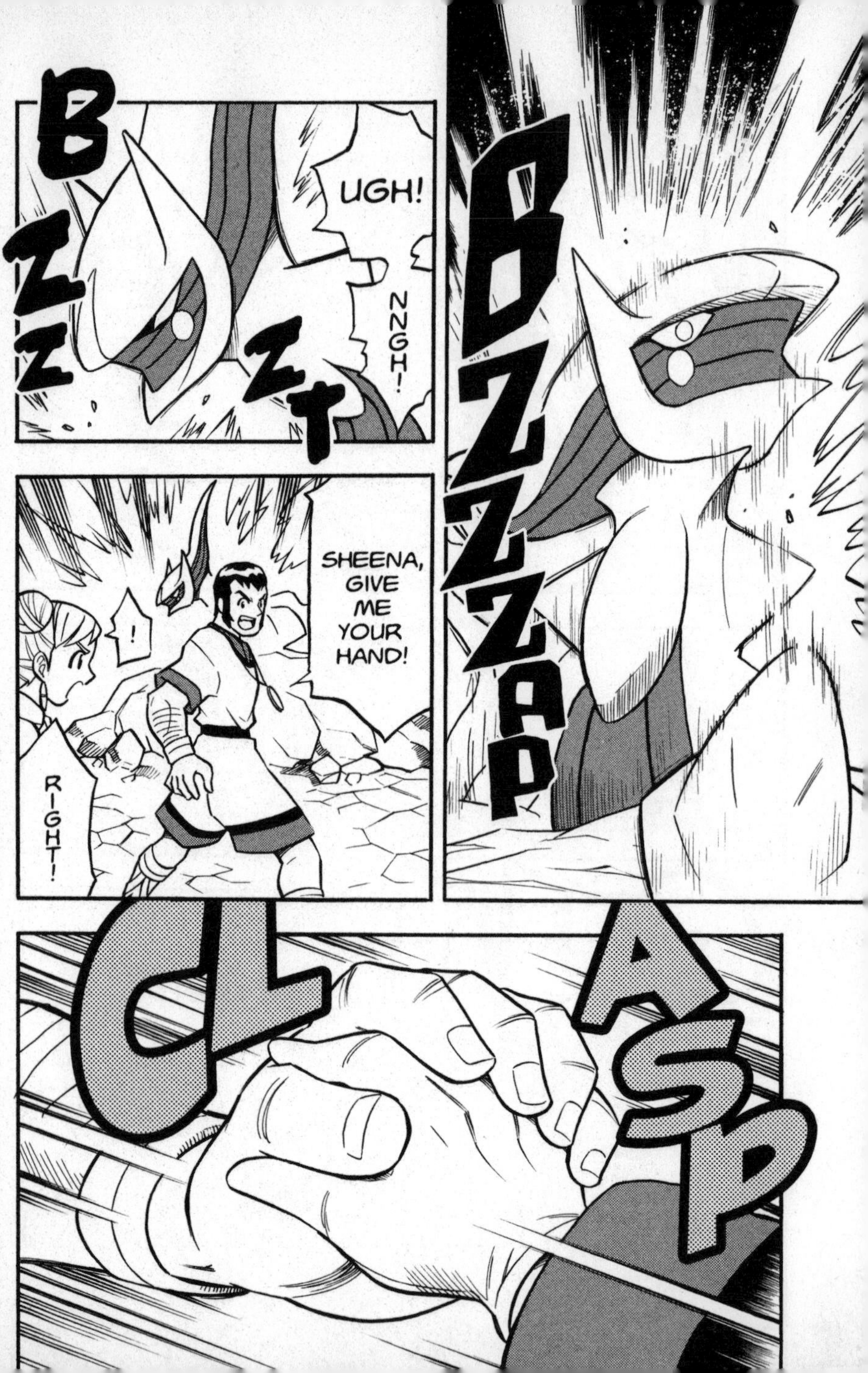
BZZZZAP
UGH!
NNGH!
BZZZT
SHEENA, GIVE ME YOUR HAND!
!
RIGHT!
CLASP

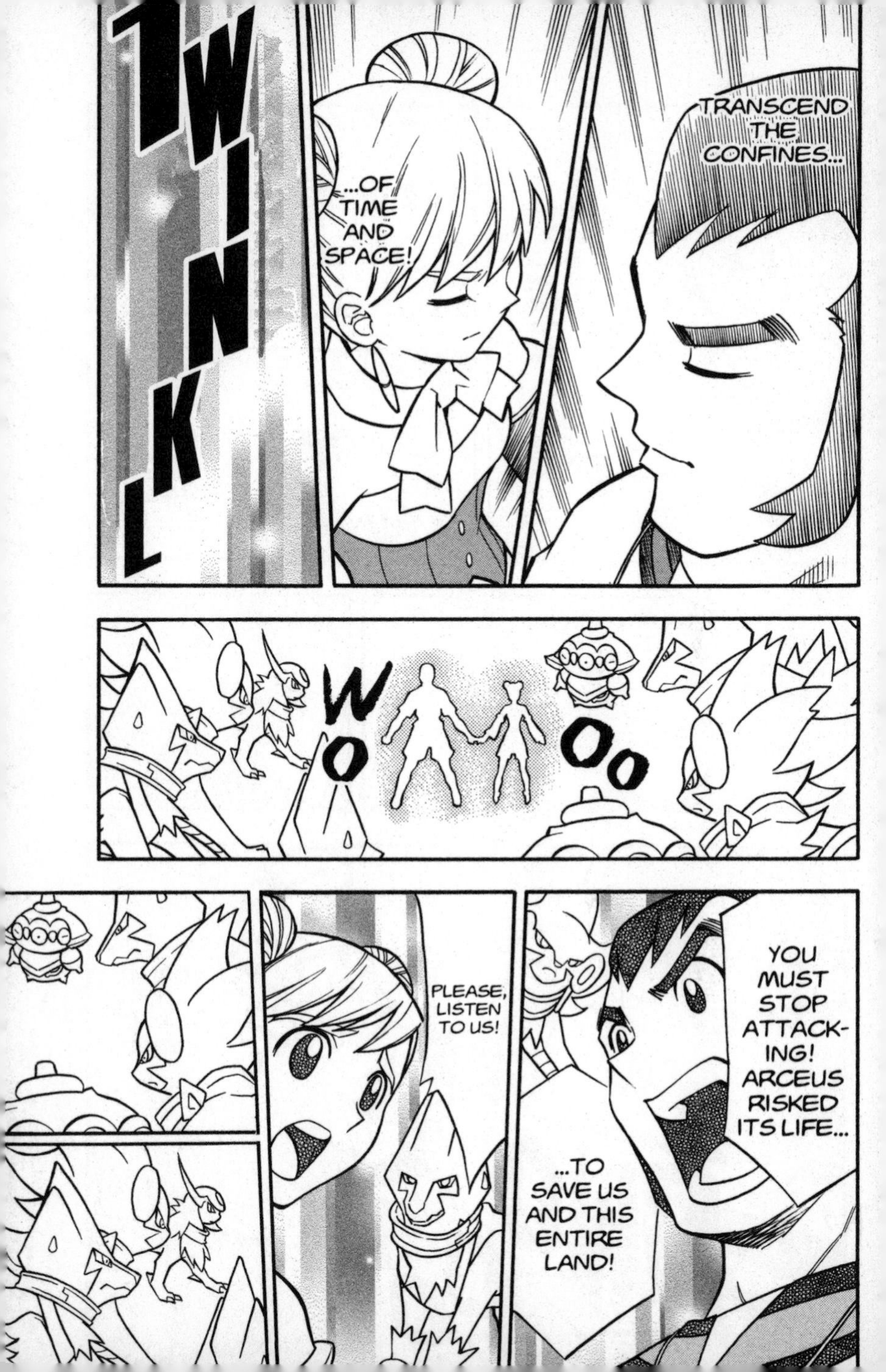
TRANSCEND THE CONFINES...
...OF TIME AND SPACE!
TWINKL
WOOO
YOU MUST STOP ATTACK-ING! ARCEUS RISKED ITS LIFE...
...TO SAVE US AND THIS ENTIRE LAND!
PLEASE, LISTEN TO US!

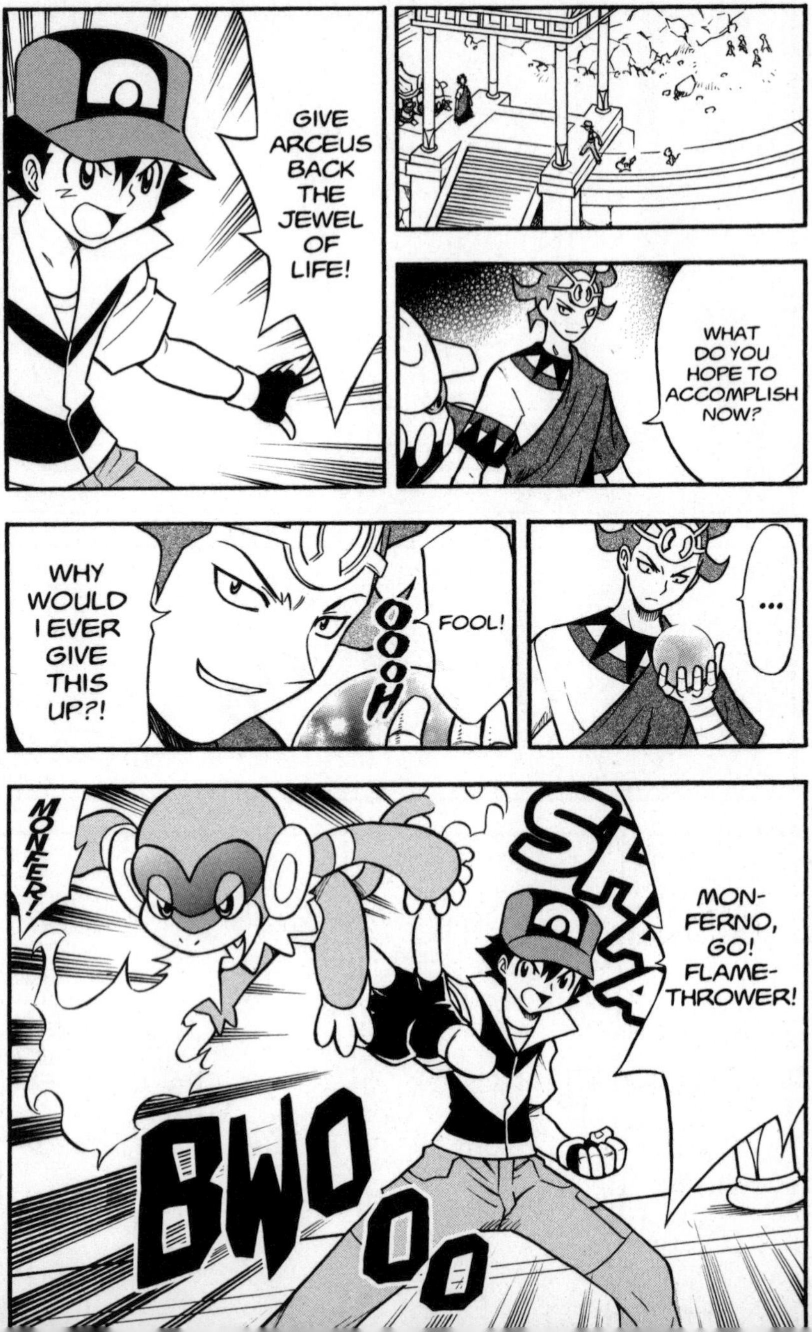
WHAT DO YOU HOPE TO ACCOMPLISH NOW?
GIVE ARCEUS BACK THE JEWEL OF LIFE!
...
FOOL!
OOOH
WHY WOULD I EVER GIVE THIS UP?!
MON-FERNO, GO! FLAME-THROWER!
SHA
MONFER!
BWOOO

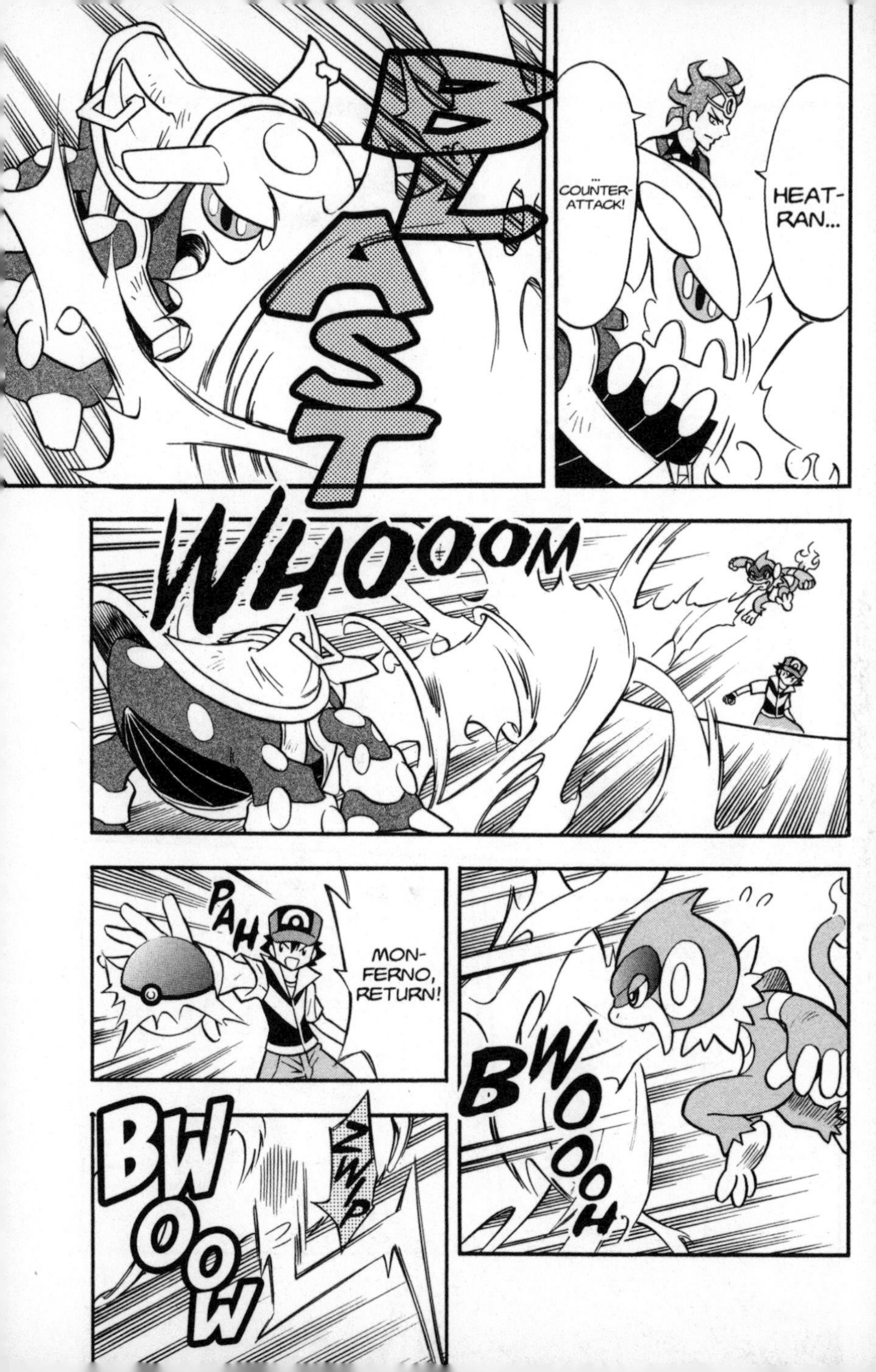
HEAT-RAN...
...COUNTER-ATTACK!
BLAST
WHOOOOM
BWOOOOH
PAH
MON-FERNO, RETURN!
ZWIP
BWOOOW

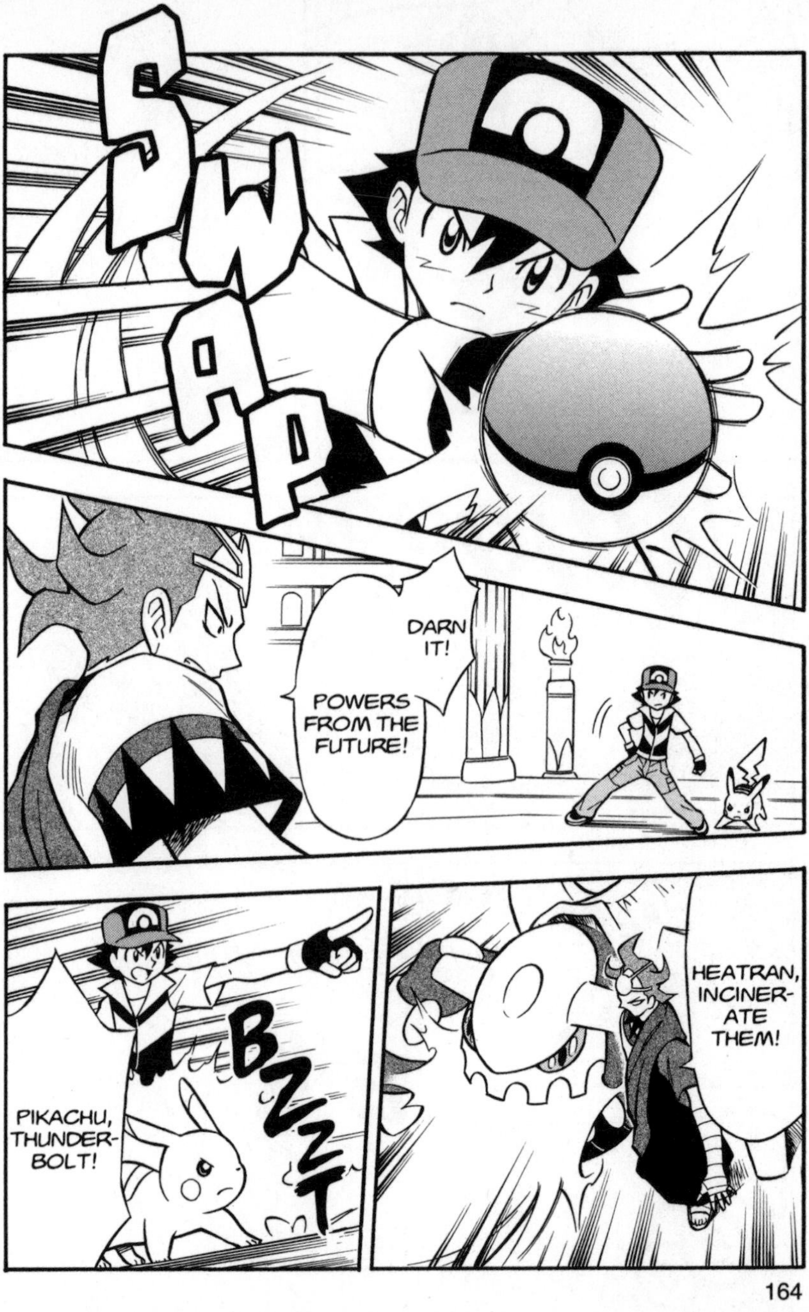
SWAP
DARN IT!
POWERS FROM THE FUTURE!
HEATRAN, INCINER-ATE THEM!
PIKACHU, THUNDER-BOLT!
BZZZT

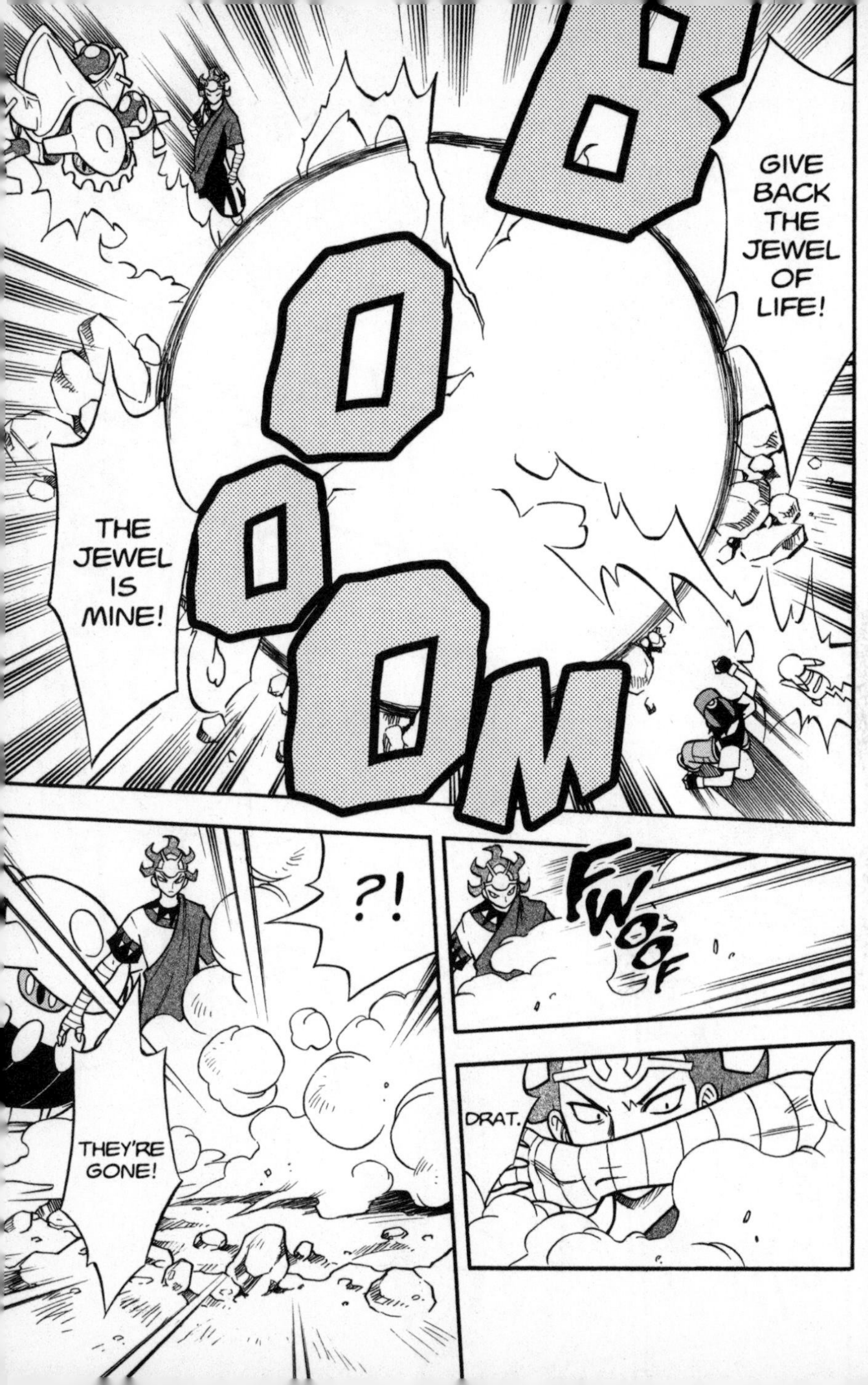
GIVE BACK THE JEWEL OF LIFE!
BOOOM
THE JEWEL IS MINE!
FWOOF
DRAT.
?!
THEY'RE GONE!

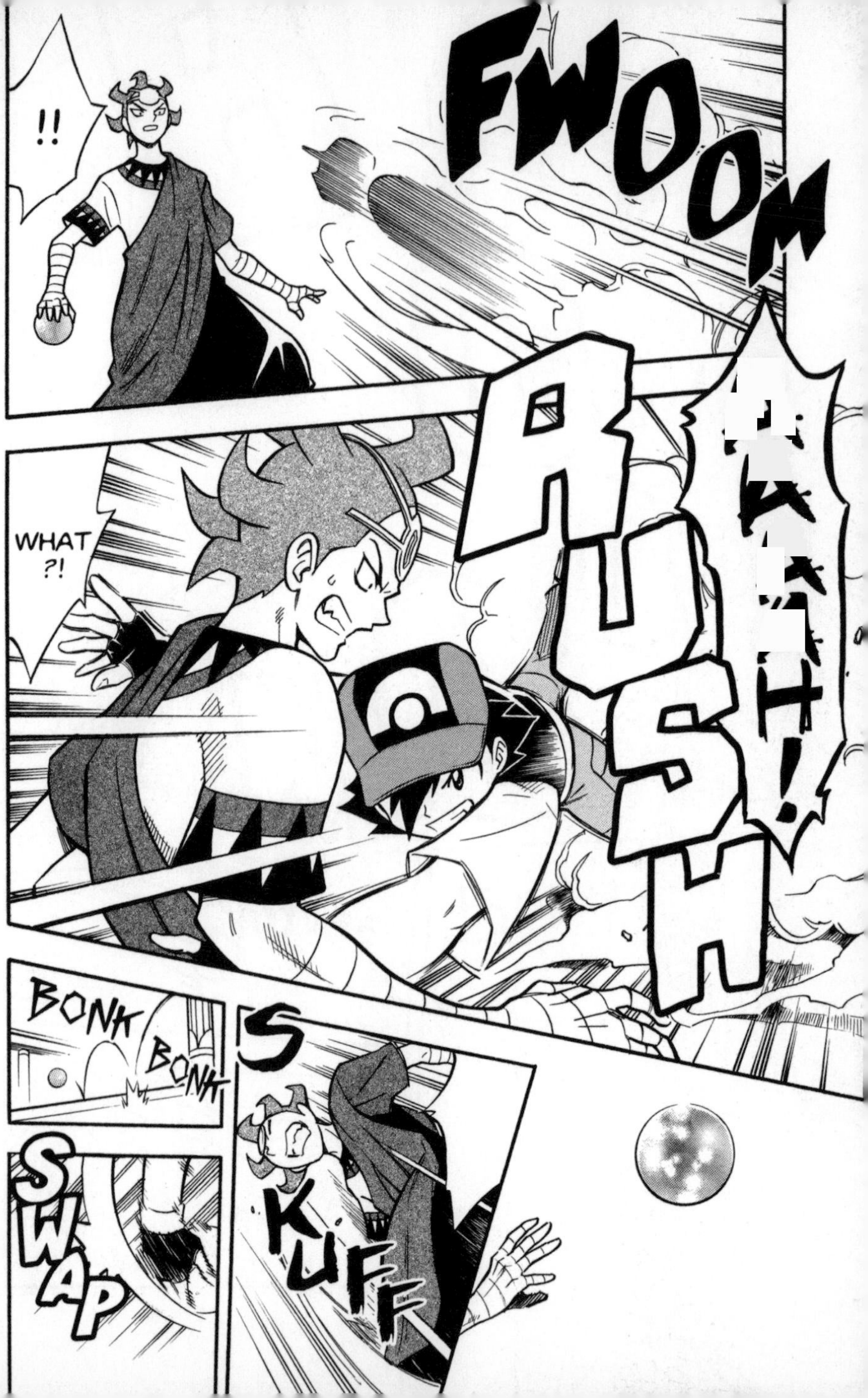
FWOOM
!!
RUSH
WHAT ?!
S
KUFF
BONK BONK
SWAP

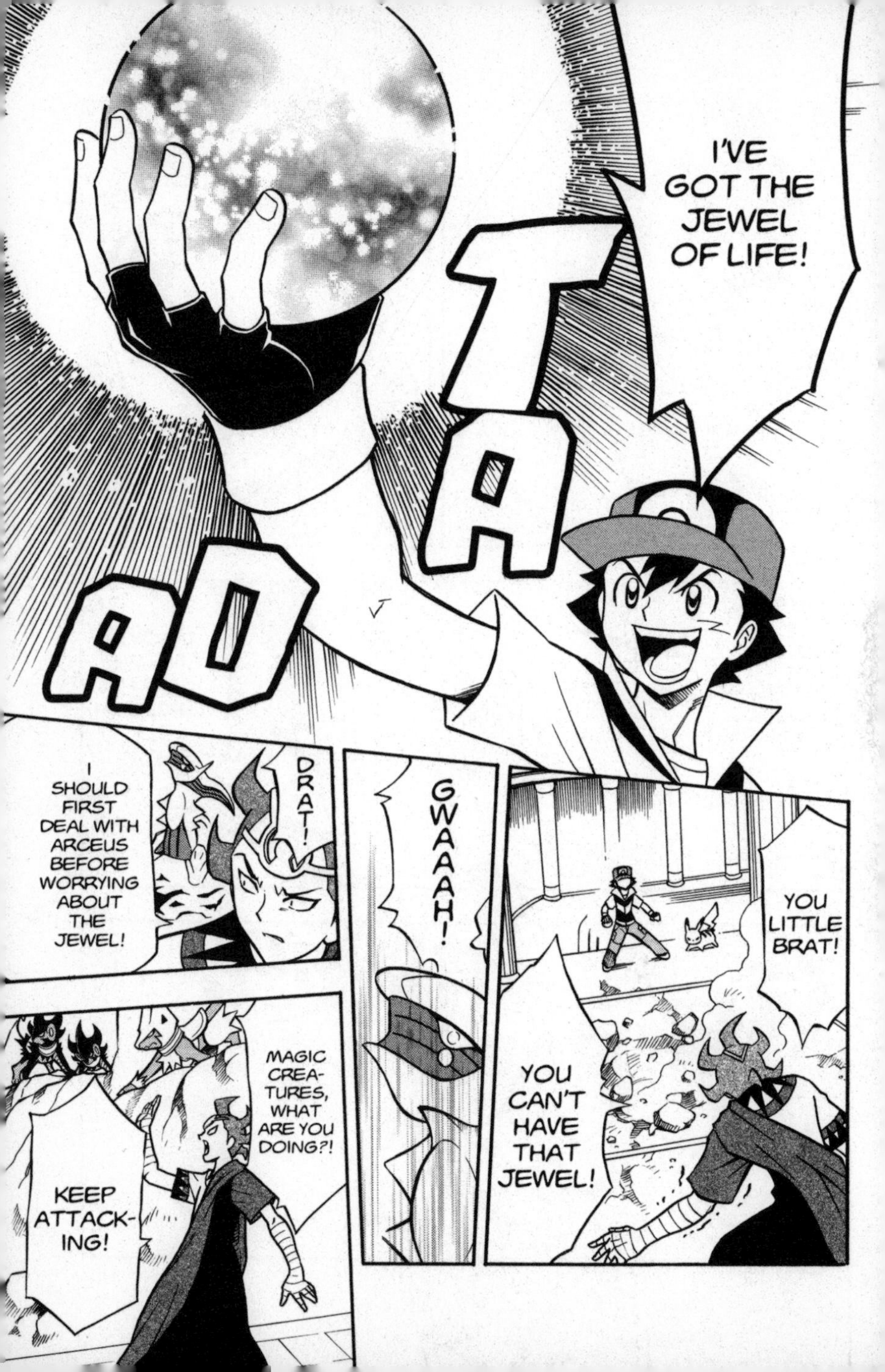
I'VE GOT THE JEWEL OF LIFE!
TADA
YOU LITTLE BRAT!
YOU CAN'T HAVE THAT JEWEL!
GWAAAAH!
DRAT!
I SHOULD FIRST DEAL WITH ARCEUS BEFORE WORRYING ABOUT THE JEWEL!
MAGIC CREATURES, WHAT ARE YOU DOING?!
KEEP ATTACKING!

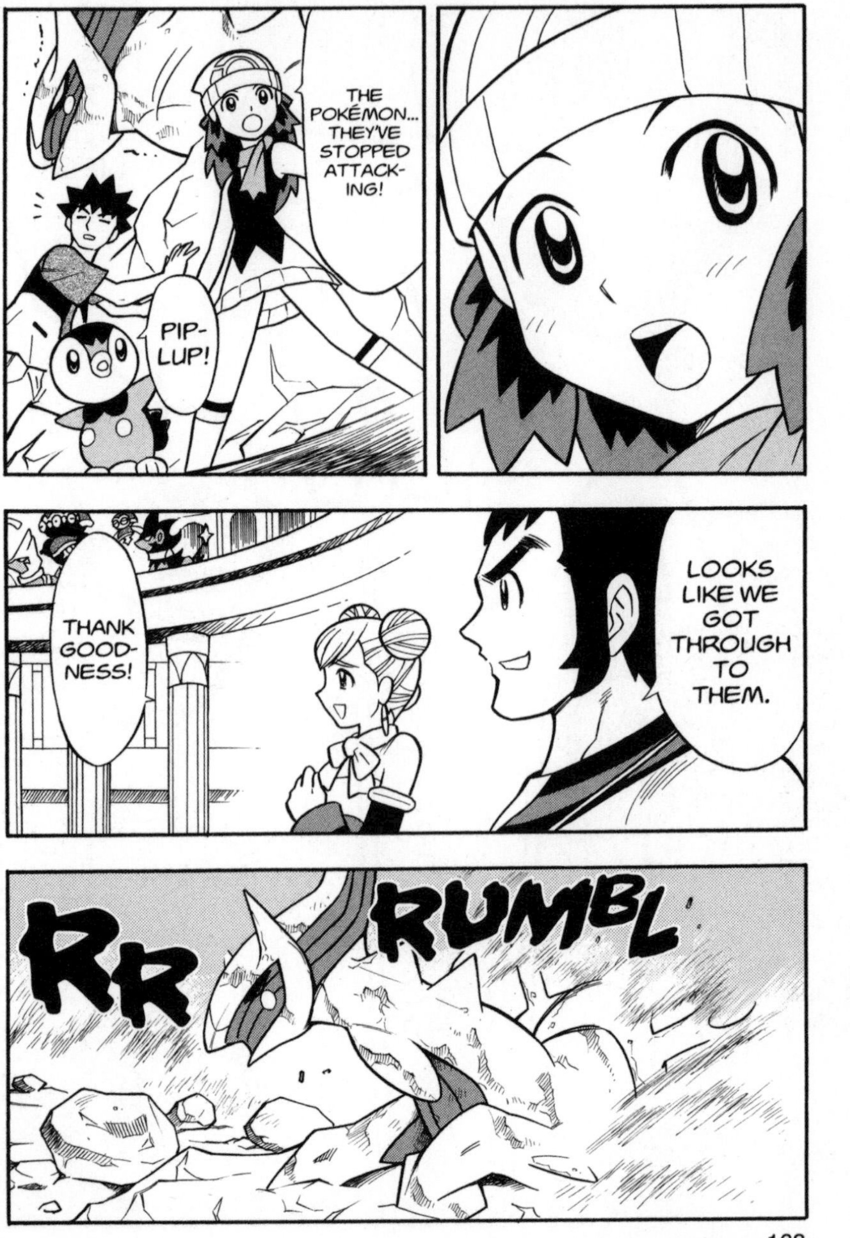
THE POKÉMON... THEY'VE STOPPED ATTACKING!
PIP-LUP!
LOOKS LIKE WE GOT THROUGH TO THEM.
THANK GOODNESS!
RR RUMBL

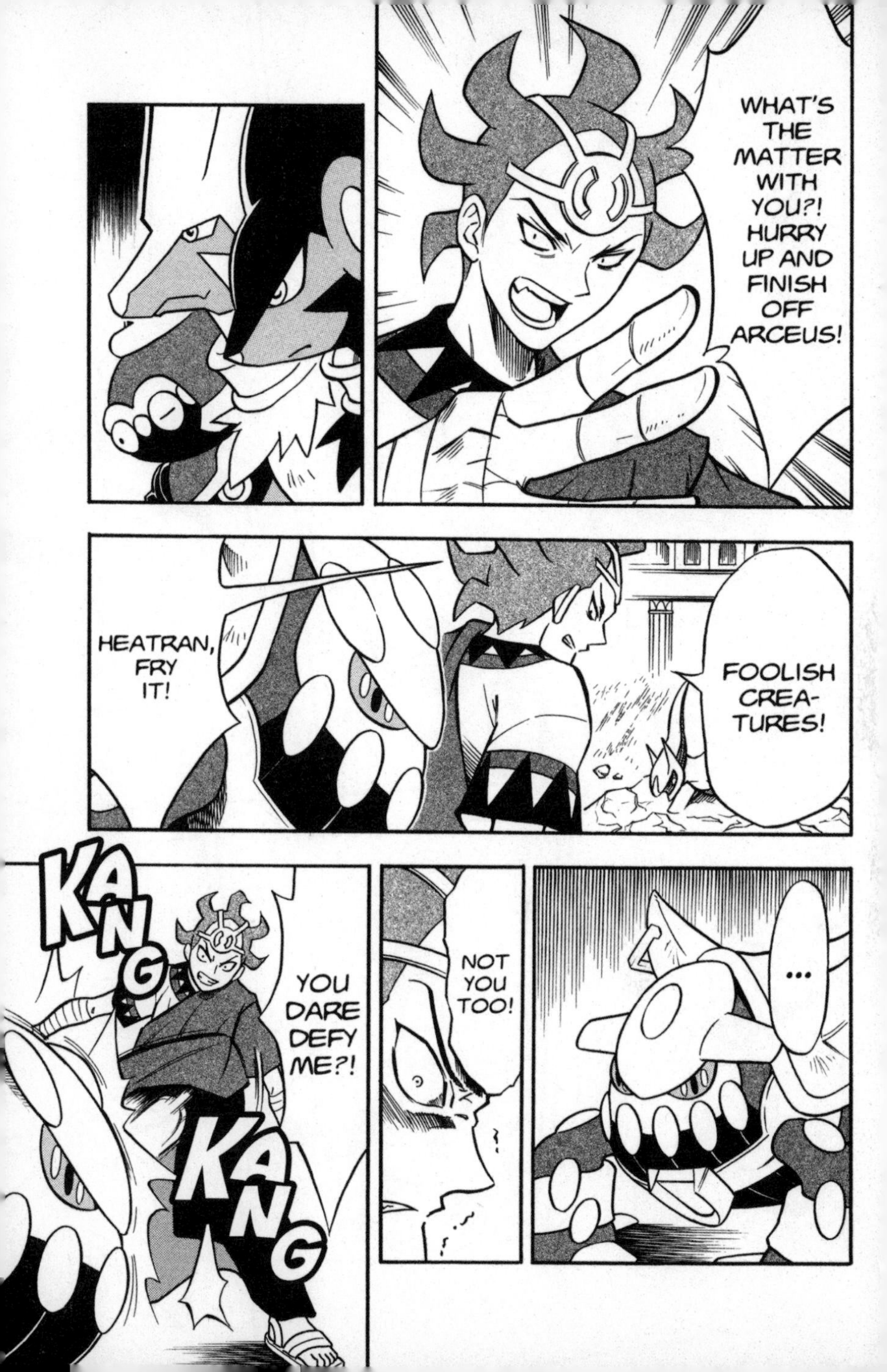
WHAT'S THE MATTER WITH YOU?! HURRY UP AND FINISH OFF ARCEUS!
FOOLISH CREATURES!
HEATRAN, FRY IT!
...
NOT YOU TOO!
KANG
YOU DARE DEFY ME?!
KANG

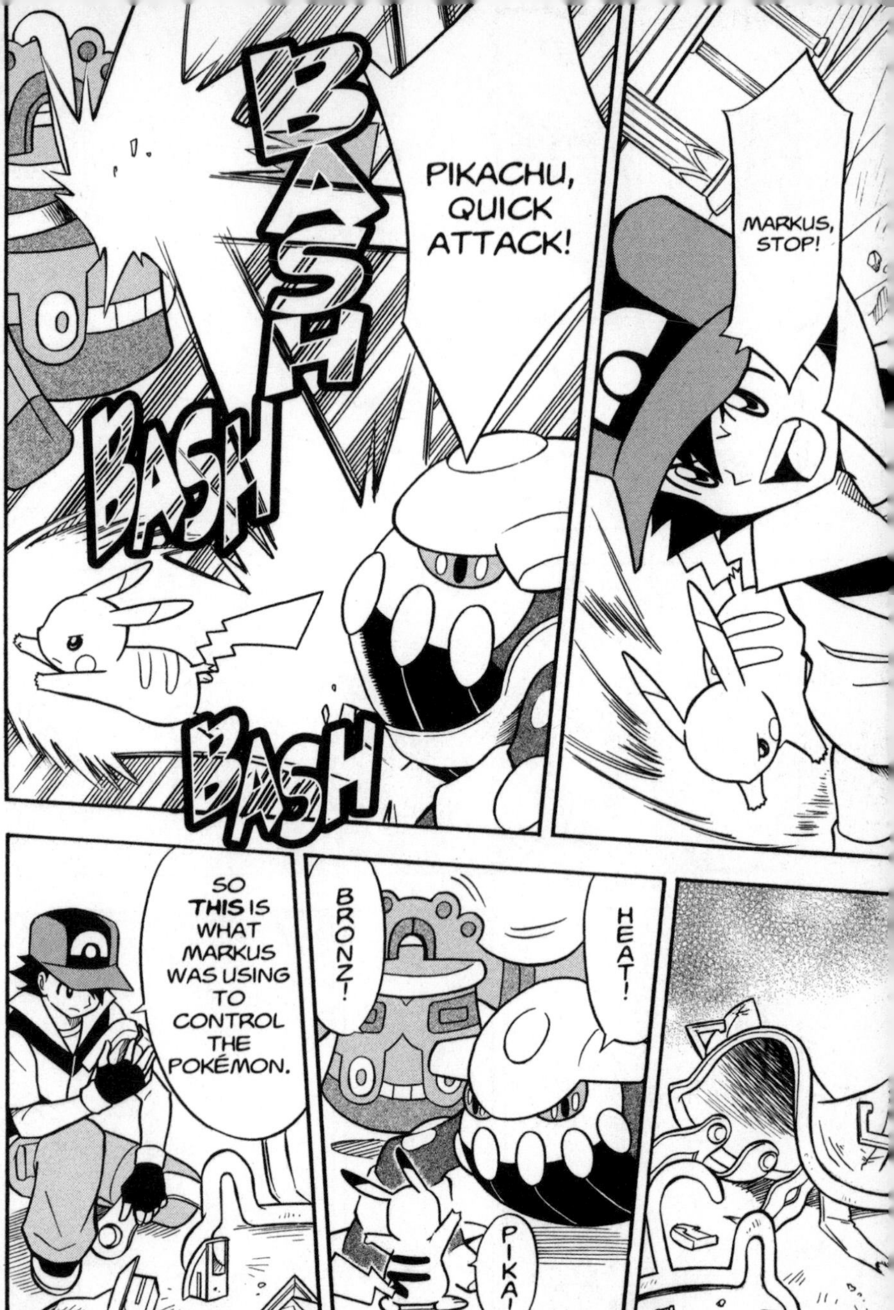
MARKUS, STOP!
BASH
PIKACHU, QUICK ATTACK!
BASH
BASH
HEAT!
BRONZ!
PIKA!
SO THIS IS WHAT MARKUS WAS USING TO CONTROL THE POKÉMON.

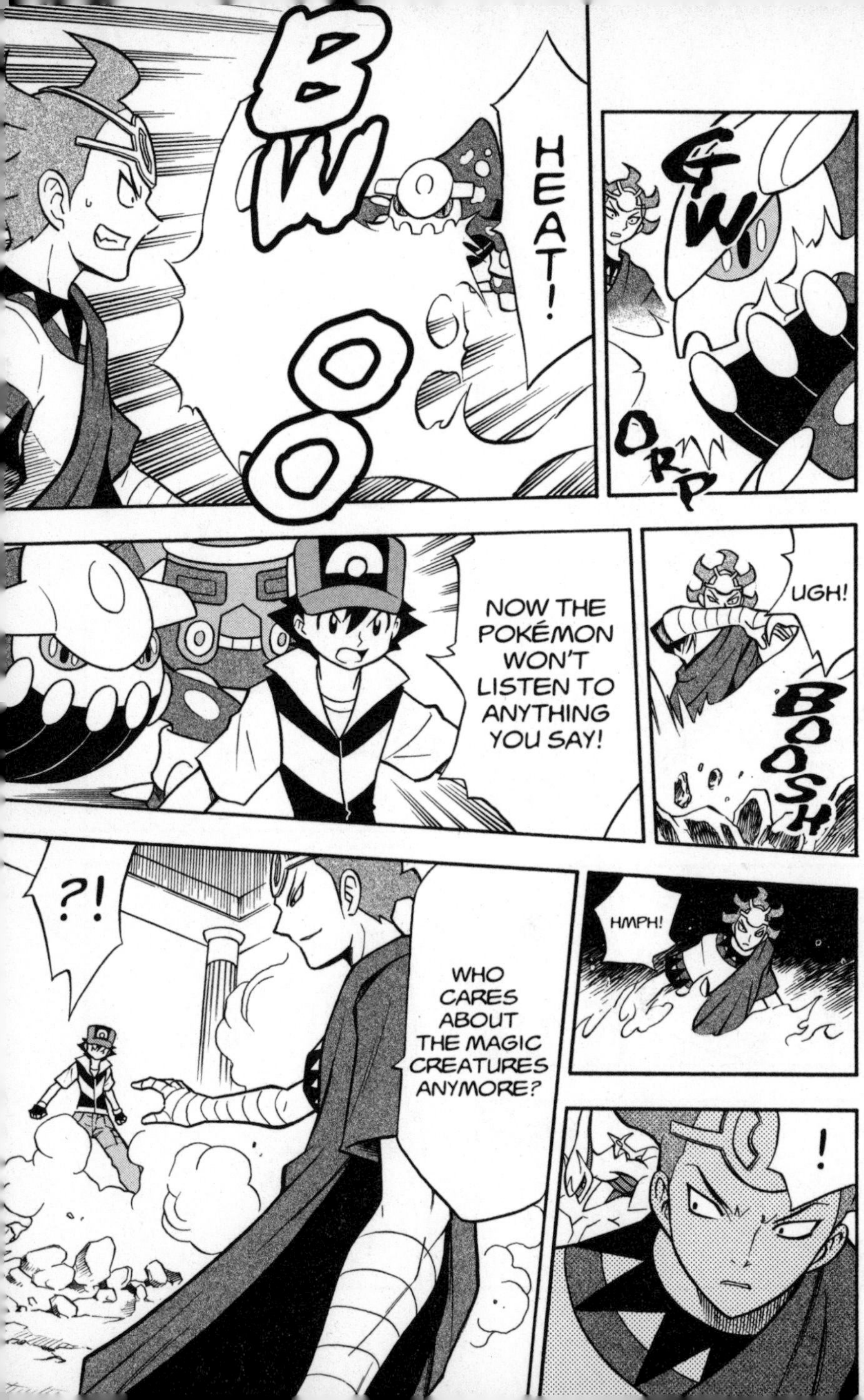
GW
ORP
HEAT!
BWOO
UGH!
BOOSH
NOW THE POKÉMON WON'T LISTEN TO ANYTHING YOU SAY!
HMPH!
!
WHO CARES ABOUT THE MAGIC CREATURES ANYMORE?
?!

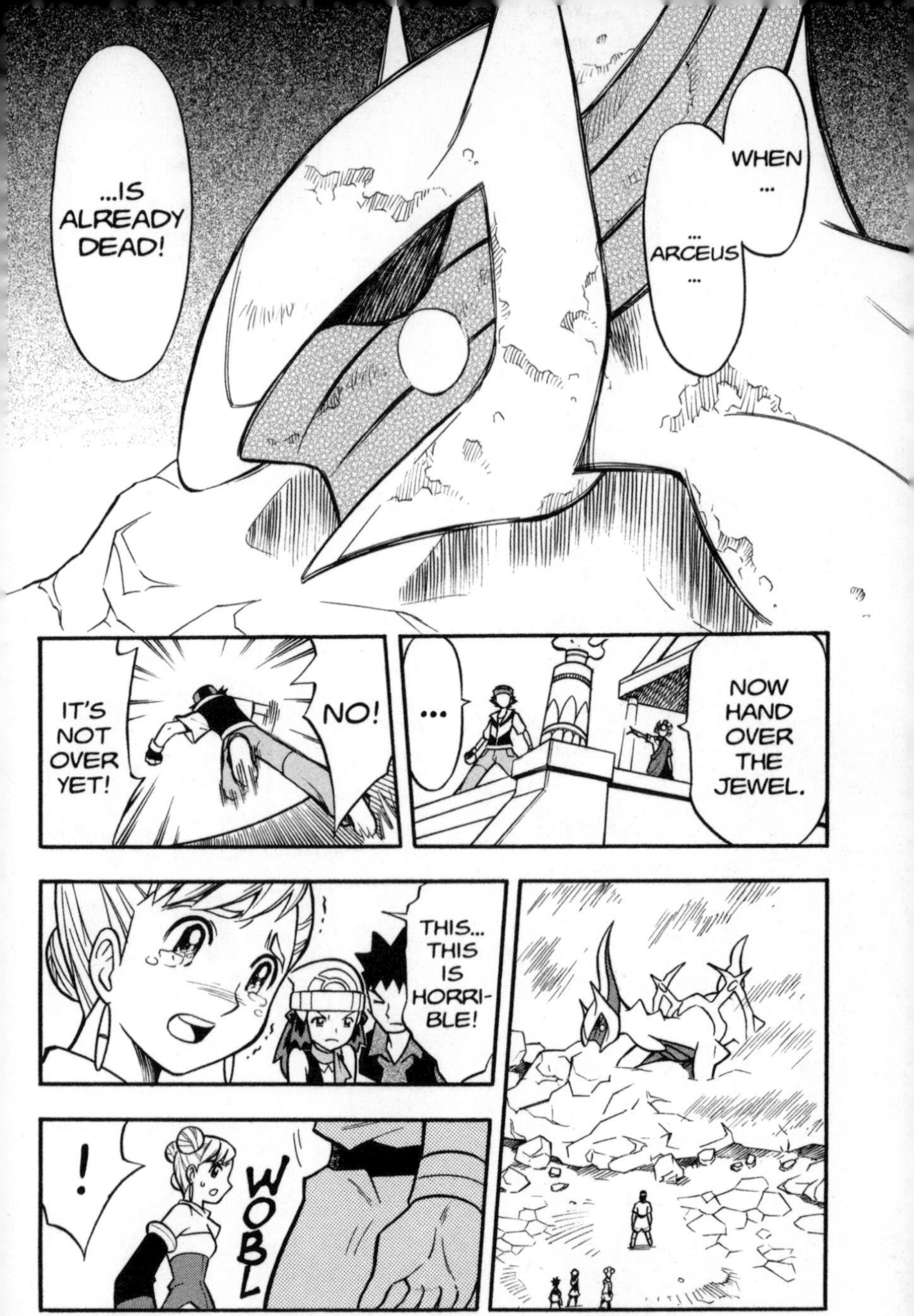
WHEN... ...ARCEUS...
...IS ALREADY DEAD!
NOW HAND OVER THE JEWEL.
...
NO!
IT'S NOT OVER YET!
THIS... THIS IS HORRIBLE!
!
WOBL

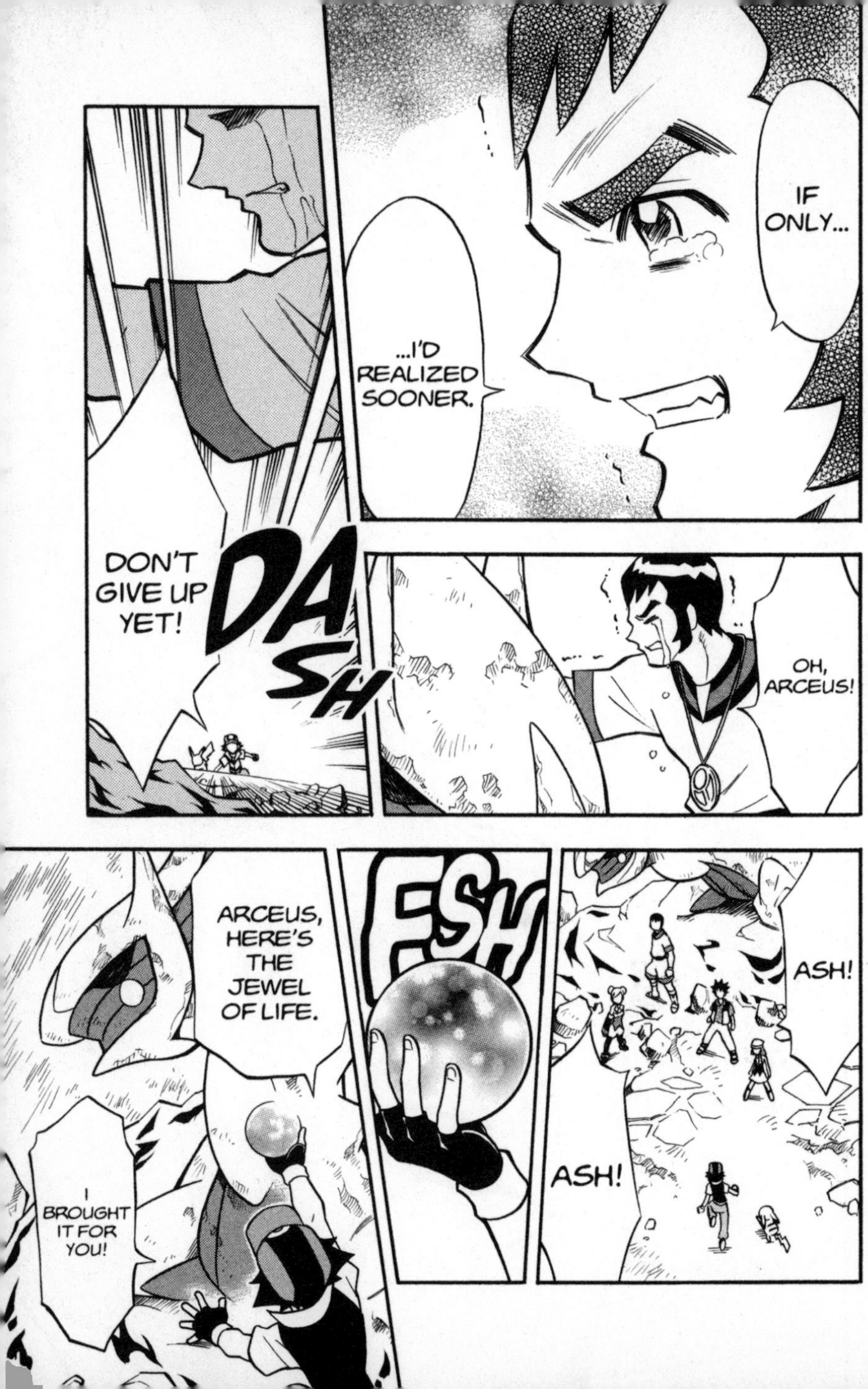
IF ONLY...
...I'D REALIZED SOONER.
OH, ARCEUS!
DON'T GIVE UP YET!
DASH
ASH!
ASH!
FSH
ARCEUS, HERE'S THE JEWEL OF LIFE.
I BROUGHT IT FOR YOU!

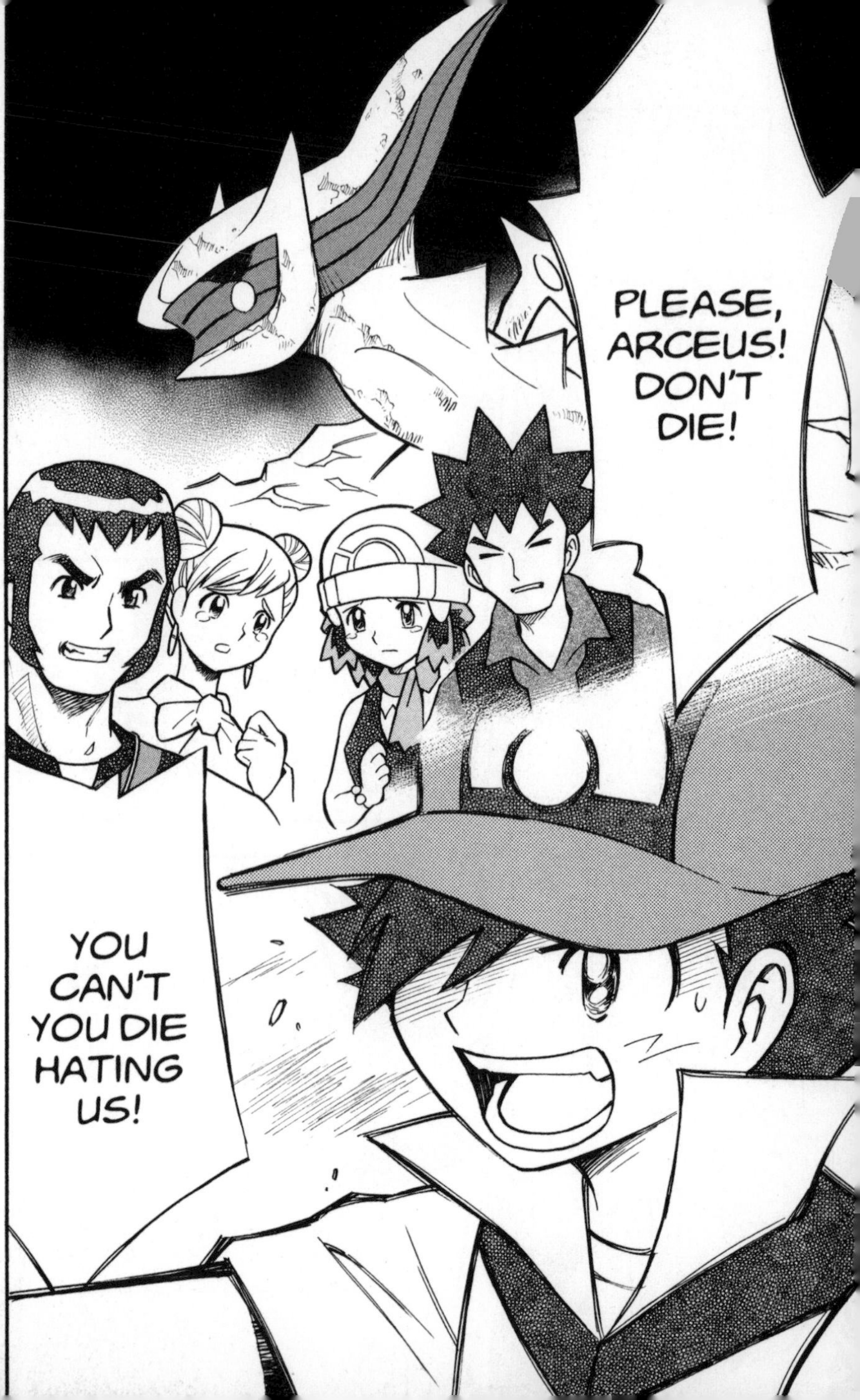
PLEASE, ARCEUS! DON'T DIE!
YOU CAN'T YOU DIE HATING US!

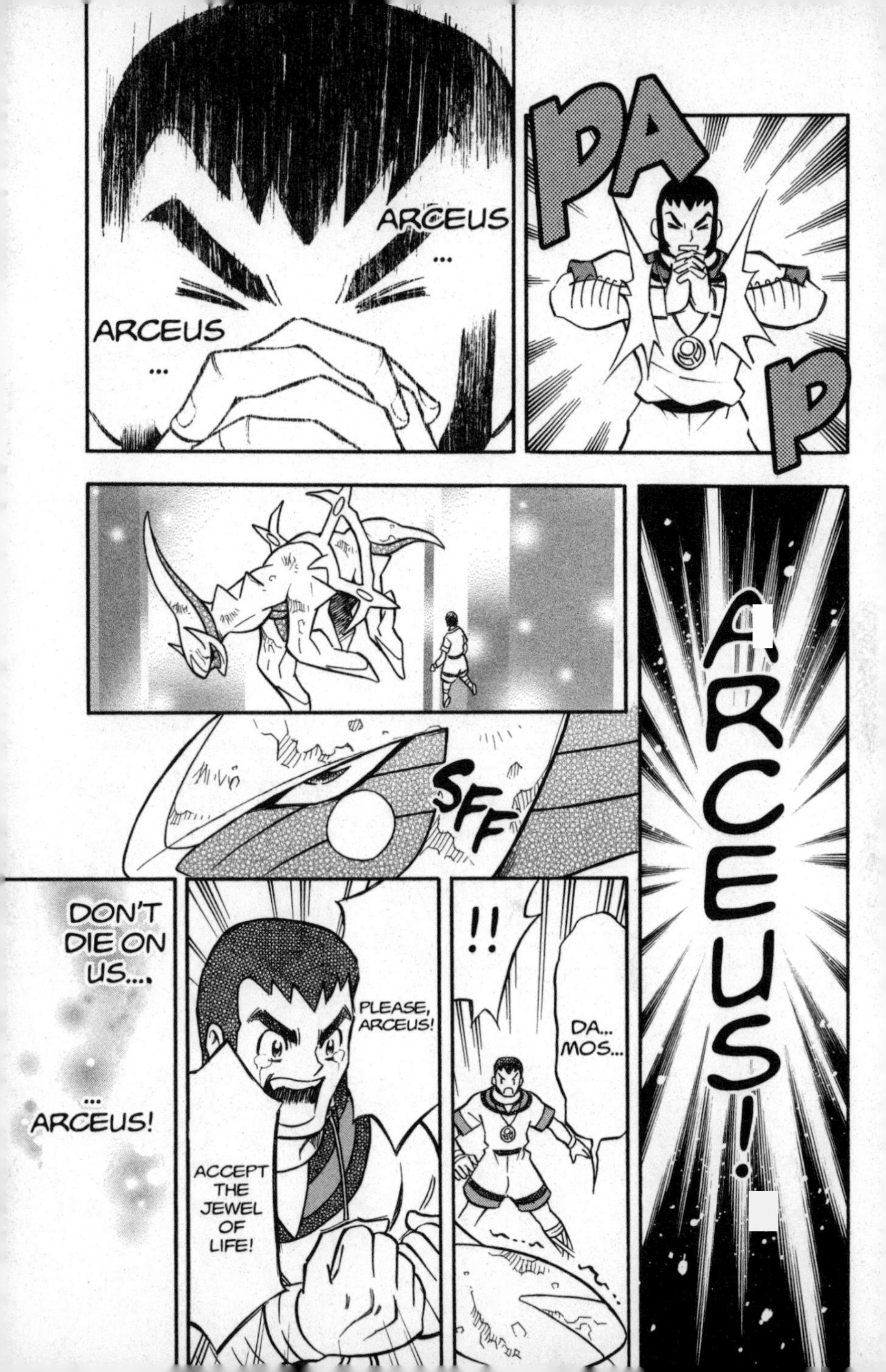
PAP
ARCEUS ...
ARCEUS ...
ARCEUS!
SFF
!!
DA... MOS...
PLEASE, ARCEUS!
ACCEPT THE JEWEL OF LIFE!
DON'T DIE ON US....
... ARCEUS!

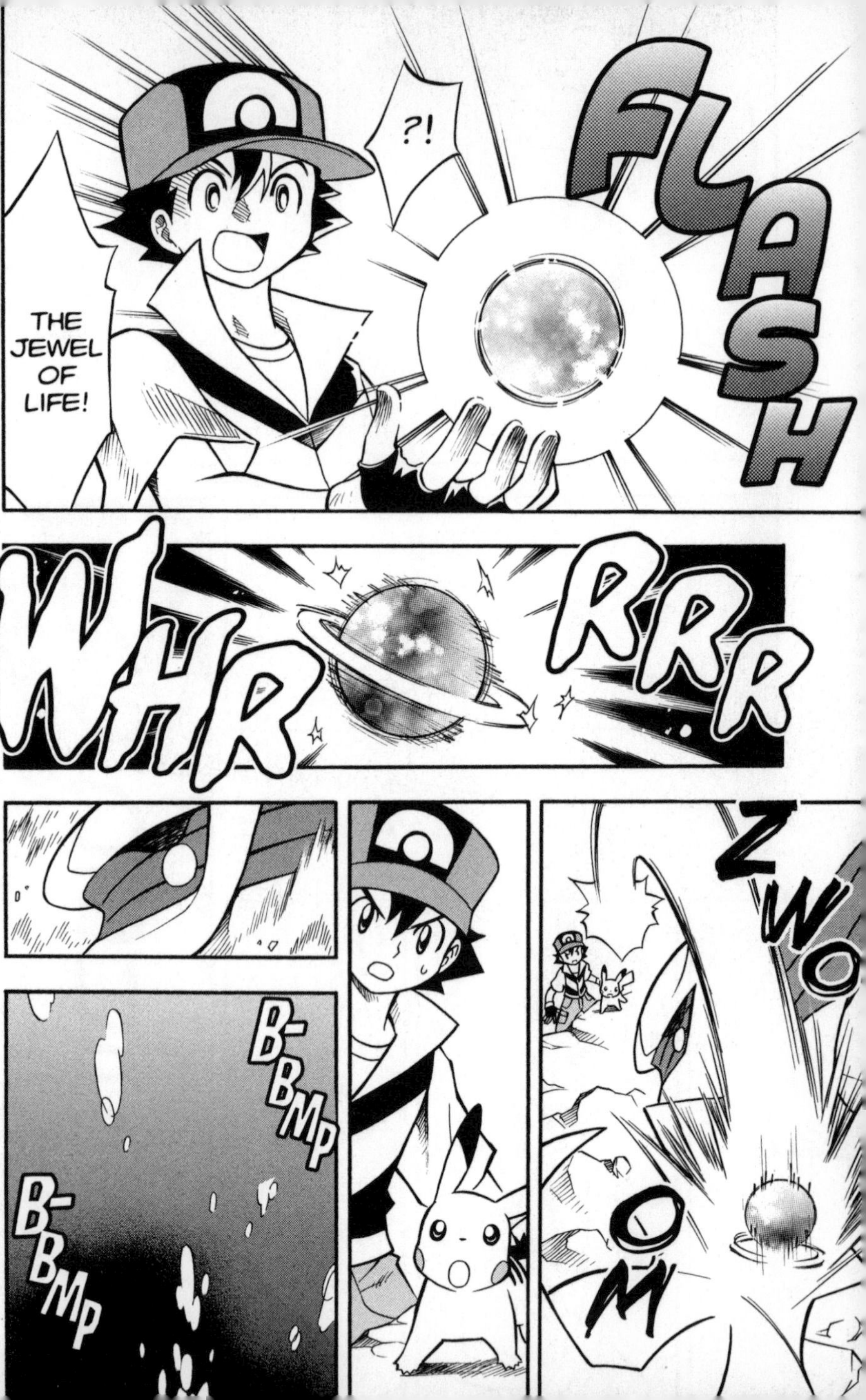
FLASH
?!
THE JEWEL OF LIFE!
WHRRRR
ZWOOM
B-BMP
B-BMP

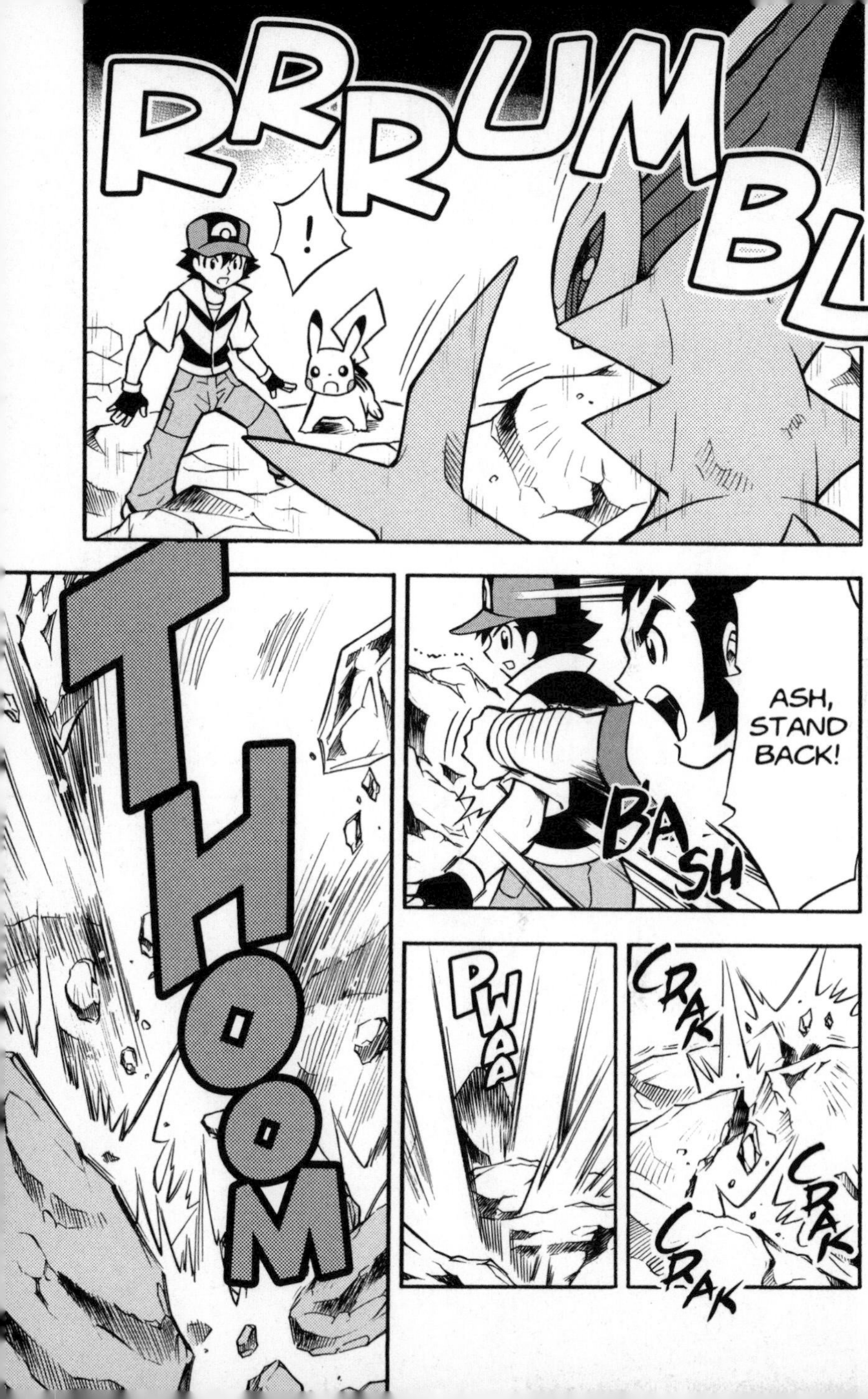
RRRUMBL
!
ASH, STAND BACK!
BASH
CRAK
CRAK
CRAK
PWAA
THOOOM

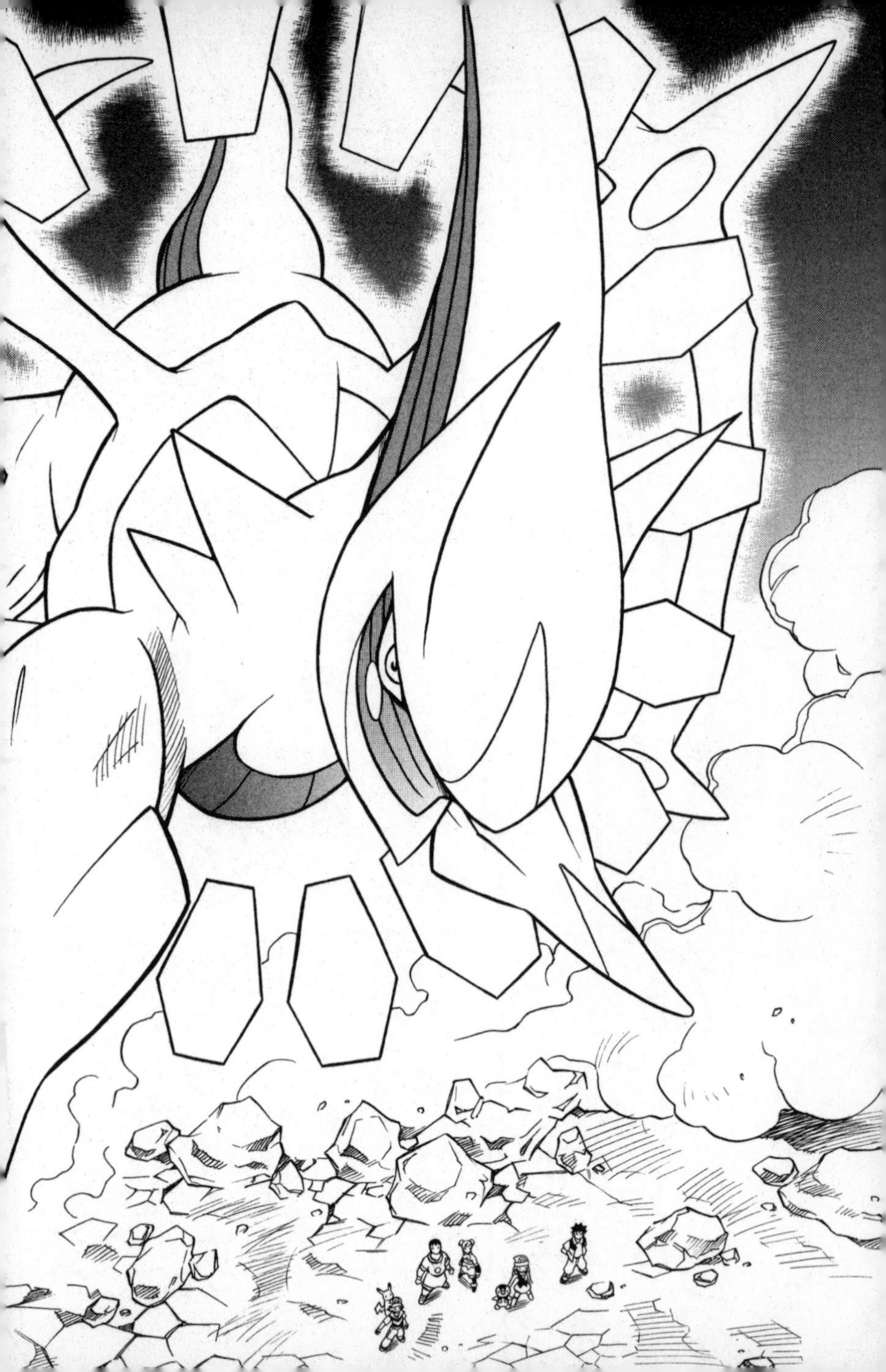

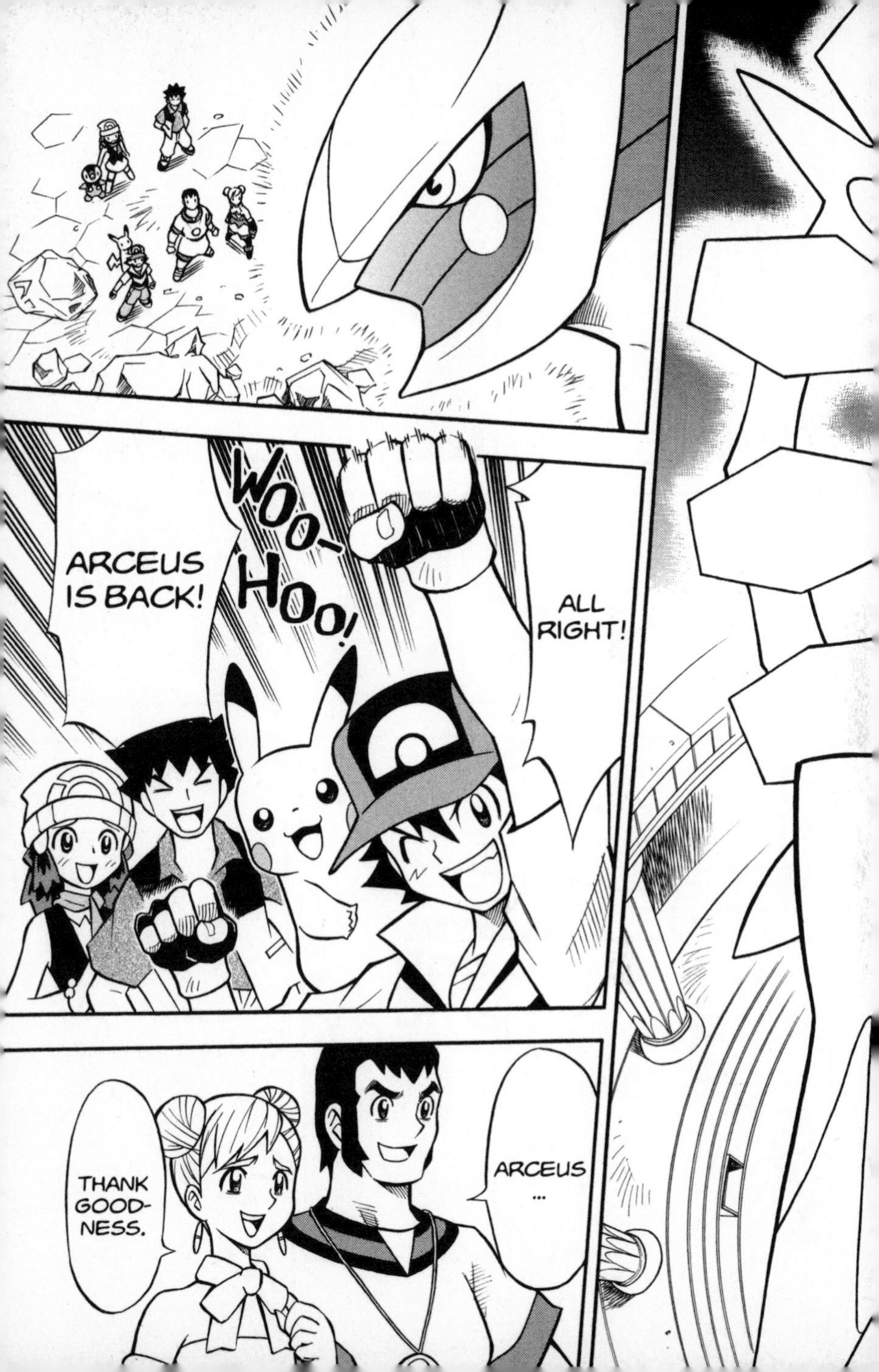
ALL RIGHT!
WOO-HOO!
ARCEUS IS BACK!
ARCEUS ...
THANK GOODNESS.

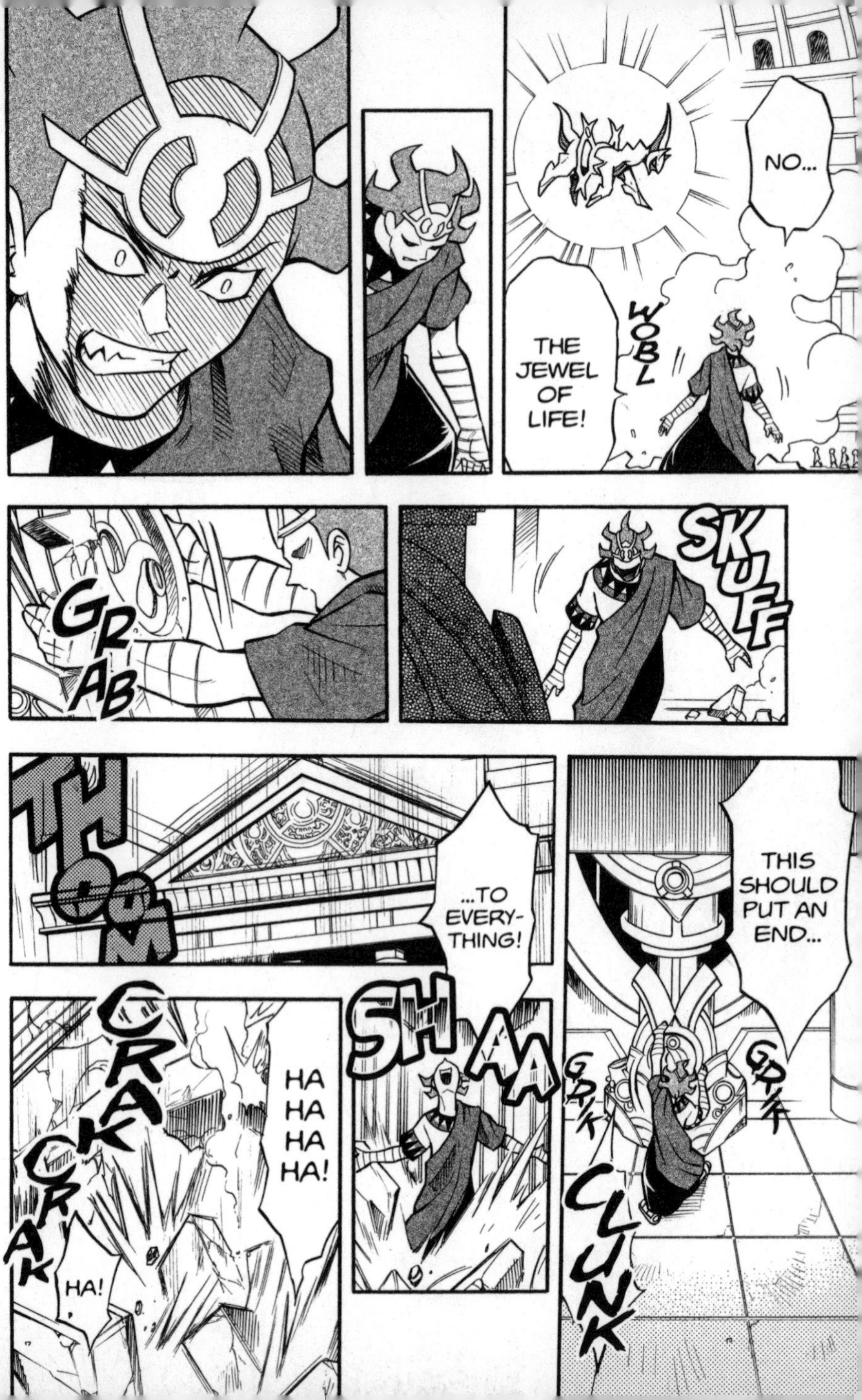
NO...
WOBL
THE JEWEL OF LIFE!
SKUFF
GRAB
THIS SHOULD PUT AN END...
GDRIK
GDRIK
CLUNK
THOOM
...TO EVERY-THING!
SHAA
CRAK
CRAK
HA HA HA HA!
HA!

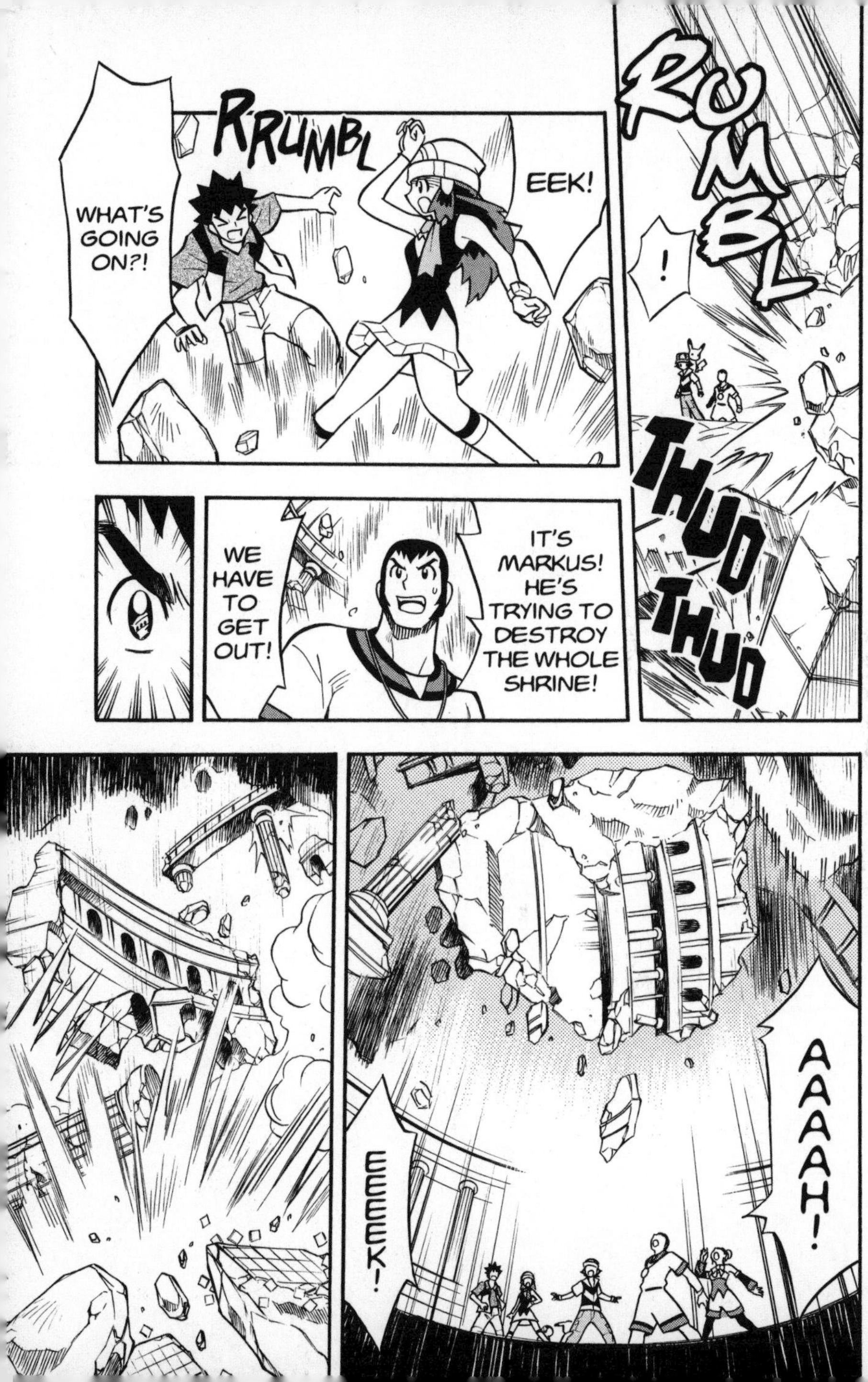
RUMBL
!
THUD
THUD
EEK!
R-RUMBL
WHAT'S GOING ON?!
IT'S MARKUS! HE'S TRYING TO DESTROY THE WHOLE SHRINE!
WE HAVE TO GET OUT!
AAAAH!
EEEEK!

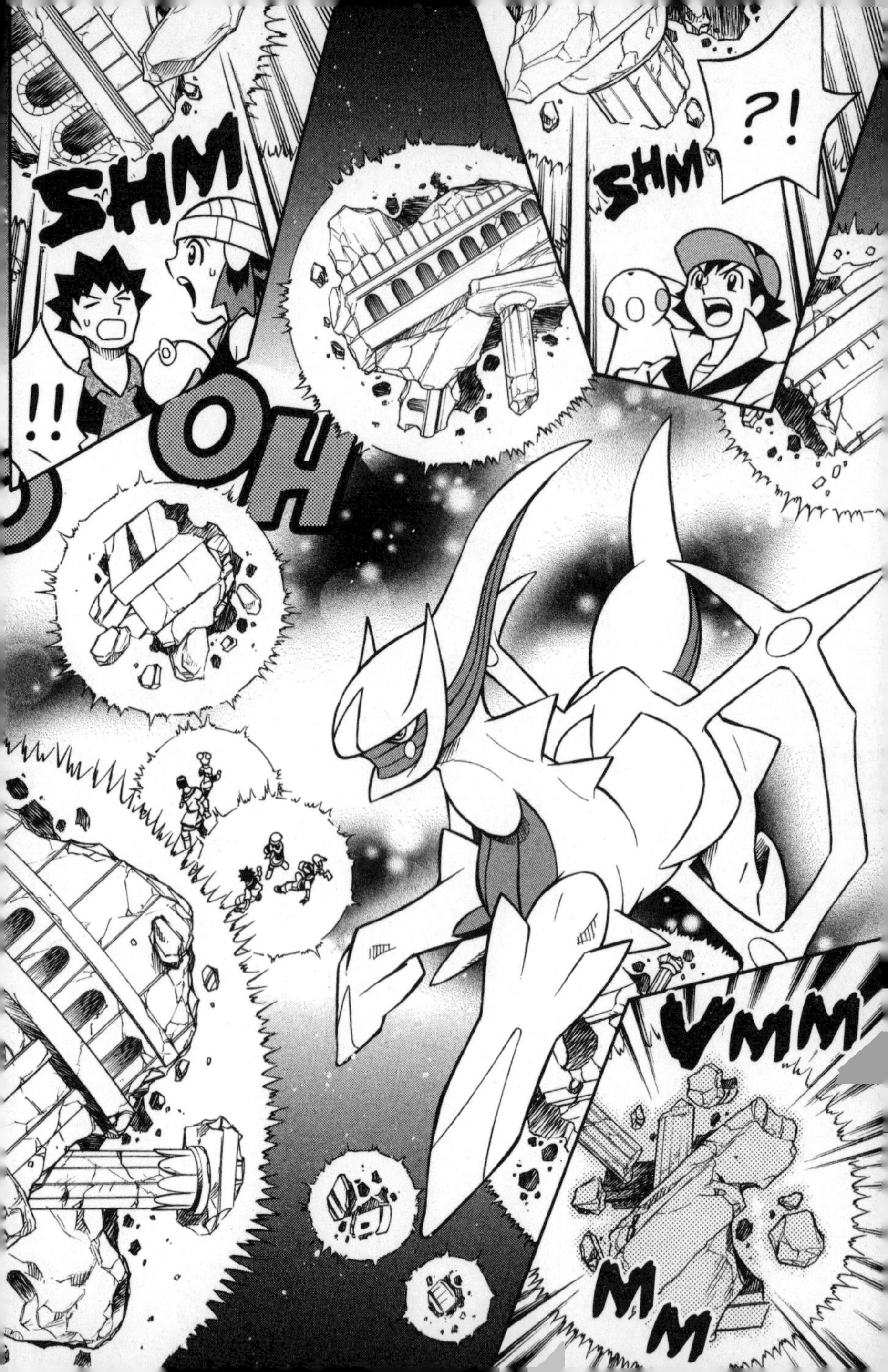
?!
SHM
SHM
!!
OH
VMMM
MM

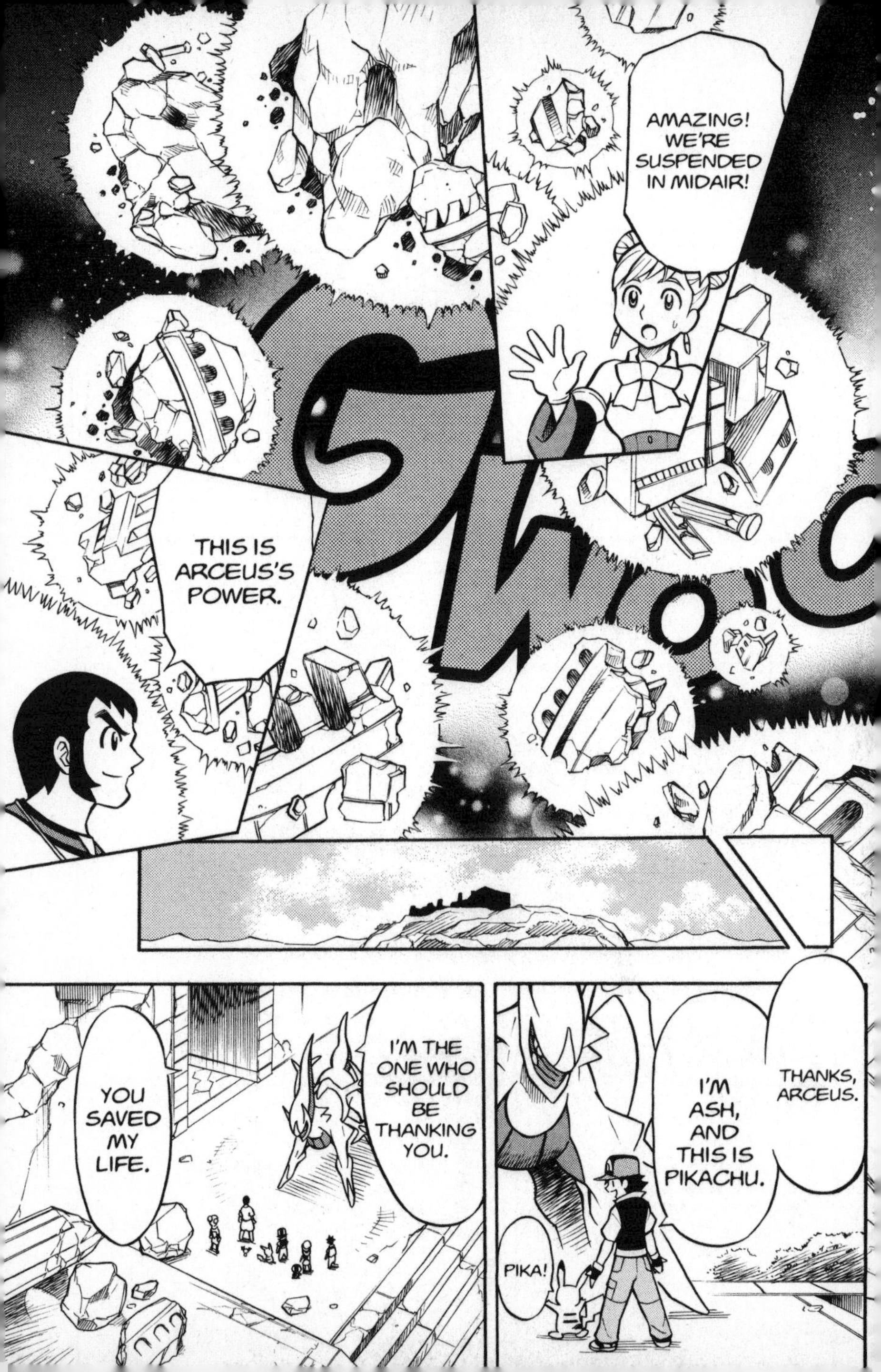
AMAZING! WE'RE SUSPENDED IN MIDAIR!
THIS IS ARCEUS'S POWER.
THANKS, ARCEUS.
I'M ASH, AND THIS IS PIKACHU.
PIKA!
I'M THE ONE WHO SHOULD BE THANKING YOU.
YOU SAVED MY LIFE.

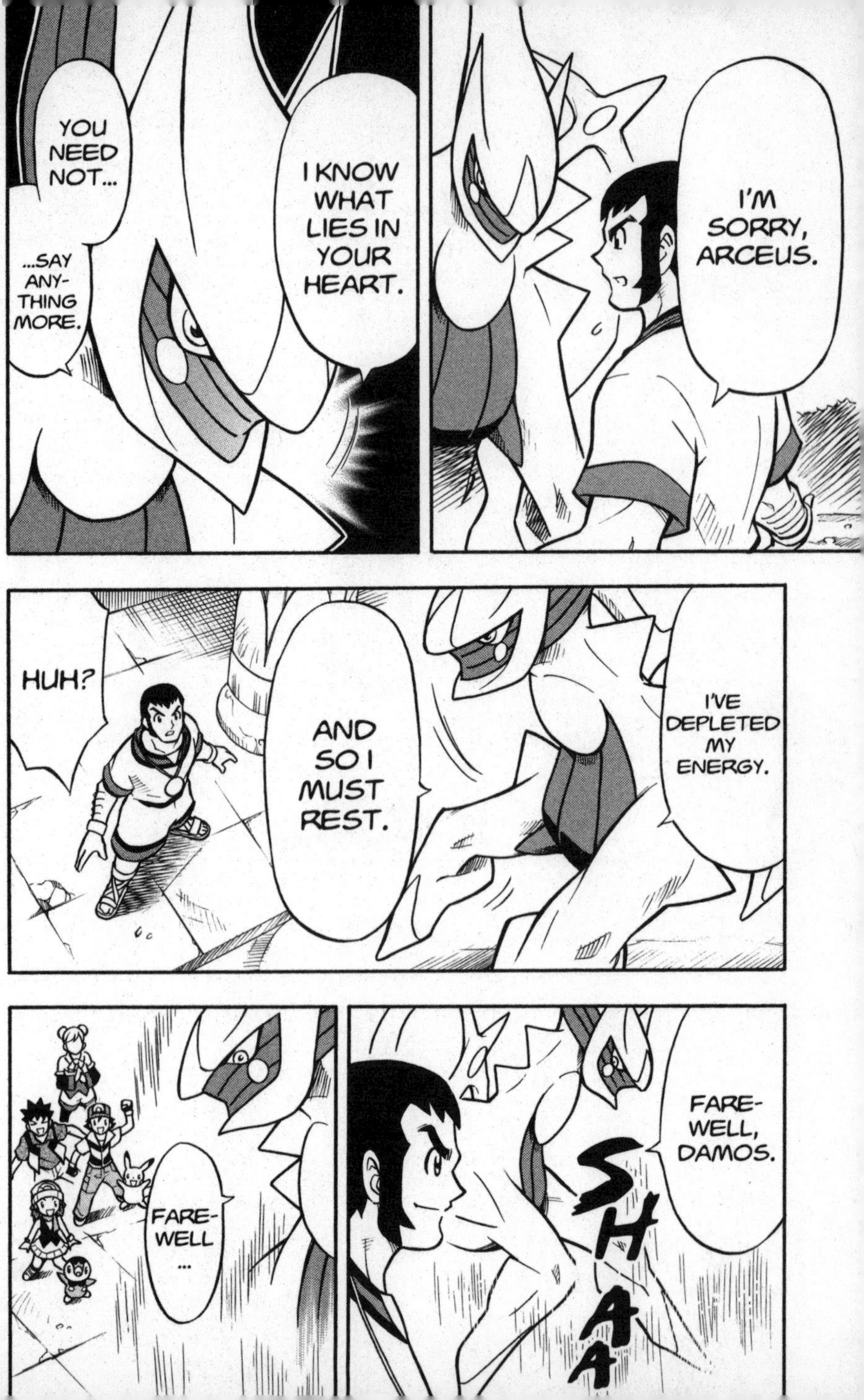
I'M SORRY, ARCEUS.
I KNOW WHAT LIES IN YOUR HEART.
YOU NEED NOT...
...SAY ANY-THING MORE.
I'VE DEPLETED MY ENERGY.
AND SO I MUST REST.
HUH?
FARE-WELL, DAMOS.
SHAAA
FARE-WELL
...

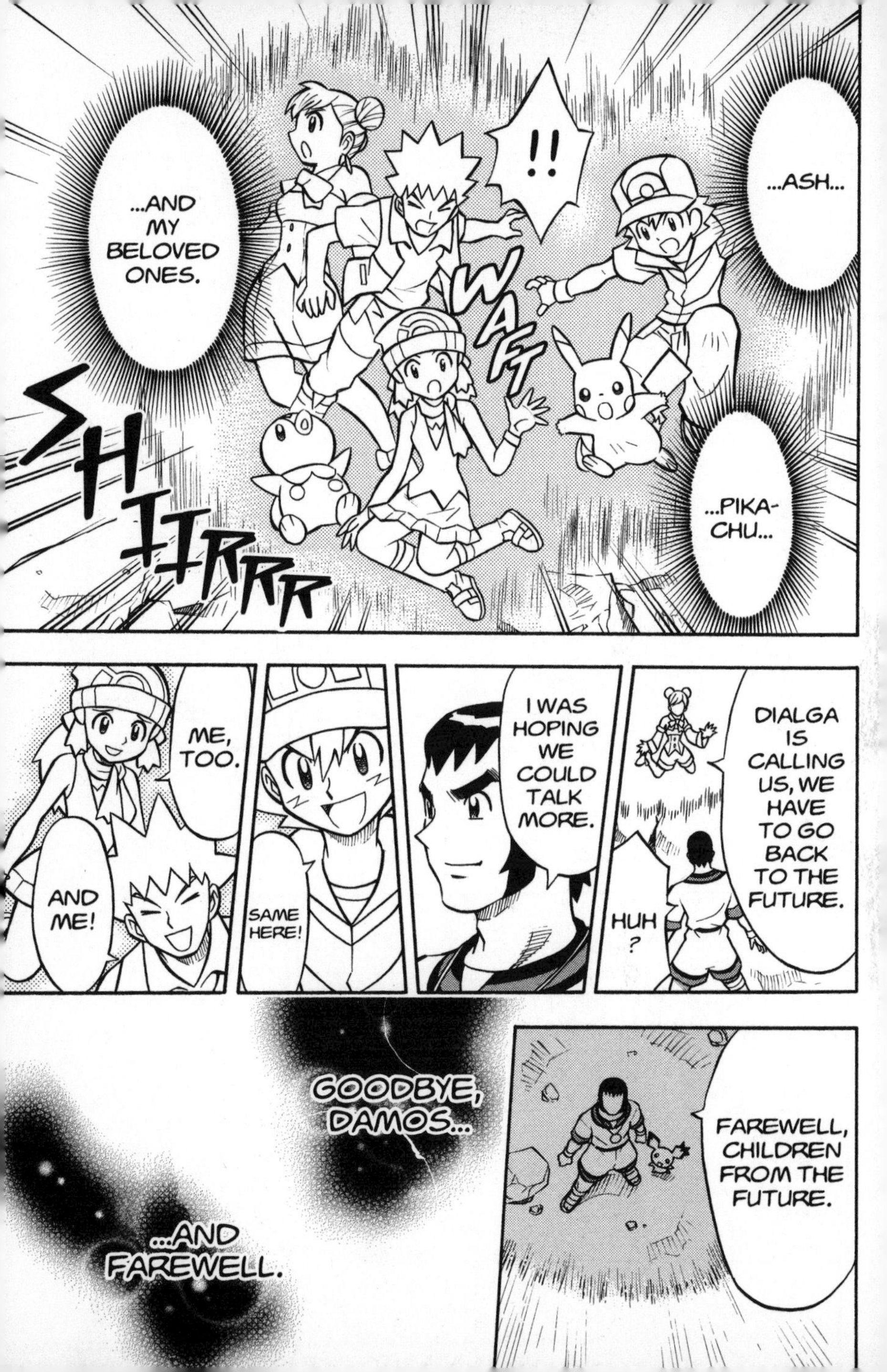
...ASH...
!!
...PIKA-CHU...
WAFT
...AND MY BELOVED ONES.
SHIIRRRR
DIALGA IS CALLING US, WE HAVE TO GO BACK TO THE FUTURE.
HUH?
I WAS HOPING WE COULD TALK MORE.
SAME HERE!
ME, TOO.
AND ME!
FAREWELL, CHILDREN FROM THE FUTURE.
GOODBYE, DAMOS...
...AND FAREWELL.

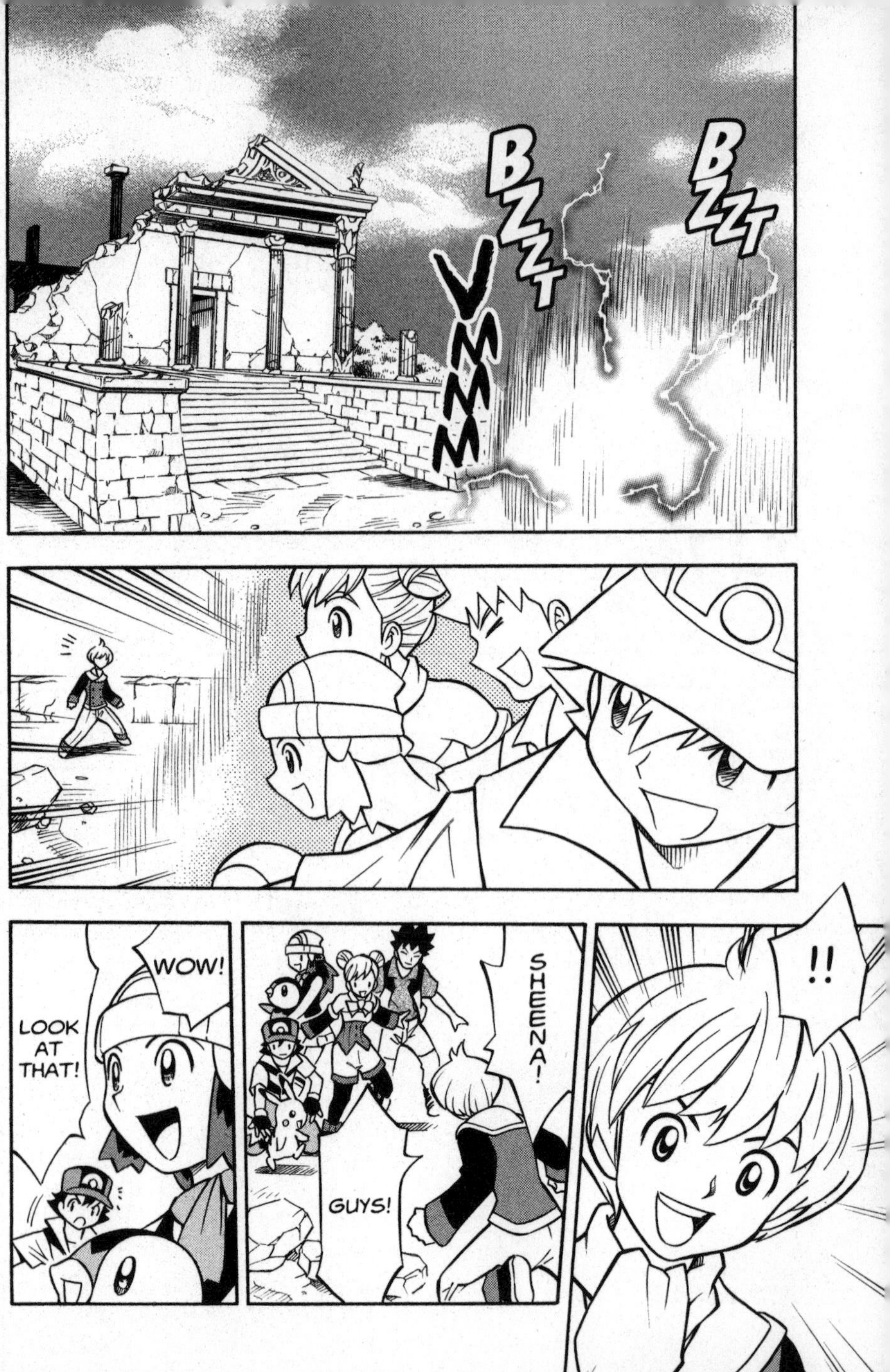
BZZT
BZZT
VMMMM
!!
SHEENA!
GUYS!
WOW!
LOOK AT THAT!

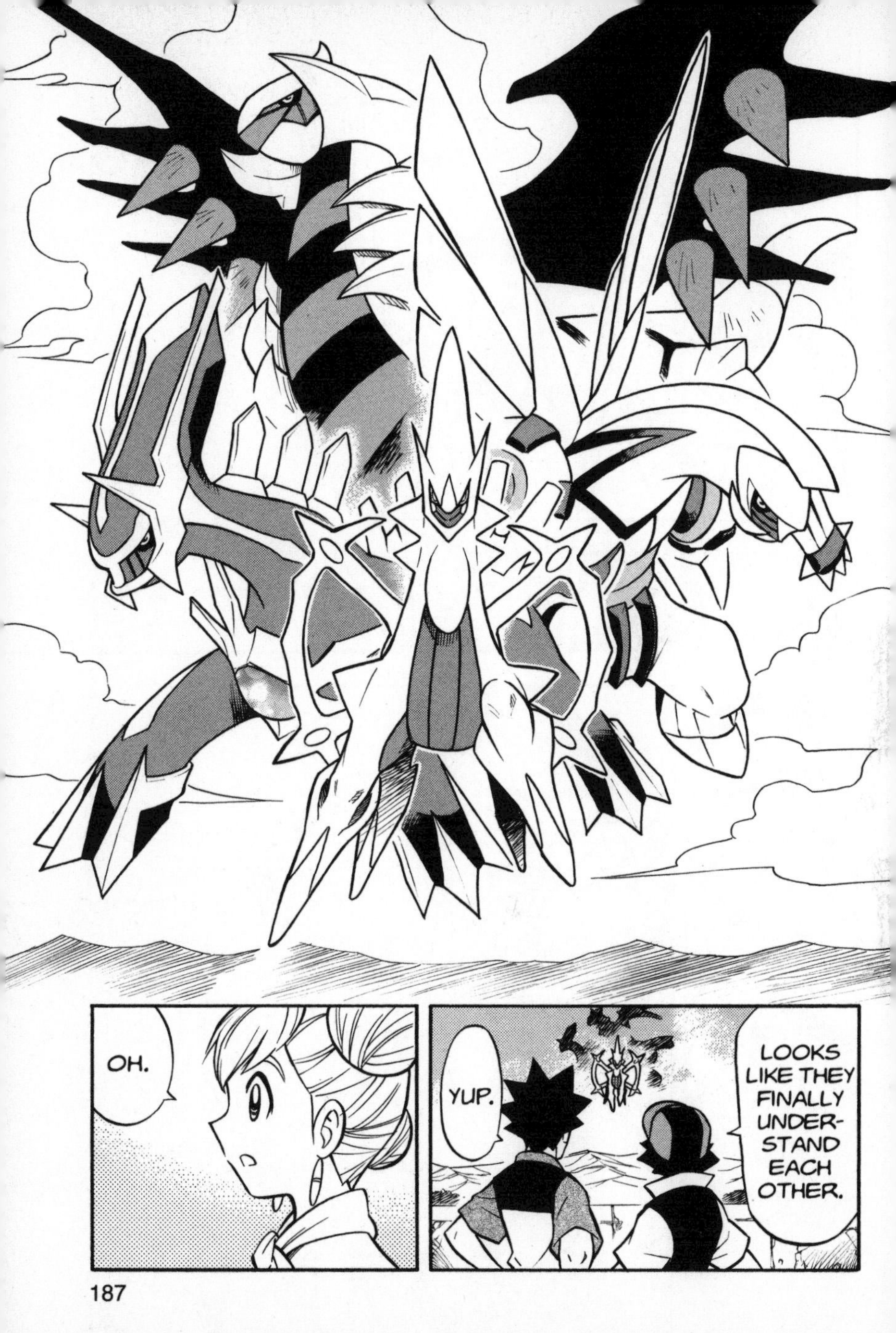
LOOKS LIKE THEY FINALLY UNDER-STAND EACH OTHER.
YUP.
OH.

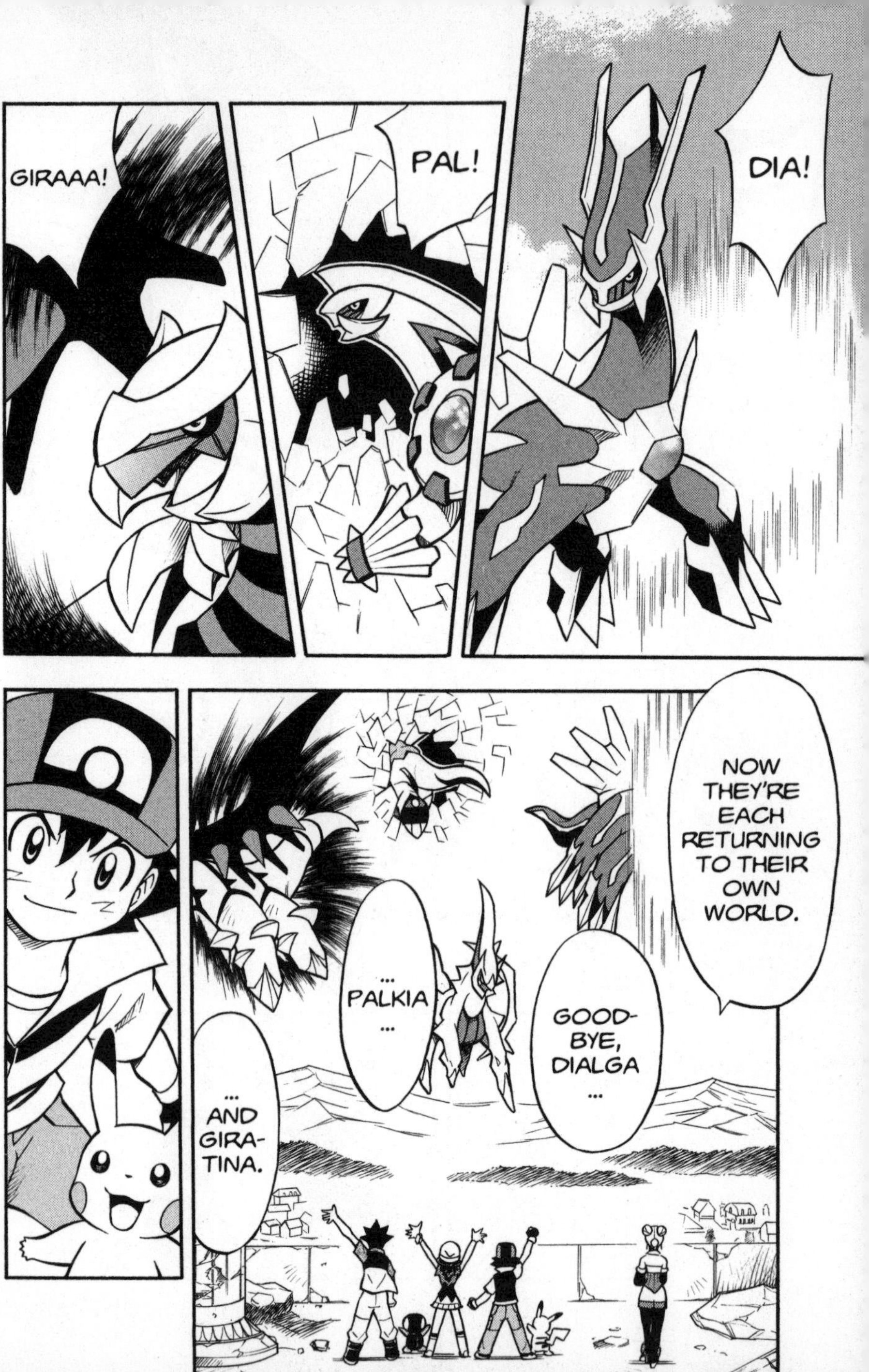
DIA!
PAL!
GIRAAA!
NOW THEY'RE EACH RETURNING TO THEIR OWN WORLD.
GOOD-BYE, DIALGA ...
... PALKIA ...
... AND GIRA-TINA.

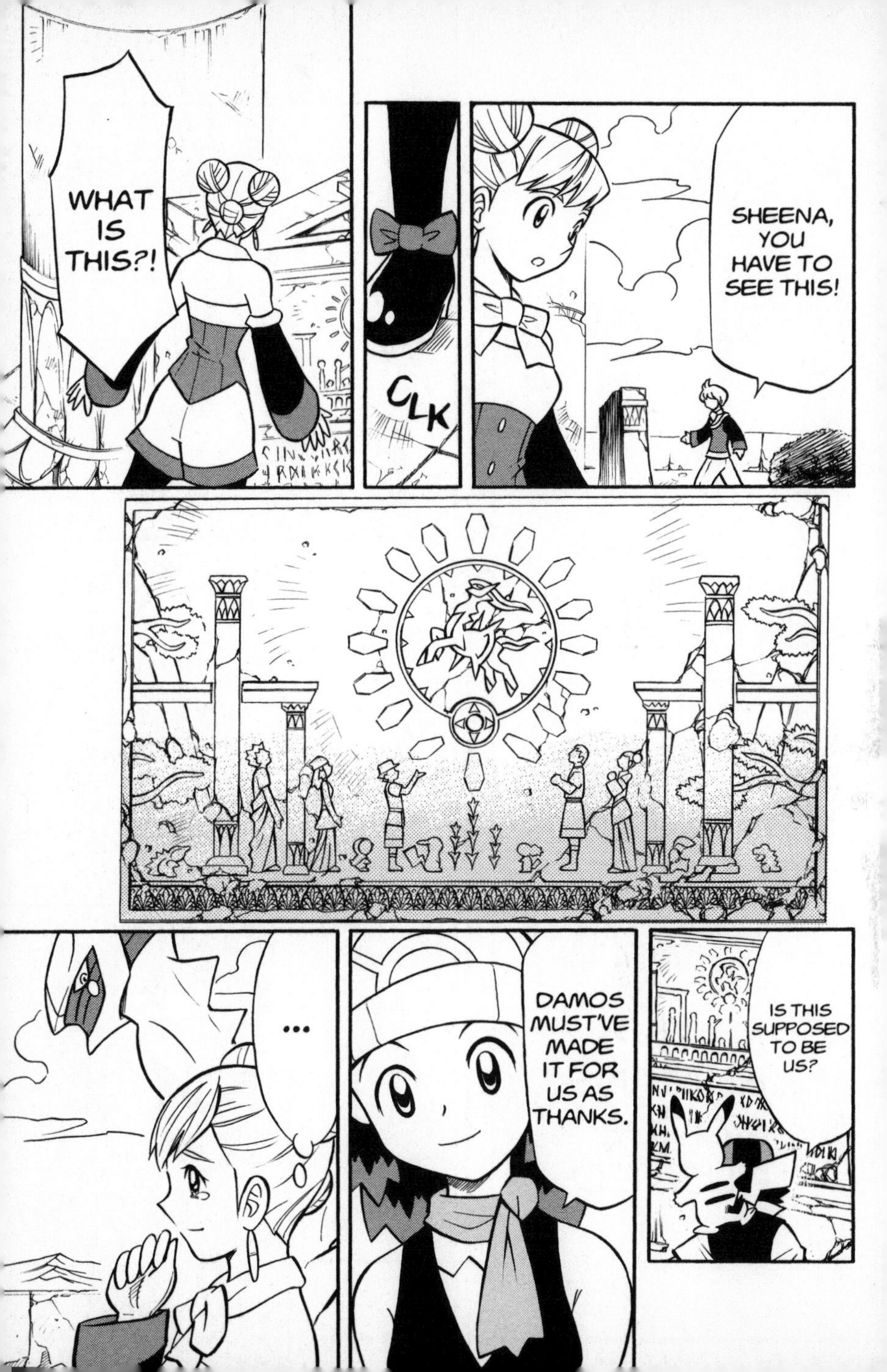
SHEENA, YOU HAVE TO SEE THIS!
CLK
WHAT IS THIS?!
IS THIS SUPPOSED TO BE US?
DAMOS MUST'VE MADE IT FOR US AS THANKS.
...

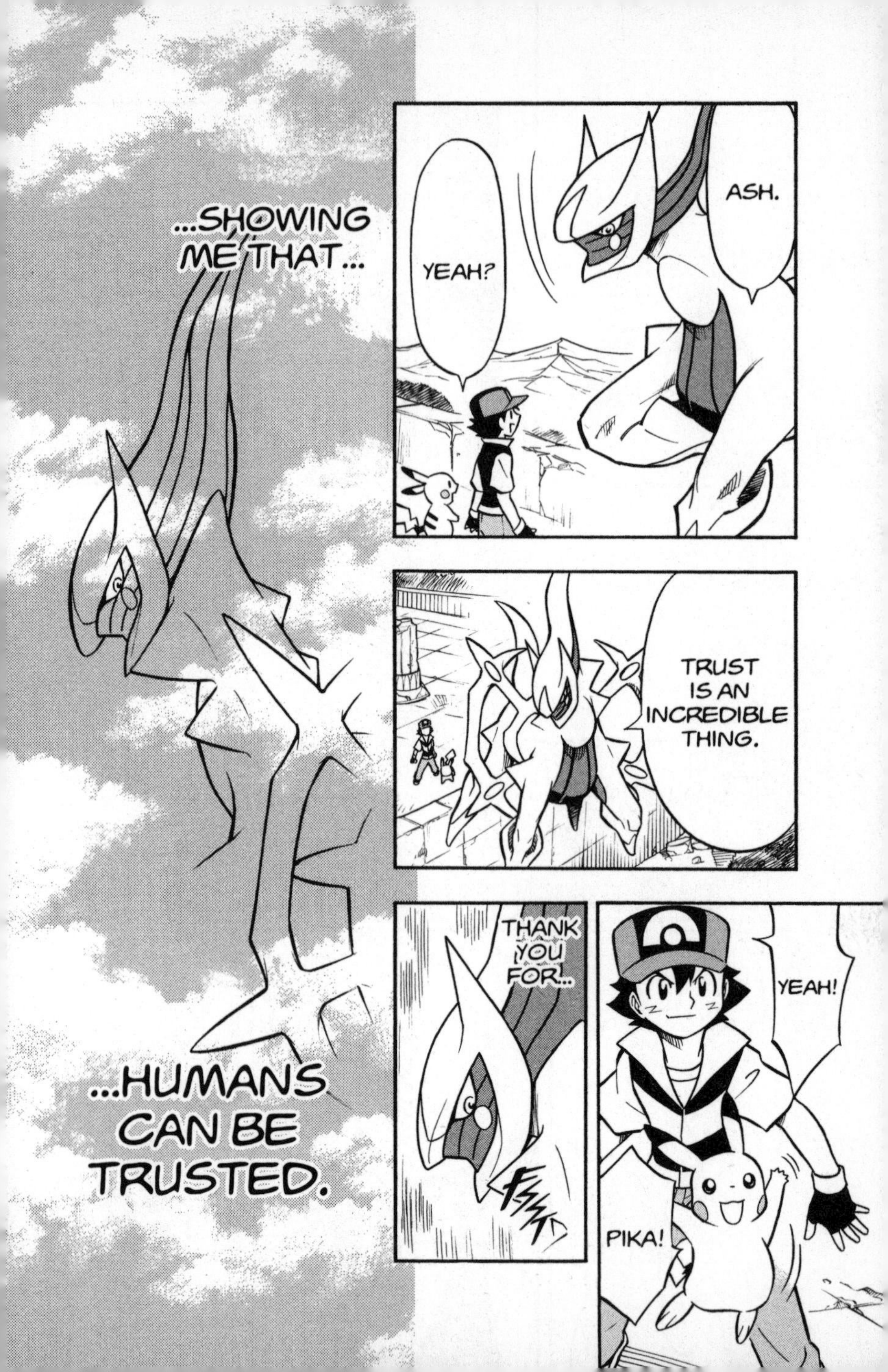
ASH.
YEAH?
TRUST IS AN INCREDIBLE THING.
YEAH!
PIKA!
THANK YOU FOR...
...SHOWING ME THAT...
...HUMANS CAN BE TRUSTED.

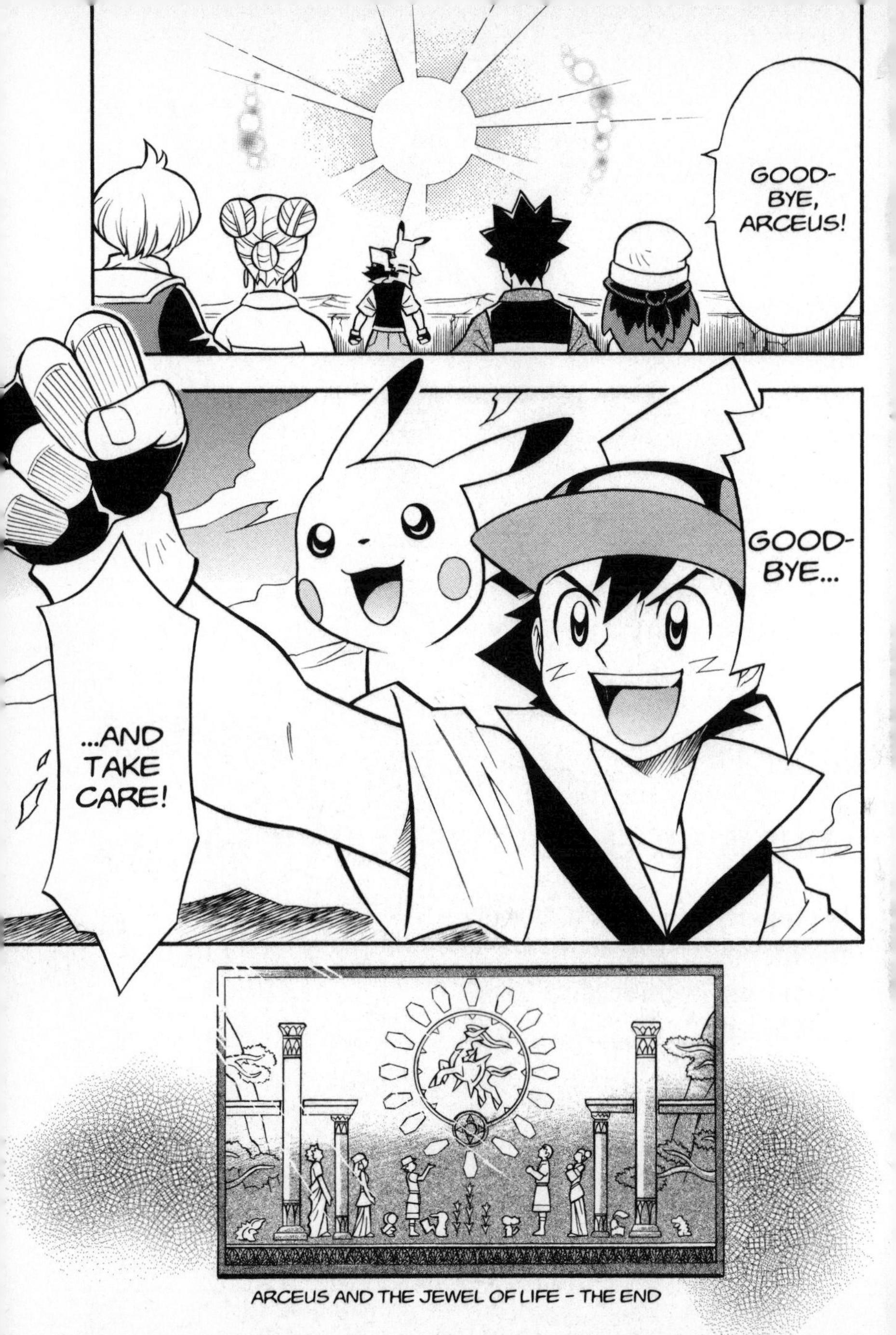
GOOD-BYE, ARCEUS!
GOOD-BYE...
...AND TAKE CARE!

ARCEUS AND THE JEWEL OF LIFE - THE END

THIS IS THE END OF THIS GRAPHIC NOVEL!

To properly enjoy this VIZ Media graphic novel, please turn it around and begin reading from right to left.

This book has been printed in the original Japanese format in order to preserve the orientation of the original artwork. Have fun with it!

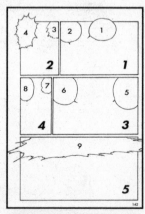

FOLLOW THE ACTION THIS WAY.